Broken Eye Books is an independent press, here to bring you the odd, strange, and offbeat side of speculative fiction. Our stories tend to blend genres, highlighting the weird and blurring its boundaries with horror, sci-fi, and fantasy.

Support weird. Support indie.

brokeneyebooks.com
facebook.com/brokeneyebooks
instagram.com/brokeneyebooks
bsky.app/profile/slgable.bsky.social

"*Trail of Shadows* is a panic-laced, spider-paced, fanged beast of a horror novel, a coming-of-age in a world of monsters. Realities bleed into each other like a Dali painting as familiar landscapes yawn open into the surreal. You don't need psychoactive substances to go tripping balls in Mike Allen's Appalachia. All you have to do is read this book." (**C.S.E. Cooney**, World Fantasy Award-winning author of *Saint Death's Daughter*)

"Mike Allen has long been a force in fantasy and horror. With *Trail of Shadows*, he's once again hit it out of the park. Beautiful prose and a haunting story combine to create a tale that will draw you in and refuse to let you go. Folk horror at its best." (**Gwendolyn Kiste**, four-time Bram Stoker Award-winning author of *The Haunting of Velkwood* and *Reluctant Immortals*)

"Hallucinatory, charcoal-dark, populated with ghosts, demons, and spiders, Mike Allen's *Trail of Shadows* is a violent fantasy-horror that pulses with atmosphere and atavistic terror." (**Matthew M. Bartlett**, author of *Gateways to Abomination* and *The Obsecration*)

"*Trail of Shadows* is a fast-paced psychedelic journey through Appalachia that's also a tender coming of age story. Allen's hallucinatory prose sears, full of wonder and terror, and his grasp of folklore and history shines throughout this Southern Gothic-meets-Weird-fiction novel." (**Craig Laurance Gidney**, Lambda Award-nominated author of *A Spectral Hue*)

"Spry and sprawling by turns, *Trail of Shadows* overflows with potent action and hypnotic, horror-tinged imagery. When it comes to dream-quest acid trips, this one's a hero dose." (**Rich Larson**, Eugie Foster Memorial Award-winning author of *Ymir* and *Changelog*)

"Allen creates a vast, intricate, and darkly imaginative world that is a chilling joy to immerse yourself in." (**A.T. Sayre**, author of *The Last Days of Good People*)

"*Trail of Shadows* is a tense, tight, and constantly surprising novel. A hike down the Appalachian Trail into a realm of shadows and surreal horror. I can't recommend it enough. It will keep you up late, and it cements Mike Allen as a horror and suspense writer to keep your eye on." (**R.S. Belcher**, author of *The Six-Gun Tarot* and *The Brotherhood of the Wheel*)

"Mike Allen's *Trail of Shadows*, set in the communities that dot the Appalachian Trail, is interlaced with strands of folk horror, high fantasy, and the just plain weird, that coalesce into a singular and fascinating milieu. Reminiscent of Manly Wade Wellman's Silver John stories, this pivotal novel firmly establishes Allen's launching pad for future literary endeavors that readers of weird and speculative fiction are sure to devour." (**Pete Rawlik**, author of *Reanimatrix*)

TRAIL OF SHADOWS

TRAIL OF SHADOWS by MIKE ALLEN

Published by
Broken Eye Books
www.brokeneyebooks.com

All rights reserved.
Copyright © 2025 Broken Eye Books and the author.
Cover illustration by Daniele Serra.
Interior illustration (paperback only) by
Kirsty Greenwood.
Cover and interior design by Scott Gable.
Editing by Scott Gable.

978-1-940372-72-3 (trade paperback)
978-1-940372-79-2 (hardcover)

TRAIL
OF SHADOWS

MIKE ALLEN

In memory of Jaime Lee Moyer,
who believed.

PART ONE:
EYES IN THE ABYSS

1

ELP ME!

A boy's shout sliced through the wind and the chirr of insects. I froze mid-step, scanning the laurels and pines to either side of the trail. No leaves rustled. Nothing moved.

With weight on my aluminum hiking poles, I slowly lowered my foot—careful to not make a noise. I held still as the seconds passed. Behind and in front of me, the afternoon sun painted the Appalachian Trail with dapples of light that danced back and forth with the breeze. As far as I could see, I was alone.

The warm air carried the scent of wood and mud, yet a chill trickled through me. When I fled the Carolina Tech campus—all that remained of my scholarship money stuffed in my backpack—there had been monsters everywhere I looked. I couldn't walk from dorm to classroom without spotting some multi-legged creature, big as a minivan and skittering across the far end of the quad, or a winged thing bigger than any bird, gliding toward the horizon. No one else ever reacted to them. No one else ever saw them.

Too much stress, I convinced myself. I had to get far away. And since I first set foot on the AT, I'd seen nothing scarier than a bear cub on a distant hillside, heard nothing stranger than a squirrel's screech. Until now.

Whatever I had heard, nature registered no disturbance. I shook my head and started walking. But then loud as a rifle shot came the scream: *Please help me!*

Not ten feet from me, the chance overlap of bark furrows, crisscrossing branches, shivering leaves—and their shadows—formed the outline of a slender boy, maybe ten or eleven, the vision so clear that I saw the rips in his sweatshirt and streaks of tears down his muddy face.

I dropped my poles. The boy's lips moved. In my head, I heard, *Don't let it get me.*

Any deer or a sensible man would've bolted. Instead, I gawked while my heart danced a flatfoot against my ribs. Behind him, a couple hundred yards down the slope, something huge slid through the evergreens, bending and breaking branches as it moved. The ghost boy ran straight at me. I ducked and raised my arms to shield my face, but the boy ran right through them. Right through *me.* It felt like being doused with ice and zapped with an electric shock all at once. A copper stink stuffed my nostrils, and my vision sizzled neon blue.

My scream cut off abruptly as I landed hard on my back on the trail's dry dirt and rock. My panicked gasping competed with a confounding déjà vu.

That cold electrocution dragged up a murky childhood memory even as the sensation faded. This memory unfurled more like nightmare: pale silvery shapes shrieked in darkness as a monster yowled, flashing claws in the moonlight—earth beneath me giving way with a thunder crack.

Below me on the slope, the snap and crack of branches brought me back to my senses. The commotion receded as whatever it was lumbered away downhill, leaving only a rotten-egg stench that made me gag when it caught up to me. A cicada buzzed past, landed in the brush near my head, and revved up its deafening song. Still panting, I stood, swaying in place.

It didn't make sense, really, that the hallucinations that plagued me on campus would go away once I hightailed it out of there. Yet they had, and that alone had been prize enough to make me feel fully justified in making this incredibly self-destructive choice, abandoning school for the trail. Even worse, it was too late in the year to hike all the way to Maine like a true thru-hiker should.

How glorious it had been though, to trudge onward while worrying about nothing more than my footing, whether I had enough water handy, and where the nearest poison ivy patches lurked.

It made more sense, didn't it, that the hallucinations would follow me—because they actually came from me, from some glitch in my brain. Contemplating this stirred a chorus of deeper panic until a new memory hushed them up, a voice scary as a snake hiss and familiar as cozy pajamas. *Leave it alone, Little Panther.*

It had been years since I'd thought of my long-dead grandmother—my beloved and feared mamaw, her green eyes blazing at me from a face baked terracotta brown. Though a tiny woman, she had always loomed over me in spirit. She had died when I was seven.

A rustling in the leaves distracted me. I would not have been surprised had Mamaw Elzbeth emerged at that moment from the bushes to transfix me with a wagging finger and that piercing green gaze.

The rustling continued, and motion gave away its source. A dust-colored wolf spider—leg span wide as my palm and back laden with tiny brown babes—so large that, as she crawled across the fallen leaves beside the trail, her weight caused them to crinkle.

My mamaw's sensible words: *Leave it alone, Little Panther.*

Maybe my reliance on dehydrated fruit and stale crackers for the past couple days had rendered me weaker and woozier than I thought, triggered something like a mirage that didn't have the courtesy to wait until I was zipped up in my sleeping bag. I would do a much better job of shopping if given a second chance to pack.

I retrieved my hiking poles, avoiding the mother spider and the thorns of a honey locust. Around the next curve bubbled a spring that some enterprising soul had enhanced with a convenient spigot. I rubbed my hands in its cold flow, drank deep, and refilled my canteens, thinking how nice it would be if I could refresh my food supply the same way. About a half mile farther uphill, past a cluster of cherry trees—their long, droopy leaves forcing me to duck—my wish came true.

A wooden sign read CRABBES SUPPLIES in carved block letters. Across from the sign stood one of those wooden boxes mounted on a pole that you see all along the AT, holding a spiral-bound notebook hikers can use to leave each other comments. The arrow on the sign pointed to a perpendicular branch of the trail that led straight up the mountain through dense thickets of laurel.

The thought of food and friendly human contact turned my head like I'd smelled charcoal and barbecue. I wrote a mental shopping list as I began the ascent.

Crabbes Supplies turned out to be an 1850s-era log home perched atop the mountain ridge. Tan chinking filled the gaps between mildew-black wooden beams. Hand-cut wooden shingles, blocky and gray, covered the roof. Structures like it nestled in the woods throughout the Appalachians, but it was a rarity to find one in use. Usually, they were collapsed and rotting.

So rusted and dented that it seemed centuries old rather than decades, a jeep sat parked by the shop—an archaeological excavation's worth of mud caked on its fenders. An old logging road wound its way down the other side of the mountain, explaining how the jeep got there. Somewhere out of sight, a gas-powered generator puttered.

Through the smudged panes of the front window, I spied a heavyset woman—her back to me, silver hair pulled up in a plaited bun—reaching for the low ceiling with a feather duster in hand. Her painfully bright pink-and-green flower print skirt made her disproportionately wide hips appear even wider. The nearby counter dominated the store's front room, a huge antique cash register standing sentry upon it. On the adjacent wall hung a board covered with flyers, posters, newspaper articles and photos, most so yellowed with age they might have been put up back when the cabin was built. A single island of shelves loaded with snacks and knickknacks and a trunk-sized cooler, likely powered by the generator, took up the rest of the floor space, leaving little room to walk.

I spotted things I needed. Leaning my poles under the window and unbuckling my backpack—so I could shrug it from my shoulders and leave it outside—I set my foot on the single front step, which creaked in warning.

Thick strands of cobweb blocked the open door. They glowed a faint blue, as if spun out of light rather than silk. But blinking didn't make them go away. I looked for the web's owner. Finding no spider, I swiped my arm to clear it from the doorway. Except my arm passed through the strands without breaking them. And an icy electric jolt stood my hair on end.

The woman in the flowered dress turned toward me as if yanked by a string. At that same moment, a rail-thin and stunningly ugly old man stood up from behind the register. I instantly, instinctively—and correctly, as it turned out—assumed they were married.

The sensation of my arm passing through the web was exactly the same as what I felt when the ghost boy ran through me. And my memories insisted that even that wasn't the first time it happened to me.

I raised my hand, palm out, pressed it against the glowing web, again found nothing to press against. My hand went right through. The cold shock made me jump.

A crowd of shrieking silvery forms, their claws raised in the moonlight, taunted my memories, refusing to condense into focus. A floor giving way beneath me. Rotten floorboards in a log structure like this one. The ruined cabin behind my mamaw's farmhouse, hidden by vines and bushes.

Recovering a physical anchor for this memory—evidence that it really did happen, however flimsy—kept me crouched in place, overwhelmed and trembling. The whole time, the old couple watched me, heads cocked at the exact same angle, saying nothing.

Again, I heard my mamaw's voice. *Leave it alone, Little Panther.*

The old man broke the detente, his drawl thick as syrup, his smile full of long, crooked teeth. "Well, son, are you coming in or not?"

Embarrassed, I hopped through the door with an apologetic response, "Sorry! Hi!" strangled by a third shock from the webbing. I staggered right into the shelves and knocked over several boxes of granola bars.

"Whoa there, tiger. You all right?" The old man came around the counter, spindly arms extended to brace me. His wife put a hand to her mouth.

Before I could protest, he steered me to a back room no bigger than a closet and plopped me into a wooden chair. His touch sent my innards squirming, though I couldn't say why.

In that tiny office, the wobbly table next to me doubled as desk and dining surface, crumbs decorating coffee-stained inventory sheets. The couple had somehow squeezed a rocking chair into the scant space on the table's other side. Above that rocker, on a dark-paneled wall, hung what had to be the homeliest family portrait in history—even in black and white. Judging by the dresses and tuxes, I guessed it had been taken on my hosts' wedding day.

"Check him for fever," the woman said.

I tried to wave him off. I didn't want him to touch me. "I'm fine. Really. Just need a little break."

He put his clammy hand on my forehead anyway, his touch so cold I thought I might be feverish after all. "Don't usually see a man this young in such a state." His acrid breath assaulted my sinuses, a mix of stale cigarette stink and recently eaten meat. Mercifully, he shrugged and backed away. "Maybe dehydrated. Might as well sit for a spell. I think you need the rest."

As he withdrew, an unpleasant new face startled me—my own, reflected in the glass of the picture frame and brought into sharper relief by an errant sunbeam from the front window. My Nine Inch Nails T-shirt stuck to me like a second skin, unwashed for four weeks.

Cheeks hollow from days of spartan dining. Neck concealed behind a bushy black beard as wild as the dark curls crowding my head. My complexion hickory dark from the sun. The green eyes I got from my mamaw stood out in a spooky way that I couldn't help but appreciate.

The reflection vanished as the shopkeepers blocked the door, shoulder to shoulder. "I could call a doctor," the woman said. "We got a phone line up here. Usually works. It's the party line to our house. We share it with the gas station down at the bottom of the mountain."

Even for the early 1990s that was primitive.

They exchanged glances, in the manner of an unspoken conversation. She smiled, as snaggle-toothed as her husband. "Or is there someone you could call?"

Instead, I asked, "Where's the nearest town?"

"Hillcrest," she said, confirming a suspicion I'd been harboring. I had kin in that Virginia town, though I hadn't seen them in years. My family dwelt in Tennessee's slice of the Appalachians while a bunch more relatives on my mother's side lived in the Southwest Virginia swath. It's all the same mountains, hardly a barrier to travel, but I don't think my twig of the family tree was missed much by the rest of the branch—with the blame for this estrangement resting on the shoulders of my parents. I had made no plans to stop in for a visit.

To my hosts, I said, "No big deal. I'll be fine."

They stayed in the doorway, and I don't think they particularly believed me, resorting to chitchat to keep me alert and occupied. Their names, they told me, were Gertrude and Herman Crabbe, not the sort of names that discerning parents inflicted on their kids when I was growing up. I debated whether to share in kind, since I didn't want to leave a trail of clues for my parents or alma mater in case they tried to trace me. But their folksy chattiness triggered my tongue before I'd entirely made up my mind, and I offered them my given name. (Let's say it's Nathan. That's close enough.)

"Well, Nathan, welcome to our little oasis in the forest," said Gertrude. "You want something while you take a load off?" She handed me bottled water, jerky, and crackers before I could answer. "On the house."

Sitting felt nice, but claustrophobia made up for it. As I tipped back the water bottle, the scene refracted through the plastic stretched Gertrude and Herman to many times their real size and gave them too many limbs. I lowered the bottle in a hurry to find them no different than before.

I very notably didn't ask them for their life stories, but they proceeded to share anyway. They lived in a log home nestled on the north side of the mountain. Born in the Blue Ridge Mountains, they both came from large families, but they were the lone introverted eccentrics in their clans. And they met when serendipitously dragged to the same saloon by wilder cousins.

"I couldn't believe how perfect we were for each other," Gertrude said. "I just looked at him, and he looked at me, and we knew. We didn't have to say a thing."

I had no trouble buying that instant attraction. Gertrude with her hunched shoulders, bulbous nose, head configured as if God had gripped her cheekbones with thumb and forefinger and squeezed; Herman with eyes set too far apart in a narrow face, spiny hairs protruding from ears and nostrils, lips so thin as to be nonexistent. They were so hideous together that they were damn near adorable.

Yet every tidbit they tossed me was embedded with a barb. I recognized the game—*we give a little, now you give a little*—and though I actively resisted playing, even scolded myself to stop, my mouth kept opening before my better judgement could shut it. My eyes popped a couple of times as I said things I had no plan to say.

I heard myself tell them how growing up a dark-skinned, bookish waif marked me as prey among the miners' sons I went to school with, but I wasn't a klutz and didn't freeze in a fight, and when I got tall enough, I convinced most of those creeps to pick softer targets. After sixth grade, my parents moved me to a different school—I didn't remember why—but things got better.

Herman floored me. "You got Melungeon in you, I bet."

"Wow, I don't think anyone's ever . . . I get asked sometimes if I'm an Arab. Or Greek. Or Turkish. Or even mulatto. No one gets it first try."

He snickered. "You ain't no Arab."

His odd leer somehow prompted me to keep talking. I swear, though it's ridiculous, I felt something sticky tug my tongue, and off I went, telling them how I had my grandmother's green eyes, and people thought *she* was Native American. My mother could pass for white and never concealed her disappointment that I couldn't. My dad made it clear her demeanor toward me wasn't his problem. If the Crabbes knew about Melungeons, my mother's attitude could not have shocked them. During Reconstruction, Melungeons waged legal fights to be classified as white. During that era, I sure couldn't blame them, but my mom I could blame plenty.

But something was wrong with me. I never opened up like this, not to complete strangers. In short order, I spilled my college ambitions, the derision my folks poured on my graphic design dreams, and even the weird things that I started seeing after dark when I returned to Tech in the fall to start my sophomore year. The Crabbes nodded solemnly while I jabbered. I wondered what drugs were in the water they gave me and kept right on going.

I would have described the translucent shapes that manifested in daylight hours, even the encounter that scared me so horribly I fled the campus, even the ghost boy that had shattered my piece of mind, but in a stroke of luck, Herman interrupted. "You're not trying to get all the way to Maine? By the time you hit Massachusetts, you'll be knee-deep in snow, boy."

"I've got friends waiting for me in Pennsylvania. A couple I met through school. Just married." Bill and Melissa didn't know I was coming, not yet. I fought to hold that secret inside and somehow won. My teeth actually clicked shut. I made do with saying, "If I stay here much longer, it's gonna get dark outside. I need to get back out there and find the best campsite before someone else gets it."

This set off one of those cutesy, passive-aggressive arguments about what was on the house and what I should pay for—with me insisting I should pay for everything and my hosts insisting the stuff I'd already eaten was their treat. They won, of course.

Gertrude returned to dusting as her husband collected my order from the shelves—bottled water, varieties of dried fruit, five days' worth of MREs. The ancient register clunked, chugged and dinged.

When Herman handed me the bag, I got another surprise. The ring finger and pinky on his right hand each had a joint too many, bending in, then out, then in again—as if the flesh wrapped insect legs instead of bones.

He grinned at my bug-eyed start. "Docs had to make me a couple replacement fingers. Took the skin graft from my stomach. Got plastic under there." He waggled them at me, making sport of my squeamishness. "This is what happens when you don't put food on the table fast enough for the missus."

Gertrude cackled loud enough to trigger a coughing fit. Alarmed by the noise, even though it was all at my expense, I started to ask if she was okay, and my gaze alighted on a face staring out from the wall. The face of my ghost boy.

I didn't drop my bag of goods, but I froze long enough for the Crabbes to note where I was looking. "You recognize him?" Herman asked.

I managed the slightest shake of my head. I could just make out a name under the newsprint photo: Thomas "Tommy" Wayne Saunders, 9, of Hillcrest.

"Sure is a shame about that boy," Gertrude said. "They think he fell off Angel's Leap, but they don't know for sure because they can't find him. You been to Angel's Leap before?"

I hadn't. Had never even heard of it. She explained, a bit eagerly, how maps called it McGlothin's Knob, but locals knew it as Angel's Leap. An outcrop of immense rocks accessed by a difficult yet popular path. An even harder climb to the peak rewards the adventurous with one of the most spectacular views across forest and farmland that the AT could offer. A one-hundred-and-fifty-foot fall awaited the careless. It lay about fifteen miles northeast of the turnoff to the store.

"Bad things happen in its shadow," she said, spurring an interruption from her husband.

"I keep telling you, it ain't the place that's evil." His eyes were on me as he said that.

I didn't ask, but Gertrude started to count off those bad things on her fingers, her eyes bright as if she relished the topic. Seven years ago, a Montana couple found dead inside their tent, their throats cut. Five years ago, a boy who wandered from his family's campsite escaped with a slashed back from a man in a white mask. Baffled police made a public plea for tips and published a sketch of the mask. They revealed the attacker molested the boy before he got loose. Two years ago, a college kid found dead—and the detail that didn't make the papers, found naked and impaled on a hand-carved wooden spear.

Two nights ago, Tommy Saunders vanished. No witnesses saw him climbing the rocks, much less taking a fall. Two teams of two dozen searchers found no trace.

"His mama and papa should never have taken him up there," Gertrude said, voice rising in righteous indignation, her gaze never letting go of mine.

"You sure you're fit to go?" Herman leaned close enough to blast me with his awful breath. "You're turning green."

They couldn't have missed the goose pimples on the back of my neck. From the back of my mind, a voice whispered that this creepy couple knew all about the boy's disappearance and his ghost, and they could tell that I'd seen him too.

"It's all just so horrible," I said. "I've really got to go." Thank goodness, they let me. I cringed as the webbing across the doorway gave me another jolt.

The sun had lowered considerably, a red orb twinkling faint through the trees. Grabbing my gear, I set off just shy of a trot, my mind and stomach churning all the way down to the main trail. I stubbed my toes a dozen times but didn't slow down.

Back on the AT proper, I opened the box containing the notebook for hikers' messages. A ratty, spiral-bound specimen lay inside, its cover a faded Tasmanian Devil cartoon. Pen scrawls filled the pages. The final message read, "The Crabbes are creepy."

Under that, I wrote, "Amen!" and signed my chosen trail name, the nickname that, despite my mother's protests, my mamaw had always insisted on calling me: Panther.

2

As the sun abandoned the forest to the night, my mamaw haunted me further, her bone-dry voice floating up from riverbeds of long-neglected memory.

She walks these hills in a loooong black veeeeeil
Visits my grave when the niiiight winds waaaaail
Nobody knoooows, nobody seeees,
Nobody knoooows, but meee-eee

The wooden shelter that I huddled inside had once upon a time been a curing shed. A fruity hint of tobacco still lingered in the place, the scent stronger the longer I stayed. I imagined my sleeping bag would reek of it by morning—not an unpleasant prospect.

I should have been spreading that sleeping bag out, pulling on an extra shirt, and sorting out how much of my newly acquired granola, jerky, and dried fruit I could afford to eat that night. Instead, I sat on the bench inside the shelter, my pack by my feet, opening and closing my Buck knife—hearing my mamaw sing, my own pulse acting as unsteady metronome. Crickets and peepers composed a soundtrack to the film my brain spliced together: *Ghost Boy*. Ghost-webs across the door. Cracking branches, scent of sulfur. Herman licking his teeth.

Pain broke the spell as I absentmindedly sliced the pad of my thumb. I raised my hand and watched the blood bead, welling until it threatened to drip.

My treacherous mind informed me, all matter-of-fact, *Either you hallucinated all of it, or you're not hallucinating at all.*

The first drop fell, and a new clot of memory came loose: a floorboard snapping beneath my foot, too rotten to support even the weight of a stick-thin six-year-old. I smashed through splintered wood into stinking mud and froze there, too scared to cry despite the blooms of pain, because of the silvery shapes gliding toward me in the darkness. A hum like a dial tone swelled in my ears, ever-louder whispers embedded in the noise. I could not, at that moment, recall what happened next, though I could fill in things that came before.

My parents claimed that, sometime in 1985, my Grandma Elzbeth's house collapsed, and though I considered them utterly untrustworthy in most things, I did not question this news. Even when my mamaw was alive, her home teetered at the edge of ruin. Wind whistled through every room.

Mamaw had no plumbing. She heated well water on the woodstove. Her outhouse, a source of fascination and terror, might have toppled with a good push. Spiders had set up shop in every nook, and even though Mom began each of our visits with an aggressive eviction via broom, the tiny eight-legged monsters always reclaimed their turf.

My papaw Henri died before I was born—when Mom was barely in her teens. She told me Mamaw let all the fields go to seed, her contempt smoldering whenever she said it. Mom never had a nice thing to say about my mamaw or about me, even when I was little, which sowed in me a sense of kinship, so everything about my mamaw fascinated me. A tiny woman, her waves of curly gray hair were often tied back in a frizzy ponytail. Her face, nut brown and latticed with deep wrinkles, made me think of cracks in clay. Her eyes blazed green.

Those eyes sometimes fixed on me with a predator's pitiless stare. Her frown could freeze me mid-skip in a way Mom and Dad's yelling never did. And when she smiled, that too had a magic effect, radiating a warmth that made me joyful for whatever made her brighten. The sight always made me forget the stomach-churning ordeal of traveling to see her—hours and hours in my parent's VW Beetle over those switchback-filled, vomit-inducing Tennessee mountain roads.

Her tiny house contained a hundred hidden corners, packed with mysterious wooden dolls that Mamaw carved and colored herself. Many were half human and half beast, birds and wolves and bears and cats—mostly cats, their whiskers and tails made from grass and brush wire. She told me that each had a story, but she never shared those with me.

Her rickety home and its satellite outhouse stood out like islands in an ocean of waist-high grass, and the line of pines about fifty yards beyond marked the shore, where field gave way to forest. A third building was nestled within the pines, its lumpen outline obscured by branches.

"What is that place?" I asked as we crowded around the teensy-weensy circular dinner table.

Mom and Dad gave me puzzled looks, but my mamaw knew what I meant. "Way back in the day, used to be the guest cabin. It fell in on itself many years ago."

"Can I see it?"

"No." Elzbeth didn't raise her voice, but her stare burned me with laser heat. "Leave it alone, Little Panther."

You'd think that would have squelched my curiosity, but of course, it didn't. Playing with blocks by the sitting room window or walking the well-worn track to the outhouse, my attention would fix on the caved-in cabin's outline. Something about it hooked my attention, the way a cat swivels its ears when it hears a mouse scrabbling. I tried asking my mamaw about it a few times more. Always the same answer: "Leave it alone, Little Panther."

During our last visit of that year, Thanksgiving weekend, my curiosity overcame my fear. On a night with stars and moon buried above the clouds and a chill wind rustling the grass, I snuck outside. That wind was my ally, sending its howl through the house, masking the noise of my escape.

I couldn't find a flashlight, so I went without. Emerging from the house, a trick of the eyes made the outdoors a hundred times brighter. The trees bit their outlines into the uniform sky, forbidding and inviting at once. The grass rose above my head in places as I pushed toward the disheveled heap of the cabin. It should have been invisible, but I sorted it from the greater shadow well before I reached the tree line.

A few hours before, my parents had made me clean my plate even though I was stuffed on Thanksgiving leftovers for the second evening in a row. But something in that cabin made me ravenous.

I found a hole in the rotten clapboards large enough to squeeze through. The rough edges tore my pajamas, but I thought nothing of it. Underneath the collapsed roof, I found a solid floor and enough room to stand—but after a couple steps, I learned the floor wasn't solid after all.

I lay face-first on mud and splintered wood, breath hitching, too shocked to even whimper. My mom would sometimes say to me that she'd bet I wouldn't cry so much if there was no one around to hear me. This once, she was almost right. Fear of who or what might hear kept me quiet.

I found the will to raise myself to hands and knees. When I looked up, eyes stared down at me, black pits with silver pupils, nested in shimmering silver faces. A hand floated toward me.

A cold, electric jolt.

What happened next, I could only remember piecemeal. My grandmother's green eyes, impossibly huge, impossibly bright, after she pulled me from the cabin. Moonlight reflecting in those eyes, even though no moon shone in the sky. The sound of a man whimpering.

More blood dripped from my hand as it trembled.

The webbing across the Crabbe's door, the sensation of the ghost-boy's body passing through mine, had felt exactly like the freezing shock from the touch of that hand in my mamaw's cabin. If I had a problem with hallucinations, it had started when I was six.

My awareness returned to the fruity tobacco scent, to the *reep reep reep* of the frogs. I clamped my bleeding thumb in my fingers, hugged my knees and shivered hard, not because of the temperature. My thoughts tumbled, unable to piece the puzzle together. How my mamaw's green eyes had glowed all those years ago, shining as if they were their own source of light. The way the shopkeepers had pegged me so swiftly as Melungeon, a word my mamaw taught me and my mother shunned, a term hardly anyone knew. How the webbing had made them *aware* of me, like I'd tripped an alarm when I walked through it. The glances they exchanged after they noticed me gawking at the boy's face.

A presence darkened the doorway. Nothing blocked the shelter entrance, nothing loomed beyond it but the blur of trees in deep twilight, but at the same time, I traced the unmistakable outline of a scrawny nine-year-old boy, crouched an arm's-length from me, his form congealed from degrees of gloom. Fear squeezed my throat closed. At last, I forced out, "T-T-Tommy?"

He rose from his crouch, his face drawing into sharp focus. His expression mirrored my own terror. His mouth moved. I heard no sound, but his voice came to me plain: *Don't let it get me!*

My own voice held no strength. "Let what get you?"

A stench of rotten eggs assailed me. The boy whipped his head to one side as if he'd heard a loud noise, though I heard nothing. He sprang away from the cabin door and vanished.

Outside, brambles rustled. A breeze disturbed the leaves, but the rustling I heard kept a rhythm, like someone moving softly, stalking.

My own breathing seemed as loud as that breeze. I locked the Buck knife open and crept forward, the sulfur smell intensifying as I approached the doorway.

The rustling stopped. At the edge of the clearing that surrounded the shelter, the afterimage of a small, gaunt boy peered from behind a tree and then dashed uphill and out of sight.

The stink remained. I walked cat-quiet toward the tree line. High above, in a gap between trees, a figure cut a silhouette from the bruise-colored sky. A man, tall and solid. He turned away from me and walked below the crest of the hill, out of my sight.

My heart jackhammering, the strangest thought crossed my mind: *Mamaw would know what to do,* accompanied by the flash of her green eyes. A woman little more to me than random scraps of memory, she'd ventured into the freezing night to pull a frightened little boy from a place he didn't belong.

As a child, I had a gift for padding across carpets and yards in complete silence, one of the many things about me that drove my mother crazy. I could sneak up on her undetected and, even more valuable, sneak past her. Even in the woods.

Determined to help this boy, I summoned that childhood talent. I stalked into the trees, ascending to a hilltop that afforded a view of a narrow gully. Despite the deepening night, I could see to the bottom, where the gully widened to a clearing.

Herman Crabbe stood there, gaunt as a Harryhausen skeleton. He spread his arms, and a ring of blue smoke stretched open in front of him, as if he'd pierced an invisible membrane and was forcing the hole larger—until he could walk through it.

A bewildering double image confronted me. Though I saw Crabbe using both hands to hold the smoke ring open, other limbs reached through the gap, spiny arachnid limbs.

He passed completely through and changed. What crawled out the other side was not human at all.

The vast spider I beheld was formed of shadow and motion—just like my ghost-boy—each leg longer than a car. The monster hesitated, flexing fangs as long as my arm, before ascending the far side of the gully with heart-stopping speed.

I didn't dare breathe. My lungs burned as my eyes fixed on the murky splotch where the outsized spider vanished. The night reduced the brush to patterns of gray. Nothing moved.

No wonder the Crabbes had grown so excited when I recognized the ghost boy. They were creatures out of a nightmare folktale—and they must have taken Tommy alive, intent on doing who knew what. Others had been murdered, molested, as Gertrude had gleefully shared.

I'd seen things on the university campus that I believed to be tricks of the mind, but in that moment, I accepted everything as real. I descended to the clearing, sure the werespider existed and sure that—once upon a time in a cabin on my mamaw's farm—I had already encountered such creatures, violent haints, and she rescued me. I wished I could step back into that memory and ask her what to do next.

The ring of blue smoke still hung in the air. I peered through it at a disorienting double image. Superimposed over the gully and the trees, a landscape of silvery rock formations defied my spatial comprehension, paralleling the contours of the mountainside without precisely matching it.

Tommy had to be in that second world, along with the spider-thing that Herman Crabbe had become. My Buck knife would be nothing more than a pinprick to that monster. Still, I held it out like a magic wand and called sotto voce through the opening, "Tommy?"

No response.

If I was in for the penny, I was in for the pound. "Tommy!" I shouted. "Tommy!"

A shriek in my mind, *Here!* At the same time, something huge made a leaf-shaking, branch-breaking commotion.

I screamed, "Run to my voice! Run! Run now!"

Uphill, distant treetops whipped back and forth as the thing chasing the boy barreled past them. I kept yelling. Tommy crested the ridge, tripped, and tumbled into the gully. In the land of silver shadow, he was solid flesh, filthy and bloodied.

I put my free hand on the smoke ring, instinctively wanting to prevent it from closing. Again, the freezing shock jolted my bones, but my hand didn't pass through the smoky boundary. My palm pressed against an edge that stretched like taffy and vibrated like an air compression motor. I recoiled from the sensation, and the smoke circle shrank, just as Tommy was regaining his feet. I pressed both hands against the edges of the ring and shoved it wide open, ignoring the twin blasts of electric ice through my palms. "Tommy, come on!"

His eyes, wounded-dog wild, found mine, and he loosed a raw-throated wail. He staggered my way, gaining speed as his pursuer popped up at the top of the ridge.

A tsunami of sulfurous stench rolled over me. The monster wasn't the gigantic spider I'd braced myself for. Rather, it stood upright on two thick legs. Thorns covered its body.

Tommy tripped again and sprawled on the gray rock. The creature chasing him leaped into the gully, moonlight bathing it head to toe. I lost all ability to think.

Spikes of bone protruded at every joint from its melted wax hide, like layer upon layer of burn scars. The pulpy mound of its head spilled over its chest and shoulders in a cascade of sucking mouths and writhing eyestalks. Spined phalluses jutted tusk-like from its abdomen.

I shrieked something—don't remember what. Tommy shrieked too and scrambled to his feet. The creature grabbed for him with impossibly long arms, hooked knuckles missing him by inches.

A vector of sensory impressions I did not fully understand burst through a psychic dam, a barrier in my mind that I had not been aware of until the moment it sundered. My skin no longer imprisoned my awareness. My vision extended wider and deeper than my eyes had ever allowed. I registered every tremor in the undergrowth, every nuance of that sulfurous stink, every sweat bead and piss stain on the boy's body, every inconsistent twitch of the approaching demon. Its movements reminded me of a puppet's, half-empty and pulled by cables, controlled from inside by a much smaller inhabitant. The demon wasn't real—its molten flesh constituted a shell worn like a costume, like a suit of armor.

The revelation kept me from bolting, as did the sight of Tommy's terror-filled eyes—even though the demon was a murder machine and I was just flesh. I screamed for Tommy to move as they both ran at me, the monster right behind its prey, arms outstretched for another grab.

Tommy bowled into me as the demon's spike-studded fist descended.

I lunged through the hole in the world and slashed blindly with the knife. An electric chill exploded through me, searing and freezing every limb.

A howl split the night.

3

I landed on my back in the wet earth, panting, Tommy's warm weight on top of me. Nearby, a man groaned, the noise muffled.

Bracing Tommy by the shoulders, I hauled us both to our feet. As I did, someone put a hand to my back to help me up.

With a yell I whirled, holding out the knife, to face Herman Crabbe. The shine from his flashlight carved his face with hard shadows. I backed away, keeping my knife between us, my other arm circled tight around Tommy, who shivered and pressed his face against my stomach. His clothes were soaked.

"Whoa, there, tiger," Herman said as his flashlight beam found my blade.

Another groan and a cough. Crabbe turned the beam in the direction of the noise. "You did quite a number on him. I'm impressed."

The circle of blue smoke had faded to a wisp. Within its boundary hung the faintest hint of that silvery landscape from moments before. Beyond it, a big man in jeans and a torn flannel shirt lay in the dirt. At first, I thought he possessed the palest face I'd ever seen. A closer look revealed a mask, made of papier-mâché and painted white. The prongs along its edges recalled the protrusions from the thorned monster's lump of a head.

Gertrude Crabbe stood over the masked man, pressing the business end of a shotgun against his chest.

The front of the man's shirt had been shredded. His exposed flesh bled from deep parallel gouges across his torso—two across his belly and two across his chest.

Claw marks. Impossibly huge claws. The gaps between the wounds were nearly six inches.

I held up my knife in wonder. The blade was clean. Despite the child pressed against me, I loosed a string of swear words.

A clear memory possessed me, the adrenaline-cranking thrill of tearing skin with razor-honed fingernails. No, not with fingernails—with hooked claws extended from a hand that wasn't a hand at all, a wide paw at the end of a powerful, muscular limb. Rippling with power that was all mine.

Panther, my mamaw always called me.

Those claw marks. I made them. I had no idea how.

With my attention disrupted, a vision sculpted from night and shadow impinged itself on my awareness, a spectral tableau superimposed over the scene in front of me. In the vision, the thorned demon lay twitching on the ground, its monstrous form dwarfed by the gigantic spider that crouched over it. Clearly female, its grotesquely swollen abdomen blurred the moon. With its forelegs, it was winding, winding—binding the demon beneath it in a tight cocoon. The webbing she bound the masked man with was the same blue thread I'd encountered in the doorway to the store.

"My wife'll take good care of him," Herman said. His flashlight beam swung back to me. "You snatched his prey right outta his jaws. Good thing too." His laugh held a cruel edge. "Get the boy back up to the store. You can clean him up, put some blankets on him. Give him some water, make sure it's small sips. If he can hold that down, maybe try him with a candy bar. On the house, whatever you need. When we catch up, we'll drive you both into town."

The Crabbes must have been watching as I descended into the gully and toyed with the rift Herman opened. I wondered, though didn't dare ask aloud, what would have happened if I'd lost the face-off. Instead, I inclined my head at the masked man. "What about him? He's bleeding pretty bad."

"Least of his problems." Herman's lips peeled back into a toothy grin. "You go on. We'll take care of him."

I could fathom what he meant, but I didn't want to. "That's a long way," I said. "Can I have your flashlight?"

His smile stretched wider. "I think you'll find you can see just fine."

Arguing seemed dangerous. I lifted Tommy in a fireman's cradle and looked back exactly once before marching out of the gully. The demon, still twitching, was almost completely enveloped in Gertrude's cocoon.

As Herman had predicted, I had no problem finding my way in the dark.

The night teemed with strange sounds, and my peripheral vision crowded with spectral shapes darting away. Familiar shapes. I'd seen their like, crossing the college campus at night, peering out a dorm or diner window after dark.

Tommy's shuddering weight, the lactic acid accumulating in my body, distracted me enough to keep me on task. By the time I reached the shop, my lungs, legs, back and arms were aflame. Tommy was in a daze the whole way. When I stepped through the webbing that crossed the front door, his eyes fluttered wide. He felt the freezing shock for sure, though maybe not as intensely as I did.

Once I stretched him out on the floor in the back room and tucked a roll of paper towels under his head, I asked for a phone number to call his mom and dad. His eyes rolled up in their sockets, and he sagged into unconsciousness. I knelt by his side, wanting to shake him awake, though not at all sure if it was a safe thing to do. The thought that he might be close to death's door squeezed my exhausted heart.

Gertrude had made mention of a shared phone line, and recalling that slowed my panic. Herman had told me to wait, but he'd said nothing about contacting the authorities. Based on what I'd witnessed, I suspected they wouldn't approve—but they were nowhere in sight, and I was out of my depth. The sooner police and EMTs got to Tommy, the better.

I searched the back room and behind the counter for a phone and came up empty. There had to be more to the building than what I could access from the front rooms. I winced through the front webbing and jogged around to a back door. Beside it, the massive diesel generator hummed, its bulk draped in a net of bright blue cobweb. More webbing covered the door's handle.

I still understood little of the night's revelations, but I had grasped enough to draw up short—that if I grabbed the handle, the Crabbes would know about it. "I have to call for help," I said to the webbing, not knowing if it would make a difference, and endured more cold shock. The door wasn't locked, but when I opened it, I found more web crisscrossing the entrance top to bottom, practically a solid sheet.

I took a deep breath, hopped through, and let out a scream as I flopped into the storage room. I collapsed against a stack of musty boxes and lay there until I stopped shuddering. Once I regained focus, I scanned more stacks of boxes, another freezer, a big plyboard desk with a lone lamp crooked over handwritten inventory sheets, a phone squatting beside it. Blue webbing covered every visible object. I took a step toward the desk, and the electric chill surged up my leg. I hopped sideways with a yelp, knocking over boxes and triggering even more web-shocks. When I stabilized, I stayed put, wary of whatever had stung me.

What I observed below me made no sense: a thread attached to one of the boxes descended to the wooden floor and continued through it, extending deep into the earth. There were many more like it, and their paths converged. A web funnel big enough to hold a van hung beneath the storeroom floorboards.

I shouldn't have been able to see this, but I could. It was as if a transparency of a spider's funnel had been overlaid across my field of vision. A dizzying duality, like seeing Tommy's face formed of shadows or peering through the hole Herman opened to see an alternate landscape superimposed over the night-lit woods. Instinct told me I should plummet into the web, and for a moment, I reeled, but the floor under my boots held solid. The threads simply passed through the boards—like a ghost—attaching to the freight, the desk, the walls. I closed my eyes, took a breath, looked again. The view got no better.

If I really was going to help Tommy, I had to suck it up. Gaze fixed on the floor, I skittered and jumped and flinched at a couple more shocks before I could nab the phone. Gripping the handset earned me another zap. I raised it to my ear. No dial tone. Instead, Herman Crabbe's voice spoke from the receiver. "Thought I told you to wait for us."

I rolled with the situation even as my heart jackhammered. "Tommy's passed out."

"The boy's gonna be fine. Did you find the blankets?"

"No, but—"

"They're in the granola crate in the room where you put him. Look, I know you mean well, but you're not gonna be able to call out right now, so just go back to the boy, get those wet clothes off and bundle him up good. Then wait for us like I told you in the first place."

In the background, I heard a man cry in pain. The masked stalker. Whatever method Herman Crabbe was using to speak to me, he was nowhere near a phone. My jaw had to be somewhere down by my boots.

"Do I need to repeat all that?" Herman said with a cheerfulness that might have been genuine. I hung up and dashed outside, no longer caring whether the strands zapped me. I half-leaped, half-fell into the dirt lot.

As I sprawled in the mud, the same way I had all those years ago in the darkness beneath my mamaw's cabin, a glint in the woods beyond the jeep caught my eye. A paired glint, two huge reflective eyes, large as footballs. Within the night, an outline sketched from deeper shadow framed those eyes. Above them, pointed ears a foot tall with black tufts at the top stood straight up from a round head about four feet wide.

A whisper. *"That's him."*

I recoiled, and as I scrambled back, I experienced the most disorienting instance of double vision yet. I stared up at those glowing eyes, but at the same time, I stared down into the surrounding trees from a much higher vantage, maybe thirteen feet off the ground. I discerned a huge feline shape amid the trees, ears tufted like a bobcat's, and a man standing beside it, who gave a panicked shout and transformed in a flurry of feathers.

I came down light on my front paws as a winged beast soared into the air, something tiny—a man—clutched in its talons. The flying beast's wingspan seemed to fill a quarter of the visible sky, though I could see the stars *through* it. Whatever it was, it fled over the mountains.

I scanned the trees, but the gigantic bobcat had vanished.

Next thing I knew, I was crouched on all fours in the mud. Those huge eyes were gone, no wings shrouded the sky, and my hands were just hands—not paws two feet wide. I was no longer by the storeroom door. With no reasonable explanation for how I'd gotten there, I was by the tree line, damn near forty feet from where I'd first stumbled out of the storeroom. "I've lost my fucking mind," I said. Thankfully, nothing spoke back to confirm or deny. I stayed in my half-crouch until the words I'd exchanged with Herman jarred me out of my paralysis.

Tommy lay where I'd left him. Still breathing: I checked.

By the time the Crabbes arrived, their captive nowhere to be seen, I had the boy wrapped in a blanket as I'd been instructed. They'd retrieved my gear from the shelter. Gertrude handed me my pack—my poles collapsed and strapped to the sides—and commenced fussing over Tommy. I sought the vast spider form I'd seen earlier, tried to spy it from the corner of my eye, but nothing. I could almost believe I'd imagined it all. No help, that I anxiously rubbed the cut on my thumb. But there was no cut, even though there had to be. My frayed mind let it go.

Tommy stirred and muttered as Gertrude caressed his sweat-damp brow. I didn't want to let him out of my sight, but the firm pressure of Herman's plastic fingers on my shoulder guided me out to the island of snacks and knickknacks.

"Let's just let her do what she does," he said. "The missus has a way with kids. Oodles of experience."

I thought of the masked man, bound in webbing. "Where's the killer?" I asked. "That . . . creep. Where is he? What *was* he?"

Herman's elongated, crooked-toothed face floated inches from mine. "Let's talk outside."

"What are you going to do?"

"Just talk, tiger. That's all. C'mon."

You would think by then I'd be used to phasing through that awful webbing, but I most definitely was not.

He walked me to the edge of the pool of light made by the front window. When we stopped, I surveyed the woods. No big bobcat eyes stared back at me, but the level of detail I could suss out in the dim light astonished me: not just individual leaves but even the bugs crawling on them. The silence dragged on, compelling me to break it. "I'm sorry about going in the storage room. I didn't know what—"

"I need your solemn oath," he cut in, "that you ain't gonna breathe a word to anyone about the things you saw tonight. Inside my store and anywhere else out here."

"I don't know what I'd say, or who I'd say it to."

"That ain't good enough. Swear it, on your grandma's name."

What a weird demand, I remember thinking. Herman's too-wide eyes glistened with an intensity that surpassed evangelical fervor. I had learned never to argue with a person bearing that demeanor. I swore on Mamaw Elzbeth's name that I would never tell a soul what I'd seen.

"Your grandma, we never knew her, but we knew of her. We're not the kind of folks who take sides, but every tidbit we ever heard made her out to be a grand old dame, worthy of respect."

"What do you mean?" In its own way, this statement yanked the ground out from under me, worse than anything else that had happened on that night. "What things did you hear about my mamaw?"

"Now, see, that's interesting. If you don't know, then maybe she didn't mean to tell you, and far be it from me to go against her wishes." He stared at the forest floor, his eyes shifting as if tracking something. "Tell me true. What you did in that gully, when you clawed that bastard. Ever done anything like that before?"

I started to say no, but the memory of my mamaw's green eyes stopped me.

On the night I had crawled into the collapsed cabin, her eyes blazing as she scolded me, her teeth flashing in the moonlight. She'd dragged me out from the mud and broken wood, lifting me with a strength that was superhuman. I remembered a sensation like huge teeth, dinosaur teeth, seizing me, lifting me, but when they set me down and I looked up, it was just Mamaw Elzbeth, furious. The whole time she snarled at me, a man inside the cabin had been moaning, wailing, badly hurt. *I* had been the one who hurt the man. That was why Mamaw was so angry.

Herman Crabbe wasn't waiting for my answer. "I would never under ordinary circumstances make this my business, but you got your grandma's blood in you, and that means something. You stepped up to help that kid when your nature might have called you to leave well enough alone, and that means something too. So I'm telling you this. Whatever plans you had, you need to make new ones. You can't stay on this trail. You can't even stay on this mountain. Things are gonna come looking for you here."

"What things?"

"Things like you seen tonight, only worse." The way he smiled, he clearly included himself and his wife among the "things."

Gertrude opened the shop door, the light behind her emphasizing her wide hips. "He's ready."

Herman's eyes held mine a moment longer. "Get all your gear. I'll warm up the jeep."

Tommy emerged from the store behind Gertrude Crabbe, tailing her with the waddle of a heavily sedated duckling. The jeep's headlights winked on to wash him zombie-pale.

"Hey, little fella," Herman called from the driver's-side door, sounding all grandpa-tender. The engine sputtered to life. He joined his wife in front of the jeep, their heads close together in conference. Then he ambled over to me, gesturing as he opened the passenger side door. "We're giving the boy shotgun." He pulled the seat forward. "Need you to get in first."

As I complied, he grabbed me by the shoulder and stuck his lips against my ear. "We're going to drop him off at the fire station and let him fend for himself from there. My wife's made sure he's not gonna remember anything that happened up here. We'll just keep our mouths shut, so her work don't get spoiled. Okay?"

Given everything I had been through that day, I had no problem accepting the notion that Gertrude Crabbe could hoodoo a boy's memory. I nodded and got out of his grip.

After they buckled Tommy in, Gertrude squeezed into the back seat and settled in beside me. The sky-eclipsing spider shape I associated with her gave me an urge to shrink away. But betraying repulsion in such close quarters had to be at best spectacularly gauche, at worst grounds for violent retaliation. Suppressing a grimace, I offered instead an exhausted sigh and a wan smile, musing that I never would receive my much-deserved Oscar for this performance.

Ailing shock absorbers made for a bumpy ride as we swerved down and down the mountain, our path an endless zigzag. More than once, the ghost of carsicknesses past attempted to possess me. When I was a kid, my delicate stomach, unfit for mountain roads, had ensured my parents never wanted to travel anywhere with me unless they had no choice.

"You gonna live, tiger?" Herman asked, his gaze locked forward as the headlights swung from one sudden clump of trees to another.

Why don't you tell me? I want to say.

Gertrude put a cold but gentle hand on my arm. "Not long now."

4

I had visited the town of Hillcrest once before, during my junior year of high school. My parents pulled me out of class for a week, so we could attend a viewing and funeral.

Riding in the backseat as the car navigated kiss-your-own-ass switchbacks over hill and dale always made me green-to-the-gills carsick, unfortunate because no other kind of road existed in the Appalachians. Neither my father nor my mother ever displayed any pity for me, likely because they were equally miserable in their own way. They certainly were on that trip. A cousin I had never met—I'll call him Charlie Evans—had died, and my folks wouldn't say how. My mom snapped at me for asking, which made me burn hotter with the need to know.

They had stuffed me in a suit too, for that long, queasy ride, and my mom warned me that I'd better not throw up on it, or there'd be hell to pay. So I arrived in Hillcrest, floundering on a wave of nausea, resentment, and fear. I remember my mother in a hat and coat of a green that precisely matched the churning in my gut, my father with his huge horn-rimmed glasses framed in the rearview mirror, wearing a suit at least as uncomfortable as mine, his underarms and back splotched with sweat. They hardly spoke to each other throughout the six-hour trip, and I broke the silence at my peril.

My dad was white, and my mom could pass for it, but I couldn't, and that led to unpleasantness at gatherings—though not this one. At first, I thought it was because those who mourned Charlie were too upset to pay my skin color much mind, but eventually, I realized that the folks who were direct kin to my ever-hypersensitive-to-status mother weren't much like her at all. They were, to put it simply, more accepting.

Her sensitivity was the source of the frosty silence in the car. My father didn't want to go. He disliked my mom's extended family on principle, for reasons never explained to me. My mother insisted we all had to go, that an absence would reflect badly on us. Given how nice my cousins were to me during that visit, I couldn't decide whether Mom or Dad was more in the wrong.

Case in point: I ended up alone in the kitchen with Phyllis, my first cousin once removed, as she cut more carrots, celery, and peppers for the snack trays.

Phyllis was Charlie's mom. "What happened to him?" I asked after making sure that my parents weren't in earshot. Beneath the half-veil of her loose brown hair, she grimaced, adding a decade of seams to her svelte yet sun-hardened face.

"The drugs," she said. "Drugs killed him. He got into some bad stuff." She focused dark eyes on me. "He was selling, Nathan. He tried to keep some of it for himself. And they killed him for it. Cops say they got no leads, but I know they're lying."

At sixteen, I had three inches on her in height. Still, when she laid a hand on my shoulder, she seemed a foot taller—and more motherly than my mother had ever been. "Your mama doesn't want me to tell you what happened, but I think you need to know. Don't ever let yourself get tangled in that kind of business. Stay away from it. Stay far away."

Her tone, her frankness, her sudden touch, sent chills shaking through me.

Charlie's funeral was closed casket. A couple weeks later, a kid in my homeroom tried to taunt me with the details of Charlie's death because he'd read about the murder in the Kingsport paper. Stab wounds. Sexual assault. Possibly buried alive. But I was steeled for it and shrugged it off because my cousin Phyllis had trusted me in a way my parents wouldn't.

Her gesture tapped a secret spring of comfort that helped me endure the awful silence of the ride home.

The Crabbes' jeep emerged from the forest onto a twisty road—the same one, I was sure, that my parents had taken to get to Charlie's funeral. This time, my stomach churned for a different reason. The more I thought about it, the more nervous I grew about what the plan might be. "Are we going to talk to Tommy's family?"

"Don't think so," Herman said. "Rescue crew's better equipped to handle that, don't you think?"

The road straightened. An occasional building materialized out of the dark, a barn here, an old house there—none of them built after 1950, some intact, some as ragged as my mamaw's cabin. After a turn at a stoplight, signs of late twentieth century civilization began to manifest: Marathon gas stations, a motel with its neon sign half-dead. Around another curve stood a vintage firehouse, plucked straight from a postcard—red brick with a bell tower on top, parking lot brightly lit. All three bays were open with two incongruously modern fire trucks and an ambulance gleaming inside. More light shone from the upper story windows.

Herman parked the jeep across from the station but kept the engine idling. Gertrude leaned forward to put a hand on Tommy's shoulder. "You go on now."

I started to protest, but Gertrude shushed me. Obedient as a robot, the boy unbuckled, slipped out of the jeep, and started to cross the road. Before he'd even made it halfway, Herman tapped the gas. I watched through the rear window as Tommy staggered across the parking lot toward the open bays, the tableau dwindling until another turn took us out of sight.

"With any luck, not a one of us will ever see him again," Herman said, and in my case, that proved true, though not for reasons I'd attribute to luck. His wife eyed me sidelong, winked, and smiled, half her face transformed into a rack of splayed teeth.

Herman swung us onto another switchbacking country lane. A sign said Hunting Hollow Road. I wondered, if the Crabbes took me somewhere remote and decided to wrap me up like a fly, could I bring back that massive, clawed presence that I'd become for just a moment, when those eyes spooked me behind the shop? More pragmatically, could I get the passenger door open somehow and roll out without splitting my skull on asphalt?

"We got a cousin lives out this way," Herman said. "We figure you need a place to crash for the rest of the night. Elwood knows you're coming. He'll help you hide out while you figure out where to go next."

"Don't take too long though," Gertrude added. "He won't tolerate it."

"I'd rather not cause any trouble for anyone. I know someone in Hillcrest." I stopped myself from saying, *I have family,* as the notion of revealing that to the Crabbes compounded my already considerable fear.

"I wouldn't advise that, tiger. You're a whole lot safer with Elwood than you're gonna be if you go trying to shack up with everyday folk."

"Safe from what?" Wherever we were, only the occasional mailboxes at the mouths of dirt driveways betrayed any human habitation amid the oaks and pines.

He met my gaze in the rearview mirror. "When you bared your claws to save that boy, that was a hell of a thing."

"Like dynamite in the coal mine," Gertrude said.

"We felt it when you took on your true shape. Anything out there like us—and I mean anything like *you* as well because you're like us—they for sure felt it too. And who knows how far and how wide."

"Pretty far, I'd bet."

"You got your mamaw's strength in you for sure. But none of her stealth."

"Wait." I shook my head, as the saying goes, to clear it of cobwebs. "I don't understand. You're talking like I set off some kind of earthquake."

"More like you sent out a signal," Herman said.

"But this doesn't make any sense. How? And a signal to what?"

Gertrude sounded almost motherly. "It's nothing you could have helped. When you gave that bad man what he had coming, you did it in the shape you were born to take. Must have been the first time you done it. When you come into your power like that, it's like a birth in the wild. And whether it's an egg hatching or a baby crowning, there may not be much noise, but the hungry things in the forest, they know."

"And you likely woke the whole forest. I've never seen that kind of strength right out of the gate," Herman said. "You're kinda scary, tiger."

I couldn't believe what I was hearing, and I mean that in every way possible. "You're scared of me?"

He turned his head to favor me with that toothy smile. "Didn't say *we* were scared."

Gertrude scolded him. "Watch the road, now."

"Whoops! Oh, whoa now, we're nearly there." A quick swerve around another gut-squeezing curve, and he pulled the jeep over onto a semi-circle of gravel. "End of the line. Or maybe just the start of it where you're concerned."

From the pull-off, a dirt road led uphill into dense pines. Gertrude inclined her head. "Elwood's place is up that way. You can't miss it."

My uncertainty must have shown plain on my face. She pinched my cheek in an alarmingly familiar way. "Young man, you don't know what you're doing. Makes you too ripe to leave out on the table. Elwood can help you stay out of sight. He's a bit more of a specialist than we are."

Pondering what might await me conjured the man in the white mask, struggling as a monster spider twined him with strand after strand. I swallowed. "I have a question. Please don't judge me for asking this."

The silence that followed let in the chill from outside the jeep, the grating chorus of peepers and crickets.

"You could've helped Tommy. Why didn't you?"

The Crabbes burst out laughing, the braying roar overwhelming in that tight space.

Herman recovered first. "Boy, you seen what we are. You know that ain't our nature. We don't go get things. We wait for them to come to us."

As Gertrude calmed down, her words weren't without warmth. "We did help in our way. And we prospered too."

"We got quite a nice stew to get back to," her husband said, making a pinching gesture with his malformed fingers.

Gertrude giggled, like a little girl told a juicy secret. "A little can last us a long time. And what's in our pot is quite a lot!"

"Appreciate you bringing him down for us, tiger. Keep up that kind of good work, you might just live a while."

"Herman. Don't make me bite off your other fingers."

He bugged his eyes in mock fear and followed that with an explosion of snaggle-toothed laughter.

I said, "Thank you—for everything. I should be going now. If you could let me out—"

To my immense relief, Herman leaned across and popped the passenger door, making room for my escape.

"Elwood's expecting you," Gertrude said. "No need to be shy."

"I won't be," I lied.

Herman got out with me and opened the back hatch. "Don't forget your stuff," he said.

As I hefted my pack, he put a staying hand on my arm. I managed not to shrink away. "One more thing, tiger. Me and the missus and our cousin, we ain't the only ones out there with a bit of spider in our steps. Most of 'em aren't so kind to strangers as we are. Not a lick of kindness in their souls, truth be told. You meet one, and it ain't one of us, you watch yourself. Understand?"

I didn't, but I nodded, desperate for them to leave me be. "Thank you."

"You watch yourself anyway. Stay alert, stay alive."

"Okay. Thank you."

Lit from below by the parking lights, he pursed his lips. "You'll learn, one way or the other. Best you get along."

I pointed up the dirt drive, which bored a hole through the trees. A few strides in, a net of that blue ghost-webbing had been stretched across the gap, no doubt to serve Cousin Elwood as a perimeter alarm. "That way?" He nodded. "Thanks again." I started walking. To my immense relief, he didn't watch but climbed back in the jeep. With an engine rev, the Crabbes did a U-turn and were gone.

Hunting Hollow Road continued only a few dozen more yards before it dissolved into dirt, just like Elwood's driveway. An End State Maintenance sign marked the point of transition. Beyond that, another glowing blue net awaited the unwary and just plain unaware. And beyond that, more shimmering strands of blue glimmered, strung within the trees. Astral spider silk infested the woods.

I wanted no part of that.

I turned a slow circle, trying to gauge how far the web extended. Across the street from Elwood's drive, a pair of motionless headlights stopped me cold, twin pinpricks aimed at me from deep within the brush.

The lights blinked. By which I don't mean they turned off and on. Rather, their eyelids closed and reopened, reflecting the electric blue of the spiderwebs. Fear spiked through me, the searing heat of an inexplicable rage cascading close behind. I burned to make myself a hundred times larger, to turn this fear against the thing watching me. I rose to my full height, arching my back and baring my fangs.

Though the watcher was perhaps a football field away, I heard, bell-clear, a man's whisper: "Shit! He sees me!"

"Unbelievable!" another man hissed. "Hang on!"

The eyes disappeared, and a huge shape launched into the night sky—the same one that had fled from me behind the Crabbes' store.

I didn't think. I focused on the thick mass of its body, bracketed by impossibly long wings, and sprang.

For an elongated second, nothing filled my vision but a ghastly, humongous raptor, outlined by the glow of countless stars. Even more stars, though muted, shone through its translucent form. I took in all the creature's details: a bare head, which was small compared to its fat gourd of a body, a wicked beak, feathers longer than human legs, talons clutched tight around a man who could have been a mouse by proportion. That man, stout and blocky and clad in black, stared with terror-wide eyes, but his terror wasn't caused by the enormous vulture carrying him off. His fear was all for me and my extended claws.

Those claws—my enormous claws—sliced through empty air. Trees rose to meet me.

Next came the most spectacularly disorienting moment of my life, at least up to that point. I landed on all fours. I should have been impaled on a hundred tree branches, but smooth ground met the pads of my paws. When I curled my lips back, the wet membranes pressed against long teeth. When I flexed my fingers, claws retracted. My arms were tree trunk thick and coated in fur. I turned my head and bent my neck to behold a powerful feline body—and a tail that twitched as I stared.

The body I inhabited wasn't the most dizzying aspect of what I had to absorb. The second layer of dissonance came from my sheer size—if my eyes were to be believed, I was larger than any panther that ever could have lived, tall as an eighteen-wheeler and almost as long. A hundred times odder, I wasn't impaled on dozens of branches because I co-existed in the same space as the forest without touching any of it. The tree trunks *did* impale me, but it was as if they weren't solid. Or I wasn't solid. Either I was a ghost or the only living creature in a ghost-world.

I had seen the likes of this when Herman passed through the ring of blue smoke and became a spider. And when Gertrude held a gun on Tommy's abductor while at the same time binding him, the shapes of spider and demon superimposed over the gully.

Far above me, the man in the clutches of the vulture spoke. I heard him plain, even though he whispered from high in the sky. "If that's Elzbeth's grandson, he's just as scary as she is."

"What does *that* mean?" I shouted back even as something in the back of my brain screamed, *Hallucination!* "My mamaw's dead!"

My voice was my own and not, each syllable blended with a basso snarl.

A response unintelligible yet full of alarm.

I fixated on the dark shape filtering the stars and gave chase. Urgency and anger fueled me, and those grim emotions gave way to sheer, adrenaline-jazzed joy as I gained speed, every obstacle an insignificant phantom, trees whooshing through me, no more a barrier than air. The sensation distracted me so thoroughly that I forgot my quarry—who eluded me easily anyhow, vanishing into the sky. I ran and ran through valleys and over hills toward the lights glowing on the horizon, the evidence of nightlife in Hillcrest.

I didn't question, in my state, the solid ground beneath my paws. The contours of the surface I ran upon followed those of the hilly forest floor, though not precisely. I dashed through a jutting rock as easily as I passed through trees. At times, I seemed to levitate, my pads pounding a faintly visible sheet of silver that existed at an elevation above the roots and brush, its texture akin to dry loam.

A paved road split the forest, and I pivoted to follow its path. Streetlights blurred past, and then buildings. In ten minutes, perhaps fifteen, I had run from Elwood's driveway to well within the town limits. I stood in an empty strip mall parking lot, my gaze level with a Ben Franklin department store sign.

Then I was staring up at it. No unearthly loam under my feet, just the hard, sweaty encasement of boots. I put my hands to my chest. All that running and my T-shirt was dry. Not a drop of sweat. I dropped to my knees, laid hands on the cracked parking lot asphalt, cold beneath the starlight.

It dawned on me then that my pack had not made the jaunt with me. I'd left it at the head of Elwood's driveway, all the possessions I'd brought with me, including the remains of my scholarship money, stuffed inside.

I'd reached town from that remote place so quickly. Maybe I could reverse the experience. I focused on the sign, the last thing I'd regarded in giant-cat form. Enough time elapsed with nothing happening to convince me I was being stupid.

Streaks of cloud blotted stars as I stared at the firmament, imagining that huge vulture carrying a man in his talons. I tried to convince myself that the stars were malevolent eyes, the portent of menace that had twice triggered my transformation. I remained solid flesh.

With a sigh, I admitted that my only recourse lay in tracking down my cousin Phyllis, whom I hadn't seen since her son's funeral. Back then, the options for reaching out still involved payphones and phonebooks suspended in protective plastic covers. Luckily, both were mounted by the Ben Franklin's front doors.

I hoped my cousin would be receptive to a collect call at that ungodly hour.

5

I've never been a good liar. So I told Phyllis a version of the truth. I had needed to get away from Tech. I didn't like my professors. I still loved art, but I needed space to decide whether graphic design was really right for me. I got a wild hair that I would hike the AT in order to clear my head but had a change of heart during the long, sweaty hours on the trail. On the way to Hillcrest, I had a close brush with a bear, at least I thought it was a bear, I only knew for sure that it was really large. I dropped my pack and ran, luckily in the right direction, toward town. On the other end of the line, her responses mostly consisted of "Oh" and "Oh my" and "Hmm."

She arrived in a long brown station wagon, the kind of car that manufacturers had to know was butt ugly from the moment it rolled off the line. She leaned out the driver's side window. "Haven't *you* grown up handsome."

What could I say to that? "Thanks for coming out here."

"You're lucky you turned up on my night off."

"I guess I am." My sigh of relief, at least, was honest. "It's great to see you."

Though she had her hair bound in a kerchief, I couldn't miss the spread of gray through her once black locks. She had a narrow jaw and sharp chin and a complexion that put me in mind of cracked terracotta. All that said, she was a striking woman, her dark eyes large and alert. "You really don't want me to call your parents?"

"Please don't. They don't know I'm here, and I don't want them to know. I'm not ready yet."

"Okay. Well, let's see if we can find your things. Hunting Hollow, right?"

My pack squatted right where I'd dropped it at the head of Elwood's driveway. "You are so lucky," said Phyllis. "You need to tell me where to find that kind of luck. I'd buy it by the bushel."

Fainter in the light of the rising sun, the ghost-webs strung through the trees still shone. I bit my tongue against the urge to ask Phyllis if she could see them.

Her wagon smelled of pine freshener. The radio was on a country station, turned down low enough to be darn near inaudible. Thank God. "You remember my brother-in-law Mike?" she asked.

I didn't but said, "I think so."

"He coulda used some of your luck," and as we rolled back toward town, she shared a story about how Mike's trip out to buy a new power drill had led to meeting an ex, a few drinks, meeting the ex's other ex, some bad decisions, and then a jail sentence. I knew none of the people involved, and it sounded to me like Mike brought on his own bad fortune, so I nodded and made appropriate exclamations while my mind, of its own accord, tried again to fit the events of the last twenty-four hours into a puzzle picture that made sense: the ghost boy who turned out to be real, the American Gothic storekeepers who turned out to be spiders, the demon who turned out to be a man who ended up spider prey. My dead mamaw must have been a sorceress because what other word could fit? Or explain the supernatural possibilities contained within my own flesh?

An urge dared me to test out my new-found abilities, prove to myself whether or not they were real, right there in the passenger seat of Phyllis's station wagon.

"Hey, Nathan, whatcha thinking about?" My cousin turned the wheel and brought us into a hilly neighborhood with modest houses perched on the peaks, the vinyl siding that sheathed them flashing shy colors in the pre-dawn light.

I started. "Nothing, nothing."

"Bullcrap. You went somewhere on me, and you didn't look happy about it."

I grinned my biggest shit-eating grin, hoping that would sate her. "You can say *bullshit*. I'm all grown up now."

She smirked. "We'll see about that. Almost home."

We turned up a steep driveway into the garage of a house a tad fancier than I remembered, two stories with a basketball hoop above the garage door and a backyard enclosed by a high wooden fence. The hoop gave me pause. To my knowledge, Phyllis had no children other than Charlie—who had moved out, I thought, before meeting his awful fate.

I followed my cousin into mauve-carpeted rooms, pleasantly lived-in but uncluttered. "I've got a hideaway couch in the TV room. We can get that set up before I have to leave for work. If you don't mind helping me and don't mind that I'm going to have to ditch you."

"Of course not." I kept my smile on. I knew empirically that it projected charm. "I think I could sleep the day through." That wasn't a lie. The hot shower I took before crashing felt so good. It could have been a holy baptism.

I dreamt of chaos. All around me, rows and rows of black pine trees scrabbled toward the sky, their rings of nude branches curling to all sides like petrified spider legs. Their fallen needles pricked the soles of my bare feet. An immense creature moved in the distance, fragmented from view through the tree trunks, muscles rippling beneath metallic blue hide.

Completing the mise-en-scène, a woman stood with her back to me, jet black hair flowing down her shoulders, her gown merging with the umber of the forest floor. As my hand inched timidly forward to tap her on the shoulder, her hair fluttered and lengthened, growing thin and gray as cobweb. The outline of her silhouette shifted at my approach, cheekbones lengthening into an animal's muzzle.

She turned in a flash of fangs.

I jerked upright in the hide-a-bed. The drawn curtains muffled my surroundings in gloom. I concluded I was still dreaming, for the scene playing out before me made no sense otherwise. Shadows formed edges and textures. What few highlights there were gleamed ghostly blue, the same way I'd perceived the Crabbes' webbing and their monstrous spider forms.

A new monster swam before me: a razor-toothed anglerfish as big as a tractor, the axis of its spine tilted vertically, the pinpricks of its pupils aimed up at two men who levitated above its fearsome maw, facing one another. The creature could have escaped from a medieval sailor's nightmare of the deep, but the men seemed oblivious to it. The space these three figures occupied bore no relation to the boundaries set by the walls and ceiling of Phyllis's house.

One of the men, short, stocky, bald, wore a long, shapeless coat that reminded me of a monk's robe. The other, younger, was naked, emaciated, and marred by grotesque wounds. A gash yawned ragged across his throat, echoing his torn mouth. His jaw hung loose.

The robed man's form grew brighter, blue light flowing like lava lamp plasma from the dome of his hairless scalp to fill all his contours. The other's wounds grew more vivid. Holes gaping in his chest resembled lips parted in surprise.

His left arm ended just above the wrist. Guts dangled from stabs to his belly. His genitals were missing, raw meat glistening in their place.

The monk raised his arms in mimicry of a crucifix. The mutilated one—whose face and frame, despite all, possessed familiar features—stepped forward.

The huge fish darted up, and the ghost of my long-dead cousin Charlie disappeared into its jaws. For an instant, his head protruded from between the monster's teeth, thrashing frantically. The fish gulped, and he vanished altogether.

The plasma glow drained upward through the robed man as if sucked out by a siphon. Maybe that was exactly how it worked, for I only then noticed that the lure-tentacle rooted in the monster fish's brow extended upward to fuse into the back of the robed man's head. He was the lure.

As the glow dimmed, so did the outline of the angler. The robed man alone remained. His shoulders shook as he wept.

He faded too. I was staring up at a corner of the TV room's ceiling, the gloom diluting, sunshine outlining the window shades. The vision of the three figures had lasted only a few seconds, but I'd been awake all through it.

My innards ached with hunger. Not the pangs of an empty stomach but a yearning that pulsed in the spaces between my cells, an emptiness in every part of me crying out to be filled. This appetite existed beyond the boundaries of my skin and bone, the cravings of a much larger beast, funneled through me. This same sensation had ached inside me as I'd approached my mamaw's cabin and after she pulled me out of its wooden ruin, her huge green eyes full of reproach. This same ache, not as strong, had goaded me as I chased after the spies who gave themselves away in the woods across from Elwood's lair.

Watching the monster fish eat Charlie's ghost had affected me as if I'd had nothing to eat for days and I'd just watched someone wolf down a burger.

This recognition had the opposite effect. I rushed to the bathroom and enacted a tragedy, barfing up the lovely breakfast my cousin had prepared for me: melon slices, English muffins smeared with apricot jelly, four different species of cheese, and a heap of bacon.

No way, I thought as I recovered, would I sleep again. Still, the jump-cut advance of the wall clock told me that I indeed had. As the second hand made jittery revolutions, tumblers clicking in the front door lock announced Phyllis's return. I pulled on my cleanest T-shirt and jeans, which weren't terribly clean, and met her at the door. She shot me a quizzical look. "You sleep okay?"

"Can I ask you something crazy?"

"Sure."

"Is this house haunted?"

 Her eyes flew wide. "Why would you ask that?"

"Bad dream I had."

She walked to a closet, hung up her coat. While turned away from me she said, "It used to be." She glanced my way, measuring my reaction, which likely manifested as confusion, as I wondered how I could possibly have seen what I'd seen.

Finally, I asked, "How do you mean?"

She left to rummage in another room. When she came back, she handed me a business card. "He told me the ghost was gone." The card read Warner Mews, Angler. "And I know he didn't lie. Nothing bad's happened since he came here and cleansed the house. He had such a kind face." Her tone turned dreamy.

"Made you think of Friar Tuck? Round face, big belly, wears something like a monk's robe?"

 She stared. "You know him?"

"No, no," I sputtered, scrambling to figure out how to explain this. "I mean . . . there's something familiar about the name. Not quite sure how I came across it. Maybe saw him on campus? Lots of weird people hang around the Carolina Tech campus . . . funny, huh?"

Her brows knitted, but then her entire expression softened for no obvious reason. "I owe that man my life," she said. "I'm so glad he came to my door."

"Came to your door?"

"He knew I needed help." Once more, her gaze went glassy as she spoke.

A chill crawled over me. "How do you mean that?"

She started to answer but shook her head as if clearing out dust. I recalled what Herman Crabbe had said to me, that his wife would make sure Tommy forgot all about his harrowing ordeal. When the boy spoke to police and parents about what happened, perhaps his eyes would glaze over in the same way. "I want to hear about the haunting," I said, hoping she could refocus long enough to tell me.

The awkward pause dragged on until she shook herself again. "And you'll tell me how you know Warner?"

Tentatively, I nodded.

"Let's take care of you first. Want a snack?"

She didn't feel comfortable sharing more until we were settled at the table in her upstairs kitchen, her with warm tea in a mug that read "Moms: Just Like Dads, Only SMARTER!" and me with a glass of diet soda. With a deep breath, she began. "After Charlie . . . died, I saw him everywhere. That was normal, I think, part of the grieving process. I felt so awful for so long about kicking him out of the house, but I couldn't let him stay here after he started bringing those awful people back with him late at night. His death . . . for a while I thought it was because of me, that I set him up for it when I sent him off on his own, knowing what he'd gotten into."

"It wasn't your fault."

"I know that. But I couldn't help thinking that way. That's not really my point. Sometimes, in the corner of my eye, I'd see his face outside the window. Or in the rearview mirror. Or I'd be out shopping and see him standing at the end of the aisle and then he'd be gone. It stopped after a while, and I guessed it was just, you know, grief. Until a couple months ago."

"You were seeing him again?"

"Worse than that. I started having these dreams at night. Hot, suffocating. Like I was him, still alive in that hole they buried him in, fighting to breathe. I don't mean his grave. I mean when he was murdered. They threw him in the ditch they made him dig and shoveled the dirt back on him while he lay there bleeding. There was dirt in his lungs, Nathan, mixed with his blood. I could feel that in the dream.

"I went back to church for the first time in years, talked to the preacher about it, even tried taking up prayer again, but the dreams didn't stop. And I kept seeing him. I'd go to work and see him in the store parking lot. A couple times I heard him say, 'Mom,' when I was alone in the office." She fidgeted, staring anywhere but at me. "Damn, I need a smoke. Too bad I quit. Five years ago, I quit.

"The dreams, see, they got worse. From being trapped under the mud to crawling out of it. To walking through the woods, walking out of them, down the road. I wouldn't always have this dream, but when I did, it always picked up right where it left off. Walking into town. Into this neighborhood. To the front door of my house.

"And when I was dreaming like that, looking out through Charlie's eyes, my skin itched like there were bugs all over me. It kept getting worse, the closer he got.

"Then just a couple nights ago, I had the dream again, and I was staring in through my bedroom window—on the second floor!—at myself sleeping. I woke up more scared than I'd ever been in my life."

My hairs practically stood on end, imagining the mutilated Charlie from my vision, hovering outside Phyllis's window. Beneath that, another thought stirred my hackles, one that made no sense even though my mind insisted on threading the connection. The strange things I'd seen on campus that no one else reacted to, the huge insects and floating faces that had me scared that my mind was going, scared me so bad that I fled to the trail to escape . . . I couldn't be sure yet, but it sounded like her dreams of Charlie had started about the same time.

That meant nothing. Surely. Except I had somehow seen his ghost myself, and many stranger things that also turned out to be real, including this part-man, part fish monster Mews. "What about the guy who left that card?"

Her eerie, glazed-over expression returned. "He came the next morning. He had the saddest eyes I'd ever seen. He said he'd heard my prayers and could help me. So I let him in."

"Just like that? You let him in?"

"I could tell. He would never lie." Her smile, aimed at nothing in particular, could have been a vacancy sign. "He told me to wait outside. It only took a few minutes, and it was done."

"What was done?"

"Charlie's ghost went away. He's at peace now. Mews told me. He left his card in case any more dreams troubled me."

Charlie was at peace. The way his head had thrashed, trapped between the teeth of a monster fish. "What made you sure he was gone?"

"The house. It had been like the air was electrified. Like there was angry energy heating it up. It had come on so gradually that I didn't really notice it. Or maybe I didn't want to acknowledge it. But I sure felt the difference when it was gone."

"Can I see that card?"

It divulged an address. This Mews had made himself easy to find. I planned to do just that.

Like that old proverb goes, man plans, God laughs.

6

I asked Phyllis, "Do you know where this is?" She told me Old Hurricane Road was across town but easy to get to. I asked if she'd been to Mews's place. She hadn't since there had been no need. I asked if maybe I could borrow the station wagon for this excursion. Her eyes narrowed, the strange stupor that the memory of Mews brought on starting to recede. Then her vacant smile returned, so damn unnerving on her wry, vibrant face.

"Charlie had a ten-speed. It's still in the shed. Might be a little rusty. Shed's not locked."

That bike had to be twenty years old. "Okay . . . I'll check it out, thank you."

Her eyes narrowed again. "Why do you want to do this?"

"I think he can help me with something."

In her state, that answer satisfied, which gave me a twinge of guilt, though I wasn't exactly lying. The man belonged to the strange new world I'd discovered, no question of that, and the thought that he had visited Phyllis right before I arrived and placed some sort of hoodoo over her disturbed me deeply. Even if Mews had indeed rid her of a haunting, his method disgusted me, and my own visceral reaction disgusted me even more.

I had accepted my half-waking vision as gospel because of how closely Phyllis's story correlated. I didn't wonder then how the vision had come to me in the first place, attributing it to some aspect of my heritage from Mamaw Elzbeth that I didn't understand yet.

That bizarre hunger motivated me more than anything. I had a half-assed notion that this Mews character could help me get my mind around it—if he turned out to be someone who would work with me rather than against me. What he'd done for Phyllis made me think he might.

Finding Charlie's bike inside the shed full of lawn equipment proved a sad affair. The chain had less rust than you might've expected, and the wheels spun freely, but the tires were flat. On a rack hung a tire pump that still worked. I hadn't ridden a bike since before I left for Tech, but my body retained the muscle memory. In minutes, I was clicking down the sidewalk.

The evening sun hovered ahead, just above the horizon, showing me streets flanked by unassuming homes and dingy convenience stores. Dust whipped past as I rolled, borne on gusts smelling of asphalt and gasoline. I crossed a small bridge over a stream banked by nettles, a cluster of beer cans submerged in its brown muck.

Dwellings gave way to warehouses. Ahead loomed the structures that served as Hillcrest's downtown, none taller than three stories. The lowering sun transformed them into toy-block silhouettes. Their darkening profiles gave me pause—as with the AT hike, I'd planned poorly. Night would conquer by the time I reached Mews's place on the other side of town.

My pulse quickened, but not out of fear. A new part of me relished the thought of confronting this fishman in the dark. Claws that I both did and did not possess flexed in anticipation. I marveled at this eager rush—and worried too.

What businesses still clung to life downtown locked their doors after five— many of the storefronts weren't even occupied. An unusually tall fellow in a navy cardigan and stocking cap watched me pass, his physique simultaneously squat and gangly. A couple cars zoomed through cross streets, alerting me to be cautious.

Beyond the dilapidated buildings, a rail yard lurked, marked off by a high chain-link fence and incongruous shrubs. Past the fence, four sets of train tracks ran parallel, bisecting the town. I paused across the street, the setting sun in my face, and took stock by mental compass. South and to my left, about three blocks down, a traffic bridge vaulted over the tracks. North and to my right, about twenty yards away, a footbridge made the crossing—with another traffic bridge visible at least five blocks farther. I turned for the footbridge as a train that was several miles off announced itself with a rumble and clang.

This footbridge had seen better days. Paint had flaked in mass quantities from the rails and bracing, as if the structure had mange. Most of the wooden boards had warped. I started up the slanted walk, and had my time on the AT not hardened me to uphill climbs, I would have probably needed to hop off the bike and ascend on foot.

Beyond the chain-link that bounded the other side of the rail yard, a man sauntered toward the same footbridge. I might not have noticed him were it not for his great height and his swollen gut. He could have been twin to the fellow I pedaled past moments before.

I glanced behind me. That very gentleman was rounding the corner, hustling toward the bridge, eyes fixed on me.

My hackles sprang to full attention. I pedaled ten times as hard, cresting onto the straightaway portion of the bridge. The train, which I had thought miles away, emerged into view from the south, a pair of diesel engines pulling double-stacked cargo containers. Its shadow blotted out the downtown side of the tracks.

I made it to the downhill ramp. The tall fellow I'd seen across the tracks stood about halfway down, right in the center of the walkway, his spindly arms loose by his sides, ready to grab. Behind him, layers of blue webbing crisscrossed the bridge railing, blocking the way forward. His eyes and mouth sat too wide in his pinched face, reminding me of Herman. The Crabbes had made no mention of Cousin Elwood running with a twin.

The bridge shook as the first fellow stomped up behind me.

I hopped off Charlie's bike and figuratively backpedaled, for all the good it would do me. The train had almost reached the traffic bridge to the south, the height of its double-stacked containers leaving only a couple yards of clearance. A fantastically bad idea bloomed in my brain.

"Easy there, buddy," said the guy behind me in a nasal Yank accent, definitely no Elwood. He'd joined me at the top of the bridge. He had those same narrow features. Behind him, more blue webbing blocked the way back.

They had me trapped on the footbridge. My heartbeat approached overdrive. I concentrated on the huge cat limbs that I'd seen extend from my own torso, the claws that put paid to the creep in the mask. My body remained as was. Above us the sky blazed glorious red. Trucks and SUVs whooshed across the southern bridge as the train emerged from beneath it. "Who are you?" I stammered. "Did the Crabbes send you?"

The guy facing me smirked. The one behind me chuckled.

The double diesel locomotives rumbled underneath us. I dashed at the north rail. Both sides of my peripheral vision filled with monstrous spider legs.

I gave myself no room to think. Slapped my hands on the rail, hopped up and over, plunged straight down at the roof of a moving cargo container. Seconds stretched into agony.

I slammed belly first onto unyielding metal. All the wind crushed out of me as if I'd been smashed by the world's biggest fist.

A glance back showed me two immense spiders skittering over the side of the bridge to join me on the train.

The pain that wracked my body dulled as I spun to face them. Abruptly, the car beneath my body shrank. My vantage changed, my eyes larger, spread wider apart. My claws clamped down on the edge of the container roof, my haunches crouched where I'd landed, and my tail arched out behind me—the threat in front of me brightening to crystal clarity as my eyes adjusted.

There was no sensation of flesh tearing or inflating. My transformation happened fast as ice heat-blasted into steam. In a blink I phased from one state to the other. As panther, my form was enormous, almost as wide and as long as the train car. Reflexes quicker than I had any right to possess kept me from tumbling off.

Two skinny black spiders the size of Buicks clung to the next double-stacked car, one on each side. Both froze in their crazy-legs advance as I stared them down.

I had not forgotten the train would soon pass under another bridge. The corrugated steel of the cargo container I stood upon registered solid and cold beneath the pads of my paws. Maybe the bridge would be just as solid.

The spiders, sensing my distraction, resumed their advance. A wicked joy spread through me at the realization that, as fast as they were, I had no difficultly tracking every move.

The one on my right scurried within my reach first. I lashed out with a paw. He reared back but not quickly enough. My claws tore through his eye clusters, ripped off his fangs and front legs in a single swipe.

As the second spider arrived, I sprang off the train car and soared over him, flipping horizontally and alighting two cars south, facing back in the direction I came from. My claws latched to the edges of the car without need to expend conscious thought on the act. My kamikaze leap over my attackers hardly took a second's time.

The spider I had mauled was human again, staggering atop the train car where I'd struck him, face a blot of gore, more blood spurting from a severed arm. That he stood upright at all was both incredible and horrible because he was tall enough that as the car passed under the northern traffic bridge a support beam slammed his already ruined head. He skidded off balance and fell into the gap between cars.

My scream burst from my feline throat as a strangled roar. I sprang off the train.

I landed in the street on the downtown side of the fence as a mix of nausea and hunger corkscrewed through me. The train continued northward, oblivious to the corpse crushed underneath its wheels.

No sign of the other pursuer. In three leaps, I was back to the top of the footbridge by Charlie's fallen bike, scanning the double-stacked cars fore and aft. A splotch under the northern bridge marked the place where the man-spider hit his head. Beneath the bridge, a small object lay on unoccupied track—a hand and length of forearm, cast red by the lowering sun. Even at this distance, my sinuses flooded with the copper smell of spilt blood.

I collapsed, my palms pressed against the dry grain of the warped boards, that awful hunger giving way completely to nausea. I rolled over, and the handlebars of Charlie's bike stabbed the small of my back.

"She'll kill you for this."

I stared up into a vomit-inducing horror—the underside of an immense pair of spider fangs, bracketing a puckered, bristle-filled mouth the size of my human fist. The monster hovered a few yards above me, rising toward the purple sky. I scrambled out from underneath and, from an angle a few yards distant, spied the thread rising from the black spider's abdomen, attached to some anchor in the heavens far out of sight.

Where he'd been a moment before, I couldn't say—cloaked, somehow, from my panther-self. At that point, I recognized the species: a male black widow. A type of spider I'd seen plenty of times playing in the barns that belonged to my childhood friends' families back in Tennessee. The spider continued to climb. "All we wanted was to talk," he said in that thick Yank accent. He pulled sideways and disappeared into the middle of the air.

"I'm sorry," I said to no one.

The webbing sealing off the bridge ramps had vanished. The whole thing could have been a mirage—except for the small, pale object on the tracks, still discernible in the fading dusk.

I could go to the police, say I'd seen the man throw himself under the train. No one would be the wiser. Or I could get the hell out of town. The *we* these creatures represented knew I was in Hillcrest—and so did the *she* who supposedly would kill me. When the Crabbes had warned me about others like them, I would bet a bottom dollar they had these folks in mind. I pedaled back the way I came, hoping I wouldn't be waylaid again, my quest to find Mews abandoned.

"Do you want dinner?" Phyllis asked after she let me inside. She didn't inquire whether I'd found Mews. I had the impression that she'd forgotten our earlier conversation or that the hoodoo Mews had placed on her made her forget. Sans the vision I'd had, and the questions it had prompted, I don't think I would have ever learned about that bizarre exorcism.

I wondered too if I could learn to understand and even control whatever had triggered the vision, and if so, might they then forewarn me against calamities like the ambush on the bridge? At that moment, alas, other worries in the mix took priority. What if someone came hunting for me at Phyllis's house?

I couldn't stay a moment longer. "Can I make a long-distance call?"

"Phoning your folks?"

That was the last thing I wanted to do. "I'm thinking about it," I said.

"There's a phone in the kitchen. Though if you want privacy, I never took the phone out of Charlie's room."

I agreed to the privacy offer. I didn't want Phyllis listening in when I called the Nesmiths, given all the ways that conversation could go wrong.

The urge to flee the increasingly alarming environment of the Tech campus by taking to the AT had sprouted gradually out of something Bill Nesmith said to me on the final day of my freshman year—the same week he landed a mechanical engineering job in Stroudsburg and left North Carolina for good.

Man, imagine all those miles alone on the trail, he said to me. *All the junk that other people tack onto you just peeling off. Every thought you can't finish finding room to breathe. Every argument festering in your head gets a chance to work itself out, and you can then cast it aside. We could get rid of all those voices that keep giving us hell even after the people who said that stuff to us in the first place aren't even in our lives anymore.*

I gave little thought to the fact that Bill himself had never set out on the journey he described in such lofty terms. To be somewhat fair to myself, I was only nineteen when he gave me that speech and still flabbergasted such cool and attractive people even allowed me the pleasure of their company, much less invited me to take part in their private frolics, intellectual and physical.

We met because they happened to sit beside me in a European history class Bill needed to complete his humanities credits as a sixth-year senior in engineering. Melissa had taken the class too, just to be near her beau. She didn't really need it, or so she said.

She sat behind Bill, quietly riffing sarcastic on every topic of the ancient professor's lectures. By some miracle of acoustics or handicap of old age the prof never caught on to what she was doing, despite her boyfriend's constant snickers. Yet I heard every word and couldn't help smirking in their direction. Rather than cutting their eyes at me, they appreciated that I got the jokes.

Both wore long, black trench coats that hung open to reveal T-shirts bearing the logos of amazing bands: Megadeth, The Misfits, Suicidal Tendencies, Jane's Addiction. One day after class, I asked what they thought of the new Faith No More, and that opened the friendship door all the way. They were outsiders too, of a sort, though their Goth-white skin was still white.

They introduced me to roleplaying games, to weed and acid, to the complex bedroom dynamics of a threesome. Were I prone to shifting blame, I might have tried to pin the nerve-wracking visions I experienced during my first months as a sophomore on the habits they taught me.

By then, they were nowhere around. The job Bill landed with some help from family started immediately after graduation. Melissa dropped out of school to stick with him, not even bothering to finish her degree.

They had wed during the summer. They'd invited me, but I didn't have the resources to go—that is, I lacked a car of my own. Trust me, I'd have given anything to get out from under my folks' roof, where I stayed a virtual prisoner in my bedroom, hiding from Mom's baleful gaze and her arguments with Dad, artillery assaults loaded with verbal abuse.

Melissa was so gracious over the phone when I told her I'd miss the wedding. "It's okay, sweetie. We'll take a raincheck. Come see us any time you want to."

So my plan, such as it was, had been to drop in on them when the AT brought me to northeastern Pennsylvania. The Nesmiths didn't know this though. I was so sure they'd take me in, I hadn't bothered to phone ahead before I emptied my bank account, bought everything from the outdoor equipment store that the clerks told me I would need, and fled to the hills.

My mind conjured perverse conversation openers as Phyllis showed me to her dead son's room. *Hey, Bill, I turned into a giant ghost-cat and killed some spider-dude. Mind if I shack up with y'all for a while?* You'd think with images of torn faces and severed limbs dancing in my head that I wouldn't have entertained such private jokes, but my predicament had shot so far past unreal that gallows humor came easy. *Hey, guys, I've learned a whole new definition of pussy-whipped. Can't wait to demonstrate. Hey, Melissa, you always said you were a cat person. Wait'll you see what I'm gonna drag in.*

Phyllis asked, "What's that weird smile mean?"

"Nothing," I said. "Just thinking about what I'm going to say."

"Want me to call?"

"No, no, no. Please don't trouble yourself. I can handle this." I gently pushed past her and flipped on the light. Immediately, I regretted setting foot in the room. "Let me just . . . work up the nerve," I said, my voice strained for a completely different reason. A cold prickling needled every inch of my skin. My stomach twinged with more of those bizarre hunger pangs.

"I'll be in the kitchen if you need me." Thank goodness she shut the door.

Charlie's room was a macabre time capsule. Psychedelic posters of King Crimson, Jethro Tull, and Yes mingled with models in bikinis whose names I didn't know. Phyllis, I supposed, wasn't the sort of mom who would bat an eye at such things. His bed sported Washington Redskins sheets. The room also held that strange energy and sense of emptiness that triggered and amplified my weird hunger.

This, I surmised, was where the scene from my vision, the consuming of Charlie's ghost, must have taken place. Maybe it was a mistake to make a sensitive call in that environment. I guessed I'd best get it over with quickly.

I didn't have the Nesmiths' number handy, but information disclosed it readily enough. Perhaps I was hearing things in my shocky state, but though the lady operator gave me the number, I could swear a man on the line whispered, "Take care of yourself, Nathan," before I was patched through.

Melissa picked up on the first ring. Her own surprise gave way to delight when she recognized my voice. "God, yes, we so want to see you. You're going to be joining us soon?" She always voiced her demands as coy questions, and hearing that affectation soothed me like the crackle from a warm hearth. She did not sound the least bit bothered that I was skipping school—but then she of all people wasn't going to find that a problem.

I suspect, though, that if I could've seen her face, her expression might not have matched the bubbly champagne cheer of her words. I might even have picked up on a phony quality to her tone were I not so relieved by the welcome. Really, though, my imagination may only be trying to revise the conversation in light of what came later.

"It may take me a day or two," I said. "I'll need to come by bus."

"Give us a collect call once you're in town. We'll come pick you up."

We didn't talk about how long I might stay—a further relief since I had no idea what I might ultimately need to ask from them. So long as I could get the hell away from Hillcrest, I'd worry about the rest later.

Phone call done, I ate dinner with Phyllis and crawled back into the hide-a-bed. I gave little more thought to this Mews character and what he'd done to Phyllis and Charlie. None of that carried the urgency of the arm on the train track and the dangling spider's strange threat.

As it turned out, I ended up crossing paths with Mews after all—under even stranger circumstances.

7

I got dressed in the windup to soul's midnight. Ideally, I'd be on a bus headed north on I-81 before Phyllis woke up. Except I had no wheels. Taking her son's bike and then abandoning it at the station for her to retrieve would pile insult on top of insult.

But I had a built-in means to travel, didn't I? I'd be mid-town in no time if I could gain some measure of control over this thing that I could do. If not, I had hours to walk the distance before dawn.

I had only performed the shift to panther as a gut reaction to direct threats. Reason told me—if such things as reason and logic could apply to my situation— that conscious command of the change *had* to be possible. The Crabbes had that power. The masked creep in the woods must have been capable of it, and the spider-twins who tried to trap me on the bridge had swapped between monster and person at will.

I put heat under half-baked ideas in an attempt to make them rise. Threats triggered the transformation, specifically threats from creatures of that other world. Correction, *people* of that other world. With the exception of Tommy, who had been abducted somehow into the shadow realm, every spirit thing I had seen so far had also been a person, even the ghosts in the cottage on my mamaw's property.

My thoughts raced—gnawed on possibilities, struggled to sort what conditions could bring about a deliberate shift in form—while I restuffed my backpack, put my arms through the shoulder straps, and slipped quietly as possible from the TV room.

A rare flash of practical insight inspired a detour to the kitchen, where I'd seen pen and paper. I wrote a note to my cousin, telling her that I needed to leave early to catch my bus, so I called a cab. I didn't want to wake her, I wrote, but I needed to leave early. I told her my parents were happy to let me come home, and she didn't need to worry. I left a $20 bill from my stash to pay, sort of, for what she had fed me.

Outside, I entertained a morbid notion that, if something went wrong, maybe I'd end up in a nightmarish situation, like with half of me on either side of a solid wall. Finally, I laughed and shrugged. What else could I do?

I turned my gaze heavenward. Hillcrest was a tiny city as cities go, but it still sent up enough light to mute the stars. I imagined Charlie's ghost floating overhead—and I gave him the wings and glowing eyes of my recurring mystery stalkers. I pushed myself further, picturing the long, curving arachnid limbs of my attackers on the bridge, the spines of Tommy's kidnapper.

All my life, I'd been prone to engaging in imaginary arguments as if the other person were physically present. That night, this crack in my sanity bore spectacular fruit. The amalgamation of all my recent unpleasantness twisted Charlie's features in a snarl. It spoke to me in my mother's voice, saying it didn't understand how its own son could be so stupid. It spoke in the voice of the snotty kid in sixth grade who thought it was hilarious to mock me with invented slurs. It spoke with the voice of the spider above the rail yard, vowing revenge.

Hunger bored through me, but nothing else happened.

I faced a choice: bang on the door to get Phyllis to let me back in or start walking to the bus stop, a distance that would be no fun traveling on foot by night. Glancing down, though, I beheld huge paws etched from shadow where my feet should have been. Looking ahead, the houses were smaller than I remembered.

I ran. Instant speed poured euphoria through me until I tumbled onto the asphalt in an unplanned roll, my body fully human and quickly covered in bruises. The ridiculousness of my situation, combined with the pain from my pratfall, caused me to cackle like a drunk.

A scan of my surroundings told me that I'd moved at least half a mile in seconds. I laughed harder, fueled with elation and amazement. My senses lit up the way they did the first time I saw fireworks, leaping and shouting, *Do it again!* My pack remained on my shoulders. I shouted aloud, "I *can* take it with me!" Lights came on in houses to either side of the street.

Once more, I pictured a specter that embodied all my sources of fear and outrage. This time, I started with the thorned demon I'd clawed in the woods and built from there. Much faster than before, the hunger returned. My teeth bared, and the hair on the back of my neck rose. My perspective changed from man height to monster height.

Again, I ran, following the route I'd taken earlier on Charlie's bike. As in the forest, the pads of my paws didn't touch asphalt but rather a shimmering silver surface, uneven yet smooth, like rocks worn down by water. Streetlights I didn't need blurred to streaks. Anything my eyes alighted on shared all its textures, colors, and minuscule imperfections in hyper-clarity, whether an object of solid world, spirit world, or both overlapping.

I had the presence of mind to ponder whether anyone had seen me emerge from Phyllis's house or witnessed my spill on the pavement—and further to wonder *what* they saw happen. Had I disappeared from Phyllis's yard, blinked into existence in the middle of the road a half mile away, laughing my fool head off before vanishing again, or could they actually perceive the mighty spectral cat that connected the chain of events? The notion made me cackle more, which my bestial throat converted to an alarming bark. Thoughts of someone hearing that noise as I dashed past them made me cackle harder.

In the forest, I'd run right through the trunks of trees with nothing more than a sensation of whooshing wind to mark their passage. The train, on the other hand, had been steel-solid when I jumped onto it. Obviously, I didn't understand the physics of being the panther, but I didn't care. My joy made me reckless, and I quit confining myself to roads. I cut a corner and discovered

I could phase through brick and plaster the same way I had phased through trees—the only difference an electric buzz that accompanied the whoosh.

The tableaux inside the houses and businesses whizzed by almost too fast to process. My crow's flight sprint took me through a whole row of houses; snapshots of humans slumbering in their beds piled up in quick-flash montage. I loped straight through one older couple wrapped up in lovemaking, and I couldn't tell if the woman reared up in shock because of me or because of something her partner had done.

I barked more laughter as I angled toward the center of town, where the bus depot nestled. With the rush I felt, the idea that I even needed a bus seemed ludicrous. Confidence bloomed in my bones that I could run all the way to Stroudsburg, all the way to New York, to the polar ice cap without slowing.

A skewed silver pyramid arose that I took to be an outcrop of this second world's landscape, superimposed over a church shouting JESUS SAVES with huge neon letters arranged in a cross. I ran right at that pyramid, assuming I'd pass through or over. Darkness swallowed me.

I landed on my backpack—the impact battering my spine—and slid on an incline that offered my boots no footholds and my fingers nothing to grip. I flopped onto my stomach, scrabbling to no avail as the slope grew steeper. My scream made no echo.

My boots collided with level ground. Perhaps the slope had flattened out, or maybe my toes had lodged against a slender ledge that heralded the lip of an abyss. Above, a triangle of gray stood out against the blackness, though nothing like light shone from it. If that was the opening I'd run through, it hung in a strange place. My slide hadn't seemed that steep.

Was this what life had been like for Tommy, scurrying and hiding in the spirit world as the demon pursued him, lost in surroundings that made no physical or visual sense? He'd been able to see into the corporeal world, though, sharp enough to spot me and call for help. Maybe he was one of my kind, gifted with that same sight, and it saved him. But what of me?

Wherever my slip had taken me, my human senses did no good. I needed my panther eyes back.

Despite my panicked state, the exercise came easier. At the moment of my transformation, my surroundings blazed into visibility. The strange terrain continued into the distance, as far as I could see, spectacularly farther than a human eye's capability, a range that seemed to span uncountable miles—if concepts such as "miles" or "distance" even held any meaning here.

The landscape made little sense. The triangular opening that I'd unwittingly dropped through hung overhead like a skylight, its position counterintuitive to my fall. It wasn't, however, an opening in a cavern ceiling. Rather, the hole jutted like a shelf from a cone of rock. No frame supported it—as if someone had snipped the shape out of the air with scissors.

The cone, smooth and massive, was one of hundreds that loomed in front and to either side of me. The view called to mind a mountain range sketched by a child—except on a titanic scale and in actual stone. Just as odd, the plain behind me seemed to stretch flat indefinitely.

But the sky, if it could be called that, took the cake. As convoluted as a crumpled sheet of paper, striated black and silver and other colors that didn't trigger associations I could name. This firmament contained multitudes, specks by the thousands moving across its many contours. Off toward an area I wanted to label the horizon—though in truth the term didn't fit, as my eyes never found a vanishing point—the moon, or something like it, glowed silver. It wasn't a sphere, though. This heavenly body had corners. More like a floating octahedron.

As I stared, those specks above expanded as if my eyes acted as binoculars—and for all I knew, I possessed such a power—and they were hordes of humans, moving across topography as gray and arid as that beneath my paws. They were dressed like reenactors, clothing a hodgepodge of fashions from bygone centuries. I was observing them as from above, even though they were above me. A man looked up—or down?—then another next to him, and another as if they were meeting my gaze across all that distance.

I snarled and looked away. Unlike my human scream, the sound echoed through the crude, conical hills, and a rustling arose in response, utterly unnerving since I saw no trees nor foliage of any kind that could serve as its source. I sprang at the triangle carved into the air, despite having no surety that I could even reach it—so high it was.

But reality spun on its axis, and I landed in a Hillcrest street, one of my paws half-phased inside a small prefab shed in someone's yard, my flesh tingling in an alarming way. I jerked my paw back and licked at it before I realized what I was doing. After shaking my head, I set off in the direction of downtown, more cautious in my pace.

A splotch drifted beside the moon. That I noticed it at all against the night sky caused me a moment of wonder.

I stared at the spot of deeper darknesses like I had at the men moving upside down across the convoluted landscape, and again, that telescoping effect revealed details. The vulture from before clutched its companion in both talons, held close to its breast the way a human might cradle a baby bird.

They were watching me back. The man *waved*. The unexpected gesture jarred me right out of panther form.

The vulture didn't stand out so vividly, but even back in my flesh suit, I could make it out.

Too rattled to try for the panther again, I started walking. My observers stayed in the heavens and kept me in sight.

From the direction of the tracks, about where the downtown bridges crossed, powerful lights outshone the stars. I pictured police and railroad officials swarming the scene like carrion beetles, scouring the dirt and gravel for mangled remains. The queasiness of those thoughts failed to take full hold. The evening's carnage seemed disconnected to my present, something from a dream.

She'll kill you for this.

She who? I asked no one.

Only then did it occur to me to speculate whether anything on the tracks could lead the authorities to me. Was I spotted at the bridge? When I leaped onto the train, I became the panther. What could that even have looked like to someone watching? I hadn't spotted anyone other than my assailants paying attention, but then I hadn't paused to inspect every alley, every window, every rooftop. My mission to escape Hillcrest gained further urgency.

An engine roared, and a deep voice screamed. I could have jumped out of my skin, but it was only a gaggle of boys in a pickup, out to scare a pedestrian caught unawares. The scare didn't make me transform, and I puzzled why.

One of them spat the N-word as the pickup zoomed away. No one had called me that, at least within range of my hearing, since middle school. To give due credit to my friends at that age, the kid who said it received one hell of a playground whooping for his sins. Or so I believed. The truth is I couldn't fully remember.

It took a beat for me to register what I'd heard, another for anger to flow free. By then, the truck had turned a corner, vanished past a thin line of trees. A cold wind whipped under the hood of my jacket, loaded with dust and asphalt. I remained Nathan.

My non-response to an affront so outrageous pulled my mind down a different chute: none of it, the rescue of Tommy, my run from Elwood's, the train fight, none of it had happened at all. Rather, every extraordinary occurrence was invented by a mind turned traitor on its owner, my amazing physical feats explained by mania and adrenaline. I needed to accept reality, to return to Phyllis's house and ask for help.

I glanced up. The great vulture floated by the moon. I saluted it with a raised middle finger. It veered and banked toward the horizon before slowly turning back in my direction. If the man in its talons made an obscene gesture in return, I couldn't see it.

I walked the rest of the way to the bus station, about an hour's trek. The ticket booth hadn't opened yet, so I took a seat on the curb behind the building. The huge bird glided in circles over the station until the first signs of dawn brushed the sky. Soon after, I glanced up and they weren't there.

Even once the attendants arrived, bus departures didn't start until 9 a.m., so I had hours more to wait inside the dingy grotto of the station, the hard benches a punishment. Exhaust soaked the air. Another benchwarmer settled in next to me, contributing his body odor. A shaggy wreck, he stared at the opposite wall—his military surplus jacket and trench coat so threadbare they probably doubled as sleeping bags and blankets.

A mountainous shape blocked the bay doors that let out of the terminal. I looked up to see a creature hauling itself into the garage, backlit so it formed one massive shadow, antlers like saplings jutting from its brow, long wings folding together to squeeze into the opening, eyes blazing at me like spotlights.

I jumped up and blinked in confusion. The encroaching hulk was just the first of a long line of buses pulling in from the street. The shaggy fellow on the bench betrayed no reaction at all. Because there had been nothing to react to.

Before long, I was nestled in a seat only a fraction more comfortable than the bench, my backpack stuffed underneath. The bus crawled up an exit ramp onto a two-lane country highway, and I left Hillcrest behind.

3

The beast wore a man's face.

It moved on all fours, the size of a city bus, and its vast blue eyes fixed on me from above a crooked nose, grim mouth, and long, matted beard. One of its ponderous antlers was broken, ending in a splintered point. The massive talons made no noise as they settled in the earth. All its fluid motion, every minor detail, registered with crystal clarity from the corner of my eye: the muscles bulging in its legs, the sunlight glinting off the scales of its spiny tail, the tall wings lowering and rising ever so slightly, like the beating of a slow, silent heart. I didn't dare turn my head to meet the creature's gaze.

Once more, I stood in a grove of pine trees that had lost all their needles, their sticky black trunks afflicted with rot. Rings of bare branches ascended each trunk like stacks of upturned spiders' legs. A path wide and straight as a church aisle sloped upward through the grove, and as I began my ascent, the beast paced me along a ridge about a stone's throw to my left, never inching closer, never looking away.

A recent rain had soaked the ground. The mud and softened pine needles squelched with each step I took. The incline grew steeper, and the black-blighted trees grew taller, older, as if they were columns that held up the arches of some primeval Gothic cathedral, its ceiling formed of the crisscrossing canopy far overhead. I marched up this elongated nave toward some unseen altar.

Though the beast never quickened its pace, it was gaining ground, getting ahead of me, its blue-scaled flank glittering in and out of view as it stalked through the pines.

Above me, a new path defined itself, perpendicular to mine and bordered by lightning-split trees that had renewed their growth in tortured curves, groping around each other in a struggle for sunlight. The beast would reach that path before I crossed it, and when it did, it would turn to block my way, the stare of its headlamp-sized eyes piercing me head on, its lips parting in its tangled nest of beard to reveal a mouthful of boars' tusks.

Beyond the intersecting path, the pine grove opened, revealing a distant cluster of dogwood and elm, a pale stone steeple rising incongruously from their midst like a signal flare.

Wood popped in gunfire rat-a-tats as the beast smashed through a ruined tree and forced its way onto the cross-trail. Its tail hissed through the air, whipping its wicked spines back and forth. I raised my hands, expecting to see great cat claws shimmering in blue outline, electric and dangerous, but instead I regarded my own feeble flesh.

I stared between my useless fingers as the horned head rose above me, eyes large and crazy as broken plates.

I woke with both hands raised, fingers curled into claws. The gray-haired Asian woman in the seat across from me shot me a fear-filled glance and looked away just as fast.

The bus reeked of exhaust fumes. The passengers, silent and siloed, unhelpfully mixed in their cigarette smoke. The cloudy sky prevented the sun from stabbing its glare through the windows. Trios of crosses sprouted on the hillsides flanking I-81, one set as tall as power towers. Car after car sped northeast past us. Hints of car sickness swirled in my head and gut.

My vision of the monster anglerfish in Cousin Phyllis's house had turned out to be something more than a figment of my imagination, so maybe this one was too. The thing from this nightmare, pursuing me between blackened trees, I'd seen it multiple times in the past twenty-four hours. I could not stop thinking about the warning from the Crabbes about predators.

If I accepted all these visions as truth, the hallucinations that spurred me to flee campus deserved a revisit.

The first and worst of those sent me running out into the night in the middle of an alcohol-soaked fuck. The girl—I'll call her Yolanda—had taken a shine to me in freshman English. I noticed, for a change, and the attention flattered me. I'd conducted some experimental flirtation test flights even as my flings with Melissa and Bill began to turn amazing, addictive, disturbing corners.

My first weekend back on campus—with Bill and Melissa far away and maybe out of my life for good—I sought out Yolanda, invited her to be my date at a party in an apartment complex a block from campus. After about four Dixie cups of some awful cherry-and-grain mash-up and about twice as many sloppy kisses, she told me she liked to picture me while playing with herself. Even though I had no matching obsession with her, I didn't need to be told twice.

My hall was all boys and hers was co-ed, and she had her room to herself that weekend. And I didn't. So that decided that.

The things we did together had faded to an unfortunate haze, eclipsed by how it all ended. We had entwined on her roommate's beanbag chair, her straddling me as my hands clamped her hips. Then a thing like a segmented serpent curled into my view over her shoulder, tall enough to brush the ceiling, bristly and tipped with a dripping stinger. It was a titanic scorpion tail. I paused in the act to stare at this gross intrusion, and that's when I noticed the claws in my peripheral vision. A monstrous scorpion had invaded—so large it filled the room—but at the same time, its substance was translucent, a ghostly terror superimposed.

Thankfully, I wasn't completely undressed as I scrambled out from under Yolanda and bolted, screaming and swearing until I was well out of the dorm.

My ability to sense this second world, this spirit world, had begun to manifest without me understanding what it was. I allowed myself a bitter chuckle at this rueful insight.

By the time we pulled into the Wilkes-Barre station, the sun had set, and a drizzle blurred the view. Bleary eyed and miserable, I hauled my pack out from under the bus and stumbled out into the night.

Melissa had instructed me to call collect once I got in. Except the operator came back on the line to inform me no one had picked up. Instead, she'd reached an answering machine. I couldn't leave a message via collect call, so I ended up having to break a twenty for change. At least it left me with one less effigy of Andrew "Trail of Tears" Jackson.

I dialed the Nesmiths, got the aforementioned answering machine. Perhaps they'd gone out for dinner. I expected some crazy recorded greeting, but instead, Bill identified himself and asked callers to leave a message in a blandly professional tone that matched nothing I remembered about him.

"Hey, guys, it's Nathan, I'm here at Susquehanna Station. I guess you guys are out. It's getting a little late. I'm gonna get a room and call you from there."

I asked the station attendant where the cheapest place to stay would be. My destination, a motel within throwing distance of I-81, turned out to be a mere rain-soaked stroll across the asphalt lot.

Rusted bolts fastened the TV to the top of the dresser. I plopped my backpack on the floor, collapsed backward onto the creaky bed, and took a moment to appreciate the decades of water stains that etched overlapping circles on the ceiling, a fossil record of neglect.

Itchy residue from the bus ride thwarted any potential for a nap. I stripped and braced myself for a test of the motel plumbing and gave thanks to providence that the showerhead delivered both heat and pressure. And I shaved, which also felt mighty nice.

Afterward, wiping the condensation off the mirror with a washrag, meeting the green eyes that were my mamaw's gift, another memory shook free. Elzbeth and I sitting at the tiny, wobbly kitchen table the morning after my misadventure in the cabin. She stared at me without blinking as I crunched dry Lucky Charms. She radiated tension that lashed me with a nettle sting.

At last, her gaze lowered, her shoulders loosened, and she muttered under her breath. I didn't understand at first that she was talking to me. "You hurt Rufus a bit, but at least, he's gonna continue. I can forgive that. He weren't worth much of a spit when he was living. If you had hurt Henri, your mama and that stuck-up college boy she married might be digging your grave this very minute. Or digging one for me."

I stopped eating and watched her, fear strangling my appetite.

She shook her head. "It's not your fault. Ain't taught you nothing." She beat a fist on the table, capsizing my cereal bowl. "You weren't supposed to be one of mine. I'm just a shell now. A hollow shell."

She noticed me gawking and grabbed me by the ear, giving a hard, painful twist. "Don't you say nothing to your mama about this. Don't you repeat a word I said."

And I saw again that mighty feline form that was also my mamaw, huge as a mountain. My heart pounded to clog my throat.

"Keep your peace, Little Panther," she whispered. "Don't go near that cabin again. Ever."

The film roll of my memory ran out, bringing my awareness back to Earth. Towel held around my waist, I shuffled toward my pack to dig out a pair of boxers.

I hadn't pulled the front curtain completely closed. Through the gap, a blue iris—big as a dinner plate—stared in at me. Its head filled the open space top to bottom, eye unblinking, beard divided by a mouth flat as the horizon. That mouth opened, exposing a crooked tusk. I screamed and hurled my towel. I couldn't have deliberately invented a more ineffective defense.

The towel smacked the glass, where the view showed nothing more than an empty, street-lit parking lot.

I scrambled for my pack, drew out one of my staffs, extended it to full length, and gripped it like a baseball bat as I huddled with my back to the door. As seconds became minutes, I started to feel stupid. Damp dry, buck naked, wielding a hiking stick against a phantom. Nothing awaited outside.

As I dressed, picking jeans and a tie-dyed T-shirt, hunger yawned open in my belly and wouldn't shut its mouth. Normal hunger. I resolved to gorge on a big meal. Properly refreshed, I'd try the Nesmiths' number again.

The motel had a diner attached to it, a place of gray wood paneling and square tables with uneven legs that threatened to tip over when you sat at them. I elected not to eat there. Given everything I'd been through, I deserved to splurge on something better.

Scanning for options within walking distance, I picked the one that held the most potential for distraction. Nestled by a posher hotel farther from the highway, its marquee proclaimed MacPhair's Funnie Faces in red and blue carnival script beneath a cartoon of a clown, grinning a grin that had to be five feet wide. As I shuffled that way, something about the place made my not-so-figurative ears prick up, the way a cat's do when something rattles inside a box.

Inside, at the vacant hostess podium, a neon-pink poster board told me, "Please Wait For Smiling Faces to Take You to Your Places." Colorful pastel caricatures, portraying dozens of profiles of not-so-memorable customers, hung on both sides of the entrance hall. I waited a minute for a host or hostess who didn't show and decided to hell with manners. I wanted to sit down. It was a Tuesday evening, not like the place was packed. I slipped into the smoking section and took a booth at the far end, putting my back to the wall.

The decor in the dining area continued the face motif. A long frieze of photographic portraits lined the brick wall above the booths, shots of people making goofy faces or wearing troweled-on clown makeup or some combination of the two. Directly above me a woman with a fantastically elongated nose crossed her already close-set eyes and made a comical O with her cherry-red lips. Next to her, a man in an orange clown collar grinned, despite the huge blue frown that covered the lower half of his face. I wondered if the portraits were done in-house with waiters accosting particularly odd-looking tourists—

or whatever sort of folks stopped over in a leftover town from the heyday of coal mining like Wilkes-Barre—luring them into a studio tucked somewhere behind the ovens and ambushing them with pancake makeup.

I pulled a paper napkin out of the dispenser and longed for a pencil. Sketching one of those faces would have been fun, a proper art class exercise and pleasant distraction. As I pictured myself drawing, an alternative subject suggested itself unbidden: the rows of barren pines with their rings of spider-leg branches. I traced their patterns on the napkin with a finger.

"Has anyone helped you?" my waitress asked. I straightened, saw her face, and almost yelped.

Dark bruises ringed both her eyes as if the blood from each blow had splattered in a perfect circle underneath her skin. A pair of Black Dahlia slits at the corners of her tiny lips stretched to her cheekbones—as if you could stick a finger in her mouth and unfold her face. More bruising made a disconcertingly regular ring around her neck. Hair black as mine, matted as if slicked with black blood. Eyes of a brown so light they could have passed for red regarded me, dumbfounded.

I felt a lurch of displacement. A familiar electric chill raised hairs on the back of my neck. My cheeks flushed beet red as I realized my mistake. In my paranoid state, my brain had supplied the worst possible interpretation of a particularly creative clown face. "I'm sorry," I said, trying to cover. "The makeup you have on looks so real."

Her eyes widened, and she took a step back, her knuckles white around her pen and pad of tickets. Two kinds of vision came into focus, and I saw two faces in the same place: one, the striped mask that first confronted me, its darknesses limned with the faintest blue shimmer, and the other, a pale, pretty girl with high cheekbones and a pointed chin, whose hair was in fact a striking highlighted blond, though the thin brown eyebrows perhaps gave her real color away. The second girl's hair was wavy and tied back in a ponytail, not dark and slicked close to her scalp. The wide brown eyes were the same in both faces. Someone else with a spirit double. Had to be. But what was it?

I willed my vision to root itself in this world, and the pale blonde—wearing perhaps a bit too much blush—grew solid.

I raised my hands in what I hoped was a humble gesture. "I'm so sorry. Please forget I said anything. I just got off the bus, and those fumes, you know, can get to you. I have one hell of a migraine. Makes me loopy."

She smiled a quick, unsure smile. "Oh-kay."

I glanced down at my blank napkin and inspiration struck. "Can you spare me a pen? I promise you'll get it back. I want to sketch something I saw today."

She complied, her expression curious, serious, calculating. I pulled out my wallet and thumbed through the bills wadded in there, remnants of the unspent student loan. I really did want to sate my urge for a splurge. I asked for a Murphy's Red. The Nesmiths had introduced it to me back at Tech. Her lips pursed in charming consternation. To my shock, she'd never heard of it.

I noticed a food-stain fleck below the starched collar of her white blouse. I had her at a slight disadvantage, I realized, because the poor woman had to wear a tag. "Hi, my name is KORI," it read.

If I let my focus drift, I could still see those markings. What the hell did they signify?

Already, I'd begun to sketch those bleak trees on my napkin. Her eyebrows rose as she watched. She asked what Murphy's tasted like, but I lack the vocabulary necessary to explain how you distinguish the flavors of beer. She stopped me as I fumbled through a series of "as sour as but more bitter than" comparisons to tell me she'd see if they had it in stock. She didn't ask if I was old enough to drink it legally. Instinct had told me she wouldn't. To her surprise, MacPhair's did have it.

The same urge that drove me to seek out that Mews character had my mind spinning in circles, brainstorming strategies to get her talking. I settled on attempting to ask her when she had started working for Funnie Faces, but she dropped a menu in front of me along with my beer and hurried off.

The dining area had gained more customers. Two booths down from me, a black family, mom and dad, two small daughters in pigtails, a baby in a highchair. A gray-haired white couple sat at a booth across from me, poring over their menus through bifocals. They required Kori's attention, which irritated me, because I really wanted to talk to her. Needed to talk to her. She was someone like me, but she seemed normal, not cryptic and creepy like the Crabbes.

The forest from my vision, the one where I'd seen the blue-scaled beast, started to take shape in black squiggles on the napkin.

"What's that?" Kori asked. Once again, she'd sidled up to me quietly. Were her eyes a little wider, I wondered, because she recognized those trees?

I gave her a sidelong glance. "Sure you don't know?"

A crease appeared between her brows. "Why would I?"

"Just, the way you looked at it." I grinned aw-shucks-like, a default disarm response. "Familiar at all?"

She leaned closer. I studied the graceful sweep of her neck. "Maybe." Her delicate features shifted to neutral. "You said you were on a bus. Where did you see this?"

Perhaps loose lips didn't matter if my ship had already sunk. "Dreamed it," I said. "Didn't feel like a dream though." Her eyes grew wider before she wiped her expression clean. Instead of commenting, she took my order.

Dinner kept me occupied: a honey-glazed chicken with seasoned mashed potatoes and breaded okra. My hunger, blessed physical hunger, yawned like a trapdoor over an endless pit.

"What, were you on a hunger strike?" said Kori when she next checked on me. I'd cleared my plate.

"Might as well have been," I told her. "I ate nothing but crawdads and trail mix for the last four weeks." An exaggeration, though not by much. I ordered apple pie for dessert and asked her to pick my next beer. I wound up with a Corona and a chaser of frustration that she didn't stick around to chat. I wanted to ask her so many questions—maybe after her shift ended. The possibilities set off mental tremors, a mix of fear she would turn me down and a different kind of fear if she was willing.

I weighed my options as I counted out cash for the meal. Though I truly couldn't afford it, I fished out an extra $20 and then wrote the motel name and my room number on a napkin and added, "Please, I want to talk to you. You've seen that place." I stuck the bill and note together and united them with dog ears. This became her tip. She collected the money without comment, that crease still between her brows, eyes focused somewhere else.

But after a minute, she returned, the $20 clutched in her fist. "Did you really think that would get you something?" She flashed teeth in what look like a smile, but from the tone of her voice, I guessed it wasn't.

I'm not too fleet on my verbal feet in an emergency. I offered what I hoped was a disarming shrug. She flicked the $20 onto the table, put her fake smile on wider, and walked over to the black family's table. I thought about insisting she take the tip but decided I'd already pushed my luck too far.

When I picked up the bill, I realized she'd kept the shred of napkin with my room number. I tried to catch her eye, but she wouldn't look my way.

Enough, I told myself. *Leave it alone, Little Panther.*

And I left.

As I walked back to the motel, I wondered what had gotten into me. Just because I'd found someone else who appeared to share my dual-world nature, I had no guarantee she'd have something insightful or profound to say to me about my condition. I had assumed too much. I'd lived in blissful ignorance myself until just a couple days ago. Maybe Kori still did. Maybe she was better off that way.

Back in my room, I tried the Nesmiths again, left another message on the answering machine with the phone number to reach me. I thought it strange that they weren't answering, but it wasn't like I had any control over the situation. I bedded down for the night, hoping I'd earned some uneventful sleep.

The waitress set the plate in front of me as I sketched on the napkin. When I saw what I'd been served, I dropped my pen. A severed wing lay across the pattern on the porcelain, its speckled brown feathers darkening to black at the tips. My startled breath stirred their edges.

The wing twitched.

I sprang out of the booth, my right knee banging the underside of the table hard enough to bruise.

I was alone in MacPhair's Funnie Faces. The dining area smelled of turned earth. A gray haze dimmed the chipper furnishings, condensing into agitated fog. The photos lined in a frieze above the booths all displayed the same image: a bearded face with piercing blue eyes, antlers rising from its temples, one broken.

I ran, but the room stretched on and on. The fog congealed into focus, unveiling a pattern, columnar, black, trunks of pine trees with spider-leg branches.

Each photo filled with one huge blue eye. In unison, all the eyes blinked.

I started awake in the motel bed, heart pounding like thunderous tom-toms.

The clock by the phone read 10:33. I had barely slept half an hour. Something struck me as wrong about the arrangement of the room, but I couldn't put my finger on it. I flicked on the lamp, half-convinced a scaly blue shape was about to emerge from the closet.

I almost missed the white scrap of paper that someone had slipped under the door. It was the note I had given Kori. On one side, my writing. On the other side, it read:

Memorytown Tavern
I'll wait until midnight

Memorytown Tavern turned out to be a couple miles distant after a right turn past the bus station, well within walking range. Unfortunately, this wasn't a beautiful stretch of Wilkes-Barre to stroll through: a gaudy procession of strip malls, auto lots, fast food joints, loudly lit signs, while cars jockeyed pointlessly for position across anywhere from four to six lanes of traffic. Hotels I couldn't afford towered to either side, bleak sentinels of commerce. I guessed that if I ever made a venture downtown, I'd find picturesque buildings with flourishes of brick architecture standing empty and crumbling from disuse, neighborhoods of decrepit old houses circling the city's core like a moat of poverty. It was the same thing over and over—in Tennessee, in North Carolina, in Virginia, in West Virginia, all up and down the Appalachians.

I didn't try to make the trek as the panther. My fall into that disorienting mirror landscape still spooked me, and that wasn't the only thing. The flickering in the corners of my eyes. The sense of unseen things watching. The same things that ate at me so horribly on campus returned with a vengeance. Once, I even thought I glimpsed that immense vulture glide into the outer range of the light pollution.

Given its wonderful name and the company I hoped to find there, the tavern proved a disappointment. As I approached, I couldn't mistake the twang of electric-guitar country. When I'm forced to breathe outside the nurturing atmosphere of industrial metal, I far prefer Duke Ellington to Doc Watson, but I can definitely handle bluegrass or Old Time music. But I'd still rather hear an accordion walloped with a paddle than listen to Garth Brooks.

I could tell already this wasn't going to be a cozy stop.

Inside, guitars grated yet failed to drown out the clumsy drawl of a particularly untalented live singer. With my wire-thin frame, dark skin, and curly black hair, I stood out like a sore thumb among the overwhelmingly white clientele, none of whom were likely to notice any of the subtleties of Melungeon heritage, nor care if they did: men in sleeveless motorcycle shirts and denim jackets that strained to hold in their guts; women with their button-down shirts tied across their breasts, revealing not-so-supple bellies that spilled over the tops of their jeans, hair 1980s-big and dyed blond. More than a few of the men sported mullets, the most frightening of which wedded punk spikes with a waist-length cascade—and adorned the awful singer's head. The flannel-shirted man serving as host gave me a once over before mercifully leading me to a table far away from the dais where the band played . . . though nowhere was far enough.

Two glasses of water later, Kori still hadn't appeared. I didn't feel brave enough to start snooping through the booths looking for her. That would no doubt draw unwanted attention.

The notion that I'd been duped sunk through me, widened into a cavern, a canyon. That Kori asked to meet me here in the first place perhaps did not speak so well of her, if she had in fact planned to meet me at all. I chided myself even as I stewed. What right did I have to believe she *would* meet with me? Maybe I had misread her entire demeanor. Maybe she was only humoring a customer who gave her the creeps.

And yet she had left that note.

My desperation for someone, anyone, to relate to had led me to make a fool of myself. I should have taken Elzbeth's advice: *Leave it alone.*

Finally, I couldn't stand to wait any longer and neither could my bladder— nor the remains of that rich meal at MacPhair's.

A constant electric crackle made the tiny restroom even more eerie. A puddle clustered around the drain in the cracked center of the cement floor. I pulled the stall door closed, fumbled with the loose lock, and sat. In that claustrophobic space, I resolved, Kori or no, as soon as I was done, I was out of there.

But where to next? Back to bed, I suppose, with a hope the nightmares left me alone this time. I'd try Melissa and Bill again in the morning.

And for the first time, I wondered if it made any sense to contact them, given the trouble following me. For that matter, it finally occurred to me to ponder whether they would genuinely be happy to see me. Maybe they were listening to the messages I left without picking up, hoping I'd take the hint and go away.

Maybe months of wedded bliss made Bill's memories of watching as Melissa and I came together super-awkward. Not to mention the night when we had agreed after many drinks that fair was fair, so Melissa could watch the two of us. Bill seemed cheerful as ever the morning after, and Melissa acted like the cat who'd had the cream, putting me at ease about everything. The water bong passed around with breakfast put us all in a pleasant state of afterglow. As far as I knew.

If they didn't want me there, though, they'd had a chance to tell me when I called them from Phyllis's house. Maybe my thoughts were spinning into stupid loops of paranoia. I'd find out one way or the other soon enough.

Okay, but say they welcomed me with open arms, even an open bed—what next? It wasn't like I could just move in forever. Maybe I could pick up a job, build up my cash reserves, get a place of my own, never go home. The absolute last thing I wanted to do was return to my parents. My mother's wrath at the damage done to her reputation—in her own imagination—would make her even more of a mortal enemy, stabbing me with the daggers of her disappointment at every opportunity. Dad would do nothing to stop her.

My racing thoughts tripped at the soft splash as someone stepped in the puddle.

The space below the stall door framed a pair of weathered leather work boots. Based on their size, the man standing outside the stall had to be enormous. I could make out the dome of his brow above the door: high forehead, gray hair swept back tight as if gathered in a ponytail. "Just a minute," I told him. He said nothing and didn't move away from the door.

A chill grew in my belly. Outside, that awful music still drenched the place. The white light in here offered no escape, and its electric hum grew louder, along with the ringing in my ears. My new friend shifted slightly, and I realized he was leaning against the stall door. I scrambled to get my boxers and jeans back in order. "Excuse me. Can I help you?" I hoped I sounded more annoyed than afraid.

The man exhaled a disturbing sigh—a sigh of satisfaction. I looked up, saw a sliver of his face as he stared through the crack in the door at me. A tangled beard. A piercing blue eye. I knew that eye. "Shit," I said, struggling to get my fly zipped.

All my hair stood on end. A glowing blue speck appeared in the center of the stall door. And that speck stretched into a vertical line, a knife slice in reality. He was slicing an opening to the spirit world right in front of me. I had nowhere to go. "Wait, wait, wait," I said.

He didn't wait.

Something like a knife poked through the opening, and I slowly realized it was the pointed tip of a claw as large as my leg. The entire taloned foot emerged, shimmering with blue phosphorescence and as tall as me. My heart battered against my ribcage like an alarm bell. I couldn't scream. I couldn't breathe.

The beast from my visions flexed its talons ever so slightly, amusing itself with the idle threat. Behind it, on the other side of the door, that mad eye burned.

I called on that locus of distress that summoned the part of me that was the panther. Under the circumstances, it was easy. Nothing happened.

I remained as I was, a skinny young man terrified out of his wits. My attacker wanted me to absorb that, understand that the inner cavalry wasn't coming. After too many seconds of blank panic, the thought arrived, *Climb out! Climb out!*

I stood up. And then the talons closed, piercing into my neck and chest and shoulders, up between my legs, through my groin. The pain was deep, fiery, excruciating—lightning wrapped around me and threaded through me. The scream lodged in my throat came loose, and I let the world know how much it hurt.

"Hello? Hey, what's happening in there? Everything all right?"

When my eyes refocused, a bearded man was staring down at me. After another terrible second, I connected that it wasn't the face of my attacker. This fellow's dark beard outlined jowls that cushioned a kind, weathered face. Brown eyes nestled in the premature wrinkles and yellowed skin of a heavy smoker. He wore a blue work shirt with his name stitched on it: Albert.

I scanned every which way. No sign of my blue-eyed attacker . . . but I had heard no door slam, nothing to indicate that he had left the restroom. "Where is he?"

"Buddy, I think you had a few too many," Albert said.

After catching my breath and rolling up my wits—I was on the floor, wedged uncomfortably between toilet and wall—I said, "Yeah. You're right. Can you please help me up?"

Standing hurt. I winced a lot and couldn't help but groan. Those claws: they hadn't cut into me, like my own claws did to the masked demon in the woods or the spider on the train. Instead, I felt baked from the inside out . . . the equivalent of an extreme sunburn in some extremely uncomfortable places. Also, I'd taken a hell of a bruising in my fall.

With Albert's kind help, I escaped the restroom, but the shadows and noise inside Memorytown took on a new timbre, one pregnant with menace. The beast was still in the building somewhere, maybe watching me from one of the booths. As I limped toward the front entrance, the hairs on my aching chest and legs prickled. The thud of his boots reached me—an inane trick of the imagination since the redneck din drowned out all else. Still, I heard them, loud as gong strikes, the same as Tommy's shouts in the woods.

No sooner had I staggered outside than a tiny gray Hyundai flipped on its headlights and screeched out from the parking spot where it had been idling. The car pulled up alongside me, stopped but with the hurried growl of the gas still depressed. Through the driver's side window peered an astonishing face—a bird's and woman's both, with flame-colored eyes ringed by haunted black.

"Get in!" Kori said.

I stepped back.

"He's coming out," she hissed. "Get in now!"

Lord help me, I did.

9

We rolled along in silence through the desolate center of Wilkes-Barre, which turned out to be pretty much what I'd imagined, beautiful buildings from the 1920s with ornate cornices, fleurs-de-lis, even a gargoyle or two, marred by great gaping wounds of exposed brick. Kori's Hyundai smelled of some vaguely fruity incense. That weird internal sunburn throbbed through my core. Finally, painfully, I shifted in the passenger seat to regard the double image of her face. "How can I trust you?"

She smirked. Her eyes never left the road. "A little late for that, don't you think?"

"You asked me to meet you."

"I didn't know he'd be waiting for you. I went home to change first. When I got there, you were already inside. So was he."

"He. You know him?"

"No. I never want to know him. I just know *of* him."

"What is he?"

"It'll be a lot easier to explain everything once we get where we're going."

I peered out her back windshield and wondered who sat behind the pairs of headlights arrayed in a stream behind us. Clothes, soda bottles, french fry boxes, and candy wrappers cluttered the back seat. A lady after my own heart.

"He's not following," she said.

"How do you know?"

"I make sure he can't see me. If he had, we'd be done for by now. That's why I couldn't go in." She breathed a belated sigh of relief. "I'm just glad you finally had the sense to leave."

Something about her cryptic pronouncements both irked and entranced me. "What makes you think *I'm* someone *you* can trust?"

The smirk again. "You're a pussycat. I've got nothing to worry about from you. And you've got much worse things to worry about than me."

"Why aren't *you* worried?"

She glanced at me sidelong. "He sees you. You're too big to hide. I'm beneath his notice."

"I don't understand what you're saying, and I need to understand. I've seen visions of—of him, of whatever he is, but I didn't have a clue what they were supposed to mean until—" *Until his claws came at me through the bathroom stall door.* I shuddered but couldn't bring myself to finish.

She pressed her lips into a grim line as she waited for a stoplight to change. Her left turn signal clicked, making her face strobe green. "I don't know anything about him. But what he tried to do to you, I've seen him do before." She fidgeted as the light stubbornly stayed red. "Come on," she growled.

I thought about the vulture, the bird-person, I'd been seeing since the night with Tommy. No way that was *her*. She had to be something else.

We passed under a bright streetlamp, and for a moment, I saw both her selves illuminated: the pretty bottle blonde in a black spaghetti-strap top, skin pale and smooth, and the bird-like creature with black bands around the neck and eyes. "Is it out of bounds for me to ask what those marks are?"

"It's not."

"Then what are they?"

"Protective coloration," she said.

"Protection from what?"

"Hunters. Enemies."

"What hunters? The same psycho fucker that's after me?"

"Not your business."

Her matter-of-fact tone brooked no argument. Which didn't stop me. "I think I need to know. Didn't you say we could trust each other?"

"I never said that."

"Well then, why are you helping me?" We'd made several turns. I had no hope of remembering the route.

"You're the first one I *could* help."

"The first?"

She briefly turned her gaze from the road to glare at me. "Just let me drive please." We weren't downtown anymore but crossing a long, well-lighted four lane bridge. American flags hung from every pole. "I suppose I should be afraid of you. It's like there's a nova hidden under your skin. Like nuclear power." She rubbed her forehead with the back of a slender hand. "But I'm not in the least bit. I can tell you're a good kitty."

"Nice of you to say, but back there, I lost my claws. Did he do that to me? How did he do that?"

"You're not declawed."

"How do you know?"

"It's plain when I look at you."

It had never occurred to me that there might be a pattern on my face visible to others—the way hers showed itself to me. "What do you see?"

She knew what I meant. "Eyes that are too bright for your face. They shine no matter how dark it is."

"Seriously? Like right now?"

"Hang on." She steered us onto a side street that converted to gravel as it curled underneath the bridge. She darted the Hyundai onto an uneven surface of dirt and pebbles, making the car shake horribly, before she ground to a stop. Her headlights illuminated one of the great H-shaped cement pylons that supported the bridge. She flipped on her brights, bringing the image tagged on the pylon into sharper focus. "We're here," she said.

"Damn," I said.

A huge, crude spray painting of an all-too-familiar monster splashed across the curved cement. One difference: the deer antlers were whole.

We sat silent in the car a moment. Finally, I asked, "Do you have any idea what that is?"

"I found the same image once, in a book on creatures from Indian myth. It's called a pie-ya-saw."

"A what?"

"*P-I-A-S-A*," she spelled.

"What kind of Indian?"

She smirked. "Native American."

I nodded. "So tell me about Mr. Piasa."

"The book said the word means 'devouring bird.' It ate young warriors whole."

I felt a prickle at the back of my neck. "Um, yikes."

"The chief of the tribe had gone to the cliff where it lived and lain at the bottom, pretending to be wounded. But all the warriors from the tribe were hidden nearby, waiting. It came out hungry, and they filled it full of arrows. It took every single one of them to kill it—after it was so heavy with arrows it couldn't fly."

"So it was killed?"

"That's what the book said. But I read somewhere else that a white man made it all up."

"Huh. That wouldn't surprise me." I opened the passenger door. "Leave your lights on. I want to look closer."

She watched a moment before following me.

The painting commanded the eye, a thing of fierce power, tall as me and long as a Ford F-150. Though heavily stylized, all its pieces were familiar: the feathered wings, the rows of blue scales, powerful haunches, the deadly talons, the long spined tail that curled above its back, the wild beard, the tusks jutting from a snarling mouth, the unblinking stare, the antlers. It shimmered with the vibrant false glow of the airbrush, like the aggressively cheerful art you see spray-painted on the sides of freight cars idle in rail yards.

I touched the painting's gritty surface. "How long has this been here?"

"Since I was twelve."

"So not that long?"

She cut her eyes at me. The headlight glare washed her pale skin a harsh white. I could at last see the jeans she wore, how they hugged the contours of her thighs and calves, the grace added to her height by plain leather boots. I wished circumstances allowed me more time to appreciate her.

She smirked and rolled her eyes. "I met the boy who painted it. Once." Her smirk faded. "I didn't really know him. He was a lot older than me."

I ran a thumb along the black lines of the creature's feathers, my own shadow floating atop the intense colors.

"It's been here as long as I can remember." She wasn't referring to the painting. "I saw it in the sky when I was little. Him. He never saw me." She pressed a knuckle against her lip. "When I was twelve, I had an older cousin who brought me down here. Wanted me to smoke weed with him. Get me stoned." She trailed off and pointed at the painting. "But I saw that and started screaming my head off.

"When I calmed down, my cousin told me about the artist. They called him Loudmouth. Because he was so quiet. When he did speak, it was with this deep, sexy voice, like some radio announcer." Her gaze was focused somewhere else as she talked. "I had a friend whose older brother hung out with Loudmouth. I was over at her house once when he was there. I'd heard he could draw. I asked him, and he did a sketch of this crazy-looking vampire for me right in my school notebook. Just like that.

"I think I could tell he was someone different. Like you. Like me.

"My cousin didn't know I'd already met Loudmouth. When he told me who painted it, he tried to make it sound all scary. He thought my freakout was the funniest thing in the world." She drew closer but eyed the painting as if it might start moving. "When I saw this . . . I wish I'd known that boy's real name. He'd been missing five months. They never found him. The police figured him for a runaway. I know he wasn't."

I put a hand over the piasa's snarling face. I imagined the frightened little girl beneath the bridge, and a twinge of anger at this cousin had me pressing the concrete, imagining that face crumpling. "I'm sorry," I said. The creature's eyes blazed from between my fingers. "You say you've seen this thing several times. How've you managed to avoid it?"

"I'm not what he's looking for. I don't take up much space in the spirit world. And I can fly much higher than he flies."

"I spotted you quickly enough."

She nodded. "You're made to see in the dark."

She sounded so confident in her assessment of what I was, something like envy clutched my heart. I redirected that energy. "There's something else I see too." I bent my fingers into claws over the beast's face. "You know that this is just a man. This whole 'creature from legend' thing is a front. Like a disguise."

A furrow of puzzlement creased her forehead.

My turn had come to tell a story. "Couple days ago, I was on the Appalachian Trail. I saw a boy who'd been trapped in the spirit world. The thing that was hunting him looked like a demon. Like something off a death metal cover. I used claws on him though, and it turned out he was just a guy, wearing that shape like a costume." Maybe I was talking out my ass, but the leap of intuition felt right. The idea came to me as if I'd heard it before, a half-remembered tutorial, though I had no memory of having had any sort of conversation like this with anyone ever. "I barely understand how any of this works. But I think, those of us who can move in that other world, some of us are born with natural shapes, and some make their own. I think that's what's going on here. This creep, he chose to be this piasa. While people like you and me don't get a choice."

"What makes you so sure I was born like this?"

I hesitated. "Am I wrong?"

Her lips pressed into a line. "No."

I leaned against the painting. It felt like defiance. "I know where I get it from. It comes from my mamaw, on my mom's side. She lived in the hollers of Tennessee. You have family there?"

She tensed. "I'm the only one like me in my family."

"Then how did you find out . . . that you are who you are?"

"When I was little, I had a friend who was like me, who showed me how to become what I've become." A little smile graced her face as a scene from memory played in her head. "Moved away when we were both ten, but I never forgot." The smile vanished. "I tried talking to my mom and dad about it. Even my brother thought I was making it all up. I think I'm just a random mutation."

"That's not how it works." I went to her, put a hand on her bare shoulder. Her skin was smooth and cool, and I caught a scent from her hair, a sweet vanilla. She looked at the wall but didn't shy away from my touch. "You're not the only one. You can't be," I said. "Based on my own experience, I bet there's someone in your family who isn't talking."

She kept staring at the painting. I moved into her field of vision, wanting her to look at me, not the monster. "I mean it. He's just a man." But was he? I'd put one hell of a hurting on that demon in the woods and an even worse one on the spider on top of the train. The piasa though, I'd not laid a claw on. Because I couldn't. Some force had somehow blocked me.

A further layer of strangeness: my claws had torn flesh. The piasa's had burned me with wounds that didn't show on my flesh, even though the pain was plenty real. I wondered if strikes from the demon would've had a similar effect if they'd hit. No way to know. "He's just like the man I fought in the woods. I'm sure of it. And that guy was a sick, sick bastard."

"So's this one," she said. "He's come after people before. People like you. I've seen it. From up high. While flying." She shuddered, and I felt it in her shoulder.

"So you really fly?" I tried to picture it. Perhaps it worked like my own exhilarating leaps when I became the panther, sans the part where gravity carried me back to the ground. "Is it like an out of body thing?"

"Don't make fun."

"I'm not."

"Yes you are."

"Am not."

"Stop it, or I'll stop helping you."

"Seriously, I'm not. If it's not clear, I've had my own share of impossible experiences. Just like you." As I said that, her turn of phrase in describing the piasa's prey popped back into mind: *People like you.* Not like her. "When you say 'people like me,' what do you mean? What makes me special to this . . . creep?"

Her face with its bands turned away from the headlights, disappeared in layers of shadow. "I told you the old story. The piasa hunted warriors in its territory, carried them off, and ate them. I've seen . . . that's what this one does." Now she looked at me, eyes red and moist, but her voice was steady. "Loudmouth's not the only one I know about." She swallowed, looking up at the bridge. "I've seen it happen twice. With . . . I don't know who they were. I never met them *here*. One of them was like you. A cat. One had too many legs. I'm not sure what he was. The Piasa took them. It was so quick. When it came for them, they couldn't fight back. They couldn't hold their shapes. They were just boys."

His eye staring at me around the restroom stall door, my hands remaining hands. So much for natural talent. I wanted to ask, *How does he do it?* but she would have told me already had she known.

In the silence that followed, I spelunked for motive. "Do you think he's trying to guard something?"

"In the story, there's no reason. It's just evil and hungry." She pulled away. "I have to help you get out of here. But I don't know if it will let you leave."

"He doesn't see you though. Maybe when I'm with you—"

"I told you. I'm too small. When I fly, I'm just a dark speck in the sky. Like a gnat to him. Nothing he cares about. But you take up a lot of space. You can't be missed."

"Do you know a good place to hide?"

"You have to hide yourself *there*, not here. That won't be easy. You're super-bright."

No such concept had ever crossed my mind. I barely knew how to make the panther appear. Had no idea I was a walking lighthouse. No wonder the Crabbes had been on to me right away. No wonder they said what they did.

"Well." I took a deep breath. "I guess it's a good thing I never planned on staying long." Not exactly the truth, but as lies go, it was a prudent one. The Nesmiths weren't going to hear from me after all.

I started toward the Hyundai. "I need to get my things. If you can take me as far out of here as you're willing, I'll owe you. Everything."

She didn't move. "It . . . he might be looking for you at your motel."

My gut twisted. That huge face staring in the window. "Yeah, he might be."

"Then we can't go there."

"Listen. From what you've told me, it sounds like he'll find me wherever I am. I need my things. Let's just do it quick."

She put her hands over her face. "Oh, God."

"Look, your battery's probably dying." I tried to laugh, to make it sound like I wasn't scared shitless. "Let's just move, okay?"

Contemplating where I could possibly go from Wilkes-Barre, where I might end up, made me want to scream. And it was therefore pointless. Best put out of mind altogether.

On the ride back to collect my things, I coaxed Kori into talking more about herself.

She grew up in Scranton. Mother was a hairdresser. Father helped build diesel locomotives until asbestos poisoning put him on disability, killing him over seven slow years. Once their lawyer excised his portion of the settlement, her mom blew it all in a candle-at-both-ends spree, the main object of which was a sleek black Thunderbird that she wrecked after a month of high-speed ownership.

Kori's family was large but not close. Her mother had been the youngest of a family of ten. Her grandparents on that side died before she turned nine. Those on her father's side had not grown closer after her father's death. Not one of them hailed from the South, so wherever my powers ultimately came from, they weren't a regional thing.

She lived at home, paying rent to her mom and stepdad. She'd tackled a few community college courses but hadn't followed through—the classes just eating her money and leaving her bored. She didn't know what she wanted, though at various times imagined being an art teacher, a paralegal, a lab assistant at a hospital, but she knew that for now she'd had enough of school.

I shared tidbits too, to draw more from her in return. How my mother had internalized hatred of her mixed heritage and externalized it on me while my father moved through life in a daze, taking my mother's side only because it forced me into silence—what he considered keeping the peace. How I decided I never wanted to be a teacher because both my parents would come home from the high school brimming with directionless anger. How, if I could magically sculpt my own future, I would live on a mountaintop and design advertisements for mega-corporations without ever having to see or speak to a soul unless I *wanted* to.

Her dream, I learned, was to fly without ever having to land.

"No husband, no children, no split-level?" I teased as we pulled into the motel parking lot. She cut her eyes at me again and made an exaggerated show of shivering.

"Oh, c'mon, it can't be that bad."

One eyebrow raised. "So says Tigger Tumbleweed."

I climbed out of the car. "You're weird."

"Don't push it." She got out after me.

"You could wait," I said, fumbling in my pocket for the room key.

"If you need help, I want to help."

"Okay," I said, jingling the key into the lock. In we went.

The room wasn't how I left it. I don't mean that a maid had cleaned up—it was the middle of the night. The covers were rumpled in a different configuration, my pack was in a different spot on the rug than where I'd left it. The bathroom door was ajar, exposing darkness.

"Someone's been in here," I said.

Kori leaned in the doorway. "Hurry."

I raised a hand. "Just a second. I don't have much." I grabbed loose clothes from the floor and pulled the zipper of my backpack open to stuff them inside. When I moved the bag, I felt a cold electric jolt, as if I'd just shoved my hand through a ghost. It felt exactly like walking through the door at Crabbe's Supplies.

I turned in time to see Kori's eyes widen in terror as talons, tall as her, passed through the wall—one to either side of the doorway where she stood, huge blue claws curling into the room, grasping for me.

I screamed as much in fear for her as for my own life.

In that split second of freaked-out awareness, I saw the great cougar paw of my spirit form take shape, thick blue-black fur stretched over massive muscle and poised to strike, but I drew short as the rational pieces of me shrieked that I was just as likely to tear open Kori.

She made a startled noise as that horrible, bearded face appeared in the door, occupying the same space she did. Just as the talons materialized through the wall moments before, the beast's face phased through her body.

Because I could see my panther paw, I also saw what happened the instant the piasa's burning gaze locked on me. The muscle and fur shriveled away, dissolved to nothing, reduced in an instant to a useless human hand.

In that same instant, as Kori slumped to the ground, the piasa's eyes widened in shock. The creature had been so focused on getting to me, it hadn't realized she was there. But I had no time to take advantage of the pause. Before I took another breath, the beast struck with both its talons.

The pain was excruciating.

A delusion of flight plagued me with vertigo. Wind battered me from all sides. The world tilted, dim and silver.

I dangled in the piasa's front claws as it bore me up with ponderous strokes of its enormous wings. I hung like a captured rodent, the iron manacles of its grip clamped around my torso and knees.

I remained Nathan. I'd been taken, the way the masked man on the trail had taken Tommy. I'd been bested by the most powerful being I'd ever encountered in my brief time of dual-natured self-awareness.

The spaces the monster carried me through surpassed the weirdness of my trip through the looking glass in Hillcrest. We passed through swirling tunnels, like passages bored through thunderheads. At times, I saw nothing but vast gray haze in all directions. More than once, intersecting plateaus knotted into cat's-cradle weaves of landscape that my human eyes could make no sense of.

Color returned. We descended toward a dark mass that resolved into a green canopy of pine boughs. And then we punched through, like a nail through skin, and I gasped at the vista below: tall, slimy pine trunks arranged in cathedral-column rows, bare branches stabbing out in rings like broken spider legs.

We dropped, dropped, dropped, squelched down on the layers of brown needles that carpeted the forest floor. The piasa settled, so its weight drove me into the mud and pinned me.

That wide, bearded face lowered over mine, its breath a gust from a locker filled with spoiled meat. Those mad eyes were half-lidded, coy, as if the creature planned to kiss me tenderly before goring my neck.

"What," I wheezed, "the fuck . . . have I ever done to you?"

Movement flickered among the prongs of the beast's antlers, silhouetted against the silver sky—a bird descending. The piasa saw my gaze shift and pressed a claw into my chest to keep me still, made me scream blue murder. The beast looked up.

Caught by the power of the monster's gaze, the bird transmuted in a confusing frenzy. Its size kept changing. I saw wings fluttering, arms flailing, heard a cry as a hand caught a branch, which broke at the weight. I pushed with both sweat-slicked hands at the weight pressing into my sternum. The creature's touch burned my chest, my palms. It pushed in a little deeper, and I screamed again.

Kori landed on her back about thirty yards uphill from us. The fall could easily have snapped every bone. She lay so still.

The piasa swung its attention back to me. It again lowered its eyelids, anticipating ecstasy. In a moment of absurd clarity, I noted the long black eyelashes that framed those harrowing blue eyes.

Kori arched her back and gasped for air. Rolling onto her stomach, using the nearest trunk for support, she struggled to her feet.

She limped up the hill, in obvious pain, dragging her left leg so stiffly I was amazed she could walk at all. She looked back, directly at me, dark rings around her eyes and neck. The double image of spirit world vision afflicted me even more strangely because in her place I also saw a bird—as large as Kori. She disappeared, leaving only the bird. Wounded, it dragged one broken wing as it hopped awkwardly away.

The piasa yanked its talon down my body, cutting deep into my belly, genuinely *cutting* this time, my skin parting, my blood burning. I gagged, howled, slumped. I was wide awake but in too much pain and terror to move.

The beast turned its attention back to Kori.

When its gaze fixed again on her, the bird vanished. I saw only a young, badly injured woman scrambling to escape my fate. She sobbed with every breath. I could hear her as if those sobs were in my ear.

Agony burned deep in my gut. Is this what it was like for the man in the white mask, for the man-spider I killed atop the train? Was this how it felt for the ghosts in the cabin?

You've hurt them enough already, Elzbeth had scolded, dragging me out of the woods.

I had been hurt more than enough. How real were these wounds? Would I bleed out in this place?

The burning, ripping pain in my chest and abdomen lowered an octave as the piasa plucked out its claw. Above us, Kori stumbled and cried out, clutching at her injured knee.

A slow smile spread across the beast's wide face. Lowering its head, it made a show by snagging a big branch between the prongs of its undamaged antler, flexing its neck, and snapping it into three pieces. Kori jerked up at the noise, wide-eyed.

Her reaction made the piasa bare its teeth in a grin. It raised itself off me, reached without looking and plucked at the groove it had torn in my stomach. I bucked in agony but did not scream. It moved its claw to the side of my neck and caressed me gently as a lover. The fire of deep pain that only someone who has been impaled or eviscerated could know burned in my chest and belly.

Kori regained her feet. The double image of woman and bird flickered, both broken. The piasa began to pad toward her, keeping its wings tight to its sides as it moved between the rows of trees. She limped onward, fully human.

The beast wasn't hurrying to give chase. As its long, segmented tail drifted over me, I lifted my left hand just an inch above the forest floor, doing my best to maintain absolute silence. I willed myself to see the effigy full of hate and fear that had empowered me in Hillcrest, all my devils compacted into one. Slowly I raised my trembling arm, hoping I would see a gigantic feline limb as thick around with muscle as one of the pine trunks, covered in the blue down of my panther self. Even the act of raising the arm stirred agonies. I bit deep into my lip to stifle another scream.

My trembling hand stayed nothing more than a hand.

Kori's ragged breath had grown more distant, though I could still hear her plainly. The beast had no trouble gaining on her, even at a casual saunter. Its wings pulsed in a slow rhythm, just as I'd seen in the vision. Despite its size, it flowed in graceful silence, making the noise of Kori's limping struggle seem that much louder.

I can't say precisely when my perspective changed. Only that one moment I lay paralyzed and anguished. And the next, I felt so much better.

As I righted onto all fours, I marveled at how thoroughly my transformation had erased the pain.

I started to silently move. So silent.

Ahead of Kori, the rows of pine trees gave way to a green glade. Beyond the glade, another line of trees began, innocuous-looking dogwoods and elms. From their midst rose a stone church steeple, strange as a giant's finger. Somewhere outside my field of vision, water lapped against a bank.

Kori had reached the glade. The piasa would arrive seconds behind her, freed to spread its full wingspan.

Which is what the beast did as soon as it left the pines, extending its wings wide like a small passenger plane, intending to snatch its new prey and win the game. As its front talons came off the ground, my own claws sank deep into the muscles connecting wings to shoulders.

It twisted and thrashed its head, stabbing at my face with its antlers. I lashed forward with a paw, extended my already bloodied claws, and raked them across the piasa's china-blue eyes. Viscous fluid slimed the pads of my paws as I robbed him of his power-suppressing gaze.

Immediately, Kori became both a bird and a woman again and then purely a bird, whooshing through the air above the glade—a killdeer with black bands around red eyes and black and white rings around its neck. If her wings were damaged in the fall, it didn't show. She had risked the piasa's horns and claws to draw its magic-killing gaze away from me just long enough.

Becoming the panther worked a faith healer's miracle on me. The fire in my gut went out altogether, replaced by adrenaline and rage.

The piasa tried to fly, even with its wings wounded and me on its back. I dug my fangs into either side of its spine, causing it to bellow and roll, hurling me off.

As I landed upright, the monster shrieked, its enchanted stare replaced with dark blood. As I circled, its awful face turned toward me, tracking me by sound alone, talons slashing out with increasing frequency as it sidled my way. I suspected the initial shock had subsided and that the pain I had just dished out was making itself known.

In my gloriously acute peripheral vision, that steeple jabbed the sky. I could tell without even looking directly at it that the structure was beyond abnormal, covered in etchings of some kind. Its presence agitated me, but I had no time to contemplate why. I stayed focused on those talons and on those antlers, broken and whole, that kept dipping and angling—so I failed to account for the speed and range of its tail.

A row of nails punched between the ribs on my left side. I roared in surprise and pain.

One of the tail's spines stayed stuck in my flesh as the piasa tried to free its tail and back away. I turned my head and bit down on the tail's scaly length. It tasted like plastic, like copper, like sinking my teeth into electrical cable. Bone broke between my jaws. The flavor was so repulsive I had to spit it out.

The piasa howled, scrambled in retreat, its broken tail a bent flower stem, flopping uselessly. The beast backpedaled down the slope, and I followed. The narrow glade widened ever so slightly, descending toward a brilliant blue lake, surreal given the sky held no sun.

The piasa's hind legs slid out from under it. I lunged and managed to rake claws across its broad chest before it flung up its talons in defense. The creature regained its feet, only to have a large bird alight on its back. Kori was tiny in her killdeer form compared to the piasa, or to me, but she was still outsized for her species—for *any* species of bird. Based on the piasa's reaction, when she plunged her beak into its back, it was plenty sharp. She flew up, taking a chunk of blue-scaled flesh with her.

Face a mask of blood, beard clotted black, the piasa swung its antlers at this new threat—and when it turned its head, I clawed three parallel gashes along its ribs.

This time, when it screamed, I recognized its voice as human.

Primal hunger yawned deep. I felt it in my belly, my limbs, behind my eyes. The prey was at bay, was going down. Above us both, Kori circled. The piasa continued to moan, a pathetic sound.

No. Its groans were syllables. Though if they were words, they were none I recognized.

The hunger changed. It was something else altogether. As if unseen lampreys had latched onto me—not to my flesh but to my mind, my animus—to draw out my energy.

Kori faltered in her flight.

The piasa screamed more nonsense. The conduits of energy, or whatever they were, widened within me, drilled and drained deep. The world blinked black, and I hurtled into the void as if I'd been thrown by a trebuchet.

PART TWO:
THE SUM OF SMALL-TOWN DREAMS

1

"FOUND YOU," A MAN SAID, HIS TENOR VOICE SMUG.

Light wavered, an underwater view. But I wasn't wet, wasn't swimming, wasn't struggling to breathe. I couldn't have told you if I *was* breathing. I perceived only sight and sound, no smells, no sensations of touch.

"Nathan, are you there? Can you hear me?"

I attempted speech. "What's going on?" I only thought those words, had no impression of jaws, lips, tongue in motion, of lungs expelling air.

"You can! Excellent!"

The patches of color around me resolved into a pattern repeating into infinity that I recognized after a moment as tarot-derived. Here were swords. Here were pentacles. Here was the ace of wands. Here was the Fool. Adding to the weirdness of it all, I knew the pattern stretched away from me in all directions because I could see in every direction at once.

The occult patterns flattened—though my vision did not—and a giant interrupted them, worn sneakers rising toward green corduroys, rising to a tan sweater, and finally up to a face I couldn't make out. My mind wrapped around the true scale of the view. The tarot pattern belonged to a carpet, individual threads wide as rail ties, though something about the way they wove together defied comprehension.

No paws or boots supported me. Like a dust mote, I just floated.

"I don't think there's much time. Here." The giant bent down and lifted me as if I were a toy. What exactly he lifted me by, I couldn't tell you. I felt no pressure of fingers, no indication of existing within a physical boundary.

The huge carpet fibers beneath me gave way to the whorls of a pale palm. The man's head became a moon—dirty blond hair, long face, and plump lips tantalizing in their familiarity. Perhaps strangest of all, no spikes of fear agitated me. Both bodiless and emotionless.

"Sorry for the interruption," the not-quite-familiar face said, eyebrows rising in what might have been amusement. He held out his other hand, empty one moment and the next clutching a large chunk of driftwood, the tips of its branches narrowing to wicked points.

He brought it closer, within my field of hyper-focus. It wasn't branch but a bone, a portion of an antler, broken free.

"Is that . . . from the piasa?"

My host smirked. "Yes. It's a long story."

"Is this a vision? Am I seeing the future?"

"Kind of. At least, I hope I'll be part of your future. Really though, this has more to do with our past."

A swell of unease proved I had access to emotion after all. "I've never seen you before." Even as I formed that thought, I questioned its truth.

"I didn't want you to remember my special house, but I think the precautions I took worked too well. Does the name Gordie Baugh ring any bells in your mind? Do you remember Black Salt Gap?"

A town in West Virginia where I'd spent a summer. A nervous, joyous interval between the sixth and seventh grades, hiking woodland trails that linked neighborhoods. At a centrally located convenience store, a truly grimy dive, I'd bought Grape Nehi sodas that cost less than a dollar and thumbed furtively through porno mags in the magazine rack, egged on by . . . a boy whose face I couldn't call to mind, no matter how hard I tried. I tested this stranger's suggestion. "Gordie?"

"That's me." He nodded his head. "I can tell the little whammy I put on you hasn't let go yet." He laughed. "Thirteen-year-olds really shouldn't tinker with magic." He didn't come off as worried—more like he found his own statement hilarious.

"What whammy?" I grew more alarmed by the second. Seeing Gertrude Crabbe put the hoodoo on Tommy had been one thing, but hearing this smirking stranger brag about doing the same thing to me triggered a pounding that let me know I still had a heartbeat.

"This mess you're in though, I don't think it's my fault. You didn't tell me the whole deal with your grandmother. I suppose you never did know who she really is. It sure surprised the heck out of me, finding out you're her kin. If only I could've known about all that when you were staying with us."

"My mamaw?" I slurred. Words had become harder to shape. "How did you know her?"

"You're gonna have to come find me when you're back in the Overland," he said. "We don't have time to work through this right now. You're in total free fall." His words started to warble. "This conversation might feel to you like it's gone on for several minutes. But really, it hasn't. This is just an instant of contact, barely enough to get this process started."

A haze approached from all directions, the carpet pattern, the giant's body, the broken antler, the palm whorls all blurring, submerged in murk. "You're probably not going to remember that this happened. At least not at first."

My thoughts blurred too. I thought I heard, though I couldn't be sure, "I gotta say, I did tell you to take care of yourself. But I don't think you listened to me."

Whoever he was, Gordie was right. I forgot all about our conversation. At least for a little while longer.

The world blinked black, and I hurtled into the void as if I'd been thrown by a trebuchet.

2

The source of the see-saw rocking that made the floor tilt this way and that turned out to be my own aching head, jostled as Kori shook my arm, repeating, "Christ, Christ, Christ—"

"Stop it," I moaned.

She gasped. "Oh, thank heavens!"

Despite the pain, I managed a little laugh. "Did you really just say, 'Thank heavens'? Are we in some old black-and-white movie?"

Peeling my eyelids open, I took in the water-damaged ceiling of my motel room. I lay by the door, which stood open. Blood in my sinuses meant all I could smell was iron. My tongue had been packed in cotton and baked. My entire body was a husk with all the moisture sucked out. A sensation of sunburn on the inside itched all through me. I imagined myself a clay golem, doomed to crack if I tried to move. "I could really use some water," I said. "Am I in one piece?"

"Yes." The relief in her voice contained its own healing. "But you have a burn on your stomach. There're blisters."

"Great. I don't think the ice machine works here." My rueful laugh died as she stood up and dashed out. "Wait—"

The minute she was gone stretched forever. "There *is* no ice machine," she snapped as she pulled the door shut behind her.

Smiling, at least, didn't hurt. "I could have told you that."

But again, she had left my side. I heard the sink running, a glass filling. "What about you? Are you okay?"

"I'm fine."

"Did he hurt you?"

"No."

By the time she came back to where I lay, I'd managed the perilous feat of propping myself up on my elbows. She helped me sit up, handed me the glass, and watched me drink. When I finished, she went to fill it up again. Over the running water she said, "I don't think we killed him."

"Didn't give us the chance. That weird slingshot thing he did got you too, I presume?" Something deeply incongruous tickled at the back of my mind, a jumble of tarot arcana and driftwood. It scattered with a shake of my head.

I gulped the next glass of water just as eagerly.

"This can't be comfortable," she said. "Let's get you onto the bed. Can you stand up?"

"I think I'll need some help."

I achieved the vertical with one hand pressing on the mattress and the other arm around her shoulders.

"Do you want under the covers?" she asked. I shook my head no. Thinking I had my balance back, I lifted my arm off her and almost keeled over. She caught me, trying to avoid the burn on my belly but not quite succeeding. "Ooh, ooh, sorry," she cried in response to my wince. I did my best to reassure her. I ended up on my back on the bed, her kneeling next to me on the mattress, trying to tuck a pillow under my head. I was more acutely aware of the pressure of her thigh against my hip than of any discomfort.

Getting the pillow under me put her face inches from mine. I reached up, caressed her cheekbone. When she didn't pull away, I ran my fingers through her hair, gingerly drew her closer.

We kissed. Neither of us broke off until we absolutely had to breathe.

I moved to her neck—quick soft pecks. She breathed deep and lifted her chin to make it easier. I put my hands on her shoulders, slid them down her tank top until I found the bare skin at the small of her back.

She straightened, eyes locked with mine. Her lips parted slightly, her expression unreadable. She pulled off her top, black cloth giving way to gorgeous pale flesh and a no-frills white bra. She giggled a bit as the garment caught her ponytail. I helped her untangle, found the catch at the back of her bra and liberated that too. Maybe pulling off my own shirt didn't require her help, but she gave it willingly.

I pulled her in for another kiss. She tried to avoid the blistered burn on my belly, but I didn't care. I craved full body contact.

She affected me like morphine: the pain in my gut, my chest, my skull didn't recede, but I simply didn't care. If anything, the pain amplified my awareness of her, tuned me completely to the places she pressed against me, her mouth fused with mine, her breasts pressed against my chest. Every inch of skin-to-skin touch electrified in an adrenaline high.

An awkward pause followed, made reassuring by giggles, smirks, and sly looks, as we removed the rest of our clothes. Naked, her body bore more markings like the rings around her eyes and mouth and neck. I followed those markings with my palms. Lying beside me, she lifted one of her gracefully tapered thighs to let me slide a hand between them. She closed her eyes as my fingers explored.

A while later, she started trying to do the same for me, but I didn't give her much chance. I pulled her on top of me and practically purred as she found her mark and slid down until her thighs pressed hard against my hips. Before it was over, I crushed her to me, our lips locked, her belly flexing into mine, pain be damned.

Afterward, we lay side by side, sweat-soaked. I kissed her a long time, both our hands continuing to explore, and the continuing electricity of touch had me ready for another attempt faster than I would've ever expected. She propped up on all fours as I knelt behind her. We didn't waste the chance.

Almost as soon as we were through, whatever spell had allowed me to keep ignoring my injury fell away like a sheet yanked from a table. I collapsed with a string of choice words and curled up like a fetus—before flopping straight as a board because curling up hurt worse.

Kori scrambled from the bed, came back with more cold water, some in a glass, more in a soaked-through towel. As I gulped down the one and pressed the other gingerly against my belly, she muttered something I didn't quite catch. When I asked, she repeated it louder. "What on earth were we thinking?"

I managed a rueful grin. "Thinking wasn't the priority." At least she laughed at that.

Though her mirth dried up. "What if it comes back? I need to get you out of here."

"And take me where?"

"I don't know," she moaned.

I put a hand on her hip. A fool impulse had taken hold of me. Kori had saved my life and more. I could not fathom going forward solo. "Let's get away from here. Leave the city. Drive as far as you can drive. I'll cover gas. I'll put us up for the night wherever we stop. I'm good for it." My heart had bypassed my brain, but I meant every word.

She replied with a derisive snort. She might as well have stabbed me.

"Hey," I said. "I mean this. I'm not trying to pull something."

"I know," she said, not looking at me. "Don't get crazy though. It's not like I can just ditch my entire life." She withdrew from my touch, started to get dressed. "I need to take you somewhere. Maybe a hospital." Her own voice betrayed her lack of confidence in that plan.

"Something tells me a hospital can't help me."

"Maybe nothing can."

"No need to talk like that." I cast about for something that would mollify her. I was bewildered that she seemed dead set on snatching defeat from the jaws of victory. "I know you didn't ask to be part of this, but you and me together, we beat this creep. We can do it again. Maybe, you know, maybe these visions I keep having brought me here to find you. Maybe I was *supposed* to find you, so we could take care of this."

Tears of frustration glittered on her cheeks as she shook her head. "Don't let yourself believe that," she spat. "Magical thinking won't make any of this better. People like us, we're not put on this earth for any reason." She pulled up her jeans, re-buckled her slim black belt. "We're not here to help anyone with anything. We just are. If anything, we're more vulnerable than people whose lives are normal. Because people like us get so crazy so easily. We're much more dangerous to each other than we are to any of them." She finished dressing, pulled her hair back into a ponytail. "There's nothing at all special or beautiful about what we are."

I winced as I sat up. "Wow. Guess I should get dressed. Or are you leaving without me?"

She fixed me with a glare, her eyes in that moment feral red. She opened her mouth, but I never did learn what she was about to say because someone rapped lightly on the window.

As we froze, a man called sotto voce, "Are you okay in there? Are you hurt?"

A flurry of whispers let us know that the knocker at the window wasn't alone. I glanced at the motel room clock. Well past 1 a.m. Not reassuring.

"Who's out there?" My attempt at a commanding baritone came out more like a wheeze.

"We've met before. Kinda." The same voice, a little louder, still a tad timid. Or maybe the hesitant pauses in the speaker's sweet-sounding tenor were just his natural cadence. "You haven't tried to claw at us yet, which maybe means you're hurt pretty bad."

Kori's brow knit as she listened, eyes wide with bewilderment. I put two and two together, realized the vulture and the bobcat were loitering outside my door.

I had not given them any reason to stop by and chat, so I asked the obvious. "Why do you care?" I groped in the general direction of my clothes. Kori stopped me with a touch and a shake of her head, grabbed up my boxers and jeans, and handed them to me.

"You're kin to Queen Elzbeth, that's why. I don't really want to have this entire conversation through a window, especially not on this topic."

Name-dropping my mamaw stopped me cold with my jeans halfway up my thighs, my heart dancing a flatfoot. Kori either recognized the name or had her curiosity fired by my flustered expression because she left off helping me and bounded to the window to pull the curtain aside.

"Hey! Don't!" I said, too late.

"Whoa!" said the man outside, confronted by Kori's red-eyed glare.

At least she blocked his view of me as I managed to work through the pain and get my pants the rest of the way up.

A Southern lilt entered the intruder's cadence. "Sorry, ma'am. Didn't know you were in there."

"You're going to have to wait," she said. "Don't try anything funny." She closed the curtain and returned to the bedside to help me up. "Another cat," she whispered. "Not as bright as you but bright enough. The other man with him, I'm not sure . . . but something about him looks familiar."

I snatched at a dangled ribbon. "A vulture. We've danced before."

She blinked, her brow creasing. "Does *dance* mean *fight*?"

"Not really . . . maybe. You fly out of here if you have to."

"We'll see. Are you going to let them in?"

"Depends on them." I moved—well, kind of hunched—toward the window. In case I needed to summon the panther, I pictured my effigy of rage and terror, which had come to look a whole lot like the piasa. "Why are you really here?" I called.

A deeper voice muttered, "I told you this was a terrible idea."

"I swear we're not trying to be trouble," said the first speaker, who I took to be the bobcat.

"I saw you, out at the Crabbe's store. You followed me all the way here."

"Yeah, okay, that was us. I can see why that wouldn't look so good—"

"And what are you talking about 'Queen Elzbeth'?"

"Oh, he doesn't know," the vulture-guy mumbled.

"I don't know what?"

Kori interjected, volume low, "I have no idea what any of this is about," which was a sort of comfort, I confess, as I didn't either.

"He heard me," the vulture-guy said. "Damn."

The bobcat-fellow spoke over top of him. "We don't want to hurt you, and we sure don't want you to hurt us. But . . . okay, this is hard to explain, but I can tell you've got an injury. It's part of my nature to sense stuff like that. Part of yours too."

Disturbing as this tidbit was, it clicked with me as sensible talk.

"I'm pretty sure our way of life is new for you. Based on what we've seen."

The vulture chimed in: "We both felt it when you made your first crossing."

My puzzlement gave way to those words from Gertrude Crabbe. *When you come into your power like that, it's like a birth in the wild. And whether it's an egg hatching or a baby crowning, there may not be much noise, but the hungry things in the forest, they know.*

"Right after you crossed, I smelled . . . I smelled a scent I hadn't run across since I was last in the Silver City," the bobcat-fellow said. "There's no mistaking that."

I looked back at Kori, whose stance hung in the push-pull between wariness and curiosity, leaning in to listen while wired to leap away.

"I feel for you," he said. "It's not easy getting used to this life. I thought, maybe if I gave you a pointer or two, you'd stop seeing us as enemies."

Guilt competed with the fear it might all be a trick. "Okay. Sorry. I've had some unpleasant experiences recently. Very recently in fact."

"Um . . . so maybe I'll just tell you what I think you need to hear now and come back when it's daylight," the bobcat said. "I'm making a guess that you're not aware of this, but if you take your shape and then release it, sometimes that helps with, you know, flesh wounds. Not always but sometimes."

"Give us five minutes before you try," said the vulture.

Silence followed. Though I practically had my ear to the window, it was Kori who stepped up and yanked the curtain back.

We stared out into an empty parking lot.

Freezing static jolted through me as Kori vanished from the room.

Confused, I dashed out the door in time to see Kori as grandiose killdeer descend magnificently from the heavens. Her form was translucent. I could see the cloud-muffled glow of the moon and the parking lot lights refracted through her body. She settled on the sidewalk and, in an instant, changed from phantom bird to woman. There was no horror film-style resculpting of the flesh: she was one, then the other.

"They're gone," she said.

My surprise dissipated. Of course, she could phase through walls. I'd done the same.

The next thought, many beats late: the bobcat and the vulture could have done the same at any time but chose not to. They'd given me a wide berth.

Traffic whooshed steadily past on the distant highway. Every contour of Kori's face, every little hair, was crystal clear, more evidence perhaps of my own enhanced eyesight. "Should I do what they said?" The burning through my torso had only gotten worse from all the activity.

"Nothing like that has ever occurred to me, but I've never done anything like what we did tonight." She shuffled her feet and peered up at the moon. "What did you mean about them following you from the store? Do you know them?"

"No. But I've seen them in their other forms, their spirit forms." I decided I had nothing to lose. "Give me a sec."

I too turned my eyes to the firmament, mentally conjuring my friend the piasa. My perspective immediately changed. I looked down, regarded my paws in the parking lot, flexed them.

"Good heavens, you are huge," Kori said behind me. I turned my head to regard her where she stood by my back left leg—my ankle level with her shoulders. She took a nervous step back.

"Oh, jeez, I'm not going to"—my voice sounded like a truck engine revving—"do anything," finishing the sentence fully human, standing in the lot between two cars about forty feet away from her.

We exchanged awkward looks. She shrugged. "Feel better?"

I did. I stretched my arms, rolled my shoulders back. The sensation of crisped innards had shrunk to a physical thirst, like I'd finished a long run in the heat, but it no longer caused me pain. "Yeah," I said, amazed. I did a jumping jack. "Thirsty, that's all." I laughed a little. "Honestly, I feel terrific."

"Come back inside," she said.

Soon we were sitting on the bed again, her not quite looking at me. "So why are those guys following you?"

I explained as best I could without sidetracking into distractions like the Crabbes or my cousin's haunting. That I had first seen them and they me on the mountain after I fought the man in the mask and then a few more times after I'd returned to civilization. I'd even chased them once. Each time, they kept their distance, though sometimes they spoke. Finally, I cut off my story. "Have you ever heard of 'Queen Elzbeth'?"

She shook her head.

"Elzbeth was my mamaw. My grandmother. She was like me. A big cat."

"You said *was*."

"She died when I was still a kid. I barely knew her."

"I'm sorry."

"Don't be. It was years ago."

"But those guys knew her?"

"I don't know. She had some kind of reputation. Those guys aren't the first people I've met who've dropped her name."

She had nothing to say to that. As she sat quietly, I studied her pony-tailed profile, her slender neck. Her beauty made me ache.

At last, I touched her arm. "What do we do?"

She sighed. "I'm *so* out of my depth."

"We could leave—"

"No," she almost shouted. "I can't. I can't just uproot like you have. Can't do this tumbleweed thing." She smirked my way. "Sorry, Tigger."

"But you could be in a lot of danger if the piasa heals—" And a flash bulb blew grotesque light through my mind. Could the piasa do the same thing I'd just done, regain his crazy china blues with a quick change?

The other two men I had hurt—the masked creep and the black widow on the train—had stayed hurt, viscerally hurt. If there were rules that explained it all, I had no idea how to look them up. I wandered a maze built from ignorance and filled with minotaurs.

Kori didn't wait for me to articulate any of this. "If it does, you're in worse danger. But you're in danger already, aren't you? And not just from the piasa. If those two followed you all this way, who else will? Would either of us be safe, traveling together?" Her real meaning I divined right off: *Am I safe with you?*

"I wish I could answer." My own uncertainty pooled cold in my chest, hot behind my eyes.

"I'm going to go. Back home," she finally said.

"Okay," I said. And for want of something better, "It has been a long night."

Thankfully, she laughed again. "Maybe some sleep will clear our minds."

"May we both get plenty."

Hand on the doorknob, she turned back. "Maybe you want to get out of this room."

I stood up, hoping a goodbye kiss was in the cards, but the door shut behind her.

I took her advice, much to the bemusement of the night clerk, and booked a different room in the same motel.

No visions plagued me.

3

The phone woke me the next morning.

My first inane thought was that the bobcat was on the other end, wanting to meet for coffee. When it occurred to me it could be Kori, hope rose, and I grabbed the receiver.

"Hi, sleepyhead," said Melissa.

I placed her voice only after a beat or two had passed. So much had happened since stepping out of my motel room door last night for dinner that I'd forgotten all about the Nesmiths. After a beat more, I remembered I wasn't in the same motel room, so the first words I actually spoke were, "How did you get this number?"

"What?" She laughed. "You gave it to us. Are you stoned?"

It didn't jibe. I'd left the number for the room I vacated. But the explanation was simple. She'd reached the front desk and asked for me. *Yeah, that's it. That's the ticket,* I told myself in a late-night comedian's voice and let the whole thing drop.

"I wish. Can y'all help with that?"

"That's more like it." Her natural laugh was low and naughty, always sounding as if she and I had just shared a dirty secret. Fitting, as she and I and her husband genuinely had, more than once.

All at once, with Kori all over my mind, a block of awkwardness weighed on my tongue. I rescued the moment with an understatement. "Sorry, I didn't sleep well at all. Bit foggy in the head."

"We have coffee here. And other legal stimulants."

"That sounds wonderful. When does Bill get off work?"

"He took the day off. We can come pick you up whenever you're ready."

"Wow, all that for me?" Guilt took hold that I ever doubted their sincerity. "Sorry to put you two through so much trouble. I hope that doesn't put him in some kind of hot water with his boss or something." I had never held down a job, but I'd heard my classmates' complaints about them many a time.

"He's worried for you," Melissa said, confusing me until Bill came on the line.

"Hey, buddy! You're a long way from the boondocks."

"Technically not true. These are Yankee boondocks."

He cackled heartily. "Welcome to the wilds of Pennsyltucky."

"I didn't mean for you to miss work 'cause of me."

"Buddy, don't worry about me, I got benefits out the yin-yang. I put myself through scientific calculator hell for six years, so I could get a job that's good to me. I take a day off here or there, and I still get paid the big bucks! And I get to see you too. Extra bonus points."

The Bill I met my freshman year would have spit in the eye of someone with such a corporate puppy attitude, though maybe he'd been posing all along. He sure hadn't loved electrical engineering for its own sake.

"I don't know what to say. Thank you?"

"Let me give you a reason to thank me first. We're in Stroudsburg, so it'll take us about an hour to get to you. Think you can be ready then?" When I said sure, he went on, "Outstanding! So what's that address, I assume you're close to the bus station?"

Before I answered, I considered flipping the question, idly speculating how fast the panther could run to them.

I waited outside in weather-inappropriate but clean denim cutoffs and an Iron Maiden T-shirt, my pack slung over one shoulder. Sunlight rendered the faded asphalt lot about as banal as memorizing multiplication tables. My motel didn't look like a place where magical creatures came calling. I didn't feel like a magical creature.

I had not told Kori about the Nesmiths. With a little twist of my stomach, I realized that for all she and I had done together in the past twenty-four hours, I didn't have her phone number. I'd have to leave a message at the restaurant when the chance arose, so I could tell her where I'd gone.

The shiny red four-door BMW that pulled into the lot had to be my ride. Gliding past the pickup trucks and tiny Japanese cars that lined the spaces in front of the motel doors, the fancy car slowed where I stood, a chariot of bling. The driver's side window lowered to frame Bill's square-jawed, clean-shaven face. He still possessed his lengths of rock-star curls. "Hey, buddy, aren't you cold?"

Melissa leaned over from the passenger seat, her dark hair trimmed in a pixie cut, long locks like sideburns in front of her ears providing a perfect frame for her huge eyes and high cheekbones. "Hello! Get in before you freeze."

I complied and savored the toasty interior, the plush seats, the new car scent laced with notes of leather, though there was no leather in sight. "Did you guys buy this on the way over?"

"Pretty sweet, ain't it?" Bill said.

He had every right to gloat—but if he spent my entire visit flaunting his success I'd have a dreary time in store. "Yeah. This is great. You should be proud. All that pain-in-the-ass studying bullshit paid off."

Both the Nesmiths brayed excruciatingly phony laughs. "Yeah, I guess it did," Bill said without a trace of humility. My heart began to sink, but Melissa turned around in the passenger seat with one of her radiant smiles aimed my way. Half the memories in my top ten list of favorites involved that smile.

"It's great to see you," she said. "And it's really great to see you following your bliss."

Follow your bliss, was a favorite phrase of hers, used both for inspiration and as double-entendre. Reflecting that the events that put me in their car had nothing to do with following my bliss, I couldn't help a sarcastic giggle. Her smile stayed put but her eyes momentarily registered surprise.

"However much time you need, you've got it," Bill said. "Notre maison est ta maison."

Melissa rubbed his arm and made a purr-like hum deep in her throat, stirring memories that made the prospect of an extended stay abruptly more exciting—and *that* notion reminded me of a practical matter that needed tending.

During the planning of my ill-considered hike, I had hedged my bet on the Nesmiths. Had they been unreceptive to my company, I had intended to keep on hiking and postpone any hard decisions about reaching out to my parents until I made it to Maine—or at least put Pennsylvania behind me. I'd mailed a package to myself at a little post office outside Stroudsburg, to pick up once I came off the trail: additional clothes, food, and some traveler's checks that would keep me independent and mobile a little while longer. Either way things went, I won a prize because if I did in effect get to move in with them, the contents of that box would still be useful.

I explained as succinctly as I could. "Can we pick it up before we go to your place? I know it's a little out of the way."

They both stiffened. Melissa's smile faltered. "I . . . dunno about that, buddy," Bill said, as if I'd asked him to rob a bank.

"Don't mean to put you out," I said quickly. "We can always get it later."

Melissa opened her mouth as if she had an objection, her brow creasing in uncharacteristically intense fashion, eyes practically pinwheeling. I saw veins bulge on the back of Bill's fist as his grip on the steering wheel tightened.

"Gee, guys, did I say something wrong?"

Bill made a garbled noise, and they both relaxed. But not in a way that put me at ease. Melissa's awful expression loosened, and she and Bill sighed in unison. Her dazzling smile returned.

"No! Absolutely no problem," Bill said.

"You sure? You sounded—"

"No, no, absolutely. We'll get your package."

"You sounded upset."

His pitch rose with indignation. "I did not. Absolutely not."

"He didn't," Melissa said, still smiling.

"Tell us about your trip, buddy. I'm a little jealous of you. October on the trail. I bet the foliage was amazing."

A quick subject change. "Yeah. Better than any painting."

"Not better than any of *yours*, I'm sure."

"No way," Melissa said.

The conversation tuned to a shallow station and remained there. Both of the Nesmiths chirped pleasantries and flattery at me without digging any deeper into my personal situations. I confess, the absence of curiosity stung.

I was sealed in a BMW with Stepford clones of my college friends. I couldn't believe that a few months of adult life would alter their personalities that drastically. Perhaps my presence plucked some nerve. Though were that the case, I couldn't fathom why they'd play coy about it. Bill especially prided himself on blunt pronouncements.

We left the interstate behind for a country two-lane lined by trees that were in the last stages of losing their leaves, their procession interrupted by the occasional stoplight. While Bill told me about the latest engineering task on his plate—me nodding along though I understood maybe a quarter of what he said—Melissa turned around to peer out the window. A smattering of gray in her hair surprised me. I surreptitiously surveyed the back of Bill's head, noticed a bit of silver and a thinning spot too. They weren't *that* much older than me. Was marriage and a "real job" that heavy a stressor on these two hedonists?

We ramped onto a new interstate, and signs for the township popped up right away. When I asked Melissa what she was up to these days, she responded, "I'm a happy housewife," and they both laughed.

"What about your art?" I asked. I'd spent hours giggling at her ganja-fueled mockeries of various professors in the art department.

"Taking a break," she said, looking out the window again.

"I nag her, you know," Bill said, a little defensively. "I love her artwork. But she insists she's not as into it as she thought she was."

She rubbed his arm again. "I'm into you, sugar booger."

I could have choked on the artificial sweetness.

We neared and passed the Nesmiths' hometown, heading toward proper mountains. Tucked within a charming pocket of country houses, we found a modest post office built of universal red brick. I asked the Nesmiths to wait while I ran inside.

When I stepped out of the BMW, I scanned the faultless blue heavens. No signs of a big vulture or an even bigger piasa.

A woman in the lobby studying the stamp racks did catch my eye.

She never looked at me, even though her features snagged my gaze and kept it ratcheting back to her—much to my own embarrassment as I waited in line. Super-fancy for this setting, the gray wool coat she wore drew up just short of the floor, exposing pale ankles and a pair of black pumps. Under a black beret, white streaks swept back from her temples and down through her shoulder-length dark hair, which framed an oddly narrow face, punctuated by large dark eyes and a lush, full-lipped mouth. The combination made her look like a foreign actress.

It was a relief to advance to the counter and ask the plump, pretty black woman manning it for the box I'd mailed to myself.

She emerged from the back room with my heavily taped box, set it down, and deposited a small white envelope on top of it. "Looks like this is yours too."

The address on the envelope had been typed using a manual typewriter. No return address.

I carried my box to a shelf on the wooden lobby partition in order to get out of the way of a funny-looking bearded man with a stack of manila envelopes waiting his turn in line. The woman in the beret still stood in the same spot, but thankfully, she had her back to me, holding two different stamp packs up to the light. I didn't mean to, but the striking sheen of her hair held my attention long enough that my vision took a leap, and I could see that both of the packs in her hands were commemorations of Columbus.

With a shudder, I tore the envelope open. I unfolded a perfectly typed letter, no signs of correction tape.

Dear Nathan,

I hope this letter finds you well.
You don't remember me, but this hint may help. You spent a summer with my family when you were twelve and I was thirteen.

I dropped the letter. The clerk and the goofy bearded guy glanced in my direction. The woman in the beret did not.

I recovered the wayward piece of paper and kept reading:

I've missed that all-too-short time we spent together, and I've always been sorry you didn't live here in Black Salt Gap. I feel that our bond would only have deepened, to both of our benefits.
I'd like you to come see me if you can get away from the mess you've gotten yourself into. I really hope you can make it. When you get here, I can share a lot of useful advice about the things you're going through.

With love and fondness,
Gordon Baugh

Gordie. That's how I knew him. Not "Gordon."

I pictured Gordie Baugh—a rail-thin boy with tousled blond hair and coke bottle glasses. His father taught English at Black Salt Community College. His dad and mine had attended university together once upon a time. I hadn't spared Gordie a single thought for many years. Not that I had any grudge against him. He simply wasn't a factor in my life, someone long gone.

The letter gave no hint how Gordie had known to send it to this post office. I looked at the envelope again. Postmarked Monday, two days ago. The day that began with Cousin Phyllis picking me up in the Ben Franklin parking lot.

I shouldn't have been surprised, given how deeply I had buried that night of fright in Mamaw's cabin, yet I sucked in breath as memories of the summer I spent at Gordie's house loomed from mental mist, relics recovered from a fever dream. Days spent wandering along trails through woods that separated scattered neighborhoods. Stomping around in the town's sole graveyard, pretending to see ghosts. Pretending. No more than that.

Gordie didn't have many friends in Black Salt Gap, maybe had no friends at all. My presence made him hyper, overjoyed to have someone to play with. And I was happy too, for I had a respite from the ear-splitting fights and poisonous silences that plagued my not-so-sweet home.

In my brain's movie house, an archive of short films unspooled: me and Gordie running rampant, racing each other up the hill to Black Salt Gap's sole library, or charging into a tiny convenience store in the middle of town to watch Gordie play Pac-Man (he was a master), or sheepishly slinking to the back of the store to peek at the porno mags while the clerk was occupied, ogling engorged organs and acts that neither of us really comprehended, that frankly looked pretty disgusting, and gave us plenty to snicker about on the return trip.

Other events wouldn't come unstuck from the fog.

Lines carved in the gray planks of a dingy picnic table under a wooden shelter. Lines that shimmered blue.

Oh, that cold prickle. It was back.

I shuddered at a cold-jolt memory, something as stomach-flipping as the silver eyes in Elzbeth's cabin. The paper in my hand shook.

A hand alighted on my wrist. The woman in the beret stood next to me. Her voice was soft, high, and a tad nasal. "Honey, you okay?"

I nodded, blushing. "Yeah, yeah, sorry."

She glanced from my face to the letter and back. "Is it bad news? You're really shook up."

Her wide mouth mesmerized me. "I appreciate your concern," I said. "It's actually—I think—good news. Just not something I expected." That was sure the truth.

"Okay then." She squeezed my wrist and smiled a closed-lipped smile that made her eyes crinkle. I couldn't even guess how old she was. Thirty? Sixty? Striking at whatever age. "Glad I don't have to call in help."

I grinned my best aw-shucks grin. "Yeah, me too." But she had already left my side. The lobby door swung shut behind her.

I looked back at the clerk, who was paying me no mind. It struck me then what a strange thing the woman had said: *Call in help.*

I emerged from the post office with my package under one arm, the letter refolded into my pocket, and half a mind to ask the woman what she meant by that phrase, though the notion was silly—maybe just an excuse to talk to her a little more. Checking the tiny lot and surrounding trees, I spied her nowhere.

The Nesmiths had parked at the front of the building, close enough I could see them through the windshield. Their expressions were utterly inexplicable—slack-jawed and wide-eyed, like corpses in a horror movie.

When I waved to them, their smiles switched on like I'd pulled a cord.

"Everything made it safe?" Bill asked as I boarded the back seat.

"Worked exactly as planned, believe it or not."

"How about that! Government that actually functions."

Melissa faced me, eyes and teeth sparkling, no trace evident of any terror-trance. My mind had jumped to the worst possible conclusion, though given the events of the past three days, I could forgive my mind for that leap.

"Hope you don't mind a home-cooked brunch?" Melissa spiced her syllables with southern drawl.

"Why on earth would I mind that?"

Gordon Baugh's letter crinkled in my front hip pocket as we headed chez Nesmith. Lines crisscrossing blacktop, glowing blue the way the Crabbe's webbing glowed. I had watched him draw those lines with chalk. His reedy voice, asking me, *Can you see the light inside them?*

4

True to their new Stepford norms, the Nesmiths owned a palatial McMansion on the outskirts of Stroudsburg. Three stories swathed in mauve vinyl siding, accessorized by box-trimmed juniper bushes and an elegant brick sidewalk, not a stray leaf or weed to be seen. The inside proved so showroom pristine I had trouble believing my friends actually lived there. The quality of the furniture, the thickness of the carpets, the size of the stereo and television, and the blandness of the art all told me that the Nesmiths had plunged down a rabbit hole of normalcy that the couple I'd shared joints with just six months ago would have run from screaming. The rebellious bohemians I'd spent many drunken, sweaty nights with could not have been playacting the whole time. I could not process that possibility.

"I kinda figured any house that belonged to the two of you would be full of black lights and horror movie posters," I said, taking in the immaculate, sunlit kitchen.

Melissa laughed nervously. Bill squinted, puzzled. "How do you mean?"

"Your apartment was."

"Ah, I see. That was temporary, though. This house is permanent. And *expensive.*" He spread his hands as if he'd said "beautiful" and we were peering out over the Grand Canyon.

Melissa set a big pot on the range. "Chicken stew sound good?"

"Please don't go to all that trouble. I'm fine with a sandwich."

Bill patted me on the shoulder. "It's no trouble at all."

"I've learned a lot about cooking since we last saw you," Melissa said. She had already spread ingredients out neatly on a cutting board.

Bill clicked the power switch on a coffee maker. "How do you like it?"

That question, of all he could ask, rattled me deeper than watching Melissa play happy homemaker. Bill knew how I liked my coffee and had made it for me plenty of times after I'd spent the night in their bed.

On principle, the worse coffee tastes, the less likely I am to abuse it. That's been my preventative rule of thumb since late night study binges drove me to start guzzling the stuff. "Black still."

His brows furrowed. "Oh, right."

"We've got some really tasty cream flavors," Melissa said. "Sure you don't want to try some?"

"Maybe later," I said. "Even water'd be fine right now, really."

"We couldn't afford stuff this good in school," Bill said. "It's great coffee. You'll see." As the coffeemaker percolated, he sat with me at the kitchen bar and maintained a smile, saying nothing.

I caved first. "Good lord, everything's so fancy. I think I'm devaluing this fancy bar stool by sitting on it."

He and Melissa both laughed at that. I wondered if they perhaps agreed with me.

The steady rhythm of blade striking wood came to a halt. Melissa swept the vegetables and chicken into the pot and joined us, patting my arm. "We have a lot of catching up to do. I'm dying to hear why you wised up and quit school."

Bill cut in immediately. "Plenty of time for that later. Let's keep it light for now. It's just good to see you, Nathan."

"I don't mind sharing." I actually was pretty nervous about the inevitable round of catch-up confessionals. The question of what I should and shouldn't share troubled me to the point of heart flutter. Putting it off wouldn't make it any easier, though.

When I opened my mouth, Bill said, "Coffee's ready!" He got up and so did Melissa, to stir the pot. I heard the tinkling of a spoon against ceramic. It looked like Bill was stirring something too—in his own cup, I presumed.

The cup he set before me bore the logo of the company he worked for. I checked to make sure Bill hadn't put creamer in my coffee. Powder swirled on its surface. "What's that stuff?"

The Nesmiths froze.

"Good thing I didn't leave this up to the two of you," a woman said. She stepped out of thin air into the middle of the kitchen, her heels clicking on the tiles, still wearing the long gray coat and black beret.

My jaw worked, but no words came out.

"Hi," she said and pointed to the coffee cup. "Are you going to drink that?"

I glanced down at the powder. The woman became a flurry of legs and fangs. Black arachnid daggers pierced my temples. White pain exploded through my skull.

I wasn't the only one screaming because the noise continued as I faded to black.

My mamaw's eyes, green as jade, filled the space that contained me—whether outside time or inside my own head, I didn't know.

Her drought-dry voice sighed. "No man can take care of himself for long."

We stood in the woods behind her crumbling farmhouse, the bare tree branches a black tangle that ensnared the starless sky. My mamaw's long black hair hung loose, rustled Medusa-like behind the clay plate of her face. Her eyes, so huge, like eerie absinthe moons. She twitched, again and again, as if bitten by bugs.

My skin itched all over—as if fleas amassed under my clothes. The forest scene grew brighter, black branches fading, fading, fading into an all-swallowing fog of light. As that light increased, my mamaw froze mid-seizure, her spine and neck twisted so unnaturally far that I faced the back of her head and its writhing nest of hair.

"Stupid, stupid cub," I heard her rasp. "You're supposed to pick them off. You're supposed to burn them all." She slapped me. Like a shock wave from a bomb blast.

A woman was singing, her soprano full of sultry character if not precisely beautiful or on key, dragging out syllables intended for much faster tempos.

The brave crew on Engine Seven never knew the switch was wrong,
And they crashed into the freight train on the Hillcrest tracks that morn . . .

My head swam in a sea of sharks. Prickly crawling things explored my skin. The sensations carried over from the dream, but that was just a fraction of what assaulted me. My temples threatened to split open. My eyes burned as if scoured by steel wool. My brain boiled with fever, a high-voltage chemical buzz.

I tried to move, but I might as well have been cast in concrete. Cold electric shocks wrapped me, ankle to neck.

The singing stopped. "Oh, hello. You'll forgive me for taking precautions."

The blur in front of me resolved into legs. Human legs. I hung upside down.

The bare legs bent at the knees. The woman's pointed chin and wide lips sank into my view, framed by her shoulder-length black hair. Between chin and knees, I observed a new outfit—short black halter dress, tight around the wide hips of an otherwise toothpick-slender frame. Her mouth moved. "You killed my beautiful young buck. Why did you do that?"

"I'm"—that maddening itch extended even beneath my tongue—"sorry."

"Everyone's sorry," she said. "That doesn't answer my question." She leaned closer and opened her mouth wide. Instead of upper incisors, she had long black chelicerae growing from her gums, and the needle-sharp fangs at their tips flexed. I yelped and thrashed, triggering more cold shocks. When she closed her mouth, she was smiling.

The sharpened threat cleared my head a fraction, enough to take in more of my environment through the fiery haze jamming my brain and the fiery itch swathing my body, a stultifying mix of agony and dizzying intoxication. An immense block of a television loomed behind my tormentor like an altar. My hair brushed the top of a coffee table, game controllers piled near my right ear.

Bill and Melissa were nowhere in sight. "Where are my friends?"

"Resting. They've had a long couple of days, poor things."

The full-body itch receded and resurged as I breathed. "What have you done to me?"

She straightened. "Answer *me* first."

I struggled to remember her question.

She'll kill you for this.

"The man on the train . . . didn't mean to . . . he was coming at me. He was a spider. There were two of them."

"And only one came back. Oh, he was inconsolable. They were twin brothers, after all. Valuable servants, impeccable lovers."

She crouched again, her long face inches from my own, the white streaks flaring from her temples like wings. As she spoke, the black fangs in her mouth flashed in and out of view. "I promised him—before I ate him—that I'd make you play in blood. But if I break that promise, he'll never know. So please answer honestly and thoroughly."

"I did see that they were twins," I said. I strained against whatever bound me, which worsened both the itching and the electric jolts. "They cornered me on a bridge. They didn't say anything about who they were or what they wanted. I jumped on the train to get away from them. They chased me." I think I was crying. I was certainly snuffling. "I struck at them. I thought they were gonna . . . I was just trying to keep them off me."

"What did you think they were going to do?"

"Kill me," I said. "Or worse. Take me away somewhere and feed on me." Like the Crabbes had done to my victim on the trail.

"Seth said you tore his brother to pieces."

I stared at her, fighting to think through the euphoria and pain. A desperate notion surfaced. My arms were pinned behind my back, held by . . . well, I wasn't sure what she had wrapped me in, but I made an educated, blue-webbed guess. I fought the urge to bend my neck and look up at my body. Given how closely she studied me, how fast I had seen her transform, and the size of the monster she became, I did not want to inspire her by making a sudden move. Especially as her more subtle shape-shift, the spider-fangs in her smile, had made me wonder if I could pull off something similar.

I wanted so badly to scratch off my own skin, anything to abate the sensation of mites crawling and chewing. I hung dishrag-limp. "I didn't mean to," I said, snuffling. "I didn't know that would happen."

She stood again, my gaze ending up level with her hemline.

She placed her hands on my thighs. The pressure intensified the cold electricity, amplified the itching to pure fire. I gasped and thrashed. She responded with a low chuckle. "Did you know *that* would happen?"

Under the sensation of shock, the skin of her palms slid down to my hips. I realized that I was naked beneath the magic she'd used to bind me.

"It sounds like my boys came on to you too strong," she said. "If you're being truthful. What you say though, that's not the way Seth told it. He said you tore into them without warning and without reason." She pressed in with a finger, drew it down to my stomach, all the way to my nipple. Where she touched me, the magic she'd wrapped me in stabbed and burned. I yelped and groaned. "It's hard for me to just let that go."

An immense darkness congealed behind her, its boundaries expanding beyond the walls of the room. A monstrous form lingered at the edge of clarity, its shiny, spiny surfaces not quite coming into focus.

She crouched down to face me again. The huge black form moved with her. Its face, wide as an oven, overlapped hers. A cluster of eyes glittered. Spider fangs extended to the floor. I was too tongue-tied to scream.

"You might think you can get away with anything," she said. As her wide mouth moved, the giant spider fangs quivered. "Your grandmother, most of anyone, knows that transgressions need to have consequences."

I shouted through the agony. "Don't you talk about my mamaw!" The sudden mention of Elzbeth, spoken in present-tense from the mouth of the monster-woman, spiked my emotions, an acid-splash of fear and anger.

Threads loosened around the tips of my flexing fingers. I focused on that sign of hope as my captor stared at me with her ten eyes.

"If I didn't love her so, you'd be dead," she said. "What would she think if she saw you now? Sweet darling cub. I bet she'd be so disappointed. She'd have a hankering to kill you herself."

She put a hand on my ribs. The smoky spider-shape behind her lifted a long, thick limb in unison with her motion. Radiating out from where her fingers touched me, bristles and claw tips settled on my skin.

"Don't . . . don't," I managed to blurt.

"Don't what?" Glee trickled through each syllable. "What do you think I'm going to do?"

"I think . . ."

I curled my claw-tipped fingers, and more threads gave. The hideous itching subsided a perceptible fraction.

"I think . . ."

I raked my hands outward, cutting into my own love handles. More of the binding gave. That was enough.

One instant, I hung from the ceiling in the Nesmiths' den. The next, I crouched over a spider squirming grotesquely on its back, spitting useless venom from its thrashing fangs, bright-blue blood gushing from four parallel slashes across its abdomen. No sign of the woman—for she was all arachnid now.

Our bodies were too large to fit inside the room, and in fact, we'd tumbled completely out of it into some other, grayer place.

Her legs tangled around my front paws. With a twitch, her fangs could strike me in the neck or chest. My panther-self flowing like supple steel, I rose onto my back legs and lunged at her abdomen. Something soft split apart and spurted stickiness.

Immediately, the spider was upright, its row of black eyes gleaming. I sprang straight back, deeper into the gray.

Where the bus-sized black widow had been, my attacker stood, clutching her side as blood streamed from between her fingers and stained her torn dress. She wore a wicked smile that wavered into wide-eyed, wide-mouthed surprise and back again. The next moment the black widow returned.

Her fangs flexed as she spoke, but her voice sounded in my mind rather than my ears. "What have you done, cub?"

"Where are my friends?" I snarled.

Our environment got weirder by the second. We were outside the boundaries of the Nesmiths' house, but there was no sign of the street lined with McMansions. The Nesmiths' den floated below and to the side, the sort of view seen through a boat's glass bottom—except this view was through the wall, and all the furniture was tilted ninety degrees in defiance of gravity. Around us, the gray haze stretched. To my right, it lightened to silver, and to my left, it darkened to black. Though my paws rested on a smooth surface, I couldn't tell you what we stood on if you put a gun to my head.

She changed to woman, then spider, and then woman again at strobe speed, laughing the entire time but finally stopping on her human setting, still holding her side. She lifted her hand to regard her blood-painted palm and forearm. "You're definitely your grandmother's spawn," she said as if she were admiring a gorgeous jewel.

I advanced, wary of her switching back to spider. "Stop talking about Mamaw. What did you do with my friends?"

She didn't give ground. Instead, she ran her blood-slicked hand across her face as if she were trying to lick it clean, smearing her own blood across lips, cheeks, and chin before flashing a deranged grin, no chelicerae visible among her teeth. "You don't know who I am. If you did, you'd know I'm your grandmother's biggest fan. I love her like a sister. I see her in you, and that makes me love you too." She put her hand back on her wounds, which were still seeping. "Your friends are fair trade for my forgiveness."

As she spoke, I'd fixed on her strange and beautiful features: the white pearls of her teeth, the way her mask of blood impossibly arranged itself in artful patterns, and somehow hadn't noticed that she's grown taller, larger. Her hips flared wide, shiny black spider legs arching out from beneath her dress. Her arms elongated, her fingers stretching into spindly talons. More eyes, human, opened above her brow, along her hairline.

I curled back my lips, dug claws hard into the mysterious surface beneath me. This wasn't the quick flip from flesh to spirit I'd become more or less used to seeing, like the sublimation of ice to steam. This was full on remolding of the skin, muscle, and bone, a slow-motion horror-film transformation.

"See you soon," she said, and she scurried sideways into the darkness. Her entire body rotated away and down as if she crawled over the lip of a crevice, her legs the last I saw of her before they too withdrew into the blackness.

I put my paw on the view of the den, and it sucked me in—I tumbled against the coffee table, human again, banged my shoulder hard, and cut my arm. Four solid walls bounded the room, their dark-stained wood paneling decorated by framed posters of Led Zeppelin and Pink Floyd, no signs of blue webbing or gates to the silver realm.

I was stark naked, my clothes piled beside the table.

"Melissa!" I yelled as I struggled to simultaneously dress and stand upright. "Bill!"

I heard a groan, faint, from the upper floor. I lurched toward the hall and lost my balance, upending between the table and the television. My head still swam, my thoughts muffled within a heated towel.

"Oh, boy, are you in a hell of a spot. You need to get out of there, Nathan."

The voice, a tenor with a dash of mountain twang, was as familiar as the back of my hand, but I couldn't tell who it belonged to or where it came from.

"Please, don't waste your time looking for me. Get out of there. Come to Black Salt Gap. I can keep you safe if you're with me, but you have to really be here. In the flesh."

The voice emitted from the speakers of the TV even though it wasn't on. When I heard the words "Black Salt Gap," my mind lit up with a room carpeted in tarot patterns and with a slender man, tousled hair and spectacles, holding a huge piece of broken-off antler.

"Gordie?"

"You remember now. Great! We can catch up later. Come find me. Over and out."

"Gordie? What is going on?"

The speakers burbled as if Gordie had plunged underwater.

"Gordie?"

Gordie had left. Not even a burble.

Too discombobulated to freak out much more that I already had, I took his message in stride—even as my own strides wobbled. My sense of balance in full trickster mode, I stumbled from hallway to stairs, calling for Bill and Melissa.

I hadn't gotten the full tour of the house, wasn't familiar with the layout. The upstairs hall hooked to the left. A door at the very end stood ajar, the corner of a king-sized bed visible through the opening, though to my addled mind it blurred as if dimmed by a veil.

I reached in, groped for a light switch, found it, and flipped. Nothing happened.

A groan preceded a disturbance in the shadows. I leaned in, alert for trouble. "Guys?"

A pale figure trembled in the distance, too far away to exist within ordinary space.

Our attacker had said she'd see me soon. I flexed my fingers, focused my vision, and strove against the wet warm chaos that scrambled my thoughts to find the mental trigger that turned me into the panther.

The figure hanging in darkness slid into clarity as my vision took a leap. Bill, naked, suspended spread-eagled. Blue webbing held him in place, the glow not leaping out over the distance because the strands were thinner than fishing line. A gloom tainted the air, and drool poured from his mouth.

A massive shape with many legs shifted above him, making him tremble again. Smaller spiders crawled over his legs, his chest.

The filaments of web made a net that extended in all directions. I spied Melissa, also strung up naked, dangling even farther in the abyss, as far from Bill as he was from me. At first, I thought a slice had been cut from her body, and I gasped as my heart spun. But when my vision leapt again, I saw the fangs of an immense spider sunk into her bare belly. Her eyes, thankfully, were vacant.

Spiders large and small, numerous as stars, moved along threads throughout the limitless web, hundreds of them turning their soulless eyes in my direction.

I turned to see the door and the light beyond recede, the space between my feet and the way out rapidly widening to cavernous dimensions. At the edges of my vision, webbing ballooned, a thousand nets cast my way.

I ran.

As either Nathan or the panther, I had no chance in that spider-filled void. That's what I told myself, over and over, in the horrible hours that followed. I left Bill and Melissa where they hung.

Only the Lord can forgive me. I can never forgive myself.

I compounded my shame by detouring into the darkened kitchen, spurred by a half-second of memory that proved correct. Our lunches remained on the freestanding counter, every dish and cold morsel left exactly where I last saw them. Outside, night had fallen. By the stove Bill's car keys were splayed.

I was going to help my friends, I told myself. I would call from a payphone once I was safely way. Far away. Safe. I didn't even let myself think about what might happen if people not equipped for the inexplicable charged into that nightmare in the Nesmiths' bedroom.

Nor did I bother to lock the front door.

I fumbled with the key ring until I found the key to the BMW. The engine roared to life as if it were a lonely hound whose master had finally come home.

5

On my frantic way out of Stroudsburg, I pulled into a Wawa parking lot and dialed 911 from a payphone. I gave the dispatcher the Nesmiths' address, as best I could remember it, and told her I saw a man jimmying the front door with a crowbar. When she asked for a description of the man, I said it was too dark, and I was too scared to slow down for a closer look. She began another question as I hung up.

One more stop beyond the town limits. The headlights revealed an old misshapen AMC Pacer, rusting in a vacant lot with "For Sale" and a phone number written in soap in the back window.

I pulled over, cut the lights, popped the trunk, and unzipped my backpack, which we'd never gotten around to unloading. I groped in the dark until I found my Swiss army knife.

In about ten minutes, the BMW sported the Pacer's license plate. Had the BMW been bestowed with any sort of soul, that car most assuredly would have blushed at this indignity.

How long would it take for whoever found the Nesmiths—and God, I hoped they would be found—to notice the missing vehicle? I prayed for them to be okay. I was out of my depth. There was nothing I could do.

The swirling warmth inside my skull dulled as I turned my stolen car south. No sleep for me until I reached the promised haven at Black Salt Gap. There, I could regroup. And maybe Gordie could tell me what I needed to do.

By the time the sky lightened, I'd been driving about five miles over the speed limit on southbound I-81 for two hours, rolling at a deliberately unremarkable pace back in the direction of Old Virginia. The warm brain fog I associated with the spider-bite to my temples had at last cleared. Simultaneously with sunup, the gray sky began to sprinkle. Figuring out how to man the wipers took a ludicrously long time. I was tempted to pull over and read the owner's manual.

A Pennsylvania state patrol cruiser, lying in wait at a median crossover, snapped any such thought out of my head. I trundled past at a relatively innocent 58 mph. He stayed put, but I kept looking in the rearview mirror, certain his lights were going to come on.

And sure enough, they did.

A new kind of fear seized me. I was totally unprepared to explain to a stone-faced state trooper what I was doing behind the wheel of a stolen vehicle. What would a cop do if I became the panther and bounded away? What would he do if I tried and failed? I shuddered as I slowed the car, waiting for the cruiser to pull in behind me and flick its lights: get off the road.

The cop came up behind me and then sped on past, answering some other emergency.

My relief swiftly died. The scare, so mundane yet so close to making me shit my pants, busted the trance of shallow survival instinct that had carried me through the night. I'd left Bill and Melissa hanging—in the most horrible and literal way—and here I was behind the wheel of their car, panicking about getting caught. A punishment that I totally deserved.

I had to believe Gordie could help them. He'd been powerful enough, magical enough, to anticipate my post office stop and to contact me directly in the middle of two attacks. He understood this strange new world better than I ever could. He'd shown me things during our summer together, though I still couldn't remember precisely what: there had been a structure standing where no structure could have been, its edges wavering as if obscured by heat haze, lights coming on behind arched windows. I remembered asking him, *Is this a dollhouse?* I'd been striving to fit a miracle into a mundane box, something that I could grasp.

Though the nature of what Gordie had conjured eluded me, I clung to the notion that he could help me, help the Nesmiths, change this chaos into order, turn my wrong into a right.

Soon after I crossed the border into Maryland, I took a risk, turning off into Hagerstown, and cashed one of the traveler's checks at an immense, eclectic emporium that sold antique wood furniture, first-edition books, and giant plush animals.

Freshly armed with coin, I dialed information in West Virginia and learned the Black Salt Gap directory had no listing for a Gordon Baugh.

He couldn't be lying to me. His family had to still live there. I couldn't possibly forget his father, a bespectacled, balding mountain of a man, the tallest person I'd ever met at that age. Everyone called him Buck, even Gordie, but that wasn't his name. Debris from the river of memory, Robert or Richard, struck a chord. Richard Baugh scored me a number and address.

I jotted down both on the palm of my hand, regarding the markings as if they might flutter up and bite me. It took a moment or two to gather the courage. I dialed.

Apparently, the phone lines to Black Salt Gap hadn't been upgraded in decades. When the phone on the other end rang, the tone gurgled as if filtered through water.

Someone answered on the fifth ring, but I couldn't even tell whether they said hello. I pictured some humanoid fish creature holding the receiver, staring at it curiously.

"Hello? Is there someone there?" I shouted into the phone.

I barely made out an irked, "Hello!"

"Buck? Buck Baugh?"

"Yes? Who's speaking?"

I practically screamed my name at him, followed by, "If you remember Jasper Mullins, you went to college with him. I'm his son. I stayed at your house several years ago. I'm trying to track down Gordie."

Silence from the deep.

"Um—" How could I explain this? "I got a letter from him. He invited me down, but he forgot to give me an address." That would have to do. "Can you tell me how to find him?"

"He's not here," the voice warbled. The connection must have been bad on both ends.

So Gordie didn't live at home at least. "That's okay. I'm trying to find out where he lives now. Can you tell me how to reach him?"

More silence. "He's not here," the voice repeated.

"Buck, this connection's really bad on my end. Can you understand me at all?"

Dial tone.

I called again, hoping for a better connection. The phone rang and rang and rang, still with that disconcerting underwater warble.

I pictured Buck with his royal hooked nose and the beige button-down sweater he wore in my memories, watching the phone as it rang, making no move to answer.

The evidence suggested father and son weren't on the best of terms. Or maybe Buck simply couldn't hear me through the bad line. Another attempt seemed a waste just then.

I paused, hand on the receiver. The only way I knew to reach Kori was through MacPhair's, and surely, at that hour, they were closed. She'd not heard from me in more than a day. She might be worried sick, or—and this paranoid, self-inflicted notion stabbed deep—not worried at all. But tenuous as my avenue of contact was, she had none. The cards were all in my hands.

Even if the restaurant had an answering machine, leaving a message would be a terrible idea. For the first time, I seriously wondered what the authorities might have found at the Nesmiths', and what it had led them to do next. I didn't speculate about whether Bill and Melissa were okay. They couldn't possibly be okay. That woman and her spider-ilk had commandeered my friends while I was still on the way to Wilkes-Barre, used them to set a trap for me.

The payphone rang. I jumped as if a bullet punched the wall beside me.

Debate raged through me as the ring repeated, whether to answer or flee for the hills.

The need to know overwhelmed the fear of consequences. I picked up. The voice on the other end immediately chirruped, "Nathan!"

My number one suspect, Gordie, the most benign of the possibilities I'd entertained. "How do you keep finding me?"

He laughed, high-pitched and blatantly arrogant. "I get why you want to know, but explaining could take hours that you don't have."

"Try me. Please. I'm a quick study."

"Okay, let's try this. Imagine my eyes can see infrared. You light up like a forest fire."

"You can see me all the way from Black Salt Gap?"

"That's the part that's hard to explain. Let's just say, I've had some major breakthroughs with the resources in the argent."

"The what?" My eyes began to sting as my voice dropped to a whisper. "Did you see what happened to me last night? And to my friends?"

"I don't know details, but I know you're lucky to be alive. You're having a terrible run, buddy. In fact, I can't think of a worse one for a newly hatched natural. First the piasa comes after you, then Lilith shows up."

"Lilith . . . the . . . the black widow?"

"Shhh. Shhh. Best not to take that name in vain, buddy. You're out in the wide open."

"Gordie, she's got my friends. She was torturing them. Her and her spiders—"

A woman leading a little girl into the emporium snapped her attention my way before she disappeared inside. Gordie said, after a pause, "I'm so sorry to hear that, Nathan."

"I've got to help them, Gordie. You've got to help them."

"If I can, I will, but what's most important is that *you* come to *me*."

"I know you can help them." I caught my volume cranking up, reduced it to a whisper. "You showed me the broken antler."

"Stop, stop, stop, you have no idea who might be listening on your end. I can't say anymore. Just get here."

"Can you at least tell me how to find you? Your dad—"

He cut me off again. "That, my friend, is a risk I really can't afford to take. Once you're with me in the Gap, I can bring you up to speed on a number of things. But you have to get here."

"Okay, but—"

A click, followed by a soft bubbling, as if he'd dropped the handset into an aquarium.

I returned to my stolen BMW and shifted into drive. By the time I reached I-68, mountains loomed blue in the distance. I took a break to gulp down a late lunch, some overcooked pork chops at a truck stop with an apple in its marquee. A couple hours after that, I rolled through the kind of terrain that rendered me carsick as a kid. At least I-79 offered a gentler ride through the mountains.

But the road had hallucinations to offer too. As the day wore on, my sleep-deprived state turned the dotted center lines into broken strands of spider web. Over the crest of a hill, a titanic fist lowered from the sky to crush me. But it was just an array of large green highway signs, announcing destination and distance, staggered so they appeared as fingers before my mind's bleary eye.

Road hypnosis proved even more worrisome as over and over I'd snap my eyes open and jerk the steering wheel to swerve the car back into its lane.

As I transferred from the exit to the twisty mountain road that would take me to the Gap, I snarled as if I were the panther. "You better make good on this safety promise, Gordie, old buddy. You better be telling me the goddamn truth."

The state government hadn't expended any funds on improving the road to Black Salt Gap since I'd last been there. It was barely wide enough to accommodate the BMW. This didn't pose the problem you might expect since, incredibly, no cars came down from the mountains to confront me that afternoon.

Those tilt-a-whirl curves stirred a sludge of déjà vu, yet whatever memories lurked underneath remained below the surface. I had ridden this path before, hunkered in the passenger seat of our VW Bug, sick to my stomach from the ripsaw centrifugal force, repeating, "Keep your eyes up," as a mantra against a car door slathered in vomit.

The seconds I had spent in that condition stretched into hours, and truth be told, retracing the route eight years later dragged out longer. Even though I was driving, motion sickness raised its serpentine head.

I tried to distract myself by chiseling at whatever barrier suppressed those memories. I'd lived with the Baughs for the full summer break, but I had never returned to that town, nor heard a peep from Gordie since. Strangest yet, so far as I could tell, I had never discussed that summer-long adventure with anyone once it was over. My time in this town cut across the path of my life like a chasm that had swallowed the bridge built to cross it.

For all the swerving, the BMW could have been navigating a Möbius strip. The crest of the mountain never drew closer, nor did the sun lower from its post, or so it seemed. My conquest of the climb arrived as a disorienting surprise: at one turn, the evergreen-gloved mountaintop loomed, forbidding as a fist. And past the next, a flat road sliced through a plane of pines as if all the stubborn mass of rock had shuffled off in a huff while I wasn't looking.

A modest white sign heralded the town limits of Black Salt Gap, and after that, the bizarre elongation of the trip completely flip-flopped.

To my surprise, I recognized the landmarks. I passed a cramped community college campus and a strip mine yawning cavernous beneath a sun lowering toward the horizon. I pulled up short at a T-intersection, facing a cracked retaining wall. Instinct told me to bear left. Buck Baugh lived on the south side of town, and though I didn't believe he'd be excited to see me, I didn't think he'd shoot me on sight either. And I had no other way to find his son.

In my head, the journey across Black Salt Gap should have taken hours, maybe because Gordie and I did all our traveling on foot that summer. Yet the drive through what served this community as a downtown took less than five minutes: there went the odd hotel with an architectural footprint in the outline of an Old West coffin, the husk of a dead strip mall, the white-columned courthouse, the boxy convenience store where Gordie had played champion-level Pac-Man. And then the cross-town trip was done.

I had Buck Baugh's address scribbled on my hand, but I didn't need it. I turned right at a fast-food restaurant, took a left up a hill. In seconds, I was there.

I inched past the untrimmed hedge and down the sloping driveway to a ranch house with a bay window. A lamp glowed between the parted curtains.

Assuming the engine sounds had already given me away, I stepped out and hurried across the walk to the front door, where I hesitated. Twelve-year-old me had needed to stand on tiptoe to peer through the upper glass panel in that door, but twenty-year-old me stared down through that same panel into the murk of the living room.

Once I'd adjusted my thinking, I savored a little laugh at my own expense. After all, I'd grown a few inches since I'd last stood before that door.

I knocked. Within the house, footsteps rumbled. A voice, gruff and deep: "Who's there?"

"I'm Gordie's friend. I called you this morning?"

The door swung inward. Mr. Baugh filled the door frame. Again, a size-related shock: I recalled Buck Baugh as a human skyscraper, his craggy nose an adze—that I once had fancied capable of splitting a concrete block with a single butt from his bald, bulky head.

Incredibly, we were of a height. He looked me in the eye, frightened. "I told you he's not here."

"Yes, I know." I felt stupid in the face of his agitation. "But he didn't give me clear directions to where he lives, and I don't have a number to call him back. This was the only place I could think of to go."

Buck put a hand on the handle of the screen door. I thought he was about to invite me in, but instead he held the door closed between us and didn't answer me.

"Sir, I realize this is awkward." I no longer believed he'd tolerate me calling him Buck, so *sir* it had to be, but I'd had an idea. "I'd like to call my fiancée to let her know I made it to Black Salt Gap safe. Could I use your phone?"

The lie slipped a bit too easily through my lips. I was gambling that it would bear more gravitas than "girl I just met."

Gears turned and then he moved aside to let me in. "You can try."

The house reeked of the scorched sweetness of pipe tobacco. With surreal clarity, I recalled hanging out with Gordie on the back deck, looking up at Buck as he lit a pipe and exhaled impressive clouds from his nostrils. Apparently, he no longer bothered going outside to smoke.

A tall stack of newspapers leaned precariously against the lamp table that held the phone. I perceived shadowy outlines of bookshelves and a TV set as large as the one at the Nesmiths'. An entrance across from the front door led into the kitchen, and weirdly, the fact that it was unobstructed made me nervous.

"Have a seat," Buck said. "The phone's right there."

A tall, plush armchair cuddled against the lamp table, its green wool upholstery well worn, the cushions dented by frequent occupation. When I had visited before, I could swim in that chair. Now, I wondered if I would even fit. I did, but the arms squeezed my sides.

My host hovered next to me, waiting. My little fib sprouted plot holes.

"I can't call collect," I said, doing my best to keep eye contact. "I'll pay you back for the charge."

Confirming my suspicions, he produced a pipe from the pocket of his sweater vest. "We'll see."

I didn't have the number for MacPhair's Funnie Faces. "She's at work right now, and I'm embarrassed to say I don't have the number handy. I'm gonna have to ask for it from information."

He nodded, lit up and took a puff. "Go ahead."

I picked up the phone, dialed 4-1-1. Could Kori have heard about the Nesmiths, I wondered. I pictured a TV news crew in front of a police-tape enveloped McMansion. Did I dare ask Kori about such a thing in front of Buck Baugh?

The dial tone faded into an underwater burble. I hung up, tried again, same result. "I think there's a problem with your line."

Buck's nostrils spewed twin streams of smoke. "They only work when he wants them to," he said.

"What works?"

"The phones. You can call in town, sometimes, but you can't call out."

The fumes made me cough. "Who—who wants them to?"

He kept his pipe gripped firm in his mouth and answered me with smoke.

I remembered the presence of a plastic gate across the lower half of the kitchen door. Once I did, I recalled why its absence made me nervous. When I had visited, the Baughs owned a cocker spaniel and boxer mix named Xeno, and that mutt had been the bane of my existence. A shaggy, ill-tempered thing, the little monster would lose his psycho mind every time he spotted me. While Xeno was indoors, the Baughs kept him in the kitchen behind a baby gate, which I never believed was sufficient protection, for the dog made no bones about his urge to murder me.

Gordie had explained to me more than once that it was Xeno with an *X* because he was convinced the beast was a dog-shaped monster from outer space.

My brain leapt at the distraction, hoping for a break in the ice. "Oh, man, I just remembered Xeno. That dog scared me so much while I was here. Is he . . . y'know, still around?"

"No," Buck said around his pipe stem.

"Well, even though I don't think that dog liked me, I'm sorry to hear that."

The phone rang. I started to get up, but Buck said, "Pick it up. It's for you."

I took him at his word and didn't even try to pretend that I didn't know who it was. "Hi, Gordie!"

"Nathan, thank goodness. I am so glad you made it! Do you remember driving by Bolling College on the way in?"

"Yeah?"

"Double back the way you came and take the access road to the campus. Then bear left at the fork. Keep going till the road changes from pavement to dirt. You'll end up at the picnic grounds. Remember that place?"

I did. Gordie's family had brought me with them a couple times that summer. We'd eaten hamburgers and played badminton, a game where Gordie's father enjoyed a tremendous advantage over the rest of us. In my mind, I couldn't bring Gordie's other family members into focus.

"You'll find a path on the other side of the picnic shelter that leads to a two-story house. I bet you remember that now. The presidents of Pittston Mining lived in it about a hundred years ago. That's where I am."

"You fixed up that . . . dump?" Heck yeah, I remembered. That old mansion had been as much of a ruin as my mamaw's cabin.

"Oh yes, I sure did. I can't wait for you to see it."

"Okay, I'm on my way."

"See you soon!" No click, just more of that underwater bubbling.

"Well"—I squeezed out of the chair and stood—"I guess I'll try to call my fiancée once I get to Gordie's place." I extended my hand. "Thanks for your help."

Gordie's father shuffled back a step. "You be careful." I couldn't tell if he meant that as advice or threat, but his eyes had widened when I reached his way. He continued to stare, lips pressed together, underlining that craggy nose.

"Okay, thanks." Message received: *Get out.* I hoped Gordie could explain why his father found him, and by proxy me, so terrifying.

As I opened the door to my stolen chariot, another memory came loose from the muck and froze me to the spot.

When I'd spoken to Buck at the door, when I'd offered to shake his hand, we'd stood eye-to-eye. Yes, I was eight years taller, but our level gazes still made no sense. I'm six foot even. Aging can make you lose height, but Buck stood straight as he had that long-ago summer. During my stay, I'd repeatedly asked him how tall he was—my immature brain couldn't process the existence of someone that tall. He'd always answered with a hint of a smile, *Six foot six.*

We couldn't be the same height. It didn't add up.

Maybe Gordie held the answer.

Gordie had not just rebuilt that old house, he'd transformed it into something impossible. The restored wooden facade was now flanked by entirely new wings that stretched at least twenty yards to either side; the venerable logs and chinking of the original structure now bracketed by stucco and ceramic tile shingles that evoked an Italian mansion. Electric light burned in the windows, though I saw no wires extending down to the house through the trees. It struck me too that there was no way to drive up to it, no sidewalk, not even a path. The house could only be reached the way I had approached, stepping carefully around bushes and roots that overgrew the path. I plucked off the burs and thorns that snagged my T-shirt.

As I neared the porch, I no longer experienced that disorienting sense of things smaller than they should be. Gordie's dwelling was larger than life—and I couldn't even gauge how far back it sprawled into the woods. I was dying to ask him how he'd made this happen, how he paid for it.

When I was about to put the sole of my shoe on the concrete stoop, a low rumble stopped me, rising in pitch and volume until recognizable as an ear-splitting growl. A compact blur lunged from nowhere, bearing its canines.

"Xeno! Xeno, down!" The front door flew open, golden light pouring out behind the slender man in the bathrobe who shouted, "Xeno, heel!"

The dog's growl stopped as quick as if Gordie had punched an off switch. Xeno retreated to sit beside his master.

"I'm so sorry," Gordie said, lifting his arms in theatrical exasperation. "I can't believe I forgot to bolt the doggie door."

Buck Baugh had said Xeno was gone. Yet here Xeno was—or if not that Xeno, an exact clone of Gordie's childhood pet. The Mark II Xeno returned my stare with dull black eyes.

Gordie noticed my astonished fixation. "He's not the Xeno you remember. He's much better behaved."

"That's a relief." My chest clenched in the opposite of relief.

My childhood friend smiled big, a master-of-ceremonies smile meant for a full tent audience. "Don't wait one second longer out there! I have illumination and central heat and food and running water!"

The spacious foyer where I ditched my shoes warmed me with air cozy as cotton. Gordie led me down a hall where wall lamps spread comforting amber light. The carpeting even soothed my stockinged feet, pressing up as if attempting to massage. I could not contain a smile at my host's unruly bush of dirty-blond hair, a thicket of cowlicks, hardly any different than when we were boys. Despite my fears about the Nesmiths, my yearning to contact Kori, the scare at the door, the tensions eased in my back and jaw, my heart rate slowed, my eyelids drooped, the urgencies that rode me dimmed.

I hadn't had a good sleep since Cousin Phyllis's house, and I was feeling every minute of that deprivation, but I couldn't just crash. Gordie stopped me, though, before I could ask a single question. "Why don't you wash off the road grit?" he said. "You'll be done just in time for dinner."

He guided me through a generous sitting room with a fireplace big enough to make Citizen Kane burn his sled from sheer envy and down yet another hall to a bathroom fit for a robber baron. "Fill up the tub," he said. "You'll love the pressure jets."

I scrutinized his thin, deep-chinned, gold-rim-spectacled face for a hint that he was joking. "How did you afford this, Gordon? You running a coke cartel?"

He laughed. "I'll explain everything over dinner."

He had not lied about the garden tub—a porcelain basin that recalled "Venus on the half shell"—sunk into the aqua-tiled floor. After mere seconds of leaning my travel-cramped back against the blood-hot jets of water, I quit questioning how Gordie had carved out this huge slice of heaven and just indulged myself.

Though I never saw Gordie or anyone else come in, somehow a comfortable black terrycloth robe and black silk boxers awaited me when I finally, reluctantly emerged and toweled off. Energy brightened my thoughts, sped my reflexes, as if I'd had a good week's sleep.

My friend met me in the hall with a cup of steaming cocoa—the best I'd ever tasted in my life. "You ready for some answers?" he asked.

"If you're ready for some questions." A list of things I had to address impinged, number one asking him to help the Nesmiths, even as an unpleasant voice muttered that it was too late, that by now it was all over.

"I need to finish conjuring up dinner," Gordie said. "Follow Xeno. I won't be long."

I looked past Gordie's feet to find Xeno's square, shaggy face regarding me with black eyes. As soon as we made eye contact, the dog turned and shuffled down the hall. I turned, meaning to say something to Gordie, but I was alone. Xeno stopped, looking back at me blank-eyed until I moved to follow.

The dog led me back to the enormous fireplace—except it wasn't the same sitting room I'd seen before. Smaller, cozier, red brick walls hung with startlingly vivid replicas in miniature of modern artworks by Pollock, Klee, Mondrian, Tanguy, and Kandinsky. A small, round table at the center was set for two.

Xeno settled sphinxlike beside the table and didn't move again, though its eyes—something about the creature made me stop conceiving of it as a dog—

tracked me as I wandered the room to study the art. Each print had a simple wooden frame that was fastened or fused to the wall. I couldn't be sure.

"Those were tough. I had to travel to New York and see the originals to get them right," Gordie said. "Staring at pictures in books did not, could not, cut the mustard."

He stood by the table, which supported a wine bottle flanked by two full goblets, tumblers full of sweet tea and lemon slices, and enough ham and vegetables for a Christmas dinner mounded on the plates. None of those things, including Gordie, had been present before he spoke.

I supposed I'd already seen stranger things. "I was going to ask how you could afford . . . any of this . . . but I'm guessing that's not the right question?"

"Correct. Won't you join me?"

The aromas of the assorted victuals had reached me by then. I didn't need to be asked twice.

Gordie already had his mouth full when I paused in the middle of slicing through the ham steak. I found the many urgent topics on my mind difficult to broach. "Maybe now's not the time to ask, but I'm really desperate to make a phone call. I tried at your dad's, but it didn't work."

Gordie's dark eyes regarded me over his glasses, a professorial look if I'd ever seen one. He swallowed to make room for speech. "I recall."

"Your dad blamed you."

Gordie shrugged. "He's right." After another mouthful, "Who are you trying to call?"

I took a leap. "The girl who helped me beat the piasa. She hasn't seen me nor heard from me since—" I counted the hours and involuntarily gasped. "Almost two days." My mind stirred as if a drape had been pulled away from it. Guilt spilled over for not bringing up Bill and Melissa since setting foot in this palace. "Gordie, please—"

He raised a staying hand. "This is my fault. I know you're having an insane week. I should have asked what *you* need." His emphasis puzzled me, as he'd expressed no wants, but he pointed to a small stand with an ancient rotary phone atop it that, of course, hadn't existed in the room when I came in. "That will call out."

Hope surged at the thought of Kori's voice. I chewed my lip. "I don't know her number. I only know where she works."

"The restaurant with the clown faces?"

I dropped my knife and fork.

Gordie spoke fast. "I told you I'm going to explain everything, but you're the one who wants to do this first."

I took a breath. "Okay, thank you." The phone had a base like a tent and a receiver big enough to use as a bludgeon. Heavy enough too, I found as I picked it up. When I put it to my ear, the dial tone changed to a ringing noise.

We'll say her full name was Kori Ross. I asked if she was working. The manager who answered offered to take a message. "Please, it's really, really urgent," I said. Watching me, Gordie scowled.

After agonizing minutes, Kori came on the line. "Nathan?"

"Don't say where you are," Gordie stage whispered. "It's not safe."

I was already talking over him. "I'm sorry, Kori. Something crazy and horrible happened. I had to run. I'm not in Pennsylvania. This is the first chance I had to call."

"What happened?"

"This woman. She's a spider. Her name is—"

"Don't say her name," Gordie hissed.

The interruption derailed me, and I couldn't unstick my tongue.

"Where are you?" she demanded. "Who's with you?"

However this line worked, Gordie could hear. Already he was violently shaking his head. "I'm safe, honest, but I can't tell you more right now," I said. "I didn't plan to leave like that. Everything happened so fast, some really bad stuff. I think you need to get away from there too."

"I already told you. I can't just leave. Where would I go?"

I glanced at Gordie, who shook his head even harder, eyes bugged in alarm. He didn't want me to extend an invitation. My fingers tightened on the receiver. "I guess I don't have an answer for that . . . have you seen anything in the news about a couple in Stroudsburg? Melissa and Bill Nesmith?"

"I don't remember seeing anything—"

"There're people like us, but they're spiders, not cats or birds. They came after me yesterday. They got my friends. I'm worried they'll coming looking for you."

The silence dragged on so long I worried the connection was broken. Then, "Nathan, what the hell is going on?"

"There's a woman. Her name is Lilith. She's tall and thin with white hair at her temples—"

Instead of a phone receiver, my hand cupped empty air. "I told you not to say her name."

"Let me call her back!"

"Calm down, kitty," Gordie said, standing up with hands raised. "Wow."

The tips of my fingers had tapered into hard, hooked claws. I stared, startled, at my own fingers.

A roar like an engine filled the room. It came from Xeno, the creature's black lips pulling back to expose teeth too large for its mouth.

My claws faded like film images gradually overexposed.

"I'm sorry," Gordie said calmly, his voice carrying despite his dog's deafening growl. "It's just like they say in the old books. Lilith is not *that* Lilith, the one out of legend, but even so, saying her name risks drawing her attention. And that risks any number of her many, many servants dropping in on Little Miss Muffet for a visit. I wasn't being a jerk. I was trying to keep you both safe." His voice held no accusatory edge, but his words still shamed me enough to stop me from demanding the phone back.

Hot with embarrassment, I tried changing the subject. "So who *is* she? And how do you know who she is?"

"Let's eat first. Then we can talk more."

"I'm not hungry," I said. The demand for Gordie to do something, anything, to help Melissa and Bill reached the tip of my tongue, but even as I opened my mouth, hunger yawned through me like a landscape split by an earthquake. Before I knew it, I'd stuffed my mouth with three forkfuls. I couldn't stop myself. Everything tasted even better than it looked.

"That's better," Gordie said, and Xeno fell silent. Gordie tucked in as well, though not as monomaniacally as I did. Man, I was so stupendously hungry.

At last, Gordie held up his wine glass, which had refilled without either of us opening the bottle on the table. "I imagine you've guessed by now that none of this is real. At least not the way most people have been raised to think of 'real.' The food, the bath, Xeno—it's all a sort of hocus-pocus. But every bit of it is as good as the real thing. Better actually."

As soon as he described the meal as a magical construct, I wanted to put my fork down. But I didn't. I couldn't.

"I hope you'll eventually forgive me for springing this behavior loop on you. You're not exactly harmless."

There. He'd just confirmed he was messing with my head. Maybe he was so cocky he believed I couldn't do a thing about it. I redoubled my effort to set my fork down. My arm shook as my hand paused halfway between table and mouth. Gordie's brows rose, eyes widened.

"Wow, you *are* strong. Okay, I'll move the agenda forward. I am going to try to undo a terrible mistake that's my fault in the first place. It's part of the reason why you're in the mess you're in. In the meantime, please don't try to hurt me. You won't like what happens."

He started speaking in another language. Or that was my first thought until I realized he was speaking backward. I don't simply mean reversing the words in a sentence. He sounded just like an LP spun backward—even the inhales and exhales reversed. Simultaneously, the reedy voice of thirteen-year-old Gordie spoke the same words forward. "You have to go. Forget what you know. Forget all you've seen. 'Til we meet a-green."

Beneath the picnic shelter, laughing at his ridiculous forced rhyme, twelve-year-old me choked on nothing and collapsed. Gordie immediately stopped his chant and knelt beside me, shouting my name—

And the memories he had shoved out of my twelve-year-old mind hurtled forward into the me that sat across the dinner table from twenty-one-year-old Gordie as he shouted my name backward.

Under the picnic shelter, only minutes before those memories were ripped from my head, I marveled at the wonder that Gordie had summoned out of thin air. Facing the woods, resembling a scarecrow as he stood with arms raised, sweat beading on every inch of pale skin, he had finally delivered on the promises he'd been making since the night I arrived at his house. Behind the volleyball net, a stunning fantasy mansion loomed, its Gothic windows and gables spanning back into the woods. I could see the trees through its walls.

With a gasp, he lowered his arms, and the vision disappeared.

The afternoon I had arrived at the Baugh house, as my dad presented me to his family, Gordie had eyed me brightly from between his mountain of a father and tiny mouse of a mother, about whose fate subsequently I knew nothing. We'd gone into his room to play with action figures, and as soon as we were alone, he'd leaned in to whisper, "You're magic. Cat magic."

And when he said that, I'd understood him. Because . . . because . . . my mamaw *had* told me what I was.

That memory had been missing ever since Gordie's spell in the picnic shelter. It returned along with scene after scene from that lost summer in Black Salt Gap.

Early afternoon, the day after my mishap in the cabin, Elzbeth stood with me in an overgrown field that had once hosted crops and cattle. "I'm only a shell of what I used to be," she said. "I don't regret that choice. I could never have been the wife Henri needed if I ain't done that. But I regret it something fierce now because I'll never even get to show you a tiny part of what you need to know."

She vanished, and in her place loomed a mountain lion straight out of a Paul Bunyan tall tale, peering at me with a head bigger than our VW Beetle.

This time, I wasn't scared. Those gleaming green eyes were still my mamaw's, after all.

She became a tiny, brown-skinned woman again, swaying, and at first, I thought she might be dancing, but she gasped and toppled into the grass.

"Mamaw!" I yelled. She pushed up onto all fours, putting a hand on my shoulder as she got back to her feet. I nearly fell over, trying to be strong for her.

"Thank you, little cub," she said. She couldn't seem to stand fully straight, and her skin had taken on a gray pallor. "I can only pretend to be what I used to be, and even that can harm me. But you needed to see. Your mama, she don't want me to show you. The power skipped her, and she hates you for it—and me too. While she's your minder, you're never gonna learn at all." She swallowed as if her throat hurt. "Remember, when you're of age, to come back to this place. The ghosts'll teach you."

I couldn't bring myself to look toward the woods and that awful cabin. "But the ghosts hate me."

"If any of 'em dare hold a grudge, I'll eat 'em up." Her smile was wicked as any witch's.

I'd no idea I'd sprung to my feet until Xeno's renewed roar blasted me back down, my dinner upending, spilling from the tabletop.

The dog had swelled to Godzilla-foe size, its head almost as large as my mamaw's in that vision from the past, a mouth full of foot-long teeth, hovering over Gordie's head. The dog shouldn't have fit inside the room, but the walls and ceiling had contorted to accommodate its new size.

"Stay calm," Gordie repeated, his voice crystal clear over the thunderous growl of his guardian. "I wouldn't advise any sudden moves. Xeno has autonomy to act in my defense."

Unsure what to do, I held still. This version of Xeno could have swallowed me in a couple messy gulps.

"You're really making me wonder if I made a mistake coming here," I finally said, the understatement of my life.

A flash of anger in Gordie's eyes dimmed to contrition. "Xeno, down."

The giant mutt receded from me, though it never moved from the spot where it sat. The room adjusted to normal proportions, as did Xeno. I didn't trust it to stay that way, so I stayed put and spoke softly. "What just happened?"

"I undid the hex I put on you."

"Why—"

"I'm willing to bet you already know a lot more than you did a minute ago about who's who and what's what and at least some of the whys. So if this question is, 'Why did I put a hex on you?' you should remember now. If the question is, 'Why did I undo it?' I'll answer that."

It began as a childish dare.

I don't want you telling anyone what I showed you.

I'm not gonna.

Really, I mean it.

I'm not.

I can make you forget if that would help.

Grown me might have asked, *Why don't you trust me?* But instead, I said, *No, you can't.* And that led to, *Wanna bet?* I'm not even sure which of us said it first.

But Gordie's arcane drawings—taped to the walls of his room, sketched with chalk in his driveway, carved with a knife on the picnic shelter posts—weren't the only things he'd snipped from my mind.

Elzbeth had tried to tell me about what I was, enough that when Gordie called me *magic* I understood how he meant it. I hadn't grown up ignorant. Gordie had made me so.

"Why didn't you undo it . . . sooner?"

"I had to do it in person, which means that you had to be here. Frankly, I didn't think you'd ever be back, and I'll admit, I messed up pretty badly. I suppose I could have written you or tried to call or something, but you wouldn't have known who I was. So it was easier to concentrate on constructing my kingdom." He tilted his head toward the fireplace for reasons I didn't grasp. "It took up all the space in my mind. I might have deliberately avoided thinking about that clumsy spell I had no business testing out on you." His hands orbited each other as he spoke. "But it bothered me a lot. The more I learned about how all this magic works, the more I understood what an awful thing I'd done. Though maybe I tried to tell myself I had done you a favor, that your life would be simpler not knowing.

"But you're a natural, a really powerful natural. I could have anticipated this would happen if I'd let myself think about it. You were going to come into your own anyway, I just—" He grimaced. "Slowed you down a bit, I suppose. When you crossed over for the first time, it was like a flare, bright as a sun. I don't mean that literally, but . . . wow! I guarantee that any natural or construct that was paying attention to the right frequencies that night got whiplash from turning their head so fast. When I tracked down the source and figured out it was *you*, I couldn't believe it. You know, I never had worked out who your grandmother really was until that moment. I can sure be dense, despite all my book-learnin'." He exaggerated his hick accent for that final phrase. "Now, where was I? Oh, yeah. Sorry. Lucky for you that by now I have the skills to reverse the hex. So then I start trying to track you, and you're all over the place. Tangling with the argents, ticking off the piasa . . ."

In my newly restored memories of the summer in Black Salt Gap, Gordie was just as prone to rambling, sans a supernatural guard dog that went Clifford-sized at will. Hopefully, an interruption wouldn't result in a resize. "Okay, but . . . the antler! Why do you have it?"

"That piasa character's both a threat and an inspiration."

"How so?"

"We're totally skipping ahead here, but I guess it's worth it because you've been to his lair." He rubbed his hands in a mockery of evil genius. "That ugly customer has built his own little paradise island, out in the spirit world. Or maybe island isn't the right word. More like an asteroid maybe, a tiny private world he flies out from when he needs another kill. A pocket universe? Something like that, I guess. He has been around a loooong time, and if anyone ever knew how he got started, they're not around to tell the tale now. But I'm proud to say, I'm already better than he is, and I didn't have to kill anyone to make it happen."

That had been Gordie's dream: *a castle in the sky, a cave under the hill, you name it,* where the kids who picked on him couldn't find him, and the adults who stupidly forced him to go to the school where those kids awaited would hold no sway. I'd thought it was the best idea I'd ever heard. And Gordie had demonstrated that he had the potential to make it happen. Like all the best mad scientists, he just hadn't figured out the formula yet. But he was getting close. He'd shown me how close, making a dollhouse appear in his driveway that was a maquette for the mansion he brought into being ever so briefly at the picnic shelter.

Gordie was still talking about the piasa. "He prefers naturals like yourself when he goes hunting, but he'll come after constructs like me too. And I'd gotten more than strong enough for him to take a shine to me, so I decided to strike first. I found him, and he got to meet Xeno."

The dog-thing sat quietly by Gordie's side, watching me. I pictured my antlered, bearded foe squaring off with Xeno gone giant-sized. "Your dog broke his antler?"

"It was beautiful to behold," Gordie said. "The coward flew away before Xeno could do anything else."

"How long ago was this?"

"Twenty-six days to be exact." He was as smug as if he'd won a sixth-grade science fair with a robot that freeze-rayed the school bully. "It was a test and a warning."

"Are you sure he'll leave you alone?" I'd left the piasa without eyes, and maybe Gordie even knew that through some arcane means, but I felt no reassurance the threat was gone.

"He can't find us here. That's why I needed you to get here. My place means protection, even from the Queen of Night. I'm still a little shell-shocked she came after you so brazenly, but I guess the way her counterpart's been acting, all bets are off all over the argent realms. So to speak. The rumor is that the Night Queen would love to roll the clock back to when all sorts of humans were on the menu, alive or not, but she—"

My head was spinning in four different directions at once, and Gordie had just added another rotation. "Her counterpart? What?"

"Gosh, I keep forgetting who I'm talking to. Your grandmother, of course. Otherwise known as the Queen of Day."

"My mamaw's dead!"

Xeno straightened at my outburst but otherwise stayed motionless.

Behind his glasses, Gordie's gaze blazed with secrets. "In this world, maybe. But she's an argent in the Silver City too. Maybe the ultimate argent. There, she's very much alive, my friend. I'm sorry you didn't know. I guess that could be my fault too, though I can't imagine why she wouldn't find a way to tell you."

He couldn't have shredded me worse if he'd ordered his dog to take me in its giant jaws and shake me apart.

7

A fire of hope and anguish ignited in my heart, even as skeptical thoughts rained down. Little about Gordie seemed sane or reliable, but this outrageous claim rang with truth. Which I wasn't ready for. My voice cracked as I asked, "How can she be alive?"

"If I knew the answer to that, I'd be God," he said. "But it's true. She's ruled the day side of the Silver City for as long as Lilith has ruled the night side. Maybe even longer. I mean, Lilith's a lot older than your grandmother, like at least a century older, but they came to power about the same time, right around World War I. It's a stretch to call them naturals, really, because either of them living that long ain't natural, I'm sure you'll agree."

It was too much to absorb. "What . . . what Silver City?"

"You may have seen it, depending where you've been in the argent realms. It can look like a moon way overhead or a jewel deep beneath the ocean. Or beneath the land. It's like all these ghost lands stacked on top of each other."

I did see a celestial body like that, a silver octahedron, when I fell through the hole in Hillcrest. The notion that my mamaw *lived* there was so disconcerting that I couldn't bring myself to explore that path. "Argent this, argent that. What do you mean by that?"

"You've been to the crossover lands. Everything's silver."

"Is that what they're called, or is that what *you* call them?"

"I don't think there's consensus really. Our kind hasn't left much in the way of recorded history. Some terms I've picked up, some terms I've made up.

"So . . . okay, the argent lands. That's where *this* house is?"

Gordie shook his head, his smug smile returned. "That's not really where we are."

"Then where are we?"

"Think on it. You become a panther, just like your mamaw. Lilith becomes a black widow. Your girlfriend becomes a bird. Constructs who have to build their own can be a little more creative. Our friend the piasa . . . well, he *chose* that form. And me, well, I'm even more creative." He pointed at the walls, the floor, the ceiling.

I swore, incredulous. "The house. This *whole house* is your spirit shape?"

"I knew you'd get it. Gold star for you!" He beamed as if I'd handed him an ice cream sundae.

"How is that even possible? How are you—are you *sustaining* all this?"

"So glad you finally asked! Before I can explain that, I need to show you something." He stood up, intoning in a fair imitation of Lurch, "Follow . . . me . . ."

The conversation had completely gotten away from me again. "Hey, Gordie—"

"I know, Nathan. I know what you want to ask me." He rubbed his face with his hands and ran his fingers through the already-tousled straw of his hair. "I need you to accept that it's out of our hands. And I need you to accept that you did the right thing by coming to me. What I'm about to show you, it *must* be your priority now. Please."

My resolve fell apart. "Okay. For now." And the next thing that popped into my mind was embarrassing in its earnest triteness. "Hey, hey, wait—before we do anything else. I don't think I want to be walking around wearing clothes that are just figments of your imagination."

Gordie smiled so big. "Believe it or not, I was expecting this request." A changing screen decorated with dragons apported within the room. On the other side of it, jeans, an Iron Maiden T-shirt, socks, undies, and hiking boots awaited, all from my pack, all freshly cleaned.

Once I'd changed, he led me down a new hallway into a utility room, complete with hot water tank and heating ducts, though it was the first time I'd ever seen one with carpeting. A closer look at the carpet caused me a double take: the pattern repeated images from the tarot. Here were swords. Here were pentacles. Here was the ace of wands. Here was the Fool.

"Glad you recognized my design," Gordie said, peacock-proud. With a magician's flourish, he brandished a titanic branch of broken-off antler and made it vanish again. "That's a prized possession. I don't leave it lying around."

An incongruous and improbably huge woodstove loomed beside a warped, brittle-looking wooden door—the first thing I'd seen in Gordie's spirit house that didn't ooze opulence. The woodstove radiated a pleasant heat with no fire whatsoever visible. Gordie tipped his head toward the door and said, "Before we go in there, you might want one of these. I'm having one."

And damned if he didn't hand me the fattest joint I'd ever seen, which I eyed warily. "Is this part of your soul too?"

"It's not really what it appears to be," he said, chuckling. "It's like an inoculation. It's just delivered in a container that I figured you would recognize." When I didn't reach for the joint, he held it closer. "You really do need it." He offered me a lighter with his other hand. Somehow, he had a lit one in his mouth already, clamped in his teeth cigar-style. I braced myself for that extra pungent cannabis odor but smelled nothing at all.

"Just trust me, sweetheart," Gordie said in a passable Bogart.

I caved and complied. My first inhale was nothing like toking, or even smoking. A silken thickness, a sort of smooth, slick pressure, filled my lungs and sinuses.

Gordie waited until I'd burned up enough of the joint to meet his satisfaction and then opened the dilapidated door and held it for me.

The round chamber I squeezed into had a cement floor, slanted from all directions toward the center, akin to a cymbal turned upside-down. An alchemist's hallucination of tubes, flasks, and beakers cluttered a full third of the room. Given Gordie's flair for the overdramatic, the mad scientist gear made a kind of sense. A dozen spherical Tesla coils made localized lightning amid the glassware, presumably for sheer effect.

The thickest of the glass tubes jutted straight up from the low point at the center of the floor. Inside that tube rose tendrils of iridescent smoke, shifting color with every wisp and curl, flowing up from underground somehow and into the eye-boggling jumble of rods, flasks, and filters. The entire contraption fed into a huge cylindrical tank lodged in one corner. The churning substance contained within had separated into different levels of sediment: turbulent steam at the top, hard crystalline cake at the bottom. Embers of light sputtered and flickered in the tank's depths.

As I approached for a closer look, I made out patterns in the play of light and shadow: buildings, bodies, faces.

Behind me, Gordie said, "You're looking at the sum of small-town dreams."

I put my palm against the tank. The substance beneath shuddered and pulsed, sometimes warming the glass, sometimes cooling it. The motions within were hypnotic. I asked, "What is this stuff?"

"I'll show you. Back away a sec."

Coils of tubing connected to the tank at different levels through translucent valves. Gordie loosened the topmost valve, and the entire room filled with a pink and violet mist. Winds blew hot against my skin. Swirling hues became animated shapes. A face lifted up, baring its teeth. Another lolled beneath it, rolling its eyes and gasping.

I must have reacted because I heard Gordie laugh. "Relax. Enjoy. They're harmless."

I stood amid a maelstrom of ghostly pink pornography, men and women of all ages and sizes coupling in every combination imaginable, the acts in progress ranging from elegant to ghastly. It was as if I'd been dropped into the first level of Dante's hell, where lovers spin endlessly in whirlwinds forged from their own lust.

"This stuff's a dime a dozen, and just about useless," Gordie said. "Sex fantasies straight from the animal brain. Even the most destitute have these. If you'd lived in the Gap as long as I have, you would notice a familiar face or two."

He cut off the valve, and I staggered a little as the interior of the cabin reasserted itself.

Gordie laughed. "Yeah, inhaling this stuff directly is pretty trippy if you're not acclimated to it. That's why I made sure to use protection." He pantomimed toking with his mouth and fingers. "You might be thrashing on the floor right now with a pair of imaginary lovers if I hadn't given you that." He turned back to the tank. "Now this," he opened the next valve down, "when I drilled this deep, I knew I had a breakthrough."

Inky whorls of indigo tinted the room. New images sketched in blue and gold swept past me, tumbling over each other, a warm soup with icy gusts twined through it. "You've got to have a little bit of a mind to make one of these, though there's still no will behind them, so they're not much use."

Moving pictures. A little boy climbed out a window and ran across an endless field while the schoolhouse he escaped from faded far into the distance. A scrawny man with a neat goatee caused a towering, thick-necked brute in a suit to collapse with a single punch to the jaw. An elderly woman shed her age, her limbs strengthening, her wrinkles smoothing, and ran with a smile to meet someone unseen.

The juxtapositions bewildered me. "What am I seeing here, Gordie?"

"Idle daydreams. Wishes that won't be granted. Desires that won't be pursued."

A tall fire-haired girl struck a softball with a thunderous crack of the bat, and it soared out into the stars. Behind those spinning stars I could see other figures moving, more leaked scenes playing out, but then Gordie cut off the valve, his smile fevered. "Brace yourself now. I was amazed at how much of *this* toxic sludge I brought up. Maybe I shouldn't have been surprised, but—" He opened the next valve down. Bolts of white and black fired through the air.

"Obsessions," he said, savoring the word.

The room flooded with violent contrast, stark shadows pitched against blinding light. I'd found the previous vision-storms more startling than threatening, but now, alarm sped my pulse. The air grew moist, stuffy, sticky. A sour stink coated my taste buds. My skin itched the way it had when I'd been wrapped in Lilith's webbing.

A head rolled past me, agony on its face. It flipped onto its neck and watched from the floor, still alive, visibly terrified, as a man made from darkness stepped forward and raised an ax. The man swung so the blunt end struck, smashing the head into scraps of meat.

"These are the things that chug on and on, keeping people awake at night. Addictions. Sick desires. Thirsts for revenge. Stuff that can possess you like a demon."

A woman screamed silently as a huge, clawed fist closed around her neck, lifting her high above the floor while another hairier clawed hand ripped at her clothes and skin. Behind her, a naked teenaged boy crouched over what looked like a mound of pus, stuffing the substance into his mouth by the double-handful.

"It's too bad you're not a native. If you recognized who these people were and what you're seeing them do . . . yeah, I don't feel the least bit bad about converting this garbage to altruistic ends."

The room returned. "And now, the main attraction!" With an exultant whoop, Gordie opened the last valve, the one at the bottom, where the substances had crystallized—and the laboratory vanished.

I stood in a forest of easels. A wild-haired, willowy man in a spattered smock attacked a giant canvas, brushes flying at superhuman speed. A scene of valleys, sunlight, and surreal animals came to life under his assault, and when he turned around triumphant, I saw inside this simulacrum of a man a different person, a small boy who wore the man's body as a phantom costume. His face beamed from inside this make-believe adult.

Applause erupted behind me. I turned to find a rapt audience in ties, coattails, and gowns, giving the boy's latest masterpiece a standing ovation. Beyond them, a balcony projected out over a streamlined cityscape. From the streets, there came more shouts and applause, a festival of praise. Behind the boy, the canvas scene expanded until we all stood within it, fantastic creatures dancing in a circle around us while the sun twinkled behind mountains blue as sapphires.

When I turned back to the boy, the scene had changed. Now he peered into the eyepiece of a telescope tall as a skyscraper. The studio stage had given way to an astronomical observatory, big as a cathedral. Across the wedge of coal-dark sky revealed through the widening gap in the observatory dome, stars and nebulae arranged themselves as if attempting to spell a message.

The panorama vanished, quick as a popped bubble.

I steadied myself against the wall by the tank while Gordie resealed the last valve.

"That was a dose of the real stuff," he said. "It's easy to lose yourself in it."

The rush of the boy's ambitions agitated my mind, my heartbeat, in a way that rolled joy and tears into one. I stared at the tank, the half-formed images boiling inside. "These all come from the town? The people in the town?"

"Absolutely." Gordie shrugged. "This whole place is so repressed. The supply is endless—no shortage of desperate daydreams in the Gap."

"That last set didn't seem like daydreams. The ones from that kid. That felt real as your house."

He offered an ear-to-ear grin and a conspiratorial wink. "That's the most powerful daydream you can have. The kind where you haven't yet learned that what you want will never happen. Put your whole heart in it, so to speak." He patted my arm. "Don't worry, it's going to good use."

That kid couldn't have been any older than I'd been when my dad brought me here. Maybe he was much younger. "When you take these, what happens to the people they belong to?"

Gordie shrugged. "Maybe they dream more dreams."

His nonchalance burned hot in my stomach. Enchantment soured into disgust. "Gordie, I don't—this is really impressive, what you've built, but—stealing from children?"

He laughed. "No reason to call it stealing if it's worth nothing in the first place."

I stayed put, peering into the spectral maelstrom held captive in the tank.

"It's better than killing them, don't you think? That's what the piasa does. Feeds on the people he carries off. Though even that's a step up from what a lot of the argents would do if they could. They have a hankering for ghosts. Specifically, the ghosts of ordinary people. I guess I shouldn't be surprised that you're a little queasy about all this. After all, your grandma tried to put a stop to that stuff. The problem is, her counterpart, your buddy Lilith, *she* encourages it—"

"What are you talking about?" I wanted to yell, though I knew. God damn it, I knew. The ghosts in the cabin, that weird hunger I felt as a child.

But my anger went beyond that awful truth. Gordie, who had complained nonstop that summer about his treatment at the hands of the other kids, laughing off what he was doing to this poor boy. My rage multiplied, but I did not forget that I had to be mindful of Xeno, even though the creature wasn't in the chamber. Nor did I forget Gordie's uncanny ability to answer my thoughts before I voiced them. Gordie, guard dog, house—all constituted one interconnected creature, and I was in its belly. So instead of rounding on him, I simply looked up. "Okay, so you're not tearing these people to pieces. Instead, you're what, killing them softly?"

"Calm down." His smile stayed, relentless, permafrozen. "I sure don't see what you have to get upset about, given everything that's happened to you since Sunday night. I built the fort I told you I wanted to build. It's completely safe. For both of us. I told you all about this idea before, and back then, you loved the thought. You had people to hide from too, remember? It's not like the world's gotten any *better* in the meantime. It's not like people have gotten any *nicer* in the meantime."

I came a hair's-breadth from retorting, *Of course, I don't remember that. You wiped my memory.* Even as I formed that thought, the whole thing came back to me.

My father had brought me to Black Salt Gap for the summer because he was both scared for me and scared of me. At the end of the school year, a kid who had harassed me through most of sixth grade told me I had to meet him on the playground to fight or else I was a coward, though he phrased it using much more offensive slurs. I didn't care about all the creative names he called me, but I had learned by then that ignoring a bully's taunts just makes him bolder. Even though my mom would confine me to my room all summer, I said I'd do it.

We met on the dry, dusty baseball diamond. I'd never been in anything more serious than a shoving match before, so I held my arms up like I'd seen boxers do on TV. His fist shot right between my hands and smashed me in the chin.

No one was sure what happened next, not even me. He landed on his back fifteen feet away and couldn't get up. I had a strange taste in my mouth, mind clouded with a lingering mirage of an impossible action, shaking a small, squirming creature in my teeth.

Lucky for me, lots of kids in my school didn't like the boy who picked the fight because if they'd lied and claimed I started it, things might have gone a whole lot worse for me. The boy was poor, but he came from a large family, and for once, my dad overruled my mom. I needed to be away for the summer, he said, where I'd be safe from the boy's brothers and them from me. He had a friend from college with a son my age who owed him a favor. That turned out to be Buck.

The sunlight glinted off the hood of the car on that endless switchback drive. My dad kept shaking his head. "Here you are, big bad fighting man, and you can't ride in a car without puking." He met my miserable gaze. "If you can find that fighting man hiding somewhere in that weak stomach of yours, I think Buck's boy could stand to learn all the self-defense you can teach him."

Gordie had endured sociopathic levels of bullying growing up. When we were out walking and spotted bigger kids coming toward us down the street or woodland path, we'd run to a hiding place. Gordie had hiding places staked out all over Black Salt Gap.

I never taught him anything. But I listened to him talk about building a safe place for the both of us and using magic to construct it—magic that turned the power of our enemies against them. He'd said that kind of thing all the time, and though I didn't really believe he could do it, I wanted him to. I wanted to have my own castle, and if it meant I never had to face off with another brute half-again my size at recess, all the better.

And after that summer, thanks to Gordie, I'd never had another thought about it. My parents enrolled me in an adjoining school district, and I thought little of that too.

Gordie though had never stopped thinking about his promise.

Light-bulb flash: my old friend Gordie was mentally unbalanced and just as dangerous to me as all the other charmers I'd met since this ordeal began.

"Sorry," I said. "It's just that I'm totally bowled over. I can't believe you pulled it off. You know, like I couldn't believe you had the power to pull off a memory-wipe spell."

He actually shuffled his feet aw-shucks style.

"This new spell"—I stretched my arms wide—"it takes over the entire town, doesn't it? Like I noticed all sorts of weird things when I came up, about how long it took to get here and how everything seems weirdly small. Even your dad. Especially your dad."

"I put him in his place, didn't I? Who's the tall one now?"

I laughed with him. "You sure did."

"I'm so glad you're here with me now," he said once he caught his breath. "I know you're going to love it here."

"I can't thank you enough," I said.

He did in fact seem shocked when I clocked him in the jaw.

I'm no experienced prize fighter. I wish I'd knocked Gordie out cold. If I had, what immediately followed would without question have gone down differently. But even were I a champion boxer, I don't think I could have put Gordie down for the count. I had no will to hurt him, only to distract him. As it was, he stumbled backward and lost his footing.

The little door flew open, the entire entrance filled by the front of Xeno's muzzle, lips peeled back to bare teeth as long as my arm. Hot, stinking breath steamed the room.

Gordie stared at the ceiling. Too huge to fit through the door, the creature shifted its head to regard me with one dead eye, a porthole into emptiness. I can only presume I scrambled Gordie's brains just enough to cause a glitch in his guardian's routine.

Seeing that Xeno couldn't get at me—yet—I lunged at the mad scientist nightmare, grabbing hoses and pulling them loose, swinging at glass tubes and breaking them. I cut my forearm as Gordie's dream concoction sprayed my face, the cold electroshock of the spirit world freezing and frying me a hundredfold. I cried out and covered my face with my hands as Xeno's jaws, shrunk to mastiff size, closed around my left knee. I could feel every tooth stab into flesh as the beast ground in.

I screamed blue murder, and when I opened my eyes, my entire view of the house had changed. The nature of my vision had changed. I had changed. I was the panther.

The house exposed all its layers to me in silver membranes and blurred blue shading. I could see out through all its walls, out through the spheres of spiritual power, even to the town beyond, outlines of real buildings engulfed and squeezed by this titanic construction that was Gordie's greedy, swollen soul. Part of that shifting mass, the lump shaped like Gordie's long dead dog, snapped its jaws at me, seeking purchase on my hide as a dazed Gordie struggled to stand up.

My attention fixed on the object that throbbed in front of me: the tangled mess of circulating energy that doubled as my friend's monstrous heart, and the object at its center that appeared to human eyes as a cylindrical glass tank. As the panther though, I regarded a quivering, egg-shaped sack of spirit tissue, a great stomach that burned with the light of the dreams it was swallowing and digesting. It shuddered and contracted, crushing and spinning the souls of the town for nourishment. Within it, I sensed a pulse—the rhythmic, thrumming pressure of spirit stuff pumped into the channels that served Gordie as veins.

I gripped the sack between my paws and tore it open.

Gordie and Xeno howled with one voice, the noise drowned out by the roar of a crowded amphitheater. Wind battered me on all sides, bodies slammed against me, smells of ambrosia and oil and sweet fruit and sewage filled my head. I heard myself roar, but even that sound was lost in the flood of dream jabber that stuffed my ears. My eyes were blinded in the explosive release of deepest dream.

At last, the flow of phantasms dissipated, solid to fluid to mist. As I floated, I witnessed that mist escaping through the rents in the architecture of Gordie's house. The entire structure was shrinking, the town outside regaining size.

Why was I so high in the air? I was too disoriented to grasp my situation until giant teeth like rows of anvils pressed against my ribs and back, squeezing the breath out of me. I opened my jaw to roar and couldn't. I swiped at the great flap of flesh that was the dog's lip, but my claws couldn't reach.

I had no claws, only fingers. The teeth bore down harder, and I couldn't breathe at all.

I'd become Nathan again, clamped in Xeno's gigantic jaws.

3

No hot breath washed over me, no drool or stink coated my skin. Gordie had no need for such props, only for the bone crushing pressure, the splitting of flesh. Whatever went down during Xeno's duel with the piasa would pale in comparison to what the monster was about to do to me.

"Asshole!" Gordie shouted from somewhere below. "Xeno, let me see him."

The dog's immense head began to lower.

"Soften him up first."

Xeno shook me. If I could have breathed at all, I would have howled in agony. Skin parted, muscle tore.

"Now," Gordie said. The beast lowered its head to the floor but did not let go of me. I struggled to wheeze. Through the smog of grinding pain, I could piece together, barely, that our surroundings had changed. We were no longer inside a tiny room but beneath a membrane the shape and size of a circus tent. Gordie hung bat-like above me, but I was the one upside down and suffocating. Behind him, smashed glass glittered, the ruins of his apparatus.

His voice, I swear, sounded tearful. "How could you do this?" He pointed outward and away, toward the town. "You're no better than they are. I can't believe it. I rescued you, and you do this to me!" He bent to grab a broken tube, which he brandished at my face as I strained for air. "Bad kitty! Oh, bad kitty! You think I can't fix this? You think I can't start it up again? I can do it in minutes. And I can take their dreams all over again. And yours too." He turned the glass tube in his hand, aimed its dagger-point at my chest. "I'll drain them out of you like sap from a tree—"

I lunged my arms forward, seized him around the midriff with fingers extended into hard claws. Xeno whipped its head side to side, but my claws were fast in Gordie. Bursts of warm red splashed my arms, shoulders, and face as his flesh tore.

The dog reared back and howled to shatter the moon, letting me spill from its jaws. The impact hurt worse than what Gordie's construct had done to me. My first fully drawn breath turned into a tortured yowl.

But like the cat I was, I got my feet under me.

The house was disintegrating in earnest, reduced to overlapping silvery outlines. Yet the woods of the real world had not reasserted. We were in a bubble of abstract that wavered erratically in size, threatening to burst and collapse at once.

Gordie lay on the floor a few yards from me, trembling, the whites showing all around his pupils, his mop of hair matted in blood, his shirt soaked dark. He tried to back away from me, leaving a dark, wet trail behind. If he died, then I would be the one who killed him, his guts torn open by the boy he considered his only friend.

"I'm so sorry," I shouted. "You didn't give me a choice!"

The thing that had been Xeno thrashed against the far wall, shrunken to minivan-size, mouths and eyes opening in its columnar trunk.

The tube embedded in the floor's central depression snapped loose as cracks split the concrete, the last of Gordie's construct giving way to entropy. The cracks widened. I scrambled as best as I could for purchase. Some new part of me tore every time I moved, the pain bad enough to make me squall.

Xeno flopped and hopped across the disintegrating floor toward its master, curling its amorphous body around him. Together, they rolled through a gaping fissure and vanished into the black.

Dreams erupted in a geyser. Maybe they were the source of all the shouting, I couldn't tell.

Talons scooped me up as the last of Gordie's soul-fortress collapsed.

For a few horrible seconds, as pine trees spun around me, I thought that the piasa had tracked me down. But the spinning stopped, and the talons released me onto a cushion of pine leaves.

A hideous vulture beak hovered inches from my face, the beady eyes above it wary. Beside the oversized bird, a huge cat with tall, tufted ears leaned in.

"Thank the Lord we found you," the bobcat said. "*Now* will you listen to us?"

Catching my breath took a long time. I knew how a chisel feels after a sledgehammer strikes it.

What my saviors wanted, I could not have cared less. What *I* wanted was an end to betrayal, to confusion, to pain.

Finally, I gasped, "Can we . . . go see . . . my mamaw?"

PART THREE: PILGRIMS IN THE SILVER CITY

1

THE VULTURE AND THE BOBCAT WEIGHED MY REQUEST IN SILENCE. AT LAST, the bobcat said, "You're torn up bad. You need to take your shape."

Shaken as I was—literally so—the potential for healing had fled my head. Mentally, I groped for the trigger that would switch me to the panther, but I found only pain, my innards a sloshing sackful of glass.

"I'm too hurt," I said, lying on the ground.

The vulture cocked his head and so did the bobcat, though in the opposite direction, a mirroring that made me bark a laugh, which ended in a strangled gagging noise.

"You can always do it," the bobcat said, gentle-voiced. "Try again."

Won't that be sad, I thought. *You go through all this trouble to find me again, and I die right here.* I laughed again, a bit more carefully.

"You need me to take off flying?" the vulture said, his tone not at all friendly. "Would that inspire you?"

I laughed and sighed at once, even though it made my ribs scream. "I deserve that."

My animal companions no longer dwarfed me. My body sprawled through trees and bushes and silvery configurations I couldn't quite make sense of. My ribs and back still throbbed.

"There you go," the bobcat said. "Maybe all you needed was a distraction."

I took a deep breath, winced, and returned to human, staring up at my rescuers. I still felt like a ruptured punching bag, yet the sensation had receded by orders of magnitude.

"Rest a little bit," the bobcat said. I followed instructions and used the opportunity to gauge where they had taken me.

Perhaps I should have grown accustomed to superimposed landscapes by then, but our place of rest achieved a new level of strange. We huddled in a clearing surrounded by pines, and simultaneously, we huddled on a structure like a flat stone bridge—which stretched half the length of a football field to the left and right of where I lay—but it connected to nothing. Two skies above: one in which the dawn sun striped clouds with crimson, the other like a filthy mirror. I rose up on my elbows, and a corresponding speck shifted in the murk above me.

"Regarding your grandmother." The bobcat's ears turned, his whole head following, his attention shifted somewhere beyond the forest. "I was hoping you would ask that. But *I* need to ask *you*, when was the last time you spoke to her?"

With Gordie's hex lifted, the answer came to me. The final morning of our last visit to the farm, two days after my terrible misadventure in Mamaw's cabin. We were packing to leave. Dad had loaded the front of our Bug with luggage and Mom had sniped for the umpteenth time, "Don't you dare get sick."

Elzbeth crouched so her face was level with mine. She didn't have to crouch down far. "Best thing you can do with your mama is smile and say yes, whatever she asks you to do. She'll never be grateful, but she won't hurt you neither."

"She's mean to me," I whispered.

"Yes, she is, but I'm meaner, so mind what I say."

"Are you gonna cut me?" I pictured the claws I'd seen, long as my arm.

She took me by the ear but gently. "Never, little cub. But when you come back, I'm gonna teach you how to hunt. And what to hunt."

My mom was calling for me. "You go on now," my mamaw said.

I never saw her again, just the plain casket they buried her in.

The motley pair awaited my answer, flanking me like guardians.

"Many, many years ago," I said at last.

The creatures shared a look. The bobcat asked, "Do you think she'll be happy to see you?"

"I have no idea. Because until this week, I thought she was six feet under in a family plot. I watched pall bearers put her casket in the grave. Can you guys tell me why I keep hearing that she's still alive?"

They shared another look. "There's a story that's like an urban legend, that she left her body of flesh behind so she'd never have to leave the Silver City.

There's another version that works sort of the same but claims she can't leave the Silver City because she deserted the world of ordinary people. What we know for sure is that every year she gets a little—"

"Meaner," the vulture said.

"I was going to say 'more eccentric.'"

"Crazier. Scarier. And it's not a *little* more. It's a *lot* more."

The bobcat made a plaintive yowl that I took as the equivalent of, *Shut up!* He went on. "I've been hoping to talk to you about it, but you were a little hard to approach."

"You kept trying to kill us," the vulture snapped.

"Just a little jumpy. I think that's understandable," the bobcat said.

I groaned as I sat up, only partly from the pain. "You're too kind."

"He is," the vulture said. "I think you're more trouble than you're worth."

The bobcat hissed. The vulture reared back, spreading its wings and lowering its neck in attack posture.

"Whoa, whoa, whoa, guys!" I raised my silly human arms. "Don't fight over me! I'm sorry! I've been a jerk. I'm new to all this. Things keep attacking me. You guys never have though. I should never have gone after you like that."

The spat settled. The vulture folded his wings and lowered its head to glare at me. The bobcat's ears and stunted tail twitched.

"I'm grateful you . . . looked past my mistakes and got me out of there. Though how did you find me?"

Another significant exchange of glances. This time the vulture spoke. "We went looking after we came back to your room and found you gone. You're not hard to spot because you've got the queen's genes, but we couldn't follow you farther once you headed into that hexed town." The bird tipped its ugly head at the cat. "He wanted to wait, so we did."

"Thank you—why did you?"

"Your grandmother," said the bobcat. "I'm hoping . . . that you can help her somehow. She's . . . not well."

"Fellas, I'm still trying to process how she got from 'dead' to 'not well.' Also, if I'm so easy to track, are we secure here? And is there something I can do about that?"

"That's something your grandmother can help you with, if she'll see you," said the bobcat. "I don't think the tricks I know will work."

"Can we at least try?" I tried to stand, winced and collapsed.

"Maybe you need to take your shape again," the vulture said with obvious reluctance.

"Yeah, maybe I do." My torso throbbed like a solid bruise.

"He needs to anyway if we're going to travel." The bobcat became a man. Middle-aged with a paunch, bushy sideburns, and coke-bottle glasses. He wore jeans, a baggy sweater, high-top sneakers, and a scarf. Nothing about him said feline to me. He offered a hand. "I'm Del."

With his help, I stood, though it made me wince. "Nathan."

Another man had joined us, his huge vulture form tucked away. Framed by his open jean jacket, his oversized T-shirt bore the Public Enemy logo. Huge and broad-shouldered, Asian—Chinese, I'd later learn—with a crew cut and a permanent glower sculpted into his jaw and forehead. He loomed protectively over his friend, watching me without blinking.

"This is Troy," Del said. Troy nodded in a not-excited-to-be-introduced manner.

"Great to meet you properly," I said. "Ow."

"Must have been a hell of a beating you took in there," Del said. "What was that?"

"Explaining would take hours."

Troy snorted.

Del eyed me up and down, worriedly. "You should try crossing over again."

I squinted, puzzled.

"Becoming your shape. Crossing over. It's the same thing," Troy said, impatience sharpening his voice. "You're really that clueless?"

Irritated by his tone but aware I had earned it, I tried to channel my misery productively, conjuring before my mind's eye the incarnation of awfulness that drew the panther out. But nothing happened.

Troy sighed. "There's a simpler way."

My exasperated laughter cut short because my ribs were still sore. "How do you know my method?" I wheezed.

"Negative animus spills out of you like sweat. It shouldn't take that much effort."

"Del, what's he talking about?"

Those sideburns made Del's face square as he smiled. "Hear him out."

"This will probably sound cheesy, but bear with me. Think of your first shape like it's a comfortable suit, like there's nothing you want more than to pull it on and fill it out and move in it. Think of how good it feels."

"Kinky."

"Yeah, I guess it is," Troy said as if my quip were serious. Del giggled. His buddy scowled, an expression amplified on his dour face. "What? You damn well know it is. That's not an insinuation of any kind."

"Ignore me," Del said. "Go on."

"I will. Thank you for the permission."

It dawned on me: these guys had to be a couple. It couldn't have been more obvious if they'd had wedding rings on, a thing that wasn't legal back then.

"The way you're doing this now, it's like you're stripping a psychic gear. It shouldn't take that much effort just to be who you are." Troy's gruff voice, roughened perhaps by cigarettes, added contrasting colors to his New Age diction. "Try it. See that big cat as an outfit you can't wait to wear. Imagine you're already wearing it, and it feels incredible."

I tried. I crowded out every thought except the joy of being the panther: the sight without limits, the strength that sliced through enemies like tissue paper. It *was* kinky, a sensual, dirty thrill.

The pain banding my chest and back lessened to the aftereffect of a slap. I opened eyes that saw for miles.

A bobcat and vulture watched me from a respectful distance atop this bridge that connected to nothing.

"Better?" Troy said.

I smiled a big toothy cat smile. "Much!"

Del the bobcat returned the narrow-eyed grin. "Now, we go see your grandma." He slunk to the edge. "See if you can keep up." He dropped over the side. Troy kept his wings folded to his plump flanks.

I crouched down and looked over. Our perch was the peak of a structure straight out of a Dr. Seuss picture book and rendered three-dimensional, bigger than a skyscraper, slender pillars zigzagging up to support crooked, curving platforms. Del padded across a platform hundreds of feet below me, looked up once, then leaped a dizzying distance to the next one down.

If he can do it, so can I, I repeated to myself as I focused on the closest level surface and carefully lowered myself over. A very human vertigo made me scramble back.

"I'm not gonna carry you, so you better figure it out," Troy said as he took to the sky. "Or this will take forever!"

Spurred by his mockery, I growled and hopped down. The landing could have gone a bit better, but it also could have gone a lot worse.

Our journey proceeded in a cat-see, cat-do fashion: if I saw Del do it, then I could too, though with occasional bouts of don't-know-my-own-strength klutziness. Distractions of all sensory kinds made my mishaps worse at first. The environments we moved through kept changing with the abruptness of a slideshow clicking forward, forest to desert to mountain to jungle to prairie to tableaux that defied gravity.

Del and I made a curious pair. The tufts of his ears were level with the tops of my shoulders—which meant he was still an *enormous* cat. Just not as big as me.

We weren't always alone as we traveled. A serpent, thick as a tire and longer than a football field, wound through the branches of dozens of trees, raising a head from its coils that flared red scales at me, a startling color in this blue and silver place. An army of small black birds that glistened like coal filled an entire copse of hawthorn, so numerous they could be mistaken for leaves. As I passed, their heads turned in unison to track me with shining silver eyes.

Every locale we scrambled through had a scent in common, or at least an aura best described as a scent, that grew stronger the farther we progressed and affected me like cool creek water after a day in the heat. I say creek water because the scent wasn't pure: threads of blood and pheromone and rot wound through it, the effect like fermentation, an enticement for hunger and lust.

Troy never joined us on the ground, but wherever the equivalent of a sky happened to be—above, to the side, or even below us—his silhouette glided within the range of my unenhanced vision, a cutout traversing the silvery haze. He and Del knew the route well, random though it seemed to me.

We were descending a series of dolmens arranged as an extravagantly impractical set of stairs. If you took Stonehenge, made the individual stones ten times taller and wedged them sideways into a sheer cliff of blue crystal, you'd have something akin to what Del and I were navigating. And something impossibly huge moved within that crystal. Focusing on it, trying to decipher its outline, made me dizzy, too dangerous a risk as I pounced from stone to stone. I registered an impression of feathers that would dwarf train cars.

In front of me, instead of leaping to the next stone down, Del dropped over the edge and vanished again. When I landed where he'd been, I spotted an opening suspended just beyond the ledge, a polygon carved into thin air like the one I'd fallen through in Hillcrest.

Through I went, my paws scrabbling at nothing before a forest floor swiveled up to meet me. My disorientation evaporated as I adjusted to the new ground level. Before me, a road bisected a forest. To my left, barren hills crested behind trees with spines growing on spines in fractal repetition instead of ordinary branches and leaves. To my right, the same variety of tree formed an unbroken wilderness of potential pain, extending dozens of miles. Concentrating, my vision taking a leap, I found a distant border where steep black mountains stabbed up like pencil points. The sky was a plateau of conical shapes, big as thunderheads, hanging over us like stalactites.

An octahedron-shaped moon hung above the horizon. The Silver City. The road sliced straight toward it.

Del had paused about forty yards up the road, his short tail and long ear tufts twitching. Instantly, I picked up on what bothered him. The trees on both sides, hostile as they looked, teemed with activity.

Troy lowered between us, phasing in from out of nowhere. "Occisors all over the Dagger Wood. We need to go back."

"Oh, *man*," yowled Del softly. "And we're so close."

"*Osiris*? What?" I didn't recognize the word Troy had used. Though Dagger Wood was self-evident.

I heard a shout. It sounded human. I couldn't tell how far away. Scanning in the direction of the sound, toward the hills on the left, I discovered I could see through everything. Solid masses of spines thinned to overlapping outlines, and figures moved among them, man-sized, cautiously advancing toward us, so many I could distinguish little about them. All the hair on my pelt stood on end as my pulse quickened.

Off to our left, hidden in the hills, a beast began to scream. I heard angry shouts. And celebratory whoops.

I crouched low to the road and peered. The longer I stared, the more my gaze rendered objects translucent, the hills as well as the trees.

In the woods, the gathered masses watched *us*. Del and Troy both sat statue-still with heads cocked, as alarmed and engrossed as I was by the non-stop screaming.

Fewer figures clustered in the hills, rendering them easier to distinguish, like microbes swimming into a microscope's field of focus. A posse of men, at least three dozen, surrounded a huge mound of quivering flesh, an animal of some sort corralled inside a cage. The creature's outlines made little sense. The men who had trapped it held long wooden spears. I noticed the spears, at least, were not translucent in my gaze. Noting how the panther's eyes perceived those weapons as opaque, I refocused on the crowd in the woods. The illusion that the tree trunks and spiked branches doubled and even quadrupled within their midst gained ominous significance.

Behind the jeering spear-bearers, another man stood by himself atop a hillock, holding a shorter, thicker wooden rod that was also opaque. A hooded robe draped his form in deep gray while the party of—soldiers?—before him were all clad in antique clothes. They could have passed for homegrown militia in any given Civil War reenactment, some in frock coats, some stripped to their undershirts or simply the suspenders that held their trousers up, all in long leathery boots. I even spotted a derby hat or two.

The creature in the cage flopped, its enormous mouth gasping, and I recognized it. My lips peeled back from my teeth. The armed mob in the trees stopped moving, the hisses of their whispers taunting my ears.

Del padded past me, heading toward the portal we had emerged from, which floated beneath the surface of the road. "Follow me, quick."

I bunched muscles and sprang, vaulting the trees in a single soaring leap to alight on the slope of the nearest hill at the same moment that a low-lying, obviously unnatural blanket of smoke rolled over the hill crest.

Behind me, within the trees, a man called, "Kill the Eaters!"

My concentration broken, the trees had returned to opacity, but I couldn't miss the surge of movement between them. A single shaft of carved wood sailed out of the cover of the forest. I stared at the spear, not registering its trajectory. Pain exploded in my hip as the spearhead embedded. Given my size, the weapon should have inflicted no more discomfort than a needle. Instead, it burned, a worm of fire burrowing into my flesh.

"Bring him down," another man yelled.

More of the wooden spears flew from the woods. One skewered me in the back, and the burning pain bloomed. I yowled and sprang into the air. Incredibly high into the air. I landed the next hillock over, and that landing, for the record, hurt like a motherfucker. A bizarre croaking scraped my eardrums.

I stumbled on all fours, swaying, as quadruple images congealed into double, congealed into one.

The croaks came from the large creature in the cage. More of those long spears jutted from between the cage bars. The monster had been stabbed along both sides at least a dozen times with the same weapons that burned beneath my skin.

An up-close look confirmed what I'd seen from the road. The long tentacle rooted in the creature's brow ended in a tip that emitted light in spurts, like a lightbulb shorting. Torn fins flapped under its belly and at the end of its tail. It was the monster anglerfish from my vision at Cousin Phyllis's house. There couldn't possibly be two of them.

A loose phalanx of about twenty or more of the spectral Civil War reenactor types stood between the cage and me. A big man in the middle of the group slipped a bow from his shoulder. "Ready your weapons," he bellowed.

More croaking from the fish-thing in the cage. This time, I made out words. "Get the wizard. On the hill. I can help you if you kill the wizard."

I scanned and found the indicated gent immediately: the man alone on the hillock. He could have stepped straight out of the Major Arcana. Gaunt and tall, he had the hood of his robe thrown back, exposing a bald pate ringed by stringy white hair. Covered with carvings, his staff was half again as tall as he was, and at its tip, the gray air condensed into a dark sphere, a will-o'-the-wisp seen in photographic negative. He muttered to himself, his lips never stopping. Dark smoke puffed from his mouth with every uttered syllable, spilled down the hillside and up, becoming the mist that half-hid my paws, that had reached all the way to the spiny trees. In his trance, his eyes were half-lidded. I don't know that he even saw me as I bounded toward him. The burning in my hips and back didn't cripple me; rather, the pain drove me harder, like lashes from a whip.

His men cried warning but too late. My teeth closed on his head. He vanished entirely as if I'd chomped on a bubble. The staff clattered to the rocks, no one left to hold it.

The smoke evaporated, and a weight that I had not even been conscious of lifted from my limbs.

Below me, pandemonium erupted.

The immense fish-thing had smashed out of its cage. I did a bleary double-take because the great piscine creature moved lizard-like and fast—its bottom fins extended into vestigial legs, its immense pug face extending a jaw like a drawbridge to expose teeth like railroad spikes. I could have sworn it was smaller than it had looked when confined, but its mouth was still big enough to gulp a man down.

The spears that had impaled it lay scattered about the cage, and it showed no sign of injury. Its maw snapped, a hungry bear trap, and a bow-wielding man shredded into nothingness.

A dozen pinpricks intruded on my consciousness and began to burn. Arrows riddled my ribs and chest, protruding like toothpicks from a ham.

The remaining men in the valley with the fish-thing were surrounding it, carved spears poised. I started toward them and yowled at the pain. One of the fish-thing's eyes swiveled to meet mine. More croaks. "Change back. To yourself. Undo the damage."

That had to be what the creature had done. Switched from giant fish to the mysterious Warner Mews and back. Something had stopped him from taking his shape before I came along. I imagined slipping out of the suit that was the panther. Then I was staggering on two legs, the ornately carved spears and arrows clattering to the slippery ground all around me.

Another croak of warning. I turned to confront a man in a white jacket and knee-length shorts, wielding a long spear as if it were a baseball bat. My head was the ball, and he hit at least a triple.

Tumbling down the hill I went. I ended up on my back, feet pointed toward the hilltop, and unsure how I got where I was. A man in suspenders stood so that he straddled my stomach and raised a spear as if it were a fencepost, aiming to plant it in my chest. A pair of huge bird talons swept down, one to each side of his head. They dug into his shoulders, and he ceased to exist.

Del dropped from the vulture's back, alighted as the bobcat, swiped the heads off three of the reenactment men, and then reared back screeching with one of the spears impaled completely through a front paw. Another of the men charged with spear lowered at the bobcat's exposed belly.

I surged at him, not even aware I'd become the panther again until my claws split him from shoulder to hip. Like the others, he instantly vanished.

The bobcat became Del. "Hundreds of them coming. We gotta get out of here!"

As if on cue, the first line of spear-carriers crested the hill. By far, I was the largest target. Troy couldn't possibly carry all three of us.

The four of us had reduced the group who had been torturing Mews the fish-thing from about twenty to a mere two. I pounced so my front paws came down beside the grotesque creature. "Can you climb on?" I growled.

The monster from a medieval manuscript became completely human, thick through the middle, short and bald with kind, wide-set eyes, the man I'd seen luring dead cousin Charlie to his doom. "You don't have a saddle."

I hunkered down as far as I could. "Improvise. Hurry."

He scrambled up my shoulder blade and must have pulled some fast transformational hoodoo because I felt long claws pulling at my hide, not human hands. Above me, Troy beat wings frantically, clutching Del, who stared down through his coke-bottle glasses.

The fish-thing circled long limbs around my neck. "Go!"

A spear thunked against the ice-like ground within inches of my muzzle. I sprang in a panic with no plan as to how to land. Another spear caught me in the knee on the way up. I landed on all fours on the peak of a hill by some miracle, yowling as new pain boiled through my back right leg.

Above me, Troy shouted with a deep, rattling roar that could have come from a dinosaur's throat. "Get to the road!"

I couldn't shift back to dislodge the spear without sending the man I was trying to rescue flying off my back. And I'd only just missed crashing into the spiny trees by a matter of yards. The road sliced a line through the forest an alarming distance away. Meanwhile, the shade between the trees was alive with a tide of movement, the hunters correcting course to catch me.

I backed down the hillside in long, rapid strides and used that slope as a ramp as I dashed full speed, focused on the incision the road made across the landscape. When I sprang, behind my ears, Mews made what had to be the monster anglerfish version of a shriek of terror, an elongated, ear-shredding gurgle.

I didn't expect to fly. I still had no sense of how powerful the panther could be, even when wounded. But I vaulted over the tops of the trees. And higher. And higher. And higher. High enough I could look down between the trees and see the hordes of hostiles, turning to swarm after us.

Mews scrambled for a better purchase on my neck. If he lost his grip now his tormentors' work would be done for them.

As a kid back in Tennessee, I'd once gotten to ride in my wealthy Sunday school teacher's private plane—he liked to show this toy off to the young boys before he got in a heap of trouble for touching one of them improperly—and the view I'd had then, buzzing along a few hundred feet above the valley's treetops, was comparable to this one. Except when I started to descend, there was no one beside me to pull up the throttle.

All my legs flailed. I twisted to aim toward the road rather than the middle of hundreds of spikes. I couldn't tell if Mews still had a grip on my fur. I did manage to come down on the road, more or less. If a plane had nerve endings for pain and pressure, I imagine a crash would have felt a whole lot like my landing did.

Mews went flying off my neck, torn off by the shift in momentum. My effort to save him had killed him instead.

Except . . . what happened next shouldn't have been so hilarious under the circumstances. But it was. Mews switched mid-air to fully human and then full-blown fish. The mouth in its giant pug face formed a comical *O* as it flopped and bounced, end over end down the road, skidding finally to a stop. It lay gasping, its scales torn away to expose gore-streaked skin—but in an instant the fish was gone. Mews staggered to his feet.

"Wow," he said. "That hurt. Let's not do that again."

What does it sound like when a giant cat laughs? Sort of like an epic basso coughing fit, one I quickly regretted, for my body might as well have been rolled in a rock tumbler. I hurt in even more places than I had after Xeno shook me. My vision went double. The ghost-men shouted behind us.

"Come on," Mews croaked, now in a bizarre two-legged version of his fish form. I'm sure I wasn't hallucinating because the vulture and bobcat rejoined us, and if they weren't hallucinations, then the hominid fish wasn't either.

"Why are we doing this?" Troy the vulture demanded. He turned on the man-fish. "Why are we helping you?"

"I don't know," Mews said, his tone serene as a meditation. "Though I am grateful."

"My cousin Charlie," I mewed through my swoon. The fish turned an eye toward me but said nothing.

Del the bobcat narrowed his eyes. "Your soul looks quite different—"

Without missing a beat, Mews replied, "I don't have time to share that story now. I need to get to the Silver City. Is that where you're going?"

"As a matter of fact," Del said.

Troy rounded on me. "Fix yourself, or we'll have to leave you."

"No, we won't," Del said. "But you do need to heal up *right now.*"

I tried. I really did. So rattled I was, no trick worked.

A human hand brushed the side of my head. "There's no reason to panic. There's no need to strike out. No need to run. Place your palms together and relax." Mews's voice was soothing as the flow of a brook after a soft rain. I did as he said, pressing my palms together before my chest. They *were* palms, not panther paws.

"Thank the Lord," Troy said. "Now get back on four legs and run like hell."

I stared at Mews, remembering with no little alarm the dreamy state Phyllis lapsed into any time she thought of him. Mews grimaced. "It's best if you do what the bird says."

"I'll give you a lift," Troy said to Mews, "seeing as you're aquatic, though I still don't know why we're risking death by Occisors to help you"—

(To me, the word, whatever it meant, had sounded like ox-SIZE-ers)

—"and the damn cats can take care of themselves."

"Much obliged," Mews said, the second before he was snatched up.

Del had already loped a mile ahead before I next flexed the panther's claws. Behind me, an army closed in, their running footsteps a steady susurrus. I tore off at a sprint as more spears clattered in the road, closing the distance with Del as the hunters bellowed their frustration.

2

We paused, exhausted. The Silver City dominated the infinite landscape the way a planet must appear to an approaching astronaut. I couldn't gauge that extraordinary structure's size—not because it was incomprehensibly immense, but because staring at it twisted my thoughts, sheets spiraling in a whirlpool.

I wasn't sure we had in fact ditched our pursuers. Del and I had run along the path for what could have been minutes or days, since the light never changed, and the diamond of the city remained a satellite hung above the road's vanishing point. I shortened my strides to make sure my fellow feline never fell behind me. The vulture's silhouette kept pace, high overhead and slightly to our port side.

When Del interrupted his headlong dash with a stubbed-toe hop, my first awful instinct was to laugh. I blame too many Looney Tunes.

But I'd completely misinterpreted Del's actions because he didn't fall back to the road. He continued hopping up into empty air. I studied the ground beneath him, noticed the faintest of blue shadows—as if someone had drawn a monolithic staircase in blue pastel and then vigorously erased it without complete success. Del offered no instructions. I raised my head to ask for some and discovered he was fading, almost as transparent as the stair. Above us, the vulture veered downward and went from translucent to transparent to gone.

I concentrated on the first stair, placed a paw on it, found it solid, put my other front paw on the next step and began to climb. When I glanced back toward the spiny forest, my footing softened and lurched. I fixed my gaze back to where I had placed my paws and didn't make that mistake again. A new landscape materialized around me, the terrain where we at last would pause to rest: another forest but sparser, the ground beneath my pads matching the texture of moss, though the texture belonged to the soil itself, not anything growing from it. Maybe the curious soil also germinated the oddities that sprouted at random around us, like Spanish moss waving skyward in defiance of gravity, some ten yards in girth.

Here, the Silver City didn't hover above the landscape but was firmly embedded, a pyramid with no reflection beneath, our progress toward it direct, the laws of spatial distance at last functional.

The nearer we got, the clearer I could see that the structure wasn't really a pyramid. Rather, it was a conglomeration of towers, shorter toward the city's outer wall, taller toward the middle, and the tallest of all rising at its center. The towers also all curved or curled in toward the central spire as if distorted by some potent magnetic attraction. And between and inside those towers—for I could see through it all if I looked long enough—life teemed. Creatures moved in there on two legs and four and more and none. Things circled in its airspace too: incredibly large birds, wingspans rivaling small planes.

Every time I tried to take it all in, I eventually had to look away to keep my mind from getting scrambled by the glorious confusion.

When we took our break, we had to have been at most an hour's run away from that ornately carved outer wall, every one of its thousands of bricks sculpted into the head of an animal, peering out at the landscape. Del said nightfall was too close—which surprised me, as I had no sense of how many hours had passed. No heavenly bodies moved through these strange skies in any way that seemed to mark time.

If we tried to enter the city after dark, Del said, we'd regret it. "We need to wait till sunup."

"Why?"

"Because the Queen of Night runs the city after sundown."

Gordie's voice. *She's ruled the day side of the Silver City for as long as Lilith has ruled the night side.* It felt like a week had passed since I destroyed his mansion, but it had only been at most a day.

I'd been so consumed with his revelations about my mamaw that the full import of that little tidbit had never hit home. Del and Troy had given no indication they were aware that the Queen of Night had paid me a personal visit, and I wasn't going to scare them off by sharing that fact. I suppressed nausea as I thought of Bill and Melissa, their naked bodies hanging in the webbing. When I saw my mamaw, I would ask her for help and hope it wasn't too late.

"Agreed," I said, "I want no part of that," as if I knew what he meant, though I suppose I understood well enough.

Del settled in that position you've seen countless cats assume, tucking his legs beneath his body. As soon as he did that, Troy joined us, setting Mews down gently and shifting to human.

"This gentleman has one hell of story to share," Troy said, regarding Mews with wide-eyed awe.

Del peered at me like a judgmental sphinx. "I do want to hear this. I take it the two of you know each other?"

"Yes and no," I said. Acerbic Troy's uncharacteristic deference worried me. I studied his face, looking for signs he'd gone glassy-eyed like Phyllis. "We have two acquaintances in common, one deceased."

"I understand completely if you're unhappy with what I did." Mews's expression remained placid, his gaze level, no hint in his tone that he needed to explain himself. "I don't like what I did. But I saved her life, and I ended his suffering."

Switching from bobcat to human when I wasn't looking, Del shifted uncomfortably. Troy shot me a look. Apparently, he felt I ought to shut up and accept that answer. "What are you?" I finally asked.

He lowered his gaze. "An abomination."

"I hope the city can give you what you need," Troy said. Del glanced toward his partner, eyebrows drawn down in consternation.

"I saw what you did at my cousin's house," I said. "Never mind how. What I'd like to know is why you sought her out." Mews opened his mouth, but I spoke first, and some part of me was surprised by my own words. "I want you to know too that I saw how you hoodooed her mind. I just found out magic is real about . . . four days ago and I'm already sick of people doing that to me. The last person who did it, I gutted him." I wasn't proud of what I'd done to Gordie at all, but anger seasoned my shame. I was, after all, speaking the truth about what I had done and what I didn't want.

"Man, you *are* the queen's grandson," Del said sotto voce.

"I deserve worse," Mews said. "But I also deserve the chance to prove I'm worth better."

He preceded to explain why.

While he told me his story, night came on, and it was hard not to be distracted by the sheer weirdness of the transition. The color of the sky, which had been a mottled gray, started stippling blue-black, the new color melding into streaks that expanded outward, like frost on a window, toward the horizon. Perhaps my rudimentary understanding of the governance of this mysterious city affected my perception because I fancied the shift in the sky an enactment of cat claws, retracting their silver wedges, making way as spider legs unfolded into tendrils of darkness.

The story Mews shared was by turns sad and sickening.

He told me he grew up in the Chicago suburbs. His father, smart enough to teach at the town's costly community college, worked there as a janitor, which gave him time for his true pursuit: he was a creature who shared appetites with the white-masked creep who I'd bested on the trail, or the joker who fashioned himself after the piasa legend. Mews's old man favored embodying a large fish, a mutant thing with shark's teeth and too many eyes.

In Mews's earliest memories, his father was already a shriveled geezer who relied on a hideous set of dentures to get the job done at the dinner table. "Your mother ran away when she saw how ugly you were," his father would say. Mews never learned what they were like before he was born and no longer wanted to know because he had every reason to believe his mother suffered.

Fathers often see their sons as a chance to shape a better version of themselves, and Mews's dad was no exception. He wanted another predator, someone to go out into the darkness and come back with oodles of food to spit up for his enfeebled old man.

They'd subsisted on ghosts, Mews said, a fine point that struck a harsh chord—the hunger that had drawn me to my mamaw's cabin. Gordie's offhand remarks about what argents eat. "Do we . . . do people like us . . . is that what we eat? Spirits?"

Troy and Del, both fully human, nodded knowingly, sadly.

"Used to be, our kind saw ghosts as delicacies. And they could fight back, which for some made them especially delicious," Troy said. "Some fight back with skill, like the Occisors. You might say, they've decided the best defense is a good offense."

"It's not in fashion now," Del said. "Your grandma expressly forbade it, many decades ago."

I hoped, under the bizarre blue lighting, they couldn't see my face flush rosy red.

Mews regarded me with an expression slightly less serene than usual, eyes a little wider, mouth almost pursed into a frown, before the surface smoothed over once more. "That's definitely what we ate. My father wanted to go several steps further."

Troy grunted. "If you can't find 'em, make 'em. It's awful."

Mews sighed. "Yes," eyes downcast. It took me a moment to recall Troy had already heard the whole tale. "My father chose my shape for me. It was a joke to him, a sadistic joke. He liked to call me his *wife*."

Little Warner never attended school. His education took place after dark, following that unmistakable scent that wasn't a scent, luring desperate souls out from their shadowy corners, hearing their whispers become shrieks as his father's jaws closed on them. His own first taste of the flesh of ghosts, nibbled from his father's rows of clenched teeth, had hooked him, so to speak.

When the yield of the hunt was sparse, his father insisted that they make their own ghosts. "Not everyone who dies leaves a ghost behind," he said. "But a traumatic death guarantees one." He paused a long time, eyes downcast. "I helped make many." He lapsed into silence.

I was in no position to judge him. Finally, I prompted, "But you got away?"

"I don't want to drag this out. There was a girl my age, fifteen, a foster child. We crossed paths late at night. What her so-called protectors were making her do, it made me sick. I picked them, her foster parents, to be our next meal, mine and my father's. When it was done, I was giddy. I found her, I stopped her from getting into a car with a . . . customer . . . and told her everything. I mean everything. And she told me I was no different from my father. After that night, I never saw her again. When I went home, my dad whipped me because he thought she should have been ours too. The whole ordeal gave me a perspective that I had never before possessed."

Mews put poison in his warlock father's denture glue. Even as his father collapsed and shuddered, the long sleek horror of his spirit construct surfaced through the table, jaws flexing as he gnashed out blind, determined to kill his traitorous child. Mews fled and never looked back.

He escaped his father, but he had not escaped a craving for ghosts. He attempted other abuses as substitute, powder and pills, but broke from that to join a Pentecostal cult. Yet nothing could tear his mind from the hunger.

He at last tried to bend those instincts toward a sort of good, making a big production of coming to the aid of those bedeviled by haunts as a means to forage for more food. Through encounters with others like him—like us— over the course of years, he learned of the Silver City and the possibility of "absolution."

I ran fingers through my curls, baffled. "What does that even mean?"

"It's a cure for what I am. I've heard over and over that the Queens of the City possess this power." His voice roughened. "I'm a thing that shouldn't exist. A thing my father made. He was a brutal monster, and I'm something even worse. I can't stomach being what I am a second more. It was your cousin that finally made up my mind."

"Phyllis?"

"No. Charlie. My last meal."

The vision in Phyllis's den hung before me. "I saw."

Troy did a double take. "You saw?"

I shrugged. "I'd say, 'You'll think I'm crazy,' but that phrase has no meaning here, does it? When I was at my cousin's house, it was like a video of what you did, playing in my mind. Though there was no video. My cousin, she was still talking about you. She was grateful, I think. I tried to find you, but—" I thought of the torn face of Lilith's henchman as he tottered off the train. "Circumstances dictated otherwise."

Mews didn't question me. "I'm grateful for that vision. On my way to the

Silver City, the Occisors caught me. Their wizard used his smoke to trap me in my true shape. The thing my father made of me. They recognized what I was, an eater of their kind. They said I reeked of ghost-rot and murder. They tortured me for days. I can't say I didn't deserve it. But I am glad that I have a chance at absolution after all."

Del leaned in. "You do know that ritual could kill you?"

Mews's voice reverted to its preternatural calm, a gross mismatch to his words. "I committed countless acts that fill me with shame and disgust. I wish to be absolved and restored to what nature intended. If the absolution unmakes me altogether, then this too is a desirable thing."

I still hadn't asked the question that burned brightest in me. My impatience overrode my astonishment. "If you don't mind, why were you in Hillcrest?"

"Gut instinct brought me there, literally. That scent that's not a scent. I picked it up strong. Funny thing was, I'd passed that way before, hadn't noticed much. The ghost of your cousin was the main reason. Something riled him up. He was strong. He had power. I think he could have hurt his mother, physically hurt her."

I wondered about the visions that had plagued me on campus. I'd guessed they started about the same time as Phyllis's dreams of her son. "About when did you—"

"Don't any of you move." That last voice didn't belong to our party. I started to turn my head. "I said don't move. You don't want to listen, I can tear your fucking head off, or you can see if your body will absorb a fucking tanker trunk's worth of venom. Take. Your. Pick."

My heart was in my throat. I could have chewed on it.

Del said, not looking up, "Sir, you just threatened to kill the Day Queen's grandson."

The man behind me laughed, long and scornful. "Yeah, lying will make this go so much easier."

Hulking creatures fanned out around us. At least five of them were spiders, but not all. One was a jet-black mountain lion. Where had they all come from?

The mocking voice continued. "So what is this all about, gentlemen? No campfire? No marshmallows? No sleeping bags?"

"We're not bothering anyone," I said, steeling myself to be struck or worse.

"The Night Queen thinks otherwise."

A cold pit opened inside me.

"Have we offended?" Del asked.

"I take orders. I don't ask questions." A hard, heavy weight settled on my shoulder, a giant cat claw. "The Night Queen wants to see this one. The rest of you, she has no interest in. Don't do anything to change that. Though I'd love it if you tried."

Mews said, his tone soothing, "I would like to see the Night Queen. I'm seeking absolution."

"Well you might, repulsive thing. You can petition the way all the others of your kind do. This one gets a special escort. Solo."

The others looked at me. I nodded my head ever so slightly and swallowed. "There's no need for threats. I'll come quietly."

"What? You're not being arrested. You should be *honored*, liar." The claw left my shoulder. "Stand up, turn around, don't grab for any weapons, and don't even think about crossing over."

"Know I'm always going to be grateful," Mews said as I stood. "I owe you for two lives." Undertones in his voice, perhaps a subtle trickle of magic, conveyed to me that he wasn't just referring to getting rescued. He meant Charlie. My bad cousin who I never knew except in nightmare visions, whose ultimate end wove black veins of guilt through Mews's words.

Del wasn't quite done. "Meaning no disrespect, but we've been a long time away. How long have the protectors of Nightside and Dayside been patrolling together?"

One of the spiders hissed in a reedy alto. "Is that a complaint, morsel?"

Making no noise, the big black cat bent its neck to cut eyes at the hissy spider.

"No, just . . . curious," Del mumbled. Troy elbowed him.

I turned to stare into the immense eyes of a spotted silver snow leopard, nearly as large as my panther shape. For a long time, I forgot to breathe. Two grossly hairy, thick-legged spiders big as station wagons quivered to either side of him.

"Walk with us," the leopard said. "The rest of you, stay put. Enjoy the great outdoors." The patrol-thug—I wasn't sure thinking of him as a "pig" precisely fit—inclined his head. "You first now. We'll follow you. Don't dawdle." The direction he indicated didn't lead straight to the city. I wasn't going to risk my companions' lives over this, so I put all thoughts of a fight aside, swallowed, and started walking. One of the big wolf spiders skittered aside to let me pass. I tried not to look at it too closely.

The posse's presence behind me was eerie in its combination of mass and silence. We approached the city at an angle—the tall Spanish moss-like growths giving way to knobby stone.

"Stop," the leopard said. "We're going to need to bind you and blindfold you. You don't need to see the Nightside passages."

I raised my hands and turned around. "Can we not and say we did?"

The other big cats in the posse had apparently stayed behind with Del, Troy, and Mews. About half a dozen huge spiders squatted to either side of the leopard, who wore the equivalent of a contemptuous smirk. "Calm down and hold still. No one is gonna harm a shaggy hair on your head unless you resist."

A trio of spiders advanced. I shut my eyes. In seconds, I was wrapped up tight. They covered all but my mouth and nose. The cold shock hardly surprised me. At least I didn't itch. Then I was borne aloft, though with some delicacy.

Even through my closed eyelids, I detected no light at all.

The woman's voice had a nasal cadence I immediately recognized.

"Set him down gently," Lilith said.

The moment my feet hit the floor, the webbing that bound and blinded me evaporated. I'd been transported to a spectacularly sumptuous ballroom, but I only took in a fleeting impression, for the so-called Queen of Night commanded my sight. She stood as if posing for a fashion shoot: one hip cocked, one hand touching her chin, eyebrows raised, teeth gleaming in her too-wide smile. The white hair at her temples glimmered with iridescence.

As for the midnight-black dress she wore, I'd never seen anything like it outside of comic books and album covers. All things considered, it probably *was* a second skin. It culminated in a high collar that covered her throat and sleeves that sheathed her arms to the wrists—but it was the opposite of modest. An oval cutout in the front exposed her pale, silken skin from below her navel to the underside of her cleavage. Two more cutouts bared the curves of her wide hips and the very tops of her thighs. Slits below her waist bared more leg, from mid-thigh on down.

A puckered scar interrupted the smooth flesh on the right side of her ribcage. She noted the direction of my gaze. "Yes, *you* did that." She sounded amused.

A whisper behind me. "Fool, kneel. Or I'll make you."

"Ignore that. There's no need." She slinked a step closer. "I apologize," she said. "The first time we met, I went about things all wrong." She placed a hand on my chest. "I can let bygones be bygones if you can."

I was honest. "I don't know what to say."

"Fair enough." She pointed. "Have a seat. I'll be with you in a moment."

Having torn my gaze away, I went where she pointed, too bamboozled to scout for an escape route. A round, thoroughly modern glass coffee table glinted beneath a chandelier big as a river raft. Concentric circles of oil lamps mounted in the chandelier's brass fluting cast enough golden light to banish all shadows from the room, which was big enough to host a high-school prom. Curved love seats ringed the table. There was no other furniture. The ceiling was decorated with plaster sculptures straight out of the nineteenth century: Roman egg motifs, fleurs-de-lis, and—surprise, surprise—a repeating pattern of stylized white spider forms. More oil lanterns were spaced along the walls, their light reflected in a wooden floor polished to the smoothness of marble. I saw no doors.

The posse that brought me had reverted to their human shapes, though the ballroom was plenty big enough to hold their spirit forms. The leopard who'd thrown his weight around with such vicious spite turned out to be a burly bruiser with a flattop, his shoulders and biceps like boulders, dressed in a white tank top and camouflage pants. The spiders were in similarly casual clothes. Three quarters of them were women. All were down on one knee with heads lowered.

"Well done, darlings," Lilith said. "Back to the wall until first light."

"Your ladyship—" the leopard-dude began.

"I didn't say you could speak," she cut in, switching from coy to curt. "Your duties call." Another cutout in the back of her dress revealed a supple spine, and the other end of the scar I'd given her.

I settled in the love seat, which let me keep all the gathered assembly in my field of vision.

"What are you waiting for? My affairs are not for your eyes and ears."

The leopard had balls. I'll grant him that. And talk about extreme code-switching: not a trace of the crude, abusive language he'd used with me. "Your ladyship, one of his companions claimed he was the Sun Queen's grandson."

"How interesting, Hubert." She looked my way and winked. "Are you done disobeying me in front of my dinner guest?"

Dinner guest. I couldn't repress my shudder.

Gradual transitions have no place in this magic. An archway worthy of an indoor Arc de Triomphe appeared, allowing the posse to exit after one more subtle ceremonial bow. Hubert the Blockhead was the last through, and then there was wall again.

With a name like Hubert, no wonder he had a chip on his shoulder.

High heels clicked on the floor as the Queen of Night walked to where I sat. With every step, her body swayed with serpentine grace.

"The first time we met, I was angry," she said. "I had tried in good faith to introduce myself, and you killed the messenger." She angled to my right, poised to sit at the love seat there but instead bent down. "I've had time to reflect. I regret the approach I took."

She put a hand on the table, and though there was no evidence a secret compartment existed beneath the glass, a shelf rose up, revealing a bottle of dark-red liquid and two goblets.

"Plenty of time to eat later," she said.

She opened the bottle and poured until each goblet was half full. I didn't anticipate that her outfit could get any more revealing, but as she sat and crossed her legs, the skirt of her dress rode up in a way that exposed the full lengths of her thighs. I averted my eyes in a hurry.

"You can look if you like," she said. "I don't mind."

"What are you doing?" I asked. "What are you going to do to me?"

"How charming," she said, "that you think I would tell you." She pushed the second goblet across the table toward me. "Maybe I will." She offered me a radiant smirk, eyes half-lidded. "Drink?"

"What is that?"

"It's delicious."

I took a deep breath and met her dark eyes. "Did you kill my friends?"

Red, red lips framed her laughter. "They're fine."

"How can I believe you?"

"I never lie." Her smile contained no black fangs. "Yes, I used them to find you, but now, I don't need them. They're going about their silly little lives as we speak. They don't even remember what happened. They never will."

Impossible. "Last I saw them, your people were using them as . . . *playthings.*"

She shifted in a way that made her thighs slide together. Despite myself I looked. She rubbed a hand over her knee and did it again. "That was illusion, dear cub. A spell I left for you out of spite. I admit that. No harm has come to your friends at all."

She put both hands behind her neck as if resting her head, at the same time arching her back and maximizing the effect of the cutout that bared her navel. She was doing everything she could to keep my eyes on her, and it was working. If this were a contest of wills, I confess she was slaughtering me. But the awful truth is that I wasn't fighting. I had permission to enjoy the view and no witnesses to check me.

"I'm a black widow," she said, "but I'm not a monster." She took her own goblet and drank from it. "I gave no thought to how little you knew about everything, including your own strength."

I tried to concentrate on her face, but that didn't help the overall cause. Her eyes glowed with an infernal mirth, and her lips were hypnotic. "You still haven't told me why I'm here," I said. "Or why you want to talk to me at all."

"You're close kin to my closest friend and biggest rival," she said, taking another sip. "Brighter than a sun, even though you're a grandson. Of course, I'd want to size you up."

I discovered the goblet was in my hand and almost to my lips. I stopped myself before I imitated her. It smelled like plum wine, which I absolutely love, though it was deep red and dense as a stout beer. "Are you doing this? Are you controlling my mind somehow, like you did to Bill and Melissa? Trying to trick me into drinking?"

She sipped again. "Be reasonable. If I were, you wouldn't get to ask those questions." She extended a long-fingered hand my way with deliberation and dipped her pinky in my glass. With slow, dream-like grace, she raised her wine-wet finger to my mouth. "Indulge me, please. A little lick is fine."

Maybe because her self-mocking, pouty-child expression reminded me of Melissa, or even just that it was the bloody opposite of what I'd expect from a supernatural being more than a century old—or even more simply that I'm too dumb to shrink from a gorgeous woman determined to touch me, even one who strung me up and tortured me—I tasted her finger. A fruity wine, as delicious as she promised it would be, and unremarkable though appealing skin.

"Fine," I said, the dam broken, and took a sip from my glass. A small one. "Are you happy now?"

When I set the glass down, she took my hand, tugging it gently, but the strength in her grip, in her pull, made itself apparent. She edged closer and put my fingertips against the scar on her ribs. "It's been decades since someone wounded me like this. I should have known better. I should have thought harder about what you are. This is a lesson I needed to learn. You've humbled me." She spoke in a rapid whisper, sounding angry and delighted at once.

I had no idea what to say to this bizarre speech, but the queen didn't seem to need an answer in the form of spoken word. I could tell you my hand moved entirely of its own accord, down to her navel, up to her cleavage, but I wouldn't blame you a bit if you didn't believe me.

Her fingers tangled in my hair, pulled my head back. I struggled then, but what they say about spider-strength is absolutely true. Her lips pressed against my neck.

Her mouth on my skin was galvanizing, electric and evil, not at all like the touch of a ghost. And not like Kori, who appeared to me as a wraith shaped from guilt as every vessel of my body surged with craving. There was witchery involved, for certain, because I wanted to howl and pull away, but that part of my brain was cast into a pit and sealed over with a stone, denied any control over my body. Her fangs stung my neck. She bit down and sucked, every bit the burlesque vampire, before she took her lips away. Adrenaline jangled my eyes, my fingers, my belly, my ankles.

She flashed me a smile full of perfect human teeth, her elongated face just an inch from mine. Then she pressed her mouth against mine. Her kiss was sweet, sweet poison, though she injected not a drop of venom. Her mouth moved to my ear. "Not so bad," she said.

She sidled next to me, holding up a goblet, and poured a swish of it down the groove of her belly. "What cats do best," she hummed as I licked her skin clean.

She undid my fly, lowered that red, red mouth, and showed me what she meant when she called me her "dinner guest." I brushed my fingers through the white streaks in her hair and ran a hand across her muscular back. What few thoughts I could marshal amounted to sputters of utter disbelief.

I came so hard I screamed. My pulse could have registered on the Richter scale. To my horror, I'd clawed her back—my fingers forged into actual claws. When she raised her head, she smiled with black fangs. She moved to kiss me, and I let her. The dress, if it had ever been real, was gone. The wine, however, remained real, and I poured it over every inch of her and lapped up every drop.

Hours and hours later, I dreamed or hallucinated that I lay tangled with Lilith at the center of a bed of cobwebs. She smiled down at me, her hands pressing hard into my stomach, her hips grinding urgently against mine, every flex inducing a mind-numbing wave of bliss. She stayed entirely human, her legs clamped around me. She breathed demands, and I obeyed them. I died the little death, again and again. Every time, her hungry mouth resurrected me.

Somewhere nearby, a muffled voice screamed in darkness, a voice that sounded eerily like my own. Around us, above and below, small white spiders by the hundreds hung motionless and watched.

3

I awoke in a cold sweat, certain I was trapped in spider webbing, but the cloth around me proved to be silk sheets. A sky-blue haze brightened a palatial bedroom, though it seemed to have no origin point. I lay alone and naked in the immense canopy bed.

After a beat, I remembered where I was and what had happened the night before, and I felt good about none of it. Did I dare believe anything Lilith said about her motives, about my friends?

Three raps, a knocking at a door, a reprise of the sound that had awakened me. I scrambled to the edge of the bed and peered out from the canopy. This room was as opulent and ornate-ceilinged as the ballroom, though smaller. I noticed the edge of a fancy tray on a stand at the foot of the bed, scrambled through the covers to reach it. A towel and a robe were folded atop the colonial porcelain. I snatched the robe as my caller knocked again.

A horse and carriage could have fit through those double doors. I opened one side. A tall, hideously snaggle-toothed man in a tuxedo stood behind it. He handed me an envelope. "Her ladyship left you a message." He had an accent straight off a genteel plantation. The imp that lives in my mind named him Beauregard.

I took it, flipped it over, and saw nothing written on the outside.

"Consider yourself lucky, sir," Beauregard said. "She left you alive." Squicked out, I started to withdraw. "I'm to wait until you've read her message."

"Alrighty then." I tore the envelope open. A scent wafted from it not unlike the previous night's wine, my body and mind responding with opposite impulses. I grimaced and read:

Dearest Nathan,

Your traveling companion Warner Mews has successfully petitioned for an absolution ceremony. I expedited it on learning he was your friend. Please join us for the ceremony. It will be of great interest to you.

You will want to freshen up and dress properly. My manservant will assist you in these things and in arriving on time for the ceremony.

I would advise against telling your grandmother about our time together. She will handle the news poorly, and you will suffer for it.

—L

My pulse heated like a steam whistle, and my face, I'm sure, boiled red. When my gaze reached her initial, the paper transmuted to black embers—as if it had caught fire, though no heat reached my fingers. The black shreds scattered, vanishing completely before they reached the floor.

Beauregard smiled with half-lidded eyes. "This way to the baths. You might hear strange noises from the pipes. They are seldom used."

Lilith either had an odd fashion sense for someone from the nineteenth century or a strange sense of humor. My attendant told me the names of the items she'd provided for me: churidar, kurti, sherwani, and chukka boots. I had to admit that the outfit, its long blue jacket and white silk pajama pants, suited me well. I might have felt a bit awkward, but I looked like a prince out of a Bollywood movie. Regarding the mirror, I mostly mourned my lost clothes, my hiking equipment, all of my money—abandoned with the Nesmiths' stolen BMW somewhere in the woods of Black Salt Gap.

Beauregard appeared behind me, though this time he hadn't knocked.

"There. How sharp. Maybe you'll keep your head another night or two." It was impossible to tell if he jested, and I didn't ask. "She wanted you to see the absolution. If we leave now, there'll be no need to hurry."

I didn't particularly want to spend more time in this man's company or in Lilith's quarters, so I said, "Let's go," and what followed was a jaunt into tunnels that would, to a city dweller, have seemed little different than walking through a subterranean metro, at least at first. A turn took us into a much more rough-hewn maze, where the walls appeared waxen and the switchback passages might have been bored by giant ants or worms. Several times, I glimpsed fellow travelers in the cross-tunnels, all of them oversized beasts: a fox, a bobcat—my heart sped at the thought it was Del, but it wasn't—two puma cubs, a snake, a trio of spiders, and once, I swear, a giant ant.

Another abrupt change of texture and architecture, and the passages recovered right angles—every surface, even the floor, decorated with carvings and mosaics that depicted, in my uneducated guess, every possible fauna to ever swim, crawl, or fly.

Our destination first announced itself by smell: a pungent mix of rotten fruit and animal musk. Without ascending, the passage curved—and curved and curved—such that we should have walked right back into the hall we came from, but we never did. The light changed, and I stepped into a round chamber, a sort of bubble or bowl scooped out of spongy stone, an indoor amphitheater. "I have delivered you as requested," Beauregard drawled before retreating into darkness in a flurry of huge spider legs. I recoiled, but there was nothing to recoil from. Beauregard was gone. So was the passage.

I surveyed the latest weirdness. A footpath spiraled around the bowl, descending in tightening, deepening circuits to the tableau at the bottom. The coiled path was wide enough that the various assembled humans in different eras of formal wear and the attendees in giant animal forms treated its ledge like theater seating, yet there was plenty of room to walk between them on the way down.

The assembled audience surrounded and gazed down upon a large pool shaped like a stylized eye, filled with black fluid, ripples spreading across the surface with seemingly nothing to cause them. Numerous huge cats—I spied the spotted silver leopard, Hubert, among them—congregated at one end of the pool. With the cats sat a couple of canine forms, a wolf and a fox, that were just as large. Spiders gathered at the opposite end of the pool, at least a dozen, comparable in size to the mammalian attendants. Among them were male black widows like the ones I'd faced on the train.

Lilith stood at the corner, surrounded by spiders and wrapped in a black robe that clung to her skin, silver patterns woven in its sides that echoed the streaks of white hair at her temples. The ground wobbled, but it was my knees going weak—and not from joy. My stomach flipped, and my head went light.

I stayed upright, at least, as her gaze flicked my way, her lips curved in a slight smile for the length of a wink.

A disturbance behind me snagged my attention.

Four scaly, super-sized lizards escorted a man in a woolen robe of no particular color, which made it kind of difficult to look at straight on. They apparently had begun their stately march from the rim of the bowl, many stories above my vantage point, but instead of following the spiral that many of the gathered were treating as bleachers, they proceeded down a groove that cut across tiers, straight to the bottom. Their course would deliver them right to the pool and the beings assembled there.

The man in the colorless robe spotted me and nodded, his placid blue eyes retaining all their zen. Mews showed not a shred of fear, but my own hackles rose, wondering what blood sport was about to unfold.

As Mews and his escort passed me, Lilith stretched her arms over the dark water and twisted her hands, so her fingers splayed in a hypnotic circle, stirring the air. For the first time, I noticed another woman at the big-cat end of the pool, facing Lilith and moving her arms and hands the same way. This woman was shorter, more compact, more muscular, and with a long, feral flow of dark hair and a heart-shaped face. She wore a simple dress, cinched at the waist, some sort of pelt wild with black stripes. Her sinewy arms were taut with power as she mirrored Lilith's every gesture.

Lilith and the other woman spoke first in unison—I didn't recognize the language—before switching to an eerie call and response, the smaller woman starting her earthy vocalizations the instant Lilith's high-pitched nasal soprano stopped, and vice versa. Lilith sounded to me like an Indian playback singer, whereas her partner could have been scatting jazz.

As Mews reached the bottom, the lizards fanned out and withdrew, leaving him alone. He walked once around the pool and its entire gathered ensemble. The mammals watched him. I presume the spiders did too, though none of them moved. When Mews paused at the pool's edge, Lilith at last turned her head to regard him, neither smiling nor frowning. My stomach clenched, but her gaze didn't flick my way. The other woman watched Mews too, and I noticed the intense green that sparked from her eyes.

I couldn't believe it, couldn't accept it. I wasn't ready.

Equidistant between Lilith and her opposite, Mews waited. The fox and the wolf left the party of cats to sidle up to either side of him.

The water in the pool churned. My own breathing heaved far too loud.

A beam of light from a pinhole in the ceiling speared the exact center of the roiling waters, etching a bright circle, and now the pool really did look like an eye, photographed in negative.

"Disrobe—" said Lilith.

"And bathe," finished her opposite, who couldn't possibly have been my grandmother. She had to be my age, maybe younger.

Mews obeyed. He slipped off the robe—stocky, pink, and vulnerable and with broad shoulders and a rump nearly as wide. He stepped out into the inky fluid, plunged in above his head, and vanished.

To get a better view, I trotted down several levels of the spiral as if it were stairs, squeezing between the seated watchers, hoping to spy Mews. My gaze fixed on the black fluid, its churning surface becoming a view into another space—as if a lens had been pressed to my eye.

That other space wavered, watery and suffused with silver and blue, very much of the argent world and fading in its depths into abyssal darkness. Within that darkness, there was a single light—the tip of Mews's lure, the rest of him near invisible. The pool had reverted him to his spirit shape.

Staring at Mews through this strange viewfinder, I caught sight of a disturbance to his left, a faint flowing, a frond undulating with the current. Though that couldn't be right, and the object had to be much farther away and much larger than it seemed at first glance. I think I spoke aloud, trying to warn Mews, but I can't be sure.

A cavern loomed ahead of him. The halves of its oblong entrance were hinging shut, the interior lined with rows of triangular stalagmites and stalactites, teeth in an impossibly huge mouth.

Leviathan jaws snapped, snapped, snapped at Mews's shimmering light. He dodged and darted to the side, surging past the teeth toward one of the monstrous predator's bulging eyes, one of a circle that ringed the creature's misshapen head. And when I saw that the round and lidless eyes were human, clouded with cataracts but still following that glowing lure, I understood what had happened: Lilith and her cohorts had somehow conspired to deliver Mews to his father.

The thought freed my mind from the vision. Beside the pool, Lilith was staring right at me, eyes wide, brows knotted, teeth exposed—not wicked glee but an unhappy grimace. Her expression conveyed urgent concepts to me as if she whispered in my ear, begging for me to act: *He's going to die. I can't help him. Ancient law binds me.*

My anger ignited. I roared.

"Nathan, no!" The shout came from Del the bobcat.

I was huge, airborne, claws fully extended. Part of me overflowed with rage and fear for my new-found friend, part of me observed with the detachment found in dreams. The creatures in my peripheral vision all scattered from me, and I landed forepaws first, dead center in the pool. The vision that had pressed against my corneas engulfed me completely.

The moment the wet abyss sucked me inside, I became Nathan again.

As child, I had a recurring nightmare—remembered in that instant—of exactly this moment, the plunge into supercold liquid, viscous as jelly yet yielding, the creature ponderously rising beneath me, huge as a kraken with eyes big as bathyspheres. I collided against the leviathan's hide, and its tooth-like scales cut my flesh in a dozen places.

I saw plain as day because the light from Mews's lure shone not ten feet away. I spun between two of the leviathan's giant glowing eyes, and both swiveled to fix on me.

The anglerfish lunged past me, jaw fully extended, and sunk teeth into one of those eyes, ripping it open with the ease of a fork bursting an egg yolk.

The universe whirled as if I was clutched in a fist arcing in a wild haymaker swing. I zoomed away from the monsters, gagging as my lungs filled with fluid.

I slammed down on hard stone. Hands pressed against my chest with rib-crushing force. A mouth pressed against mine, blew air into me with a snarl, and the hands crushed my ribs again. I vomited, and it was as if the whole ocean spewed out of me. How could I hold so much fluid inside?

The mouth against mine again. This time I protested. The woman in striped skins stood up, backing away from me, green eyes ablaze with fury.

I couldn't deny it anymore. The resemblance ached, despite every jarring discrepancy, the smoother, paler skin, the supple yet intimidating muscle. Her eyes were exactly the same. Mamaw, Grandmother, Elzbeth. I wanted to say those words, but my tongue stayed tied.

"Stand up," she said. Her voice boomed and rasped, more panther than human, fangs flashing in her human mouth.

I faltered as I struggled to my feet. She grabbed me by an elbow and pulled me all the way up. My God, was she strong. She couldn't have been my mamaw. This was some mythical monster wearing her face.

But it had to be her. The timbre of her voice. The curve of her chin. The tilt and spacing of her eyes.

Once she had me on my feet, she snarled, "Stupid cub. You came to witness this absolution. Now witness."

Fearing what awaited, I peered into the pool. The panorama, much changed, overwhelmed my vision once more.

An amorphous source of light shone, far distant. Illuminated by that light, a vast corpse drifted. The mutant megashark rotated its flank into view, revealing pits of stringy flesh where eyes once protruded, a ragged crater where a gill had flexed.

I had to squint before I finally spotted Mews as the anglerfish, a tiny thing swimming laboriously toward the new light source, his own glow diminished. He listed to one side, and a dark stream trickled in his wake.

A fist tugged at my hair. The sudden sharp pain dissipated the vision.

I had dropped to my knees. The avatar of my mamaw was holding my head up, keeping me from toppling back into the pool.

"He's going to die," I said.

Lilith stood to my other side. "That's a risk he chose to take," she said—as if she'd never given me that fear-filled look that egged me on.

Elzbeth talked over her. "He may. He has another debt to pay." Her voice, normal volume, was a whiskey voice if ever I'd heard one. "He's slain the demon that sired him. You saw that. The absolution requires one last atonement that won't be ours to see."

I wanted to ask what she meant, but she jerked me to my feet as if I were a paper doll, even though I was taller and I presume heavier. She dug her nails into my elbow, and it was as if five knives stabbed me. "Stupid cub," she growled, all her teeth grown into fangs. "Hard to believe we are kin, but the blood-scent tells no lies."

"I'll take him off your hands, my lady." The spotted leopard, Hubert, had padded to the edge of our tableau. "We all know the punishment for interfering with absolution." Glee amplified his inhuman voice.

"You'll do no such thing to my grandchild," Elzbeth snapped. Her fangs clicked together as she spoke. "His fate is mine alone to decide."

Lilith leaned in, lips curling in a beautiful, predatory smile. "I am told your man was quite unkind to your kin on first meeting. Disbelieved his lineage claim, spoke to him rudely, handled him roughly."

The surprised look I gave Lilith likely was twin to the wide-eyed expression of Hubert the leopard.

"I'll take my leave, my dear sister-in-arms," Lilith said, still smiling.

My mamaw didn't respond or even act as if she'd heard. Still gripping my elbow, she grabbed at the leopard with her free hand, showing no fear of his size, and our surroundings changed in a hurricane whirl.

Wind whipped long grass, which rippled like the surface of a sea. White boulders interrupted the plain, some glistening with smooth curves, others stabbing deadly edges toward a sky where clouds churned with the vigor of storm-blown tidal foam. A shriek of agony continued for what could have been seconds or hours.

I blinked. I sat in a large, white-washed room on an oak divan, its stiff upholstery packed with straw. The light shining through the curtains wasn't the silvery ambiance of the spirit world but plain old sunlight.

A canopy bed dominated the room, though this had more to do with the size of the room than the size of the bed, which was much humbler than the one in Lilith's chambers.

Footsteps swished and clicked across the floor.

Elzbeth stepped around the corner made by bedpost and canopy—her green eyes so bright they could've been lamps. She clutched a huge pelt, its length slung over one shoulder. The fierceness of her gaze was aimed somewhere other than the place I sat. I couldn't tell if she'd even seen me, though I roosted in plain view.

With a mighty heave of her arms and twist of her waist, she hurled the pelt at the bare wall between two of the windows. It spread flat and fastened as if stretched and nailed, displaying an animal pattern of blue-and-gray spots. The pattern matched that of Hubert, though it couldn't have come from him. It was too small to wrap his animal form.

Blood seeped down the wall from the pelt's bottom edge.

"Cross me like this one did, and there's plenty of room for your hide too, cub."
This too-young doppelganger of my mamaw still didn't look my way. "Don't
think us being kin'll save you."

I took in the bleeding hide with new understanding, and the many others
like it that decorated the walls in haphazard placements.

Troy's voice. *Meaner. Crazier. Scarier.*

"I'm sorry . . . Mamaw, I didn't mean to offend—"

"You *are* sorry, and you *did* offend." She crossed the room in a blur, her fangs
gnashing an inch from my face, her breath reeking of blood. "No cub I raised
could be so *stupid*." Her fist slammed my ear with the strength of a wrecking
ball. I tumbled over hard floor into an even harder corner, picking up 360
degrees of bruises.

I curled in that corner, dazed. The Elzbeth I remembered would never, could
never, have done that. The Elzbeth in the room with me continued her rant,
advancing on me with claws extended from her human fingers. "Barging in on
an absolution like some brain-blind child. I should have left you in there and
let you drown!"

To my own surprise as much as hers, even with the daggers of her claws
poised above me, my anger hardened into something wounded and sharp. I sat
straight, staring past her bared fangs and into her eyes. "You didn't raise me.
You did nothing at all to help me."

Her fingers crooked. "What did you say?"

"You died when I was seven years old."

She uncurled her fingers. Blood beaded on her wrists where she'd
inadvertently pricked herself. "What about Henri?"

Her husband, my grandfather, my papaw. The name of one of the ghosts in
the cabin, not the one I hurt. "He died before I was born."

Her teeth and nails had shrunk to stubby human proportions. Her eyes
dimmed. "What year is this, cub?"

I told her: 1991.

She stumbled back toward the divan and collapsed on it as if I'd shoved her.
The cords of her neck stood out as her eyes squeezed shut and her shoulders
heaved. Her question came out as a single sob. "What year did we die?"

I couldn't say off the top of my head which year had contained my seventh
birthday, or how many days after that date I'd learned of her death. As for my
papaw, I'd never even seen his headstone.

Her sobbing continued. I wanted to go to her yet didn't dare risk it. I stayed quiet as she covered her face with her hands. Her anguish subsided to hitching breaths. She whispered, "Oh, Henri, has it really been so long?"

"I don't understand," I said softly, not at all sure she heard. "How you can be dead and also be here?"

I blinked, and she regarded me with a radiant smile, no sign that tears ever wetted her cheeks. "How many children did we have? What are their names?"

I explained gingerly that she had one daughter, Nathalie, and that I was an only child.

"And what has your mother shown you?" Her smile remained unnaturally bright.

Even as I answered, "Nothing," a delightful and terrifying notion distracted me. I imagined confronting my mother with this rejuvenated clone of *her* mother. How my mother's pinch-lipped glares of petty contempt would dissolve into panic as this green-eyed demon seized her by the scruff of the neck. My schadenfreude died as I pictured the gory acts likely to follow. "She doesn't have powers like you or me. She wanted nothing to do with it. Mamaw—you—told me my mom despised me for being like you, though when you said it, I didn't understand what you meant."

Young psycho Elzbeth's smile collapsed into puzzlement. My imp of the perverse kept words flowing from my mouth. "You said that I'd gotten your strength, that it skipped mom and she resented me for it."

Like I had thrown a switch, the Queen of Day stiffened with rage, eyebrows rising, eyes bulging. "You have my strength!" She barked a laugh. "Shall we test that out, cub?"

"No! No! No!" I raised my arms as if she were already showering me with blows. "I couldn't match your strength in a million years. I didn't mean it that way at all! I have no idea what I can or can't do. No one's ever shown me. I don't even, at the bottom of it, have a clue what exactly I *am*."

Instantly her anger melted into sorrow. Del, if anything, had undersold how unstable my mamaw's moods were. I speculated whether her death in the world of flesh had made her like this and whether I'd live to figure out the cause.

She muttered, rocking back and forth. "My cub untaught. My cub untaught. My daughter blind in the head. How could it come to this, Henri? But you're a ghost now, aren't you—if any part of you is left at all." She shut her eyes, sighed, and turned her face back to me, her expression startlingly serene. "And so am I."

I said nothing, but she went on as if, even with her eyes closed, she read my expression plain enough. "Of course, you don't understand. How could you? When I avenged my father's death, I sealed my fate. I was queen of the lands that thrive in the day, and if I stayed on Henri's farm, the city's light would have passed to other clans and come undone because not one of those fools could stave off the hungers of them that thrives in night. Henri wanted what I wanted, bless him. He offered to live *here*, where he'd have gone mad and been eaten, soul and all."

Her eyes stayed shut as she recited, as if she had given this speech before, perhaps to herself. "I loved him like a madwoman, but he could never come here. I couldn't keep him safe. Not without him living like a prisoner, locked away, and that he could never abide.

"But I knew a way, and I invoked it. I was queen and could not be denied. I dove into that same pool where your friend found absolution and called down a rending. The part of me that was flesh went back to the farm with Henri. The part of me that was spirit never left the Silver City again."

She had described an astonishing self-mutilation. No wonder her temper and behavior veered so erratically. I had only been aware of the panther for a few days and couldn't fathom what severing that part of me would entail.

I remembered green eyes floating above me like twin moons. "So you . . . you split in two? But how did she . . . you . . . change into the panther? She did it when I was little. More than once."

"It's like the stub left when the tail gets chopped." Her eyes opened. "There is still something there to wag but little more than that." Her flippant tone chilled me. Like a child disclosing she'd stomped on a worm.

Her voice held none of the creaky dryness of the voice that spoke to me from memory, yet deep in its cadence, I detected commonalities, enough to make this version's casual cruelty even more unsettling.

My mamaw *did* have trouble maintaining that big cat shape for long, but the opposite didn't seem to apply. I hoped curiosity wouldn't get me killed. "What about you? You don't seem to have trouble walking on two legs."

She snorted. "Within these walls, I can look however I please."

"And outside?"

Her demeanor swung on a hinge—from smug to shattered. "There is no outside. I can never leave."

That windswept plain where someone, I presumed Hubert, had screamed his last. "But I thought . . . we went somewhere else before we came here."

"Poor ignorant cub," she said, shifting instantly to contempt. "Our ancestors hunted those grasslands before flesh and time were born. They lie in the heart of the world, and this city was grown tower by tower around that heart."

At last, the question I had burned to ask. "Can you help me understand all of this? Can you teach me?"

"No. It's not possible." Her eyes blazed green, her teeth lengthened. "You think you matter more to me than the Silver City? You think I should let it spin apart, just to wean an ignorant cub?"

Indignation trumped wisdom and survival instinct. "I don't know what you're talking about. All I know is that I need to learn, and who am I going to learn from if not from you?"

She advanced on me, but I didn't shrink. Not because I was brave but because I was annoyed and incredibly stupid. But also because her demeanor changed mid-stride.

Her shoulders slumped. Her spine curved. When she reached me, I could for a moment have believed she was the woman I'd last seen on a farm hidden deep in the Tennessee mountains. This close, her hair glimmered with a gray sheen, so faint it faded with the tilt of her head.

The face that turned up to regard me had skin smooth as a teenager's but eyes that were ancient and alien. Pain cracked her whiskey rasp.

"I can't. I can't. I can't. I would have to leave, and I can't leave for you. Just like I couldn't leave for Henri."

No tears streaked her cheeks, but the agony bleeding out from her cast water on my own match strike. Still, I needed an answer. I wanted to ask, *What do I do?* Anticipating even as the thought formed that this strange, dangerous creature that shared my mamaw's face probably wouldn't or couldn't give a straight answer.

At the same time, a scene that had been tied up in Gordie's hex floated to my mind's choppy surface. *Remember, when you're of age, to come back to this place. The ghost'll teach you.*

"Who are the ghosts that live on your old farm?"

Hope brightened her gaze. "Are they still there?"

"I hope so." The thought of reminding her it had been years since I'd seen them made my stomach writhe. "You . . . the other you . . . told me they can teach me. Can they?"

Her compassion slunk away, and she hissed, gums studded with fangs, "Of course they can, stupid cub. Why are you wasting my time?"

I kept my cool. "Can you tell me how to get there from here?"

Her teeth shrank, her eyes dulled. Sorrow cracked her voice when at last she spoke. "I can't take you there, but I can send you. Come."

A door opened where none had been, though by then such a development hardly surprised me.

Elzbeth led me through the dining room of a home that would have been extravagant during the time of the secession from the Union. There was a thick wooden slab of a table and a fireplace large enough to stand half a dozen plump children inside shoulder to shoulder. Daylight shone through windows: daylight that could only have existed via magical fiat, for when she took me out a back door, we were back in nuances of blue and silver, ascending a slight incline to emerge in the bowl-like amphitheater where Mews's absolution had taken place.

The chamber had emptied. A fox and a wolf flanked the pool. Above and around us, at least four dozen silent cats in all shades of gray and cerulean rested on their haunches and observed.

The queen—the living half of my mamaw—descended to the pool and waded into it. No. She walked atop it. The waters stayed black and smooth as onyx underneath her feet. When she reached the center, the white beam enveloped her, transforming her into a silhouette of burning white.

Her voice projected, loud and fierce. "Hurry, grandson."

When the shoes Lilith gave me touched the waters, I didn't submerge. The surface had little traction, as if I stepped onto a freshly waxed floor.

Shielding my eyes, I reached the beam of light, stepped into it. For a moment, the world tipped sideways.

I stood in the woods outside my mamaw's cabin. Queen Elzbeth was nowhere to be seen, nor any other remnant of the Silver City. The gold sun blazed at high noon between a gap in the clouds. Gnats squiggled between the trees.

The dwelling I remembered from my childhood—the separate living quarters and kitchen, slumped in a state of graceful decay—had collapsed into piles of worm-chewed wood. The cabin of the ghosts, already half-caved in when I'd prowled the woods in childhood, lay buried under unruly brambles.

And yet . . . between the trees, a shadow.

Improbably, two posts stood out from the brush, side by side, weatherworn pylons of rotted timber—the remains of the cabin's doorway. A figure stood between them, visible only as the faintest outline stitched from the surrounding shadows.

Others stood behind him, invisible in sunlight to all but someone like me.

I went down on one knee because I couldn't think of another gesture more appropriate.

"I hurt you once," I said. "I was young and stupid and didn't understand why I shouldn't. And for that, I'm sorry. I will always feel guilt for this." I kept my eyes on the ground. "I swear to you that I am no danger to you. My mamaw, the part of her that lives in the Silver City, she sent me back here to learn from you. I need to learn. Everything wants to kill me, and I've done stupid thing after stupid thing. I'm as dangerous to myself as my enemies are to me. Please help me."

The ghost of my papaw flowed toward me through the trees and bid me welcome.

PART FOUR:
THE LONG ARMS OF THE LAW

1

BEFORE LEADING ME TO MEET THE OTHER GHOSTS, MY PAPAW ASKED THE question that had been on his mind since his wife died in this world: *How is she?*

What to tell him? The entire Silver City lives in fear of her temper? She grows fangs and claws and tosses men around like rag dolls? "She's fierce and strong and just about invincible," I said.

Henri's long, weathered face wavered out of focus and returned with wistful clarity, his smile a sad one.

I added, "She thinks of you often. I saw firsthand."

He tugged at the collar of his loose flannel shirt and adjusted his coverall straps—nervous habits likely retained from life—and nodded. His French-seasoned drawl flowed with warmth and mirth. *Quite a story she and I wrote together. Passionate, complicated, sad story.*

"Still are a story, looks like," I said.

He smiled ruefully. *I know why she sent you here. It's something we talked about many times before she died. Come meet the rest. We need to get you started.*

I stood between the broken doorposts at the edge of the overgrown mound that was all that remained of my mamaw's cabin. A crowd of unmistakably human shapes layered from the play of light and shadow watched from the nearby trees. These ghosts weren't so eager to see me, remaining in the woodland shade as Henri called their names.

The first of them to acknowledge and approach me was the last one Henri named, Alisgida. A tiny woman and extremely young, I thought at first, yet a second look told me that though she perhaps died when not much older than me, she was prematurely withered, harshly sculpted by a brief and brutal life. Her hair and eyes shaped by clusters of deep shadow, she carried herself regally, despite a raiment of tattered animal hides. Her carriage, to be blunt, was no different from my mamaw's, which made the resemblance that much more striking.

She didn't speak English, yet I had no trouble comprehending her. *I for one am glad to see you again, older and wiser.*

Behind her, a mustachioed man stepped forward, glowering at me from under the brim of his bowler hat with eyes made of sunlight speckled on leaves. Rufus, Henri's cousin. He lifted his hat in sardonic greeting to reveal a scalp shredded by claw marks. Marks from my claws.

My mamaw's words arrived as shielding against his glare. *I can forgive that. He weren't worth much of a spit when he was living.*

I smirked before I caught myself. Rufus noticed and, based on the disapproving murmur, so did the other ghosts hanging back.

My mood sank quickly to shame. I found Rufus's eyes. "I'm sorry," I said. "I didn't know what I was doing, but I never should have done it."

Please forgive them, Henri said. *They're frightened.*

Stop it, barked the tiny woman, who had turned toward her cohorts in the trees. *We are not children. We don't let petty things get in the way of what we know to be our duties.*

Thank you, Alisgida, said my grandfather. *My wife wouldn't've sent him here if he wasn't ready.*

Rufus laughed in disbelief. *Whatever sent him here ain't your wife no more.*

Some of the other ghosts gasped. Henri's smile shrank, and he pointedly avoided looking at his cousin.

Rufus's taunt had truth at its core—the queen I met might well weep with joy at the sight of her husband one minute, devour his soul the next—but I couldn't let the insult stand. "With all due respect, you're wrong. My mamaw would love more than anything else to be here, and if she were here, she'd be the first to let you know how wrong you are."

The smirk beneath the bowler hat faltered.

Another ghost came into full view. In life, Chidike's complexion must have been pretty close to jet black, but the deepest concentration of shadows demarcated a burnt hole over his heart, a fatal wound from a black powder rifle. He cut eyes contemptuously at Rufus. *Better to get our task over with than bicker.*

Another stepped forward, a sailor, Paolo. Tattoos etched the contours of his torso: dense patterns of stars and birds above an immense turtle, akin to the one from legend that carries the disk of the world. The other ghosts began to follow his example.

Henri's hand lightly touched my shoulder, accompanied by the slightest electric crackle of spirit.

It broke her heart when she knew that her time had come and you weren't ready, he said. *She only had moments when the pain in her arm began. But I was there with her. Even then, she had her mind, she knew everything, and she made me promise for the ten thousandth time to teach you when you came. She said she knew you'd come.*

He shed no tears. But I did. The ghosts said nothing as I wept.

I stopped when my papaw's gentle hand touched my shoulder again.

C'mon, he said. *We go.*

"Where?"

To the hidden falls. That's where we do this.

One more mystery from Elzbeth's past. I took a deep breath, and said, "Okay."

Not easy, tracking ghosts in sunlight, even with preternatural vision. I followed their faint outlines into deep gullies and out again, braving a few precarious jumps to keep my shoes from squelching into leaf-choked creeks. More than once, I had to cling to the underbrush that populated the steep slopes in order to maintain my footing. Branches scratched my arms, my face, nearly stabbed me in the eye more than once. The clothes Lilith's manservant had outfitted me with proved ill-suited to the trek, tearing with every snag. The brightness of the noonday sun proved to be of little help without a path to follow. No living feet had trod this land in decades.

The panther could have passed through every obstacle unscathed, but the fragile trust of the ghosts would shatter if I crossed over. The ordeal agreed with me, a penance for my childhood transgression.

After an hour, with the spectral crowd hovering ahead of me, I heard rushing water. I shoved my way through a wall of evergreens, my clothes and hair instantly sticky with sap.

The waterfall roared out of a cavern in the middle of a cliff face that must have concealed an underground spring. The torrent struck a shelf and spilled over into a pool about the size of a basketball court, which must have drained somewhere far underground because no stream snaked away into the forest.

I inhaled the cool, clean smell, opened my eyes to spy shimmers on the frothing surface. My ghosts were swimming.

Follow us, my papaw called.

I debated whether to brave the swim nude and decided I'd be better off having dry clothes for later. As I pulled off the tattered silk shirt, Alisgida's round face emerged from the thicket crowning the pool's sheer bank. My surprise obviously amused her.

Find us behind the falls, she said.

"What's back there?" I asked, but she had melded with the glimmer of sunlight on water.

I stripped and took the plunge. The water was cold, cold, cold. And dark. Beneath the surface violent currents churned.

I thrashed toward the bank and put a hand on its red clay loam to steady myself. I half-swum, half-tugged my way toward the cliff wall as clay yielded to limestone. Against the cliff face, which continued who knows how deep beneath the turbulent froth, I made out a dark opening veiled behind the cascade and thought I spotted the milling shadows of my ghost guides.

I kicked off from the bank with all my strength, pushing myself at the waterfall with everything I had.

The downpour immediately slapped me deep underwater. A fist of unyielding stone slugged the back of my head.

The impact might have rewired my brain because my surroundings shifted from mud black to radioactive green. Panicked, I flailed toward the spot where illumination seemed brightest and broke the surface, gasping.

I floated in the middle of a subterranean pool beneath a domed ceiling—though not a man-made dome. The cavern had either been hollowed out by erosion or by something really large and worm-like. Huge patches on the walls glowed the same green as the radium numbers on an old clock. That glow revealed a semicircular platform, rising from the water with broad natural steps which led up from its bottom ledge to a rounded stalagmite that resembled a lopsided chair.

Behind it stood ten ghosts, their outlines fainter than ever in the uranium pall.

As I pulled myself out of the water, one of the men muttered, the sound audible in my head despite the waterfall's roar. *He lacks his grandmother's grace.*

She would slice you to nothing for speaking that way, Alisgida snapped. I smiled, knowing she had to be my mamaw's forebearer.

My hands slipped as I sought a foothold on the ledge. Dropping and rolling saved me from falling back into the water, though my shoulder caught the lip of the first step with a hard thump. I lay on my back, catching my breath and collecting my dignity. That was when I noticed that the glowing blotches on the ceiling contained patterns.

Picture a planetarium lit up in full glory. Then imagine that outlines of constellations had been etched by the light and then spread like mold—the original designs smeared and distorted but still perceptible.

I studied the patterns as I got back on my feet but could only guess what they were. Runes? Pictograms? Prehistoric cave art?

The ghosts stood in a ring around that slow-grown stalagmite at the top, which looked less like a chair up close. They parted to let me walk a circuit around it.

The seat of the chair was worn smooth as a saddle, and when you settled in it, you weren't supposed to have your spine pressed against the conical "chair-back" but rather your belly—as if sitting backward in a normal chair. Some parts of this chair had clearly been altered by hand because the odds of a precisely placed chin rest being scooped at random out of the cone seemed slim, much less having marks gouged out of the rock such that placing your chin on that rest had you staring right into a pair of crudely drawn eyes.

On the other side of the cone, a shelf had been carved out and smoothed. The shelf sported two clear handprints. The way to sit in the chair, it appeared, was to perch backwards in its saddle with your chin in the scooped-out chin rest, facing the carved eyes, your arms hugging the conical chair-back, your hands pressed palm-down into the hand-shaped depressions in the shelf on the other side of the cone. Dark glyphs surrounded the hand-shaped depressions, akin to the designs on the walls, reminding me of astronomical and astrological symbols. The depressions were stained dark too. I just knew, with my luck, what those stains had to mean. The cold scoured my naked flesh, independent of this chill of realization.

The tattooed sailor, Paolo, squatted and gestured at a sharp triangle of flint lying by the base of the chair. His grin was a bit too self-satisfied for my comfort. *You brought no blade with you, so this will serve, like it served your grandmother.*

I stooped to pick up the flint. "When Mamaw went through this, you all were here?"

Not me, son, Henri said. *And not everyone with her was a ghost.*

Watch closely, Alisgida said. She held up a barely visible hand and, with her other hand, drew a line across the ball of her thumb, the pads at the base of her fingers, and each of her fingertips. *You have to cut both hands the same way and place them there.* She pointed to the handprints on the shelf.

"And? Then what happens?"

Perhaps this question had been asked and answered innumerable times before. Alisgida spoke as if reciting. *To spirits like us, most living people pose no obstacles, their minds as open as the plains. But one like you or your grandmother or the one I took that sired your line, dwellers from the Underside, you have walls of protection around your souls that cannot be breached by the likes of us unless you take steps to bring down the barriers.*

My confusion remained evident, so Henri picked up the thread. *It's the way we teach you, fella. We get inside your head and share our memories of our loved ones. Your blood kin. The ones who are like you, who can do what you do.*

"You mean you possess me?"

If that's the word for it, then yes, he said.

"I don't know about this."

Your grandmother did this, and her mother before her, and her mother before her, Alisgida said.

I pondered that, hard. My mamaw, much as I loved her, didn't appear to have come out of this process sane. Admittedly she had taken some drastic additional steps.

On the flip side, I'd seen how strong she was. I needed to be the predator, not the prey.

"Okay," I said. "Let's get it over with."

If you haven't made it a habit, deliberately cutting yourself ain't easy. Luckily, if you want to call it luck, the flint was quite sharp.

My blood dripped black on the cave floor as I took my seat on that freezing saddle of stone. My teeth chattering, my skin a harvest of goose pimples, I settled my hands in the depressions, which were a size too small for me, better fitted to a woman's hands. I imagined how my blood looked as it filled the hand-shaped spaces and trickled out into the runes inscribed around them, coloring in the lines.

Even as I pictured this, the grooves of the hieroglyphic eyes darkened with fluid, and then they were no longer carved but instead real—black-irised, shiny in the half-light, staring a hole in me. A torrent of other minds poured through that hole, and then I was no longer in the chair, no longer in the cavern.

Around me, trees towered, huge and ancient in a primal forest. Roots jutted from the mountain slope, mighty enough to split boulders in their quest for water. A roaring filled my ears, not like the cascade of the waterfall—not like any sound I'd ever heard before. Smoke stung my eyes. A fire burned in my belly. I lifted hands covered in blood, but the blood didn't come from the self-inflicted wounds I'd made. And no ritual cuts marred my palms and fingertips, though they stung from splinters.

The hands I held before my face weren't mine. They hardly seemed human, their skin a mottled gold.

The haft of a spear jutted from my abdomen, broken off at about a foot's length—the splinters in my palms suggest I'd broken it with my bare hands—and though the skin of my bare belly was as gold and as powerfully muscular as my hands, the blood coursing out around that impaling weapon was plenty red enough.

A woman's voice called to me from higher up the slope.

An unfamiliar word formed in my head that meant *human* but also meant *other*, a wily creature regarded with fear and contempt.

The woman shouted again. She peered around the edge of a boulder many yards above, dark eyes wide with alarm. In my brain fired two separate sparks of recognition. I beheld an even younger, less-weathered Alisgida. This being whom I had become, who shared a mindscape with me, also recognized this woman, and that recognition ignited a storm of conflicting impressions and emotions. I witnessed flickers of memory: lurking outside a village, spying on a dance that unfolded in a regal pageant of beads and bison-hide robes, noticing a young girl that had noticed me at the edge of the bonfire's light and who said nothing as we regarded one another. Other encounters too: in the forest, her watching me warily from the thickets, just as I watched her, repulsed yet fascinated, not raising a hand to harm her or to ward her off.

The present-day me learned from this shared mind that the spearhead slowly burrowing into my gut was thrust into me by one of my own kind, though of a different heritage: a monster with snaggle teeth, graceful speed, and gray skin that bristled with hair like a spider's carapace. Others with him had pinned me down as he wounded me. The death stroke dealt, they fled.

A bright, angry flicker in the valley below, smoke billowing up to affront the sky. The forest was burning. Set by my assailants? I couldn't know. I couldn't sit upright, much less flee, until the girl arrived and grabbed my wrist.

The heat baked our backs as she ran, and I struggled to keep up, the spear in my belly a tether of fiery pain that restricted every movement.

The fire hissed and cackled, enveloping the trees, and the smoke blinded us as the ascent grew steeper. If I stayed on two feet, we would die. I seized the back of Alisgida's deerskin tunic with my teeth like a lioness nabbing a cub, and I reared back on my haunches and sprang, carrying her with me. The power in me was like the earth itself, hurling a punch at the sky.

Every second of the leap burned with agony, hot as the forest fire. The spearhead held its own malevolent magic and remained embedded within me, the hex it bore devised so its wounds would harrow me in whatever shape I took.

We landed on the crest of the cliff. Inside me, a dozen new things had torn loose, and when the broken end of the spear struck a stone and shoved the spearhead deeper, I loosed a bellow that I'm sure could be heard for miles. I dropped her and collapsed, mewling, shrunk from great cat to useless flesh.

When my consciousness clawed out through the agony, she was still with me, dragging me along trails left by deer, boar, and bison. I cried out in shock when we plunged into dark, freezing water.

As we came to the surface, her mouth was against my ear, telling me not to struggle. I did as she asked, and the girl proved to be a strong swimmer, hauling a youth twice her weight through the violent current and under the waterfall.

We emerged in the phosphorescent cave where, more than three centuries later, I shivered with bleeding hands, consumed with this vision of my history. The rock formation that would become the ritual chair was still a short stalagmite—with a single wickedly pointed stalactite dangling over it.

After Alisgida pulled me up onto the natural dais, she took a flint that I recognized as the very same I cut my hands with and used it to cut the wound in my belly wider and pull the spear loose. My screams birthed spectacular echoes.

She broke the necklace she wore, used the cord and one of the fangs strung on it to suture the wound. Her bright smile helped me endure the surgery and the days that followed.

My future self lived every moment of my predecessor's life, even though those moments poured past like sand through a bottleneck. Alisgida brought me fish and wood dried of its sap by the forest fire. My ancient self made sparks to ignite the wood, using mind, fingers, and tongue. The modern me, living it from inside, learned how it was done.

She brought rabbits, chestnuts, even berries. We became lovers, moving together under the unreal light. I accompanied her to her village where I was greeted with cheerful welcomes, naked hatred, and various gradients in between. Much was made of my eyes, as bright, reflective, feral as any cougar's.

I tried to live among them, tried to convince Alisgida to leave with me, and left her when she wouldn't, and when I did, time skipped to our tearful embrace the night I returned to her. I understood then I lived the life of my ancestor in Alisgida's memories, and when we were apart, he didn't exist as far as this magic was concerned.

This axiom was to hold for the whole of the spell.

When I returned, Alisgida's family celebrated. She and I danced, and smoked, and that night our bodies became reacquainted. Later that same night, I awoke as a man was slitting my throat. My ancient self's final thought was to wonder whether the killer was one of Alisgida's kin or one of mine.

The journey of memories resumed without pause as I became Alisgida's daughter, suckling at my mother's teats, learning words, learning who my father was, why my skin was different, a red-gold like no one else's in the village. Why, when angered or frightened, I could without thought take the form of a huge mountain cat.

When I was years older, though still teenaged, my mother took me to the cave behind the waterfall and told me everything about my father, that he was a young man from the land deep under the world and that he had doubly rebelled: first by defying his family and emerging from the caves to explore in the sun, second by taking a human girl to wife. He had returned to the Underside to join his father and brothers in a feud against the spider tribe but had rebelled again and rejoined her. He vowed to her that this time he would stay until death, and those words proved prophecy as he was killed the night he said it.

It was his own father who ordered him killed and his own brother who carried out the order.

I listened to all these things from the hunched figure of my mother, who for all the dampness in the cave seemed too dried out for tears. With a vow of vengeance, I became a great and terrible cat and phased away into the spirit realm to find my murderous uncle. I never saw my mother again.

But my life in this body from the past resumed. I found myself approaching the strangest man I had ever seen as he walked a path between trees in the Overland. His skin, dark as some of the banding of the birds, had tattoos covering every inch. He sported hoop earrings and wore an open tunic and baggy breeches, though these were tattered, and cloth wrapped his feet.

The man had killed a deer, which he then skinned and cooked. He shared the meat with me. The odd jar he carried with him contained a drink—sweet yet pungent—and it burned like nothing I'd ever tasted before, even more potent than the fermented fruit I remembered trying in the teeming chaos of the Silver City. He spoke a language I'd never heard. The first word I understood was his name, Paolo. He kissed me, his mouth sweet and salty, and I giggled into his throat as I let him take me.

Paolo, the lost sailor, traveled with me to places in the Underside. He stood by my side on the bone-strewn plain where I faced down my murdering uncle and conniving grandsire and, in panther form, fought them both.

I lived inside her as she twisted and spun, as she tore her uncle's flank wide open from hip to rib, as she clamped her teeth down on her grandfather's spine and broke it. I could have screamed, not just from the violence but because I recognized the place—where Elzbeth had skinned Hubert alive.

Paolo and I returned to Overland, exhilarated, and that night, after making love to him once more, I left his side and his life—until I tracked him down again to show him my swollen belly.

I had returned to the Silver City, this time as a ruler of my tribe, and come back with knowledge of my heritage increased a hundredfold. I returned to the little cave behind the waterfall, called forth my mother's ghost and spoke of vengeance complete, used my claws to gouge symbols in the stone, carved the shrine where I would educate my daughter. Paolo cowered beside me, terrified witness to the full extent of my power.

I left one more time for the Underside—or as Gordie called them, the argent realms—and Paolo's memories of me ended.

For the modern me, a passenger hooked up at the nerves, the novelty of being a woman and experiencing sex and pregnancy subsided at speed, for from this point, the narrative accelerated, jumping further and faster, and the majority of my ancestors who possessed the power to cross over, up through my own mamaw, were women—fierce, forward women at that.

I became Alisgida's granddaughter, engaged in a stormy tryst with a rugged French trapper. In that life, I became the first, though not last, of my ancestors to undergo a ritual that split human life from that of spirit. I learned little of the ritual itself, for it took place away from my partner; and after the split, though I presumably went on to lead some sort of life with the trapper, his ghost offered no more memories to the lesson because, I suppose, that new life contained nothing of the powers of the argent lands. My tutorial instead continued in other hosts.

For those like me who bore the genes of the Underside, the isolation of the Melungeons with their dark skin, black-curled hair, and eyes blue or green, provided an ideal community to blend in. A revolution took place in the world of flesh, and the territory we lived in topside gained a boundary and a name. The hybrid peoples in the Tennessee valleys took in a few slaves who'd gained their freedom. One of my rebellious grandmothers bedded a man on the run from a tobacco farm before he was hunted down and shot point blank in the chest.

The women in my family continued to rule the great cats, warring ruthlessly with other tribes, most of all the spiders, within the spires of the Silver City and in the gray lands outside it. Through the memories of a Union soldier turned faith healer, I learned of the truce forged: cats ruling the day and spiders ruling the night, a pact enforced by powers even older.

The ranks of the spider tribe too had swollen with the offspring of human matings, and the most troublesome of all those was the witch who claimed the name Lilith, who murdered her way through her own kind to achieve the Queenship of Moon and Night. Her real name she never shared, even with her own kind. Back then she wore black wool with a starched lace collar, and the white streaks at her temples weren't so prominent, but her too-wide smile remained the same.

When a mischievous sprite of a girl named Elzbeth first met a gangling, kind-eyed boy named Henri at a town dance, Lilith's reign was just beginning, but I, now in my mamaw's body, chased thoughts of that monster away to pursue my infatuation. In Henri's small flat above the town grocery, the one he took over from his uncle, I learned a lot more about my mamaw's youthful dalliances than I ever wanted to know—among them the unfortunate, unwise fling and frightening miscarriage that bound surly, seething cousin Rufus into the spell, even though he had next to nothing to teach the modern me.

I begged forgiveness, Henri forgave, and the river of life flowed on. I thought of Henri's bed as home, though duty called me all too soon to the city, and I would vanish for days at a time. I showed Henri what I really was, and he didn't run. As I peered down at him through the eyes of a feline titan, he told me I was beautiful.

I—my mamaw—told Henri how, were it not for Lilith's warning, men with serpent shapes would have killed me as I slept, but my cats and owls were waiting for them. The serpents had refused to surrender the name of their master before they died, and I couldn't rule out the notion that Lilith herself masterminded the scheme.

I had told him many such tales, but this time, the terror and sadness in his voice broke my heart as he begged me not to go back. The sorrow born in me could have torn me in half. I decided then that I would undergo the rending.

Once I—once Elzbeth—descended to undergo the ritual, the memories ended altogether.

I bolted up from the limestone chair, hands throbbing from the scabbed-over cuts. I looked up at the markings on the cave walls, and I could read them.

2

I hollered. I whooped. I laughed. I didn't even bother to wipe the tears from my cheeks.

The amount of information twining and leafing through my mind absolutely overwhelmed. I spoke three words of power, and all the excess phosphorescence burned away, leaving the runes on the walls and ceiling outlined, clear and sharp.

Then I was the panther, and I stretched my huge blue claws, reached the ceiling with ease, added symbols to what my ancestors had already carved there, writing my name in an alphabet I had never known before that moment.

A bedrock understanding stabilized me, one of many: that what my claws could cut, what my paws could grip, was a function of willpower and intent, and the things I had managed to do up to that moment by blind instinct alone paled next to the possibilities opened by certain knowledge.

The ghosts had left me. Their task was complete, their obligations to me finished until I chose to call them again. I would have their cabin rebuilt—or even better, rebuild it myself. I had never undertaken or overseen such a project, but the euphoria that filled my massive chest and limbs made me certain nothing was outside my abilities.

Surely, if I ran long enough, fast enough, took the right shortcuts through the spirit lands, I could cross Pennsylvania by nightfall and see for myself whether or not Bill and Melissa were alive and well. If not, Lilith and her followers would have hell to pay. I could find Kori, explain everything that happened, and guarantee her safety, whatever she decided to do. I could find Gordie and show him the real meaning of power.

Perhaps the spirits of my ancestors stayed close after all. I thought I heard high-pitched shouts outside, my long-dead kindred-by-love calling me to come join them.

I decided I would, and one bound sent me out through the waterfall.

A dash of cold water doused the fire of my arrogance. Barreling through the falls, out of the magic-infused cave, I reverted at once to Nathan. I landed with a big ol' naked cannonball in the middle of the pool.

I bobbed to the surface. The sun was still out, though it had lowered to fraternize with the clouds above the western horizon. A huge bird circled up there, though too small to be Troy—maybe a real vulture. I wondered what dead thing might have drawn its attention.

The ghosts of my ancestors were nowhere to be seen. Most likely they had all returned to the cabin, and the voices I had heard had been tricks of my giddy mental state.

That same mental state, I guessed, prevented me from leaving the pool as the panther. Bamboozled because my new learning told me I should have crossed over with ease and humbled because maybe I didn't know so damn much after all, I scrambled and clambered up into the brush where I'd left my clothes, nettles adding their stings to the bruises on my ego. A chill wind harassed me while I dressed.

As my aggravation grew, for the first time in many hours I wondered if—despite all I'd experienced—there were problems in my head, my mind, that had nothing to do with monsters and queens, that instead stemmed from categories of disorders.

Soon, I regretted the absence of the ghosts for a purely practical reason. With all those newly embedded memories of these lands, I should've had no difficulty finding my way back to the cabin, but nothing looked like I remembered. I called out names—Henri, Alisgida, Paolo, even Rufus—but no silhouettes etched themselves from shadow in response. I started in the direction of my best guess.

The leaves around me fluttered in the cold breeze but went still with my first step. Blessedly, the air warmed. A shadow darkened the ground as I crossed a clearing, but when I looked up, I saw that circling bird, nothing more. I tried again to shift into the panther, but it didn't work. I pushed faster through the ravines and hillocks. If something had gone wrong, the ghosts could tell me—I hoped.

For all the anxiety that churned in me, my cat instincts guided me true because the shapes of branches, bushes, and rocks became familiar, and I found the collapsed cabin, quicker and with fewer obstacles than I'd first encountered when following the ghosts to the cave.

I called to my ancestors again. No answer.

I tried shifting shape and still couldn't. I voiced a few choice words then for all my forebearers, even for the Elzbeth that was dead and the Elzbeth that ruled the Silver City. If I couldn't become the panther and if I couldn't find the ghosts to help me, my only way out was on foot. I hadn't been to the farm since I was six, didn't even know where to find the nearest road, much less the nearest town.

Past the ruins of my mamaw's house, dead grass almost concealed old tire ruts that led around and up a hill and into more woods. At the top of that hill, a metal object, obscured behind a clump of cedar, glinted in the setting sun.

I couldn't tell what that object was until I was right up on it. Then I couldn't believe what I was seeing until I laid my hands upon it. The BMW I'd stolen from Melissa and Bill, complete with the Pennsylvania tags I'd swiped.

Oh man, did my heart start pounding crazy.

I thought about where I'd last seen it. "Gordie? GORDIE?" I tried the driver's side door. Unlocked. The keys dangled from the ignition.

How could this even be? Who could have known to bring it here?

I searched the woods around the car for any sign of another person's presence. I called Gordie's name some more. I called the names of the ghosts. I called my mamaw's name. I tried again and again to cross over to the panther—to no avail. I ransacked my newly acquired memories, scrambling for any instance when my ancestors might have faced a similar problem with taking their shapes. Nada.

I wanted to scream. Wanted to punch something solid. The BMW mocked me, a monument to fear and guilt.

I sat behind the wheel, mind a panicked blank, as the sun quit the horizon, leaving a wedge of moon behind. The stars were the brightest I'd seen since I set out on the AT, a whole lifetime ago, or so it seemed. At last, I decided that whatever this meant, however it was orchestrated, I desperately needed transportation and had best use my gift horse. When I turned the key, the engine roared to life.

I had to roll out of the woods and onto the hill to turn around. I had no idea how far the overgrown ruts snaked through the woods, and I wasn't about to try it in reverse. About-faced, the world narrowed to a tunnel of trees, bored out by the BMW's brights.

When I was a kid, I'd experienced that winding, bumpy ride as drawn-out torture. Even given that experience, the distance from mamaw's farm to any country road anywhere stretched longer than I remembered as I carefully negotiated switchback after switchback, long enough that I wondered whether I'd turn in a circle and doubled back.

I didn't put any trust in signs the forest had thinned, but a strip of black at the edge of my cone of vision tantalized me with the possibility that I'd found a state-maintained strip of asphalt.

The explosion of blue blinded me.

I stomped the brake, spinning off into the grass. My dazed brain failed to process what the salvo of spinning blue lights meant until a white beam blared through the BMW's windshield, and a man's voice shouted, "Nathan Mullins! Get out of the car! Put your hands where I can see them!"

Behind the blinding spotlight, shadowy figures hurried forward.

I bailed from the BMW and bolted into the woods.

"Suspect is running," someone barked into a radio.

"Drop or I'll shoot!" another hollered.

I begged all the powers in the universe to remove the block that kept me from becoming the panther.

My ankle snagged on a root, and I went sprawling. A boot came down on the back of my neck and smashed my face into the dirt. A knee landed in the small of my back, heavy as a pylon. My mouth filled with earth as I screamed.

Meaty hands twisted my arms behind my back. Cuffs bit into my wrists. The scabs tore free from the cuts on my palms, and they joined in the chorus of pain.

One of the deputies kept his boot on my neck while another read me my rights and told me I had outstanding warrants in Pennsylvania for grand larceny of a vehicle and for the first-degree murders of Bill and Melissa Nesmith.

"Looks like those Yankees have one thing right," he drawled, voice as droll as if he'd cracked a joke. "Just like here in Tennessee, those are death penalty crimes."

5

They tossed me in the back of the police cruiser with no care as to how I landed. The doors slammed, and the cruiser drove off as I struggled to right myself. The silence didn't last long: the deputy behind the wheel spoke first. "We're so damn far out. Can't even pick up dispatch on the radio."

The one in the passenger seat craned his neck around, so he could regard me with eyes of an unnerving pale blue through the mesh divider.

The driver's next question addressed me. "Just what were you doing all the way out here? No one's lived on that property for years. Were you hiding something? If you did, you might as well tell us because we're going to find it anyway."

The cuffs dug in like they were fixing to pinch my hands off. "These cuffs really hurt. Do they have to be this tight?"

"You tell us why you're out here, maybe we'll loosen 'em up."

The deputy in the passenger seat turned forward for a minute, and I noticed a huge bulge on the back of his neck. As if something implanted an egg there.

I tried crossing over to the panther. Nothing.

I could swear the lump on the deputy's neck twitched. I froze and stared at the malformity but looked away when he turned to glare with those blue wolf's eyes.

"What the fuck are you looking at, kid?" It was the driver who spoke.

Maybe I'd only make things worse for myself, but I decided to take a chance. "I didn't hide anything. My mother owns that land. It used to be my mamaw's farm."

The driver guffawed. "That so? Does your mother know her son is a car thief and a wanted killer?"

I didn't know what to say to that.

"So you're telling me you offed your friends up north, stole their car, and drove all the way here dressed in those stupid clothes 'cause you miss your mamaw?"

The idea that Lilith had lied to me, that Bill and Melissa really were dead, sent a toxic wave flooding through me. Anger lodged in my throat. When the obstruction broke, I blurted, "I didn't kill anyone. I didn't even hurt anyone. But I know who did."

The blue-eyed deputy finally spoke. "Tell me a new one." His accent wasn't Southern. Midwestern maybe—I couldn't place it. "There *are* no other suspects but you."

The impossibility of explaining what really happened sank another nauseating wave through me. Old Blue Eyes continued to stare at me as I fumbled for anything I could say that could help my situation. I resorted to picturing the monster made of my own fears and hates, hoping to bring the panther out. But to no avail.

What I finally said: "Will you please at least loosen these cuffs? I'm not going to try to get away again." I hated betraying such weakness, but the pain in my wrists sliced harder by the minute.

"Sure you won't." Old Blue Eyes continued, mumbling, "Didn't hurt anyone my ass."

I braved a bigger question. "How—how did they die?"

Both deputies bellowed laughter. Old Blue Eyes went quiet first. "You study acting in school?" the driver said when his own giggles subsided.

I needed to calm down because they were trying to bait me into saying something they could twist into an admission of guilt. I told myself to hold my piece, but as the minutes dragged on, I couldn't. "Jesus, these handcuffs hurt!"

"Maybe we can help you with that once we get to the jail, son," the driver said with Good Cop kindness. "But not before then."

The pain in my wrists crowded out rational thoughts. What little space remained inside my mind gnawed on unanswerable questions. Why wasn't the magic working? Were all those lessons I learned in the cave useless in the real world?

I couldn't even look to the stars for relief: either the windows were tinted or else clouds blacked out the usually glorious country sky. There might as well have been endless abyss outside the cruiser's windows.

The deputy in the passenger seat finally turned his gaze to the windshield. And no, I hadn't imagined the grotesque lump on his neck.

The night grew so dark, you'd think we'd gone underground, though the tunnel retained a country road's nauseating hairpin turns. I daydreamed about puking in the cruiser as an act of vandalism. The gleeful rush of defiance might've been worth whatever the deputies did to me in retaliation. The fantasy helped to keep my mind off the state Bill and Melissa had been in when I last saw them. I had left them to die.

Hours passed, or so it seemed, before we arrived in a tiny town, its streets empty. It was the dead of night. We pulled into the parking lot of the jail, and the driver actually said, "We're here."

The jailhouse we'd pulled up to was a dead ringer for the narrow, whitewashed building that stood sentry behind the courthouse in Black Salt Gap. An architectural twin, right down to the vertical windows, thin as arrow slots, with horizontal bars cemented in. Oddities like that you don't forget.

The driver opened the rear door on his side. "You gonna make this hard for us, son?"

Old Blue Eyes stayed in his seat, watching me again. "No one around to bear witness if you resist."

His point about no one around hit home. The lot was deserted and mausoleum quiet. "I'm not going to fight."

"Smart boy," the driver said.

The two men dragged me out and flanked me, each gripping an elbow, their identical dun uniforms making me think of Tweedledee and Tweedledum.

Someone inside opened a door into a short gray hall that stunk of urine and disinfectant. At the other end, a thick, metal gate clattered up on rollers. My escort half-pulled, half-shoved me through. We paused in a sort of anteroom lined with lockers. The gate awaiting at the far end was formed of classic iron bars.

My back and neck throbbed. My flayed wrists screamed. "Can you please loosen the cuffs?"

In response, Old Blue Eyes twined his fingers in my hair and tried to wedge my head between the iron bars. When that didn't work the first time, he tried again and again, several times more.

The other fellow—shorter and dark-haired, gut jutting out like a shelf—talked all through the assault as if it wasn't happening. "We're a small department, see, and our magistrate won't be in 'til morning. Same as the guys who do our fingerprintin' and photos. So we're just going to have to hold you here for the night 'til we can get all that done to start on the extradition process."

I fell, dazed and bleeding, to the floor.

"Hope that's all right with you, son," the short fellow said. "Because that's how it's going to have to be."

I accepted at that moment that, despite everything I'd been through in the past few days, plain old non-magical reality had me in a fix far beyond my skill to handle. It was time to swallow whatever pride I might have left.

"My parents live outside Kingsport," I said. "I want to call them. They'll get me a lawyer."

Old Blue Eyes laughed, and as he grinned, I noticed something wrong with his eyes. They were underscored by thick pink scar tissue—as if someone took a red-hot poker to his lower eyelids. Maybe those injuries explained his cruelty.

Recognizing the first flickers of Stockholm syndrome, I doused mental ice water all over those thoughts. I still was, despite my skin color—which maybe these assholes perceived as license for additional abuse—a snotty, middle-class college brat. So I tried bluffing. "Do you really think the way you treat me won't have any consequences? My parents are gonna get the best lawyer in Kingsport, and when they come down here, they're gonna *see* all these bruises."

Blue Eyes kept staring and smiling. The short fellow didn't say a thing.

"I'm not fucking kidding," I said, amazed at my own gumption. "Let me talk to them now, like you're supposed to anyway, maybe I'll cut *you* some slack."

"I guess we can do that," Shorty said.

"All right, boy," Old Blue Eyes said. "But since you're such an escape artist, we're going to shackle you too. Then we'll get all that stuff done for you and put you in a cell for the night."

"How'm I gonna dial the phone?"

"Since I'm such a nice guy, I'll dial for you."

So they took me through the jail proper, past a half-dozen cells, all but one empty. The single occupant lay in a cot with blankets pulled over. I couldn't make out anything beyond their hair, which would have been dirty blond if it wasn't so mud-caked and greasy. Or maybe, given what I just went through, it was clotted blood.

They led me to the other end of the building, to an office that held nothing but a desk and a phone and the chair onto which they shoved me. Shorty withdrew jingling shackles from a drawer and clamped them to my bare ankles. Old Blue Eyes nabbed the phone, a rotary, and asked for the number. I recited it, he dialed, handed his partner the receiver. "See, we're full service."

Shorty pressed the receiver to my face. And as the other end of the line began to ring, Old Blue Eyes chuckled, "This should be good."

So much for my bluff. My heart stuffed itself into my mouth as my parents picked up on the other end. Or someone did. As I repeated, "Hello? Mom? Dad?" into the phone like a stupid parrot, silence stretched until at last a voice started to sob.

I had not spoken to them in weeks. Maybe Mom and Dad were worried, even terrified. I'd been utterly selfish and thoughtless, disappearing the way I had, and karma was due. The sobbing continued, definitely a man's voice. "Dad?"

"I'm sorry," the voice choked. "I'm so sorry. He made me do this."

That voice, so familiar, belonged to neither of my parents. "What?"

"I'm sorry," the man on the other end of the line repeated, and in disorienting stereo, I heard the same words, the same muffled sobs, coming from the occupied cell down the hall.

And then I realized whose voice it was. *Gordie?!*

"Fucking hell," Old Blue Eyes spat.

The most astonishing thing happened next. Shorty dropped the phone receiver, pivoted, and drew his piece on Old Blue Eyes, shouting in Gordie's voice, "Stop this now!"

Old Blue Eyes lunged across the desk with an animal roar and tore his partner's face off. There was no scream, no blood, no noise. Shorty unraveled from the point of rupture, converted to empty air as if never there to begin with.

The receiver clattered to the floor. Old Blue Eyes shattered it to powder with his boot, and the voice down the hall screamed. The deputy turned his head toward the row of cells and roared. I saw with a shock that a third blue eye still stared at me, its bright, mad iris smack in the middle of the boil-like lump on the back of Old Blue Eyes's neck.

His face had changed when he turned back to me. The scar tissue now filled his sockets, and those insane blue eyes speared me with their gaze as they migrated up his splitting brow. The crests of his cheekbones also split open, and two more eyes stared at me, unblinking. He opened his mouth, exposing incisors that were lengthening to tusks. His forehead stretched up, up, bulging impossibly tall.

My scream choked off as he closed clawed fingers around my throat, hand completely encircling my neck as he lifted me from the chair, held my face up to his—now larger than human—and four china-blue eyes bored into mine. Through a tusked smile, he said, "Remember me?" Antlers sprouted from the peaks of his forehead. The left one, formerly broken, was now healed.

He roared again and flung me like a sack.

I should have slammed into the wall, but instead, I hurtled right through, the cinder blocks no more substantial than fog.

I landed on a cold, stone floor and rolled, my horizontal momentum the only thing that kept the impact from transforming me into a bundle of broken bones.

The piasa had tossed me into a long room lit by electric lights strung from the ceiling, all the wiring exposed. Crumpled, I came to a stop by a low stone table, the first of several in a row. Someone lay on it, chained. Though the chains were overkill since the prisoner's legs were missing below the knees, arms missing past the elbows. The mutilated man sobbed. "I'm sorry."

Every tile in the floor, every block in the wall, held an inscription: a name, a date of birth, and a date of death. Some were inscribed with epitaphs. The letters in the tile beside my head—"Her father's joy and the comfort of his last years"—were filling with my blood.

My captor lumbered toward me, his healed antlers threatening to scrape the ceiling. The man who styled himself as the piasa dropped to his knees beside me, his faux-deputy uniform peeling off like old skin. A fist the size of a pumpkin bounced my head against the gravestone floor, and out I went.

4

When I came to, I heard the voice of Old Blue Eyes. The piasa was in a chatty mood. Perhaps hours had passed, perhaps only minutes.

". . . never tried it before, but now, I understand why beasts like you like it so much."

A raw shriek of blunt force trauma enveloped me head to foot. I spat blood, so I could answer. "Tried what, creep?"

He loomed over me, leather boots making silent threats to either side of my head. I glimpsed a checkered shirt, denim coveralls—a nightmare Paul Bunyan. "Eating ghosts," he repeated. "I've never tried it before. But I understand now why you beasties do it." He lowered to one knee, the monstrous silhouette of his misshapen head and wicked antlers blotting the incandescent bulbs. "Not much nourishment, but the rush. And the taste. It's sugar syrup and hashish in one quick slurp."

His meaning hammered at my heart even before he held up all his fingers. "Ten little piggies make a hungry man's stew."

The ghosts gone when I came out of the waterfall. The "bird" in the sky, following my progress from the cave. The way my powers didn't work, just like in Wilkes-Barre whenever his accursed gaze fixed on me.

The ghost of my papaw, gone. Nine others whom I had shared lifetimes with in the course of a day, gone.

I bellowed, kicked, thrashed, squirmed—would have bitten his crotch if I could get to it, I was so crazy angry—but he pinned me down effortlessly, keeping a hand pressed to my chest.

"No point in struggling. Those cuffs are real. So are the chains. And so is this." He pulled a hunting knife with a long, long blade out of his boot and held it so that it reflected my swollen and bloodied face. Then, he put the blade in his mouth and flipped me onto my stomach. He sat on my shoulders, crushing my face to the stone. "Now," he said. "We'll see about making these cuffs more comfortable."

I snarled, "Get off me!"

"Time to declaw," he said. He gripped my wrists and squeezed the cuffs tight enough to cut off circulation altogether. He wound something else around my forearms as I shouted, "Fuck you, motherfucker!" over and over again.

A ripping agony sawed into my left wrist. My words strangled into a scream. Abruptly, my left arm was free, but though I bucked against him, his grip on my right arm was solid as iron and heavier than granite. I screamed again as my right wrist seared—this agony ten times worse. I twisted my arm to escape his grip and felt muscle tear. Felt a final rip. Inside, I was one endless howl.

He jerked, and something plopped about a yard from my head.

My howl dried out and died.

Centered on another headstone tile lay a pair of hands, cuffed together, blood draining from the stumps of smoothly severed wrists.

I gasped. I gawped. My mind told me the piasa had played a trick, that those weren't my hands cast off like the heads from a fisherman's harvest.

The piasa's weight lifted from me. I flipped onto my back, and the ends of my wrists exploded in agony as I pushed against the concrete. I howled again, holding up my arms, taking in the black-leather tourniquets, biting deep into each forearm below cross-sections of raw meat where hands should have been attached.

He grabbed the chain strung between my ankles and yanked it like a handle, dragged me toward the tables—their bases also cobbled together from headstones, their tops huge stone slabs, fitting as sacrificial altars. I flailed pointlessly, unable to fight, unable to grip anything, though my addled, terrified brain couldn't seem to come to terms with this.

We passed the first table. The pitiable figure chained there struggled to raise his head. "Oh, God, Nathan. Nathan. He found me, and he made me do this. He made me set the trap and watch for you."

The piasa sniggered with pit-of-hell mirth. "You'll both have plenty of time to chat."

He grabbed one of my ankles and hauled me up onto the next vacant slab as easily as hefting a bag of dog food. I screamed again when I landed—to his obvious delight.

He stooped. I heard the rattle of heavy chains.

Beside me, Gordie's breath rasped, the sound of a man being slowly crushed by a boulder. I said, "I'm sorry too, Gordie," because if it weren't for what I had done to his house, what my claws did to his body, he'd never, ever have been there on that table.

I thought I heard him say, "Get . . . the fuck . . . out . . ."

A grinding noise, like thunder.

"*. . . of here . . .*"

An opening as ragged as a hole torn in canvas appeared between Gordie's table and mine, filled with the black and silver of the Underside. Hidden from my view, Gordie retched and gurgled like his innards were boiling out through his throat.

I didn't think. I pushed off with my legs and rolled, flipped into the gap Gordie had created, defying his torturer with all his remaining power.

It didn't go like you'd think: I scraped on a hard edge, like I'd dropped through a fissure blasted through a concrete floor. Behind me, the piasa roared. A claw snatched at my back, but I slipped his grip and tumbled into darkness.

The piasa's bellows followed me, and I learned Gordie had survived casting the spell, could hear him wailing as the monster took out its frustrations.

Gordie's screams cut off as the hole between realities closed.

Lost in the abyss, back at square one, solid surface beneath me in the silver haze. I understood at an instinctual level that Gordie had sent me somewhere physically far, far away from wherever the piasa had trapped him but had not a clue where I was.

Crossing over to the panther had healed my wounds before. The shackles on my ankles fell away as I changed without difficulty, from human to cat.

The transformation made the agony as fresh as when the piasa first sawed into my wrists. I squalled in pain.

My blue-furred forelegs ended in raw stumps. My front paws were gone.

I yowled in rage and terror and heart-spearing grief and became a man again. Part of a man.

My breath hitched until I wept in despair. The bastard had hobbled me in both worlds, robbed me of my best weapons against the argents, robbed me of the means to make art, damaged me beyond all repair. And my newly minted memories told me that for all my might in feline form, if I couldn't run or leap, I could go nowhere.

Beneath the tourniquets, veins bulged purple. Above them, my severed stubs clotted black.

Kneeling, I trembled. Blood smeared the leggings Lilith had given me. The smears called up a memory of blood streaked down my bare legs, a strand of my guts dangling from a slice in my belly. No, not my memory: one from Alisgida's daughter. A memory from her time in the argent lands, one that came to life as she described her ordeal to her wide-eyed lover.

After her first unsuccessful attempt at avenging her father's death, she had been abandoned to die in a remote cranny of the Underside. She had spoken words of power over her own blood to summon help.

Poor Chidike and Paolo. Poor Alisgida. Poor Henri. All of them. Devoured.

I had no shortage of blood. I was covered in it. I knew the words. I spoke them aloud.

My mind stretched out and up and down and in a thousand directions, searching, searching for anyone who might know me, who might help me. My mamaw in the Silver City. Del and Troy would do, or Kori, even the Crabbes, even Mews, if he was reachable wherever he was now. Kori. How badly I wanted to see Kori one more time.

I touched a mind. Someone who definitely knew me. The worst outcome imaginable. I felt her seize on the contact and barrel my way, legs moving like lightning.

I was done for. Totally fucking finished. I couldn't fight. Outside the sanctuary of the city, nothing would stop the black widow from killing her mate.

I felt no pity for myself. I was a complete failure. A useless waste. I would never be the child who would make ferocious Elzbeth proud. I had brought death to Gordie and to my mamaw's beloved ghosts. I deserved what was coming.

The only thing left to do was meet the end with some pretense of dignity.

A nightmare meteor, she raced toward me from above, her bizarrely graceful legs crawling at terrifying speed along an invisible thread, a bloated black fiend with gleaming coal eyes. She slowed as she drew closer.

I held up my useless stumps. "Finish it. Kill me."

Lilith halted and then inched forward—slowly, slowly, closer, closer, drawing out the moment. I shouted, "Get it over with!"

She seized me with her elegant forelegs. Her fangs found their mark, her poison flowed, and at last, I knew mercy.

PART FIVE:
THE CHAPEL BUILT FROM GRAVESTONES

1

WAKING UP WAS THE FIRST SURPRISE.

The second came when my eyes focused, and I registered the worried woman staring down at me—her blonde hair dark at the roots, her delicate, pale features superimposed by ghostly marks, dark bands around her eyes and mouth and neck. Those eyes were red from crying, her cheeks moist.

"Kori?"

Kori's smile brightened and faltered. Then came the third surprise, for a long-faced, wide-mouthed woman with white streaks at her temples leaned into view. "Good. You're awake," Lilith said.

I lay on a futon situated against a wall in a room even tinier than the dorm rooms at Tech. Strung from the ceiling light, a mobile of paper birds slowly rotated. Posters of Duran Duran, R.E.M., and Radiohead watched over me. Opposite them, Kori knelt by my shoulder, dressed in an oversized, faded T-shirt, hair loose and frizzy.

Lilith stood. She wore a jacket and pencil skirt, fancy enough for an executive suite. A white dresser with a mirror mounted on top barely squeezed into the space past the foot of the bed. I knew where I had to be: Kori's bedroom in her folks' apartment. "How . . .?"

"You were delirious when I found you," Lilith said matter-of-factly. "You told me bits and pieces of what happened when you started to regain your senses. I asked you where you wanted to go"—she smiled wryly at Kori—"and you told me you desperately wanted to see your friend again. You gave me just enough to go on that I could divine the rest for myself."

I was both overjoyed and appalled. I wanted to tell Kori how happy I was to see her again. I wanted to yell at her to run, to grab her family and run. Where was her family?

The confusion, anger, fear, and joy that thrashed across my face must have looked like agony. "Oh, Nathan, are you hurting?" Kori cut eyes at Lilith. "You said he wasn't in pain!"

I held my hands up to my face. I had no hands.

The tourniquets were gone from my forearms. Instead, webbing coiled tightly around each wrist, covering and sealing the wounds. The spider-gauze shimmered with that familiar blue glow.

I goggled at Lilith. "What did you do to me?"

"Kept you from bleeding to death," she said.

My disbelief and dismay did not subside. Kori's look grew sharper. "You said the piasa did that to him."

"Which is what he told me when I found him like that."

"It's . . . that's . . . yes." I struggled to line up jumbled thoughts. Whatever else happened, I didn't want Kori to start an argument with the Queen of Night. "It's true. The piasa did this to me." I stared at Lilith, who maintained a slight smile, inscrutable as a mask. "Thank you . . . I didn't . . . how long will these hold?"

"As long as I want them to," she said. "Perhaps forever if need be."

I was so confused. The full implications of her statement flew over my head. "You—I'm—why didn't you take me back to the Silver City?" *To my mamaw,* I almost said.

"You're safer here," she said.

"What do you mean?" I asked. At the same moment, Kori asked, "What are you talking about?"

Lilith tilted her head. "If I'm not mistaken, you know a lot more about the Silver City now than you did two days ago. What do you think will happen if you go back there in this condition? Wounded, unable to defend yourself, a lame cub?"

When she said *cub,* I got the gist. She wasn't just talking about the creatures that lived there, she was talking about Elzbeth. I pictured blazing green eyes, fangs and claws that appeared and disappeared at will, pictured her asking about her beloved Henri. Pictured what she'd do when I told her that her husband's ghost had been eaten by a monster. That the piasa had massacred our ancestors. I couldn't defend myself from *her.*

I wasn't going to weep in front of Lilith. Despite—or really *because* of our tryst—I was more frightened of her than ever, mortified that she was in the same room with Kori. And not because of any potential for soap opera drama. I remembered that I had managed to give Kori a warning before Gordie cut me off.

I held up my webbing-wrapped stumps. "Lilith, is there more you can do? Can you heal me?" I knew the answer—of course, she couldn't—but that wasn't why I spoke.

Kori didn't react as I said Lilith's name. Either she already knew or hadn't heard my earlier warning. Or she was one hell of a poker player.

Lilith's answer made my jaw drop. "If we had your hands, reasonably intact, I could. No surgeon needed."

Kori's eyes bugged. "You can't be serious! What *are* you?"

"I told you," Lilith said, never losing that *Mona Lisa* smile. "I'm a witch."

"I . . . don't doubt that, but—"

My mouth finally caught up to my spiraling thoughts. "You're not lying? You'd do that? You'd help me fix this?"

Lilith's smile widened a fraction. "Of course, I would." And a little wider. "Are you implying I've lied to you? If you think that, give me an example."

And here I'd been worried about Kori starting a fight she couldn't finish. My pulse spiked. "That's not what I meant, honest. I'm just . . . that this is even possible . . . but this knowledge is useless, right? Can we even get them back? That bastard, he's probably—"

I couldn't finish the thought, picturing what the piasa had likely done with my hands after my escape. Even worse, imagining what he'd done to Gordie. Those screams I'd heard. The memory, or my fight to shut it out, made a pattern of tarot figures flicker before my mind's eye, like the one woven into the carpet in Gordie's ruined dream home. All the dioramas moved: the Fool teetered at the cliff edge, Temperance upended her jug, screaming souls fell from the collapsing Tower.

I twitched to shake off the mirage. Deeply unsettled, I almost missed what Lilith had to say. "I would bet that that one preserves . . . keepsakes."

Kori asked a question of Lilith that chilled my heart to hear and that simultaneously made it swell with gratitude for a largesse I had not earned. "If that's true—will you help us get his hands back?"

Lilith's slight smile bent into a subtle frown. "I don't expect you to understand this." She sat on the edge of the futon, jostling me ever so slightly, though I felt no pain. "Even if I knew where that monster hides his lair, and I don't, I'm no warrior. As Nathan can verify, I've got enormous responsibilities in the Silver City that I can't casually abandon. And getting myself killed counts as abandonment." As she talked, she absently rubbed her ribs where I'd scarred her, though I suspected she knew what she was doing and wanted to make sure I saw. "I've gone dangerously out of my way already." She patted my leg. Kori's eyebrows rose. "Though I had to. I couldn't leave him like that."

"But you can't leave him like *this* either," Kori said, her voice rising. "It's going to come back for him."

Despair compressed my chest, overwhelming all caution. "So it's hopeless then?"

"Not at all," Lilith said. She spoke a word of power. *This is taking too long,* she continued, though her lips didn't move. All motion in the room stopped, not a breath or eyeblink. The mobile that dangled from the ceiling light stilled. *I can't waste my time explaining to your feisty little friend all the things* you *need to do to get* yourself *out of this mess.*

My ancestors' memories of magic contained nothing like this, but the sensations duplicated the experience I'd had when Gordie first spoke to me in the room with the tarot carpet. I couldn't even feel my body, much less make it move. *Don't you dare hurt her!*

However this spell worked, she heard me. *Ah, but she's scrumptious. Spiders eat birds, you know.*

I would have screamed if I could move my mouth. *Don't you dare!*

Calm down. I'm not going to touch a single feather.

How can I believe that? Where's her family? Are they bound up in webs like my friends? Are they even still alive?

Now, sweetie. She addressed me as if I were six. *I told you. Your friends are fine. They don't remember a thing. If it's such a matter of life and death, you can call and ask them yourself after I leave—if you can get your girl to dial for you.*

Calling Kori "my girl" angered me more, and on top of that, I still didn't believe her. *The police told me they were dead!*

Stupid. Impatience heated her disembodied voice. *Your friend the piasa and a complex illusion, created by the boy he captured and tortured, told you that your beloved Bill and Melissa were both dead. You credit that over me?*

She had me there, but scoring points off my rage and panic didn't calm me down. *Why are we here? Why didn't you take me to mamaw? What are you planning?*

My goodness. You'd think our lovely night together never happened. Maybe I won't help you after all.

Too flummoxed to respond, I wondered if she could read the mass of confusion, guilt, and anger her head game stirred. Her words hinted that she could. *Think this out. You've met the part of your grandmother that lives on in my city. Even if she wanted to help you, she can't leave. And that's assuming she doesn't stretch your hide on her wall for whatever she perceives your failure to be.*

If I could have waved my mutilated arms in her face, I would have. *What other choice is there? I can't fight the piasa like this!*

Stop arguing and hear me out. I could swear she turned her head toward me a fraction, though nothing else in the room stirred. *You're not helpless. Not at all.*

I didn't know how to process that obvious falsehood.

You're not limited to two shapes. You can improvise.

She could make her fangs come and go at will, as could Elzbeth. *You want me to fight the piasa by nipping at him? My claws are gone.*

You're lucky patience is innate to my nature. Cheer brightened her words for some unfathomable reason. *It's within your power to make your own claws. Didn't you tell me the piasa made many new eyes to make up for the ones you tore from his face? Your new claws might not have the power to wound in all worlds, like the ones you lost, but you* do *have your grandmother's strength, so they'd be plenty powerful enough.*

I—I don't remember telling you—

You did. Has anything I said been wrong?

No, but—you think I should become like him?

In the past lives I've absorbed, my forebearers altered their shapes on a curve between human and cat when extreme needs arose: sprouting claws, baring fangs, narrowing pupils to slits, even extending tails. But none broke the mold altogether. From these past lives, I unearthed reservoirs of disgust at the very notion.

Would you rather the piasa murder your pretty bird? Because I'll bet she's no longer beneath his notice.

I weighed whether to tell her off for threatening Kori or demand that she tell me how to do this thing she proposed. Because I knew she was right. Before I reached a decision, Lilith spoke another word of power.

"Not at all," Lilith said. "It's well within both of your abilities to put this animal down. I recommend you don't wait for him to come to you." She lifted her hand from my leg with a broad, toothy smile, and with a leap, she phased through the ceiling in an explosive flurry of expanding black carapace and immense arachnid legs. Kori reeled backward, and I cringed against the pillow.

Neither of us screamed, to our credit. When Kori caught her breath, she said, "That was the scariest person I have ever met." She put a hand on my shoulder, and I thought she was about to say, *You need to get the hell out of here,* but instead, she said, "You need to tell me everything."

A woman called from outside the room. "Kori? Are you talking on the phone? What time is it?"

"Oh, shit, my mom," Kori whispered. "She had some kind of silencing spell up. Must have come down when she left."

"Kori, it's two in the morning." A door opened. Footsteps shuffled down a short hall.

For the first time, my ancestor's memories did me good. I rolled toward the rock posters, crossing over to the panther as I did, and phased through the wall much the way Lilith had departed through the ceiling.

On the other side lay concrete and bedrock—Kori's bedroom was at the back of a basement apartment apparently. Had I phased completely into the Underside, a drop of considerable depth awaited, so I remained corporeal enough to float in the rock, a huge feline specter, peering into the room from outside. Another skill that underscored my debt to my cruelly lost ancestors.

But theirs wasn't the only gift that kept me alive. Not for the last time, I sourly noted a debt to Lilith. Her magic bandages adjusted to my shape and state of existence.

Kori's mother barged into her bedroom. "Why are you up? Were you on the phone?"

"Mom!" Kori protested. "Privacy, please! It's not your problem."

Kori had claimed there was no one in her family like her. But that absolutely wasn't true. A slender, handsome woman—a little thicker through the middle and quite attractive, her hair the umber shade I imagined Kori's would be if left undyed—Kori's mother definitely bore the same markings that Kori did. If the two women's skins could be thought of as layers of translucent glass, Kori's marks were right on the surface while her mother's were two or three layers deep, still noticeable but diffuse. I wondered if I could have perceived her mother's bands without the teachings of my ancestors, those poor slaughtered ghosts.

"Is it that Justin, bothering you again?"

"No, it's nothing. Go back to sleep, Mom."

After about ten minutes of variations on this exchange, Kori's mom exited, pursued by glares of exasperation.

"Well, that was embarrassing," Kori muttered.

I whispered to her through the wall. "Who's Justin?"

The exasperated glare swung my way, though it was clear she didn't know exactly where to look. "Not your problem, Tigger. Where the hell are you?"

"Outside, kind of." I had what felt like a lifetime of explaining to do—and maybe some begging because the schemes boiling in my mind couldn't be executed without help. "Can you meet me outside? Is that possible?"

Her expression grew solemn. "Um. Yes. Definitely. Parking lot. By my car."

"See ya there . . . um, any chance you could find me a coat or something?"

She uttered a little half-laugh, a single syllable that conveyed without words, *I can't believe this is happening.* "Why not? Okay."

Phasing toward the surface proved hellaciously challenging. My instincts directed me to swim as if I were in quicksand, which without front paws proved pretty difficult. The textures sharing the same spaces as my body grew soupier until at last I raised my panther head through the tarp over a swimming pool. I'd emerged in the central courtyard of Kori's apartment complex. Climbing out also proved grounds for slapstick: by instinct I focused my will and thus my grip in my claws, which were gone. I crossed over to Nathan only after several failed attempts to flop out of the water and onto the artificial turf by the poolside. I also managed to soak myself, icy temperatures biting through the thin fabric of the clothes Lilith gave me. The deeply unpleasant sensation reminded me how I'd acquired that outfit.

My stomach churned as I contemplated explaining that to Kori. For better or worse, I resolved not too. At least not yet. Whatever that night meant, I couldn't take the time to face those implications, not with a chance to restore my hands, not with a chance to save Gordie.

I succeeded in clambering to my feet because the magic Lilith invested in those creepy bandages allowed me to keep my balance despite my lack of hands. Opening the gate to get out of the courtyard, however, turned out to be an insurmountable obstacle. Or at least I hadn't yet managed to surmount it when a stout fellow with bushy mutton chops trotted up the sidewalk on the other side and said, "Here, let me help." I should have known. It was Del.

I watched him lift the latch. "Thank you! Am I still that easy to find?"

He nodded sadly. "Yeah . . . holy crap! What happened? Is that spiderweb? Where are your hands?"

"The piasa cut them off," I said, surprised how calm I sounded.

Del swallowed. "What are you going to do?"

Stairs descended a sloping lawn to the parking lot where, I presumed, I was to meet Kori. "Mind helping me down?"

Above us, the few stars shining through the city's light pollution twinkled with sadistic amusement—or so I fancied as I reached level ground. Del spotted me as I walked. Kori had dressed in a denim jacket, T-shirt, jeans and boots and was warily eyeing Troy, who wore a long black coat and camouflage pants and warily eyed her back. Troy turned my way and did a double take. "Holy shit!"

"I can't talk about it here," I sighed. I longed for a silencing spell like Lilith's— and the plumes of an arrow from my ancestors' quill of tricks flashed through my mind. "Is there somewhere close we can go without people, like a park or an empty lot?"

By luck, a neighborhood park was about a block's walk distant. Kori had brought a wool parka that I guess belonged to her stepdad. I gratefully put it on and hastily made introductions. "Everyone here is a friend," I said, and my ragtag crew nodded but continued to watch each other warily.

We made the trek to the park in uneasy silence. The three of them gasped as I made the entire world outside the park fall silent.

"Even folks in the Underside can't hear," I said. They all looked at me quizzically. "You know, the argent lands?" Obviously, none of them had heard either term. "Whatever, it doesn't matter."

Kori first: "How long have you been able to do that?"

"I want to answer all your questions," I said, and that was mostly true. "But we can't stay here long. I have another friend, Gordie, and if he isn't dead already, he's going to be soon. There's stuff I can do to help him and to fix myself, but I have to get it taken care of fast. I'll do my best to explain."

Our unlikely council convened, Del and Troy sitting side by side on the unfancy merry-go-round, me seated at the bottom of the slide, Kori standing by the jungle gym, gripping one of the crossbars as if she wanted to break it free and use it as a weapon. Del was there because he came from a family loyal to mine, and he still held on to hope that I might repair whatever was wrong with the head of our tribe; Troy came out of devotion to Del and nothing more, helping me against his better judgement; and Kori—she couldn't possibly have yet made up her mind what I meant to her, but maybe pity inspired by my horrible injuries and evident grief provided the tipping point that overcame her caution. Maybe my quantum leap in magic prowess impressed them, or maybe they all really did genuinely like me—Lord help them—but when I explained what I wanted to do in the sketchiest of details, they all agreed without questioning me about the why.

I'm always going to be grateful for that. And sorry for all the horrible things that followed.

2

Kori volunteered to carry me. I didn't believe she could do it. I thought that Troy would carry me while Del dashed across silver landscapes and Kori followed.

She turned directly to Troy. "We'll be faster if we all fly, right?"

He nodded, expression grave.

"But how're you going to carry me? Your feet don't work like his." I pointed to her boots to make my point. "You can't grip. No back talon."

Troy interjected before she could answer. "I think there's a way." He turned to me. "It won't be easy, and I'm sure you won't enjoy it." His tone implied, *This is more than you deserve, so put up and shut up.*

So it turned out that Troy and Del met through a caving club based in Christiansburg, Virginia, about fifty miles west of Hillcrest. Their first descent together went deep into a network of natural crevices near Mountain Lake, poetically called Hogs' Hole because farmers used to drop the bones of slaughtered hogs into its depths. Troy programmed for a software company, Del was a college librarian, and they lived together in a house in the backwoods, close enough to the AT to notice when I crossed over that first time.

He swiped a coil of clothesline from one of the patios in Kori's complex and used it to tie a full-body rescue harness on me in under a minute. Hardcore cavers I met at Tech kept multiple carabiners on them just because they found them so damn useful, and Troy was no exception.

While he worked, I learned how Lilith brought me to Kori. In the middle of the night, a woman's voice woke Kori, asking if she knew Nathan Mullins. When half-awake and seriously freaked out she gave a nod, the lights turned on of their own accord, and the voice said, "He's badly hurt and needs your help. Please, don't be frightened." A shadow had engulfed the ceiling, and I lowered out of it, suspended on blue threads, like the ones that wrapped my wrists. Then that darkness covering the ceiling congealed, and there stood Lilith, dressed as I'd seen her. "She was the scariest person I've ever met," Kori said.

"She *is* scary," I said, though reflecting that my own mamaw might be scarier.

Moments later, we flew into the Underside, me dangling like a kitten from a loop gripped in Kori's beak. I couldn't help but hoot and holler the way you do on a carnival ride to vent your fright.

My shoulders and hips started to smart like hell in short order on account of how the harness dug in. I tried a variation on the claws-and-teeth trick— something Alisgida's granddaughter did under curiously similar circumstances, when an avian ally carried her from a battlefield. I lightened my legs and strengthened my arms, shoulders, neck, and back, not with the panther's full might but enough to hold myself steady in that horribly awkward position. And so we flew.

Silver and black flickered past us in a sky as convoluted as wads of crumpled paper. Nothing like a moon showed its face. High above, points of light akin to stars couldn't be trusted to stay in place. Other markers had to guide the way, though Troy had no difficulty navigating. Much larger than Kori, he kept Del tucked close.

Bearing up weight like mine, even redistributed, started to wear Kori out. Carrying offspring or prey wasn't woven into her nature. She descended to a ledge that projected like a diving board from one side of an odd stone spire, set me down, and called her killdeer cry. Troy circled back to join us.

According to my new memories, the ledge where we took our break corresponded roughly with Bluefield, West Virginia, in the Overlands. We hadn't even been airborne an hour—or so it seemed to my still-human sense of time—and we'd covered the equivalent of an eight-hour drive. I asked Troy if I was right about where we were. He shrugged. "Short cut."

Kori stayed in bird form, black bands striping her chest, neck, throat, and brow. She panted, beak open, tongue protruding, wings held away from her body.

"Sorry I'm so heavy," I said. "Crossing over and back might help."

She acted on my suggestion, and it did help. She still panted but not as hard. "I'll be ready soon." She cocked her head, red-brown eyes scanning our environment, and trilled. "All of this, it's . . . it's beautiful. And it's really, really weird, which I also like."

"I'm glad you're getting something positive out of this," I said.

"I've never gone so deep into the silver that I've lost sight of Wilkes-Barre," she said. "I didn't want to get lost. I had no guides, you know." She cocked her striped head, her eyes growing redder. "If I met someone who might know their way around, I didn't get to know them for long."

"That's going to change," I said. "After tonight, and from now on."

She cocked her head in the other direction. "How can you be so sure?"

I let a nervous laugh slip. "I don't guess I am that sure. I'm trying to be the 'Little Pawless Panther that Could.'"

She replied with a nervous laugh of her own. "At least that wasn't a crazy answer." Half to herself, "I don't guess you're the crazy one."

I picked up on who she meant. "I'm so grateful you're here, but if you don't want to be here, I have no right to demand that you do this."

To my shock, she talked over me. "I cannot stand that you left my sight and this happened to you."

"You can't hold yourself resp—"

"Whatever you need me to do, I'll do."

I took a deep breath and said, as much for my sake as hers, "Once we get Gordie away from him, we end this—" A half-assed speech queued up in the jukebox of my mind, thanking her profusely for joining me in this crusade even though she hardly knew me and knew Gordie not at all. Thanking Del and Troy for being so doggedly helpful when I'd dealt them nothing but hostility in our first encounters. My fear for Gordie and white-knuckle terror of what the piasa had done to him came gushing out of the background, a smothering panic that stilled my tongue.

At the same time, as if invoked with the utterance of Gordie's name, my vision filled with the repeating tarot patterns of Gordie's carpet, spun into kaleidoscopic motion, images from the suites and the Major Arcana revolving around each other in a grand clockwork procession.

The pattern surrounded me on all sides. In the spaces between, blind women crossing sword blades, angry mobs fighting with blazing staves, cups emptying oceans into one another—a scrawny man with tousled hair adjusting his glasses. He, like them, repeated endlessly, part of the swirl.

Gordie! I shouted. *You're alive. We're coming for you.*

His lips didn't shape words, but his smug smile offered all the confirmation I could want. *I knew you would. Glad I was right.*

Where are you now? Where is he? Can you see him?

Why had I thought his smile smug? As he shook his head, I found it wistful, even rueful. His voice in my head again: *I see nothing. To paraphrase the poet, my eyes shall be lifted nevermore.*

To say I reeled might sound redundant with all that constant spinning, but it's the truth. Disembodied, I howled in denial. He fidgeted with his glasses but otherwise held the same sad smile.

My mind at last quieted enough to puzzle out what was happening. *Are you a ghost?*

He started to shake his head but paused. *I was about to say, "Nope, I'm not even a ghost," but then it occurred to me the distinction might be academic. Let's say I'm leftover magic that still works because the late great Gordie Baugh was just that damned good.*

Despite myself, I laughed.

His eyes seemed to widen, and his smile straightened out, though I could swear his expression stayed fixed as a mask. *With any luck, our piasa friend hasn't figured out how to make my magic work. You need to get what's left of me away from him, or he'll become something even worse.*

Can you tell me where his lair is?

His eyes darkened behind his glasses. *Xeno will show you.*

Gordie, I need to do something first. I had no idea whether he could see the condition I was in. *He hurt me really bad, and there's a thing I need to get done before I can fight back.*

Even as I formed the words, the swirling symbols withdrew to somewhere out of time and sight.

"... we end this—" I gasped and staggered.

"Nathan!" Kori crossed over to human but not fast enough to keep me from falling. I tried to catch myself with my stumps. You can guess how well that went. Once again, I owed Lilith because the binding held and kept pain from exploding through my arms.

"I'm okay. I'm okay!" I shouted as the other three huddled around me. "Little help?"

Troy hefted me by the midsection. Kori inspected my wrappings, wonder creasing her brow as she found no breaks and no blood.

Del, bless him, actually said, "You sure you're up to this, boss?"

The news of Gordie's death, a fresh, raw wound, propelled a wave of rage through me. "Whether I am or not, I have no fucking choice." I looked them over, my motley band. "Thanks, all of you, for coming this far with me. I don't deserve one bit of your friendship." My gaze met Kori's as I finished that phrase.

"Stupid Tigger," she said. "That's my choice to make."

I stretched out my arms to brace for her beak's grip on my harness. "Let's get to the next stop." Softer, I said, "Thank you."

Below, slump-shouldered mountains unveiled a ghastly secret, visible only from above. The cracked open slopes revealed a network of gaping chasms—each crossed by acres and acres of blue-cobweb spirals. We had returned to the Overland, emerging in the Blue Ridge Mountains near the Appalachian Trail, somewhere between the Crabbe's Store and Angel's Leap.

"We need to land," I called. I craned my neck to look up at Kori as she slowly beat her wings.

Troy glided near. "We're back. Creepy enough for you?"

I pulled a face. "Don't know that I'd have tried to hike it if I'd seen it from this angle first."

"You get used to it," Del said, like the ride in his boyfriend's giant clutches was no more stressful than a countryside stroll. "Big webs are everywhere."

"I didn't need to know that," I said to Del. And to the general company, "I need to get down there."

Troy's laugh of disbelief was like a prehistoric shriek. I did sympathize.

I changed my eyes, made them completely panther while keeping the rest of me mostly Nathan. The sensation was unnerving—as if my eyes vibrated cold in their sockets. But I could sort every single strand of webbing and the gaps between with crystal clarity.

Deep, deep, deep under all those perilous nets of spiderweb, I homed in on a figure cocooned at the very bottom of the black hollows.

There were several possible paths down, all much better suited to spiders than to a cat without functioning front legs. "See that furrow in the trees? There, where three webs overlap. I need to get to the bottom. The very bottom. There's a rock that overlooks it with a big cleft right through the middle. Let's land there."

Del, bless his heart, must have used the same trick I'd just employed. "There's something down there." As he spoke, Troy began a careful descent.

Time to bite the bullet. "Yes, yes there is. And I have to see if he'll talk to me."

Kori lingered for a few beats too long. I presumed she'd put two and two together—and then confirmed it once she finally followed Troy to the landing spot. As soon as her beak was free, she crossed over to human. "That's the creep who was chasing after the boy you saved?"

Troy and Del watched in silence. I hoped she wouldn't force me to explain what I had in mind. "The very same creep."

"He's still alive?"

"Yes. He is. He has information I need."

"Since when? Why didn't you mention this before?" Even though this predicament was my fault, the reluctance and worry in her voice upset me. I couldn't afford hesitation here.

A memory asserted itself, one of Elzbeth's, demanding that a reluctant stoat spy for her. To force compliance, she pushed the direction of her recalcitrant scout's thoughts in a manner that I suspected had been done to me over and over again those past few days. The spell felt like brushing fur against its natural direction.

I refused to do it.

"Please," I said, "the only way for me to find out whether or not this thing I need to try is going to work is to actually try it. And to even do that, I need to shake this asshole down for information. *And* if my idea's a bust, we need to be able to get out of here fast and come up with a new plan even faster. Del, I need you near me in case I have to climb out in a hurry. You winged ones need to take special care to steer clear of the webbing. Maybe you should stay airborne."

The confidence in my voice, the sound of a man with a plan, however faked, did the trick.

Perhaps this would all have been easier had I tried going straight to the Crabbes and making my case. Or perhaps they'd have fought full fang to stop me. On balance, I didn't want them to know I was here, much less why. A natural, as Gordie had termed them, of *any* stripe might well object to what I had planned. Hell, even if they approved, knowledge of my plans could be dangerous to them, and I didn't want to risk that either.

Once Del and I were alone on the outcrop, I needed his help to descend. The natural stone path twisted down through the rock at alarmingly steep angles. Crawling made for the safest approach, but that wasn't so easy for me. I poured as much of the panther into myself as I could without changing my outward shape: the strength, the eyesight, the reflexes. Even doing that solved next to nothing.

Del, human himself, offered assistance as a sort of living crutch, only grabbing my harness when he absolutely had to. He stayed a little below me, bracing himself on the closest outcrops of lichen-blotched stone, watching and guiding the direction of my steps with nudges and nods of his bushy-haired head. I privately gave thanks that his concern for my mamaw made him so willing to share this risk with me.

No blue strands obstructed the way. I suspect Herman and Gertrude had never imagined intruders approaching from above. Peering up at the web spirals among the trees, I could see how they were deliberately arranged, parallel platforms like the floors of a high-rise office building.

We emerged from the cleft in the rock to set foot on soft woodland loam.

Spying with the panther's eyes, I stared hard at a clump of webbing, suspended between two venerable oaks. Within hung the still-living remains of the man in the white mask. His breathing was so slight I would never have detected it without the aid of magic. He lay supine in his demon form, slung at an upside-down diagonal, sheets of web coiling around and around his shriveled husk of a body, pasting his arms to his torso and his legs together. His head remained uncovered, a bulky bloom of fangs and eyestalks. Additional strands wound through his horns, functioning like rigging to keep his head fixed in place. Most of his eyes had wilted, fruit gone rotten. Rank drool oozed from several gaping mouths.

The Crabbes were making him last. Had I not been aware of the context, I might have felt pity for the piece of shit. Even knowing the context, I felt a twinge of . . . sadness? Dismay? Whatever you feel when you spot a horsefly twitching in a spiderweb.

"Holy fucking Jesus!" hissed Del beside me. I'd forgotten this was his first sight of my old acquaintance.

"Shhhh," I said. Soft as I could. "Stay here. I need to try talking to him."

Del swallowed. "Can that thing still talk even?"

Breath, heartbeat, bloodflow—still present. One of the monster's good eyes began to twitch. It had heard us and was scanning the dark.

With my enhanced sight, all Del's broad contours shone silver. "I think it best he doesn't see you. Could you go back up the way we came? Just a little ways?"

"What if he tries to hurt you?"

"Hopefully I won't have to get that close." I reflected on my last encounter with the masked man, my claws slicing into him through Herman Crabbe's ring of blue smoke. How quickly that had unfolded. "I doubt he'll even recognize me."

"How long will this take?"

"I don't know. Just bear with me please." I pondered how to cajole further and still avoid lying. "I just . . . I need him to talk, and my gut tells me it will go better if he only sees me."

As if on cue, the demon opened one of its mouths wider to spit out a wet, rasping sigh. That seemed to help Del make up his mind. "Okay. Please, please, don't take long." He clambered back into the cleft in the rock.

I didn't want to do this but putting it off wasn't going to make it more pleasant. Ducking my head to avoid the lowest strands of web, I crept closer to the monster, sidestepping to crouch behind a tree trunk once I'd closed the distance to about nine yards. "You there," I stage-whispered. "Can you still speak?"

The thing made a gagging noise from three different orifices and shuddered inside its cocoon. Folds of skin about its head pulsed, and black saliva spattered on the ground as it tried to twist its head against the bindings to see me better. After a moment, I realized its drought-dry croaks were words: "Help me . . . help me . . . help me . . . help me . . ."

"Be still," I shushed. "Do you want to bring *them* here?"

I didn't need to explain who I meant. The thing stiffened and went quiet, though two of its good eyes darted back and forth frantically, seeking me out.

"Show me you can whisper," I said.

"Who are you?" The monster could indeed whisper—and from more than one mouth. It was one of the most disgusting sounds I'd ever heard.

"A friend," I said, though it made me sick to say it. "I want to help you. But I gotta have your help too." Made me even sicker to say *that*.

"Get me out of here," it whispered, "and I'll do anything you want."

I risked approaching a little closer, shuffling around the tree, still keeping the bulk of the trunk between myself and the demon. "I have to have something from you first."

A frantic whisper: "What? Tell me!"

"I need to know how to be someone like you. How to sculpt myself into a monster. So that I can defend myself. I need to know how you did it, how you made . . . your true self. The form you hunt in."

The thing's eyes squirmed, both the whole ones and the rotten. "Who are you?" it whispered again.

"Ask me that one more time, I'll leave you here."

After a long silence, the thing's multiple mouths let out a pitiable moan. "I can't explain it to you. No one can explain it."

I left my cover. "I bet you can," I said, edging closer. "Think about it. Think about how you'd say it. Think hard. If you want me to get you out." I had to make sure he swallowed the bait whole. "If you can tell me how, there's a bastard I'm going to get. A man with big cat's claws. He tried to kill me just like he did you. I'm gonna kill him first."

The creature in the cocoon grew still. Its neck went stiff. It tried to raise its misshapen head but with little success.

"Yeah. The same bastard who did you got me." I inched a little closer and held one of my severed stumps up in a faint patch of gray light, where his drooping eyestalks could focus on it. "I need to know how to fix myself."

"Let me go," the creature rasped. "Get me out of here."

"Not until you help me. Tell me what I need to know."

"I've . . . never talked to anyone about it . . ."

"Think! How would you say it? And hurry, before those spiders come back."

Bless the little sicko's heart, he did try. "It's like there're two of me. And one of me isn't real, and I can pull that me out of shape like taffy, force it to be what I want—"

I lunged forward to inflict one of the most twisted and evil hexes in my ancestors' arsenal, one that would steal the knowledge I needed, one that required his blood. With my claws taken from me, I had but one method of acquisition left. Nathan and the panther couldn't've been more sharply divided than they were at that moment: Nathan triggered to gagging convulsions as I shoved my face into the slimy, putrid pulp of the monster's head, even as the panther thrilled as my teeth found the weakened throat of the real man beneath the construct and tore open the tepid meat. My mouth filled with hot, coppery broth.

I ran back to the rock as the interconnected webs shook behind me with the force of the masked man's death throes. I assumed the blood smeared around my mouth and streaked down the parka I wore inspired Del's bug-eyed stare until he whispered, "I heard every word. What are you going to do?"

I had no time for the regret that shuddered in my heart. I spoke with a mouth full of bloodied fangs as spectacular as my mamaw's. "Help. Me. Up! To the top!"

He was less gentle as we scrambled back to the crest of the outcrop, though it wasn't entirely his fault. My own impatience drove me to push harder, make unwise steps. Del had to be using a strength more spirit than human, given the many times I slipped only to find him braced firm as a wall behind me.

Against my instructions, Tory and Kori both waited atop the outcrop, fully human. Kori gasped as Del hefted me over the lip of the rift. "What happened to you?"

She dashed to my side as I got my legs under me. "No," I said as she tried to help me up, my voice more panther than Nathan. She backed up a step as Troy grabbed Del's hand and pulled him up.

Kori stared agog at the bloodstains. "I'm almost ready to leave," I said.

From the masked demon's blood, I learned his real name, which wasn't important, but I also absorbed the explanation of how his own magic worked, which he'd been wrestling with as I dealt the deathblow. Though hardly perfect— in my memories, the hex was never perfect—drinking the blood transfused a dose of the creep's understanding of his own nature that delved well past awkwardly chosen words. Enough to teach me what I needed to know.

The piasa had done me a warped favor, mutilating me body and soul. At the edges, where he'd sawed through my forelegs, my true shape had now been rendered malleable.

I tore at the matter of my soul and forced it out of true, discovering quickly that these first alterations would not be enough to accomplish my aims. Giving myself new paws, new claws, wasn't going be enough. I had to fully transform myself.

Holes opened in my soul, tissue stretching and muscle tearing as I pushed my blood-bound self in ways I had never dreamed. These lesions existed only in spirit, not in flesh, shielding me to a degree from the pain. Otherwise, I'd have been bawling like a toddler. No sound ever left my throat, though a huge cat's agonized shrieks slashed constantly through my mind.

I crossed over to the new version of my spirit form.

Kori stumbled back and nearly tripped—but thankfully not over the edge. Troy swore, and Del yowled. "Oh my God! Why? Why?"

While my human self remained handless as ever, the huge cat I became had some new additions.

The normal cat's claws had become more like massive bird's talons, though unlike any you'd find in nature. Thick, knobby pads now ringed my severed wrists—the wounded stumps and Lilith's bindings concealed within their leathery creases. Six talons radiated out from the pads like the tines of a snowflake, each more than two feet long and tipped with a retractable claw. Fully extended, they stretched large as a window, shutters thrown wide.

As my blue fur flattened into silvery scales, I arched my back and rippled my shoulders as reptilian wings unfolded from behind and between my shoulder blades.

Kori was on her feet again, eyes and mouth wide in shock. "You look . . . like *him*. Like the piasa's bastard cousin."

"Still me," I said.

"This is horrible!" Del wailed. "Do you know what the Day Queen will do to you when she sees you this way?"

"What the fuck were you thinking?" Troy spat, arms circled protectively around his partner. "Involving *us* in this?! Del's right. Your grandmother will kill you. And us too for helping!"

Kori rounded on them. "What are you even talking about?"

Memories provided hints. For a natural to carve up their own soul, invent their own shapes in the manner of constructs, was as much a taboo as suicide to a devout Catholic. Repulsion and revulsion that didn't belong to me stirred under my soul's crust, threatening to erupt. I addressed my ancestors as much as I addressed Troy and Del when I said, "I can change this. When we're done, when I'm back together again, I'll turn back the way I was. But I have to be this now, or we don't have a chance."

Del's mouth struggled to find words. Troy spoke for him. "Ain't no *we* in this."

"What the hell is he supposed to do then?" Kori snapped. She studied me closely, head to tail—both of which were still feline, though scaled. What she said next made my heart lurch behind my breastbone. "Teach me how."

"We won't be part of this," Troy said. And Del chimed in: "This is abomination."

"Then *go!*" I snarled.

Troy crossed over, snatched up Del, and they ascended.

Kori didn't watch them go. She jabbed a finger at my broad, silver-scaled chest. "You show me how to do this. Because I don't want to run, and I don't want you to die. We'll be twice as strong against that son of a bitch. We'll bring him down together."

I rumbled disapproval. "No. No, no, no. You have to be . . . *hurt*. Like arms-chopped-off hurt, like me, for this to even be possible." Having now performed the self-augmentation, I knew this to be only a half-truth. The damage to spirit didn't have to extend to the flesh. But I wasn't going to say that. No way. "I can't show you. I'd have to mutilate you first, and no way will I ever do that."

She glared grimly. "It might be worth it. Maybe I should—"

"Stop! Don't even say it!"

She fell silent. A sensation faded from my mind of fur stroked the wrong way. Revulsion boiled hotter as I comprehended the wrongness of what I'd just done to my last ally.

She blinked, clearly confused, and shuddered.

"Please. Don't." I hunkered down on the elbows of my forelegs in a manner more typical of dog than cat. "Don't even think about doing this to yourself. Stay in one piece."

"Okay, I guess." She glared at me for another agonizing, uncomfortable minute. "So now what?"

"We find the piasa." As I said that, I envisioned the worst possible price for confronting that monster again, one I didn't want to pay—even though I was desperate to have Kori by my side. "Or I find him. If you don't want to go through with this, I don't blame you. Maybe you should go—"

"I *do* want to go through with this, asshole. Excuse me. I meant, 'Stupid Tigger.'" She turned her back to me. "I'll do what's my choice to do." And she became a killdeer. Lifted up into the argent spaces. An exhilarating sight. Joy filled my heart. I'm not sure my love for her has ever burned as hot and pure as it did at that moment.

I waited until she shrank to a speck and then sprang after her. My wings pressed air beneath them, again, again. My will made it so. My augmented body flew as if it had always known how.

Below us, a huge spider moved across the treetops, likely Gertrude Crabbe. I hoped she'd be understanding of what I'd done to their long-term meal.

Whatever consequences befell me, I was grateful to be gifted with Elzbeth's strength. In no time, I was on Kori's heels, so to speak. Soon, I overtook her.

I thought of Gordie, who had told me that Xeno would lead the way. I said his name.

In the distant silver haze, a figure rose on four legs, swung a ponderous head, and broke into a trot, receding in the direction I presumed we needed to go. Kori gave no sign she shared the vision. I presumed it was for my eyes alone.

She swooped to follow me as we headed north.

3

Dark fluid trickled down corrugated hillsides, culminating in a silvery lake that would have been crystal blue had we flown over it in real space. And that's what tipped me off that something wasn't right about the whole tableau, for at the northward end of the lake, I did indeed spy a glimmer of blue that widened as we glided closer.

We were deep in the argent lands, way out of normal space, yet along that shoreline, the trees were green.

In the forest of blackened trees from my visions, I had seen in the distance a steeple, rising from a friendlier-looking copse of elms and dogwoods, and heard water lapping at a shore.

Lo and behold, we canted down toward a swath of elms that began at the edge of this blue spot of lake. And from the middle of the trees rose a pale steeple.

Well past the elms gaped a clearing, everything gloriously sunlit, even though the sky contained no sun, no visible source for any of the light. Beyond the clearing marched rows of tall, sickly pines that only held green needles in their uppermost branches. Beneath the needles, I was sure I'd find trunks ringed with dead branches like upturned spider legs.

The knowledge my ancestors gave me allowed me to study this freakish landscape in a way previously beyond my ken. It was akin to the kind of constructed location that Gordie, poor Gordie, had built in Black Salt Gap. A place that the piasa could retreat to and have his uninterrupted way with prey—and what he took from them, he used to shore up his hideaway. Instead of stolen dreams, stolen lives fed this pocket universe. Gordie's curious warning to me about the piasa stealing his power after his death made sudden, horrible sense.

Right after that realization came a notion far worse. Could the mental contacts from Gordie, the visions of Xeno marking the way, been orchestrated by the piasa to lure me back? I couldn't be sure, but even if so, I had an ugly surprise ready for him.

What the chapel might signify to the man who patterned himself after the piasa bird, I couldn't divine. No path led toward it through the trees. As Kori spiraled higher, scouting, I circled down to inspect the incongruous building.

The steeple rose from one corner of a square, peaked roof. The blocks that formed the entire structure, every stone mortared into that grim chapel, were all gravestones. Some bore only inscriptions, some bore angels or crosses, some bore Arabic lettering, some bore Stars of David, some even had stained glass windows inset. *They couldn't possibly all be trophies,* I thought, for if they were, his victims would number in the hundreds, maybe even in the thousands. A darkness beyond the visible spectrum wrapped each stone, a force that cried out with the pain and dimming that comes with death.

I circled the chapel three times. Its four walls rose to identical Gothic arches that framed round windows like giant black pupils. A great furrow in the earth had been dug around its outer walls, a dry moat with dirt walls black as tar. The chapel's macabre gravestone masonry continued down into the pit—and likely below ground. Nowhere did I see a door, much less an opening large enough to let a monster the size of the piasa through.

The piasa had to have constructed this place over centuries, it seemed, given how extensive and detailed. The chamber with the surgery slabs, where he'd killed Gordie and dismembered me, must have lain deep underground.

Kori stayed above me, gliding in a circle that covered more ground, keeping watch.

The actual peak of the roof, boxed between the four Gothic arches, I'd at first thought to be the only part of the structure not made of headstones. Up close, this proved untrue. Broken pieces of tombstone were tumbled into the sculpted concrete, artfully arranged into mosaics that created mirrored portraits of the piasa: two sets of sweeping wings, eight talons, four tusks, two beards.

I wondered if the roof could part like a clamshell to loose the monster within, but I found no seam.

I decided it would be easiest to get him to come to me. I landed on the roof. The stones were ice cold under the pads of my back paws.

I gripped the steeple of the chapel with my talons, King Kong style, leaned back my head, extended my feline jaws, and roared for everything I was worth.

I almost cost Kori her life.

From the rows of blackened pines, a huge shape launched into the sky, straight at the killdeer circling high above. And when the piasa's eyes focused on her, Kori lost her bird shape. Now human, she plummeted.

I raised my wings and surged toward my enemy.

Kori fell without a sound, her head and legs and arms pulled in, rolling in the air, but from that height, a simple tuck and roll couldn't possibly save her. And I couldn't catch her, not even with a rocket strapped to my back.

The piasa drew in his vast wings and dove toward me. I beat my own wings with all the strength in my shoulders. Kori dropped from my line of sight.

I spread my wings their widest as the piasa brought all of those burning blue eyes in his malformed head to bear on me.

I taught him the virtues of self-mutilation.

The ghosts of my ancestors had supplied me with a mental encyclopedia of magics, among them the reflection of hexes. Even a hex that stripped one of all powers of the spirit could be turned on its maker if met with the right frequency and volume.

As I stretched out my silvery-scaled body and extended my shimmering wings to their maximum, the piasa found himself staring into a hundred-score reflections of his own mad gaze. And all at once, he was human.

I could only hope Kori felt his curse lift.

I took my first real gander at the man behind the monster facade, his mouth gaping in a delightful *O* of terror: thick-shouldered, pale as a moon, pink scars for eyes beneath bushy brows in a face flat as a trowel and puckered as a prune from age, bald with a comically crooked nose, crinkled neck bulging from a checkered collar, clad in lumberjack overalls and the heavy work boots that had intimidated me so in the Memorytown Tavern.

The monster who sawed my hands off was just a man, arms windmilling cartoon-like as my front talons closed around him, as they dug into his flesh.

I spun at the fastest speed I could muster—no sign of Kori anywhere—and plunged into the elms, clutching the piasa-man beneath me. I dragged him through the uppermost branches too quick to duck or ward off any blows or stabs or gashes.

Now he was screaming. Music to my kitty ears.

However, he snagged on something too solid for me to pull him over or through. The abrupt halt nearly pried my grip loose.

But not quite.

We ended up in a prickly elm treetop, me with one talon clamped around one of his legs. My back paws, my panther claws, hooked into bark and held fast.

My "friend," however, was in an awful position. The leg I grasped by the thigh was wedged up to the hip in a fork, where two massive branches spread apart. I couldn't see his face, but I saw flailing arms, heard gasping sobs.

I helped him out, pulled his leg loose. An explosion of thrashing leaves as the remainder of his body tumbled away from me.

The shrieks from his throat, the stench of his blood, affected me like ambrosia.

I looked up and witnessed a miracle: Kori gliding above me, restored to killdeer form, which she must have regained when I neutralized the piasa's gaze.

My delight at the sight of her was such that I noticed—a heartbeat too late—that the sound of a body pitching through leafy branches stopped just a little too soon.

Talons raked my belly from below.

I leapt away. Beneath me, the piasa glared with all his sets of eyes, hauling himself out of the trees on his three remaining limbs, lunging at me with his antlers. He'd saved himself from death by retaking his spirit shape.

I hovered above him, my silvery wings flapping, but he remained a monster and kept coming. That gaze that made his victims powerless was something he apparently could use at will, and if he used it now, it would kill him. Unless he killed me first.

I let him know how this was going to go down. I stared him in the eyes, took his human leg in my six-taloned grasp, brought it to my mouth, and bit it in half—let him get splattered with his own blood.

The blood told me what was on his mind, brought me a vision of my limbless body strapped to a slab, my human mouth shrieking as he twisted a metal instrument deeper and deeper between my severed thighs, my intestines spilling out through the opening.

The piasa blasted up from the trees. As grievously as he'd just been wounded, he had no damn business being that fast. He grabbed at me from below, but I shook him loose and lifted up, up, up. He recovered instantly and surged after me, stabbing for my heart with his antlers. I grabbed them with my talons, and we flipped end over end as I tried to sling him away.

He wound up atop me, squeezing my neck with his front talons, his remaining back leg clutching one of my ankles. His immense wings beat like thunder, lifting us both toward the hazy sky. I scrabbled at his massive chest, ripping scales loose. Their knife-sharp edges sliced at the pads of my talons.

Even with a leg missing, his balance was impeccable, and his strength was overwhelming. I beat my wings frantically, trying to capsize him, flailing with my loose back paw in hopes of striking his belly. He dug his talons into the muscles of my neck, and when I left off tearing at his chest to rip at them, he lunged upward and let go of my back leg, whipsawing my neck with intent to break it. Bones in my spine ground together in exquisite agony. My wings flopped without coordination, and I squalled in pain.

Then he screamed and let me go.

I fell nearly to the treetops before I reoriented and regained altitude. I hurled myself at the piasa, who had climbed high in the air, raking talons and swinging antlers at Kori's darting form. She kept fluttering just out of reach, and as I drew near, I spotted a bloody hole where the eye in the back of his head had been.

She jabbed with her beak, trying to add more to the tally, but the piasa parried too quickly with the prongs of his antlers.

He had not tried to make her human, though he could easily have killed her if he did—so he must have known I'd be back in an instant. He tried to grab her neck like he'd grabbed mine. She barely slid her head out from between his talons before darting away.

I was directly above him now, so I contracted my wings and dove.

He sensed me coming and did the same.

He plunged toward the pines, toward the exact place he'd sprung from, me a full body-length behind him. Our trajectory plummeted right at the real entrance to his lair: ringed by the tallest of the haunted pines, an effigy of the piasa's face with its lower half hinged open to either side, a yawning gate below blind eyes of blue stone. He dropped through the mouth into the dark gullet beneath. The gate swung closed but not fast enough to keep me out. By the time it occurred to me that charging head on into the piasa's labyrinth might indeed be a terrible idea, I was already sealed in the darkness with him. The entrance hall rapidly narrowed to a more human scale, and I gathered my prey had shifted size accordingly to give me the slip.

I hit the floor running, stopped to track my quarry. The panther's senses were on highest alert and heard him scurrying down a passage to my right. Given the lopsided rhythm of his footfalls, I took satisfaction that the loss of one of his real legs was causing him difficulty.

As I'd seen Lilith do and as I'd seen the piasa do, I tried to adjust my own scale and form to humanoid without losing my talons and hex protections. I remained a thing of silvery scale, folding my wings back under my shoulder blades. I made my legs nearly human, my head larger than normal, my muzzle extended for the full benefit of smell and bite. My eyes and ears remained feline. My new talons, substituted for a missing piece of me, resisted this half-transformation, shrinking only to about half their original size, and if I hadn't retained the panther's strength in my arms, I wouldn't have been able to lift them.

Chasing the noise, I caromed after my enemy, and Lilith's spell cast on my wounded wrists again proved its usefulness because I didn't trip over my own oversized fingers as I sprinted into the catacombs.

Even the panther's preternatural vision could only make out variations of gloom in the passage ahead. But my quarry must have been in an even worse predicament because he triggered something like a magical light switch, and strings of lanterns hanging from the ceiling flared to life with false flame.

The hall was a horror show.

I ran between walls decorated not just with gravestones but graves. Alcoves the length and height of coffins were carved out of the walls, each containing bones sprawled in arrangements that had nothing to do with their original function and formation. Some smashed to pieces. Some meticulously sliced through and strung together as nightmare marionettes. Several in a row, obscenely positioned with the skull in the bowl of the pelvis. Many with shreds of desiccated flesh still clinging, like algae to driftwood.

There were always more around every corner, enough moldering remains to account for all the stones and then some. But instinct told me that I couldn't accept anything I saw as real. These catacombs, this chapel, and even, I suspected, the stones themselves were organically constructed out of dreamstuff—a nightmare setting to aid the piasa in making sure his abducted victims spent their final days in stark, meat-sweetening terror.

And speaking of meat-sweetening terror, if the piasa thought to lose me in the maze, he didn't understand what was hunting him. I might as well have been tethered to him by a rope. Every maimed flop of his flight reached my ears, and the heady smell of his blood had me slavering. Passages branched off right and left, and I dashed right past them, knowing they were wrong turns.

I reached a semicircular chamber where the catacomb's tunnels converged. A short ramp led to an open door. Beyond the doorway, illuminated by light bulbs, were rows of bloodstained slabs—the room where I'd been tortured. It reeked with the scent of my prey.

I sprang through.

The ax smashed against the left side of my face.

He was standing right beside the door. I'd fallen for the oldest fucking trick in the book.

Had the skull he struck been more Nathan than the panther, my story would have ended there. The blade cracked bone. My left eye went dark.

My momentum kept me reeling forward. I stumbled against one of the stone slabs, the tables he used for butchery. The chains heaped upon it clanked and slithered to the floor.

The next table over supported a mound of bloody meat and bone fragments, a skinned skull balanced atop in it a nauseating mockery of a memorial—a pair of glasses nestled askew on its glistening face, a wad of bloody, blond hair stuffed in its mouth.

Heart pounding, mind shrieking, I grabbed the edges of the slab in my talons and, powered by adrenaline, lifted it completely off its base, spilling Gordie's remains. I spun, catching the multi-eyed and antlered piasa-man with both arms raised, his wicked five-foot axe poised to split my spine.

The slab struck him in the midriff. The velocity and weight swept him off his feet—he had only been able to grow a vestigial spindle of a leg on short notice, little more than a stilt—and he and the slab struck the wall as one. The slab smashed into four pieces with a demolition-loud crack.

I didn't wait to see if he got up. I grabbed another slab and hurled it to join the rubble of its compatriot.

But if being crushed against a wall by six hundred pounds of rock slowed the piasa down, he didn't show it. He was already up on his crazy legs, one wide as a tree trunk, one skinny as a sapling, and running pell-mell for the door at the other end.

The ceiling was low, but I sprang anyway, returning to my full size. The racks of tools and torture implements and mildew-stained sinks and meat lockers blurred past as I expanded to fill the room like a demented feline Alice from Wonderland.

My talons ripped his overalls just as he made it out the other side of his custom abattoir. My roar was a curse.

He slammed the door behind him.

I smashed it from its hinges.

He was hobbling up a narrow set of stairs toward a spooky violet radiance.

The flood of adrenaline kept me from fully registering how badly my head hurt—a good thing since there was no time to cross over and heal. My entire awareness homed in on catching the piasa before he could escape.

When he reached the top of the steps, something else appeared there—a twisted creature made completely of spirit stuff, about the size of a pit bull, hairless and pink as a rat's tail.

Didn't see that one coming, though Gordie's non-ghost had warned me. The thing resembled a Xeno reborn from radioactive acid—maybe it was the piasa's crude attempt to repurpose Gordie's construct. It had no eyes, and its face was all muzzle and twisted teeth.

It snarled and hopped down the stairs to greet me.

To keep it in sight, I had to turn my head and track it with my right eye—and the sharp spike of pain at the base of my skull reminded me that I'd been given whiplash only moments ago when the piasa tried to snap my neck in mid-air.

The creature sprang, aiming for my throat.

I caught it in one talon. It snarled and slobbered, and the saliva burned. I gripped it in both outsized hands and ripped it apart, and as a memory triggered, I tossed in a single power word that undid its magic, hopefully permanently preventing my enemy from reforming it and retro-engineering more.

I dashed up the stairs and into the chapel tower, a violet glow washing down from the quartet of round windows.

All the piasa had wanted his minion to do was delay me a few seconds. He had reverted to full monster form, batting his wings with a force of wind that flattened me.

As I resumed full crypto-panther and unfolded my wings, he thrust his antlers into one of the big circular windows and crashed through it, a nimbus of white casting him in silhouette as he escaped. Stained glass rained down, covering me with tiny cuts as I rose after him. By the time I reached the window, he had dwindled to a black blotch bound for the lake. I didn't see Kori and could only hope she was safe.

I gained more cuts as I pushed through the window, my back paws lacerated by the glass still mounted in the sill. I jetted after the piasa, flapping my new wings at a speed painful to maintain.

He was too far ahead. He could fly on into the argent lands, and I'd never catch him.

Kori sliced down on him from directly above, straight out of the vast gray nowhere.

He swung his antlers up to meet her. I heard him scream what I once thought were nonsense syllables, when Kori and I had him cornered after I blinded him. I recognized them now as power words. Kori vanished.

I roared. Rage flowed lava-like through every blood vessel, searing every rope of muscle. Wherever he'd sent her, the distraction slowed him just enough to let me close in. And he knew it.

He swung around—so I couldn't pounce on his back—while lashing at me with his tail, a strike I easily ducked. Below him, at the strange demarcation where the lake water moved from blue to spectral gray, an object danced on the surface. I had no time to register details.

The piasa came at me talons first.

We grappled again over the lake, two wounded demons out of a Boschian apocalypse.

My single eye had to do all the work, so vision was a blur of fang and sky, talons and the piebald surface of the lake. We jerked away from each other after a whirl of desperate scrabbling and regained our equilibriums, gliding around each other in cautious circles.

I took a risk and scanned the water for the anomaly. I saw a man. Running on top of the lake. Waving at me frantically.

The piasa punched into my blind side. The points of his antlers speared my belly. I twisted in mid-air to get away from him. His talons tore at my haunch, my ribs, but I broke loose and flew sideways. He kept pace, staying on the side of me that couldn't see.

With my good eye facing the lake, I spotted the man again, standing sure as Jesus on the surface of the water, an inexplicable glare of not-sunlight flashing off his glasses. Gordie.

He waved his arms back and forth in unison, like a marshaller on an airport runway, signaling a plane to land. He kept the gesture up as the water around him began to scintillate. His eyes made contact with mine. He smiled broadly, happy as a thirteen-year-old tramping through the woods with his only friend. I felt the connection, a wordless mélange of regret, gratitude—a farewell.

I drew my wings to my sides and dove right at him as he faded away.

I wonder if the piasa saw the same thing I saw as he lunged after me. If he did, I can't imagine he understood what he was seeing because I sure didn't.

Where Gordie had been, the waters brightened, and a geometric shape etched itself on the lake surface: a design akin to an eye, its pupil right where Gordie had stood smiling up at me. The shape was familiar, though I had no time to think about why because I hit with meteor speed and was promptly dozens of feet under.

And immediately regretted it.

Below me, a leviathan drifted up—a monstrosity huge as a submarine. Through the murk rose an immense, hideous maw with rows on rows of teeth, big as my own talons. My wings weren't made for swimming, but I did my damnedest to propel away.

The lake monster listed at an angle, no urgency or purpose to its motion, and I could see how its misshapen head was girded by eye sockets and how every eye had been ripped free, reduced to tendrils of flesh. What drifted below me was an immense corpse. One I'd seen before.

Something glowed in the murkiest depths of the lake, an outline in the shape of a human eye, the same shape I'd just seen on the lake's surface. The shape of the pool in the Silver City where I'd last seen Mews.

I had no time to sort heads nor tails, only to roll with the madness.

I swam for the surface and sucked in a wet gulp of air.

The piasa was ready for me.

He'd pulled up short, beating his wings to tread air, so the talons of his three intact limbs stayed poised just inches above the water. He grabbed my wounded head in a vice grip, crushing my skull into a ball of bestial agony. I floundered, scooping water with my wings, as he ground the breaks in my bones together and shoved my face back underwater.

Immediately, he let go, howling nonstop.

I'm amazed I had enough sense or stamina left to sputter back to the surface. The piasa was flapping its wings with all its might, thrashing its tail through the water—all of his inhuman eyes bulging, that bearded mouth with its wicked tusks stretched disturbingly wide as he cried out. But as much as he strove, he couldn't lift off. Something in the water had hold of his good rear leg.

Below the surface, an orb glowed.

I kept my throbbing skull above water and stared agog, confused and fascinated by my enemy's struggle. He redoubled his efforts to lift off, succeeded in rising just enough that his trapped leg pulled the creature gripping it up to the surface.

I beheld that muscular lion's leg, blue and bloody, clamped in the jaws of a freakishly large and incredibly ugly fish, one with an angler's tentacle sprouting from its brow, a glowing orb at its end.

The absolution requires one last atonement that won't be ours to see.

Had my mamaw known all along what awaited Mews at the end of the ritual? How could that even be possible?

Were it not for the way the knowledge of my ancestors had enhanced my perceptions, I could never have marked when the piasa's eyes re-lit with that power-suppressing curse. But I did notice. All the blue orbs deforming his face regained that mad pinwheel stare that had repeatedly terrorized me since we first crossed paths in dreams. He meant to make Mews human again and tear off into the sky.

I heaved myself up in a burst of spell-reflecting scales.

And a trowel-faced man in overalls had time for one more shrill scream before he vanished below the surface of the lake, a cloud of blood blooming to celebrate his final moments.

Warner Mews repaid his moral debt to my family by consuming his first and only living victim. Such is the cruel logic of the Underside.

4

The eye shape made by the pool of absolution lost its glitter and dissipated as I used my wings to heave myself aloft. I struggled to stay airborne, touching down on the bank where the elm trees sunk roots into the water. I became Nathan.

Alone in the piasa's lair, exhausted, my agonies considerably dulled when I crossed over, though not completely. I didn't think about trying to recover my hands, or how long that chapel would hold together with its creator dead. I gave hardly a thought to the further whereabouts of Mews, in the shape of monster or man, when he didn't emerge from the water—though I wallowed in a quagmire of bewilderment at the mystery of his intervention. I simultaneously quailed at the thought of explaining to my mamaw what had happened to the ghosts on her farm and burned with a hungry delight, knowing they'd been avenged. I thought how Gordie and I had teamed up for one last adventure in the wilderness, and I wanted to weep. I wondered where the piasa had sent Kori, and fear spiked a stake through the eye of my emotional hurricane.

But I could find Kori. I knew a seeking spell. I just needed more of my own blood.

I sighed. What was one more wound? I began again to cross over, making my fangs grow.

A noise far above. A killdeer call.

I opened my eyes, leaping from Nathan to the panther, my wings beating.

A disturbance overhead. For a fraction of a second, I believed a sun had appeared—though instead of illuminating, it ate light. What had tricked my eye was the phenomenon's circular shape. It was a blue-limned ring, like the one I'd seen Herman Crabbe open six nights and a full lifetime ago.

When I was high enough that the piasa's domain spread below me like a map, its edges of blue and green fading to silver and black, four figures came into view within the smoky outline of the gate. Lilith stood on the other side, wearing a high-collared gown. Above her hung three people wrapped head to toe in electric-blue webbing, two men and a woman suspended upside down.

"What a mess you've made of yourself," she said.

The shorter of the two men, Del, twitched inside his cocoon, shouting muffled syllables made high-pitched with fright. Broad-shouldered Troy hung completely still. No sign even that he breathed. A tuft of Kori's blonde locks dangled free.

I shouted, "What the hell are you doing?"

"Solving many problems at once," Lilith said, projecting her nasal voice as if she declaimed to a sold-out theater. "Showing you your place."

Her smile sparked a rage in me like an exploding sun. I roared, ignoring the ache in my skull, and rushed right at her.

She crossed over to black widow as I passed through the ring, levitating as if raised on wires, and Kori, Del, and Troy were yanked out of my sight as if drawn up into a fly tower by stagehands.

I was no longer in the sky above the Gravestone Chapel.

Around me, grassland stretched in all directions, a strong wind causing the chest-high grasses to ripple in great waves. Though sunlight bathed the field, clouds billowed overhead, roiling unnaturally fast. The entire mise-en-scène had the feel of a movie on fast forward. The air crackled as if every particle was charged with that cold, jarring spirit magic.

I had been to this plain many times in memories not my own. And once in person, as Hubert's shrieks drowned out the susurrus of the wind.

Lilith dangled above me, body perpendicular to the ground, all eight limbs outstretched, black eyes gleaming.

She spoke in a normal tone of voice, yet it was louder than thunder. "You see, sister. It's just as I told you. He's an abomination. A shame to your family."

I started to demand what she meant when I heard a low rumble from the grass. Deep in the ever-swaying stalks, a pair of green eyes blazed at me.

I'd been tricked. I'd been had.

I became myself again. My skin brown, my heart fluttering, my hands missing.

"Mamaw," I said. I held up my severed wrists. I think I was crying. "Look what he did to me."

My grandmother stood from the hiding place where she'd crouched, and as she did, she continued to rise, swelling into a towering giantess—a monster out of a fairy tale, green eyes focused on me, pupils contracted to vertical slits, her muscular arms ending in nails like sickles, baring fangs as she spoke again.

"What," she asked, "have you done to *yourself*?"

"Tell her!" I shouted at Lilith, but the Night Queen had disappeared.

I stared dumbfounded into green eyes wide as cars, a mountainous cascade of hair that shimmered from gray to black. My mamaw crossed over, became a great cat in full regal glory, the largest beast I'd ever seen, four stories high at the shoulder, her hide golden as the sun. Her gaze never wavering, she again rumbled the word I hadn't quite heard the first time.

"Abomination."

She sprang, eclipsing the sky.

PART SIX:
BONES IN THE GRASS

SIX DAYS AND NIGHTS HAD PASSED SINCE A GHOST-BOY CALLED TO ME FOR help on the Appalachian Trail. This is how the seventh day began.

Instinct moved ahead of thought, and I took to the air while Elzbeth was still in mid-leap. As soon as the majestic panther that my mamaw had become landed on all fours, she bounded after me.

I fled higher and faster, soaring toward the roiling clouds, and she chased me on the ground, never lagging, in what must have been the strangest cat-and-bird pursuit in the history of the world: a great panther, four stories tall at the shoulder, sprinting after prey nearly a third her size, a silver-scaled catbird with reptilian wings.

She leaped at me again. Her paws brushed my tail. *STOP IT,* I yowled. *STOP IT, MAMAW.*

FOOL CUB, she roared.

The clouds enveloped me in churning fog. Phantom creatures tumbled within like the dreams I'd seen trapped in Gordie's tank, everything from horses to worms to eagles to eels, crawling and swimming over one another in the cloud current. I kept climbing, hoping to get out of Elzbeth's reach, praying to spy an escape route.

Every particle of air that touched my scales charged up to a burning static shock, and in the reptilian part of my brain, I understood this was Elzbeth's will and Elzbeth's fury unleashed.

The entire world flipped like a flapjack.

I mean that exactly as it sounds. The ground and the sky swiveled, so one moment, I was escaping through the clouds while the next I was rocketing upside-down straight into the windswept field with Elzbeth in mid-leap, bearing down on me from above.

I dodged her and corrected course just in time to keep from splattering like an egg. In the near distance, I glimpsed a cluster of large white rocks, the bones of one of my ancestors, slain in the shape of a great cat. White boulders dotted the endless plain, and the ghost memories I had absorbed informed me none were stone. All were bone—the ribs and femurs and tarsals and skulls of countless giant felines, cracked, gouged, and strewn throughout the windswept grass. This was the place where all the great cats in my line ended their disputes in blood and death.

Elzbeth touched down right behind me and snapped her jaws at my retreating tail. No way I could outrun or outfly her now.

I landed, skidding to a halt on my hind legs. I raised my front talons to ward off a strike from her claws, sure to slice me open like a mewling fruit. *STOP!*

She clamped me in her jaws, engulfing my head in moist, oven-hot darkness. Her teeth crushed my chest, my back, my wings.

She shook me. My flesh tore. I cried in pain.

She tossed me like a toy top. I spun, both wings broken, and bounced when I landed.

Stunned and winded, I lay in wait for the killing blow, however it fell, tooth or claw. Nothing could stop her from killing me.

Immense hands clamped around my neck. Not paws with claws extended. Her hands, fingers fully human, still big enough to lift a forty-foot-long birdcat by his neck. She hefted me, so my back paws dangled a yard above the ground, the cords in her neck bulging with the effort of strangling me. With a snarl, she pitched me like a rag doll.

This time, I landed on all fours. Beside me, the skull of a giant cat gleamed in the sourceless light. The vacant sockets of its eyes yawned in a sad testament— that even in the argent lands, death is death. And the dead are forgotten.

My mamaw stood ten times as tall as the woman I remembered from the farm, her skin more gold than clay-red, her wide body rippling with muscle beneath her waist-cinched robe of animal hide. Her green eyes burned with fury around the dagger slits of her pupils.

"How could you *do* this to me?" she snarled.

I winced from the pain as I retucked my wings. "I didn't—"

"Our kind will never see what you've done to yourself," she bellowed, "see this filth you've let yourself become."

I moved to put a giant plate of jutting shoulder blade between myself and her. "Mamaw, listen to me—"

"Killing you myself is the dearest mercy I can offer."

I kept backpedaling. She kept advancing. By now, my mouth had taken over. "But this doesn't make sense! You knew, didn't you? You knew that Mews was going to kill the piasa. So that can't be all that you foresaw. You must have visions, like me! You saw that the piasa was going to chop my fucking hands off! That he was going eat your husband's ghost—"

Her fangs visibly grew. "No. You. You *let* him die!" Her voice grew loud enough to shred my eardrums. *BECAUSE OF YOU HE'S GONE—*

She grabbed for me.

By my front feet, a vertebra tilted, one from the part of the spinal column found between the shoulders, possessed of a long, protruding spur. I seized it with my talons and swung at her head. She caught it with both hands and lifted. As my back feet came off the ground, I kicked at her abdomen, reached flesh, and drew blood.

She hurled me away, roaring so loud the ground shook and the bones shifted. I rolled in the grass, came up on my feet.

She came at me again, still human, still giant.

By a miracle, I still clutched my impromptu club. Beside me lay an immense scapula, brittle and ancient. I used the vertebra to smash the shoulder blade into several huge pieces. I snatched up the largest and sharpest of them.

I couldn't believe what I was about to do. I wanted to bawl.

My mamaw roared and rushed me, grabbing at my face as I stabbed up with the shard of bone. I felt it sink in up to my deformed knuckles. With a scream, I recoiled, drew the blade back, and stumbled against a pile of ribs. Nearly two feet of the shard's length was slick with my mamaw's blood.

She clutched her side where more blood bubbled through her fingers. And panted. And grinned at me. Her voice a basso rumble. "Too scared to fight me?"

I became completely human. I lifted my severed stumps. "Stop it."

She backhanded me with all her strength. The shock and pain triggered instinct as it had before. I understood how my powers worked, and I halted my sudden flight in mid-air, the panther again—my healed wings outstretched and flexing just enough to keep me hovering, level with her midsection.

DISGUSTING, she roared as she tackled me from above. She pinned me beneath her, both hands squeezing my neck with an iron grip. She slammed my head against something that crunched with the impact. I raked both my front talons down her sides, deep enough to strike bone, and gashed her belly with my back claws, shredding skin, tearing meat, spilling blood.

She stayed locked in place, crushing out my breath, making my sight go black. Her blood soaked my scales.

She could have cut off all my air, all the flow of my blood, but as badly as the pressure of her fingers hurt, I remained aware and struggling.

I comprehended then the full depth of her dementia, the utter wrongness of everything she was doing. As I tore at her in every way my mutant body would allow, she did nothing to defend against it, just kept single-mindedly, brutally, stupidly attacking, going for the greatest pain and least effect.

She wasn't trying to win. She was forcing me to fight for my life.

She was forcing me to *kill* her.

"Why are you doing this?" I croaked.

She roared to shake the earth, letting go of my throat with one hand, so she could use it to crush my muzzle with her huge, human fingers. The pain was white-hot, was too much.

I raised my talons to her neck. That close to her, focused with life-or-death level adrenaline, a glimmer caught my eye, the same silver sheen I'd noticed in her hair when we spoke in her bedchamber.

Were it not for the knowledge of magic I had gained in the cavern, I don't think I would ever, ever have understood what I was looking at, what it really was. Gossamer thin, even with Elzbeth grown to giant size, thousands of pale strands spun tight through my mamaw's hair, woven all through it with such subtle delicacy as to be all but invisible, the slightest hint of silver when the light struck just so, easily mistaken for the natural graying of age. These threads were so sophisticated in their sorcery that they stayed wound in my mamaw's hair whatever form she took—in the same way Lilith's webbing stayed around my wrists.

Melissa and Bill, who had acted so strangely: I'd noticed the very same sheen in their hair.

A single strand—so economical in its power, so microscopically thin, that only one of my line might have a chance of seeing it—led off in surreal fashion from the crown of my mamaw's head to some point above, far out of sight into the aether. Whatever, whoever it attached to at the other end, it was a magical connection that needed to be broken.

I swiped my talons through it but to no effect at all. I tried again, and again, I failed.

As I stopped clawing her, Elzbeth hissed and shook me with tremendous force. I fought not to lose sight of the single puppeteer thread, to keep my eyes on it and not her rage-contorted face, focusing all my attention as if my gaze could ignite it.

I spoke a word of power, past my mamaw's palm, and plucked again at the strand. It broke with a lightning crack—loud as Elzbeth's raw shriek.

She let go.

Roars transmuted to squalls, to the screams of a human woman, to sobs.

She was no longer a giant, just a tiny woman so much smaller than the panther. Dust spilled from her hair. Spore-like clouds puffed out from her eyes.

I crossed over to Nathan and reached toward her. The dust motes that alighted on my fingers began to crawl. Crystal mites, tiny spiders no larger than pinpoints. They dissolved and died as I repeated the word of unmaking.

Elzbeth wrenched away from me, both hands clutched to her head. "Mamaw!" I cried, kneeling beside her. Nothing in my life or the lives of my ancestors had taught me what to do to help her.

She convulsed as I watched, helpless, horrified. Her green eyes rolled up into their sockets, and drool foamed from her mouth. I couldn't even take her in my arms.

I stared up at the endlessly churning clouds, unable to watch as my mamaw died a second time.

A gentle hand touched my knee.

Tears had blurred my vision. I blinked to make sure I saw correctly: my mamaw had sat up, was wiping off her face in a rather cat-like fashion. She regarded me, clear-eyed. Her gaze lowered from my face to the web-wrapped stumps of my forearms. Her lips curled back, though her teeth remained human.

The gray was gone from her hair. But for the intensity of her stare and the tremendous strength radiating from her frame, a stranger might have mistaken her for a teenager.

When she spoke, her voice retained its whiskey drawl. "I'm so sorry," she said. "I never meant for anything like that to happen to you."

Her apology took me so far aback, so I skipped out on feeling any relief over her calm demeanor. "What do you mean?"

"It took me over so slow. Months slow. Maybe decades. When I realized I was hexed, it was too late," she said. She spoke carefully, giving me time to absorb the meanings stuffed between the words. "I cut myself and used the blood to call for help. A call to my kin straight from the fires of my heart. That's all I had time to do before the hex took my mind completely away. I didn't know who I was calling to—if there was even anyone alive to help me. Didn't know if it would work at all. Then I forgot I even did it. 'Til now. 'Til you broke the hex."

I shook all over. "How long ago?" But I already knew when, tallying how I became plagued with visions on the NC Tech campus and bedeviled by an inexplicable urge to flee to the mountains. And how by a coincidence that was no coincidence at all, the ghost of my poor cousin Charlie rose from the grave to start his own ill-fated journey home.

"I couldn't say," she said. "Time passes differently in the Silver City. Can you stand?" She had already done so, and even as she asked, she took me by the elbow. Goddamn, was she strong. "We got a lot we need to talk about," she went on, "and a lot of sadness to share. But first, we gotta settle an account. Cover your ears."

She screamed at her mightiest volume. Directly above her, the clouds whipped into a whirlpool, shock waves spreading from the spiral as if the entire sky were a pond and my mamaw had just thrown a moon-sized pebble into its center. Within those ripples, blue turned to black.

As the clouds rolled away, they revealed a night full of spiderwebs. Imagine if all the stars in the Milky Way were strung together with cobwebs. And from those webs, spiders dangled, numerous as raindrops in a storm.

Lilith arched over us in spider form, in all her hideous, graceful glory— venom dripping from her fangs, her onyx abdomen swollen as a hot-air balloon, the black moon in this infested sky.

I had seen this place before too, had a vision of it before I fled the Nesmiths' home.

"Sister!" Lilith's voice came casual as a street-corner conversation, a soft and silken sound that whispered unwanted in my ear while at the same time booming loud as a goddess. "What's this uninvited intrusion?"

Elzbeth's smile was coy as a tiger's. "So it's still *sister*. Is that right? What were you aiming for, witch? Him to kill me, or me to kill him?"

Lilith's legs spanned the heavens. It wasn't one thread that supported her in her night but thousands, stretching to all the celestial corners. "Don't try to claim this was my idea. The only way your people will tolerate one like him is if he *rules* them."

"This *was* your idea," I roared. "Telling me I should make my own claws, luring me here with my friends as bait, knowing what my mamaw would do because she was under your hex!"

Don't take her head on, Little Panther, Elzbeth said, though her lips didn't move. *It's what she wants, how she plays. She thinks ten moves ahead because she could never otherwise best us.*

"I won't dignify that accusation with a response," said Lilith, oh so sweetly. "There's the truth, and there's whatever lies you choose to tell yourself."

"Where are my friends?" I shouted as Elzbeth gripped my shoulder, keeping me human with my feet on the ground. "You let them go!"

"Lilith, deary." My mamaw's raspy voice mirrored Lilith's poisoned sweetness. "Where are my boy's companions?"

With all the legs crawling through the webs stretched across the hellish cosmos, it was hard to concentrate on Lilith's form alone as she hung perfectly still.

"Lilith, deary, I remember *everything*." My mamaw's voice grew a little louder, a little harsher. "Let them go."

"I never had them," Lilith said. "Your grandson falls for simple tricks—"

With a roar, Elzbeth transformed from tiny woman to great panther, sending Lilith scuttling up, but my mamaw didn't pounce at her fellow queen. Balanced for a fraction of a moment on two legs, her massive torso twisted, and one of her titanic forelegs vanished to the shoulder as if she reached into a trick mirror.

Her paw came out covered in webbing, a wriggling spider of smaller size impaled on her claws and three thickly padded cocoons spilling out onto the grass.

She flicked her feline wrist as she fell back to all fours, and then, she was beside me again as a human woman.

The webbing had vanished. A short, mangy-haired man lay in two pieces about twenty yards away from us. Where the cocoons had been, three very familiar people stirred.

I started toward them when Lilith said, "How dare you! I should let the boy's wrists bleed."

Elzbeth grinned. "Try it."

My heart flatfooted in my throat, but nothing changed. The blue strands remained around my wrists.

My mamaw wasn't following her own advice. "See, witch? I'm completely free of you."

"I *don't* understand what you're—"

"Parasites in my head, Lilith darling? What you did to me, this was your cleverest curse yet. I should exact a blood toll from you for every single one of my people who died while I was under the influence of your pests."

"They were not mine, dear Sister Queen. I'll root out whomever made them and put them all to death. We can feast on them together if you like."

Elzbeth's lips curled. "As if you didn't know all along. Your lies are like eggs within eggs, planted in innocent hearts to hatch hordes of vile maggots. They murder their host and lay eggs of their own, and the dead can never know which mouth birthed them."

The Queen of Night's demeanor changed. She lowered in the sky. Behind her, en masse, her brood made their webs tremble. "My patience has run out." Her voice dripped with hate. "Your family owes mine. Especially now with that whelp murdering my consorts and me sparing his life, even saving it." She lowered further, and hundreds of her eight-legged children began their own descents.

Elzbeth waited as that horrifying horde dropped slowly toward us. Del was holding a dazed Troy by the shoulders. Kori, who was up on her knees, met my eyes, her own like saucers.

My mamaw spoke quietly. "We owe you nothing. And you mind your subjects. Lest you forget whose place this is."

And just as she had when I tried to flee, Elzbeth roared and spun the world. Once, twice, three times. I never lost my balance, fixed in place by a will not my own. Kori screamed and so, I think, did Del.

Lilith's army tangled into sheer chaos. As far as the eye could see, huge spiders struggled, piled on each other, their own webs coiled around them. Lilith herself shook violently in her harness of star strands.

"Crazy bitch. You weave so many schemes and counter-schemes you don't know anymore what end is up," Elzbeth said calmly. "Guess what's coming next."

Even as she said it, boulder-sized bones lifted from the grass, falling toward the sky.

From that sky full of spiders came human cries of terror. Lilith screeched frantic words of power.

Like a curtain yanked shut, the roiling cloud cover full of half-seen animals returned.

My grandmother watched the sky a while longer as the bones returned to the earth that cradled them.

She turned to me and shocked me the worst yet, for her cheeks were soaked with tears. She hugged me fiercely, but the ferocity was that of a mother embracing a long-lost son.

"I'm so sorry," she sobbed. "For what I didn't do. For what I did."

Bewildered, I returned her embrace.

As she pulled away, she gripped my forearms where Lilith's usurped spell still kept me whole. "I'll tend to this soon. Make you a mending of my own." Her eyes found mine. "She's right, you know."

I did a double take. "What do you mean?"

"You've crossed a line that our kin will only tolerate if you undergo absolution. And I do not want you to attempt such a thing. I don't want you in danger anymore. There are ways you can come to visit me in the Silver City. Secret ways. I'll teach them to you."

I tried to make a joke of it. "If there's one thing I've learned, Mamaw, it's that I'm always in danger."

She didn't laugh. Her gaze and her grip on my arms grew more earnest.

I nodded toward Del. "I think maybe our fellow cats can come around with time. But what will do you about Lilith?"

She answered as if by rote. "We are forbidden to harm our counterparts. And that one is always seeking ways around the rules. It is a fact I live with, no different than breathing. I hold myself to blame that I wasn't more watchful."

"But—" I couldn't believe what I was hearing. "But she made all this happen. My friend Gordie dead. The ghosts of our ancestors gone." I raised my arms. "The piasa butchering me."

My mamaw was already shaking her head. "No, Nathan. My magic, my call to kin, set you on this course to cross that brute's path. That's not Lilith's doing. That's mine." I couldn't tell if she held more anger for herself or for her enemy. "Lilith just saw opportunities. That's her way."

My jaw worked. I wanted to shout at my mamaw, to slash at her for blaming herself. I couldn't bring myself to go that far. "She can't be that damn smart. She actually thought I would kill you."

My mamaw looked away. "She knew I would let you."

As I stared, poleaxed, she went on. "I've been so long without Henri," she said. "And now, because of my own magic, there's nothing left of him at all." Her eyes told me she wanted me to grasp every nuance of her meaning. "If her plan had worked, maybe it wouldn't have been so bad."

And the longing in her eyes broke my heart.

"No, Mamaw," I said. "I'll never, ever do such a thing. I've hurt you enough already."

POSTSCRIPT:
QUEEN OF NIGHT AND DAY

THE EIGHTH DAY HAPPENED TO BE MY TWENTY-FIRST BIRTHDAY, AND YOU can bet I had a drink or ten.

On Halloween, I told Kori everything. Talking to her about the night I spent with Lilith—what I did with the Night Queen and what she did to me—was the hardest, scariest thing I'd ever done. That's because I was sure that once I finished the telling, if she let me finish, I'd never see her again. Our new lives in a snowbound Oregon town, where we didn't answer to the names Nathan and Kori, had barely gotten started.

She wasn't cool with the revelation. I can tell you that. She was angry at least as much at me as for me. But she didn't leave me.

After the Queen of Night and her brood beat feet, my mamaw's green eyes had blazed across that wind-blown, bone-strewn plain as she warned me and my friends that we wouldn't be safe while Lilith's humiliation burned hot. We had to make ourselves difficult to find, as humanly and magically as possible. I grasped right away what that meant, and I'd been sure Kori would never go along with it. But she did, not entirely unhappily.

The first hexes I taught Kori were the ones that feel like stroking fur the wrong way. And the next were more permanent in their effect, feeling like peeling back skin and replacing the layers with your own concocted pelt. Our earliest days in this new life were spent traveling via Underside shortcuts to the necessary places in the Overlands, tying up loose ends in the minds of humans whose lives intersected with ours.

To my shock, Lilith told the truth about Bill and Melissa. They remembered next to nothing about the circumstances surrounding my visit. With a little additional push, they forgot me altogether, and though that made me sad, I have to believe their lives were better for it.

I confess, I expected to take grim satisfaction at snipping my mom and dad out of my life, but I've lain awake a surprising number of nights after, haunted by their vacant eyes. Kori did not share the same ambivalence toward her own mother, and when we left her apartment complex, she flew off without telling me where she was going. Given the catastrophic effect that crossing paths with me had wreaked on her life, I didn't chase her down. I had no right to demand she come back to our trailer in Oregon if she didn't want to. But she did.

The truth is, though we'd been through hell together, we barely knew each other. Having her around made me happy, and I think the same was true for her—and at that time, that was enough for an unspoken agreement to face the travails of the refugee life as a team. She took a job waiting tables at an upscale steakhouse. She used the hexes I taught her to get the job and told me afterward that doing so made her feel a little scummy. Though only a little.

At home, I spent my hours getting used to living without hands.

Whether or not Lilith lied about my hands being recoverable, I don't know, but I never got the chance to find out. The piasa's chapel and surrounding lands disintegrated while I fought to keep my hex-ridden mamaw from murdering me. As with the Nesmiths' BMW—the real one, not the illusory bait the piasa set for me—we never found what the piasa took from me.

Because my ancestors' memories hinted it was possible, I worked on making myself prosthetic hands. Certain kinds of wood possess innate magic—which is why the Occisors who hate our kind wield carved spears and arrows against us. I started there, using hawthorn. Carving the right runes using the panther's immense, unnatural talons turned out to be really, really hard. Again and again, I had to restart from scratch, so to speak.

Coming up with fake IDs and social security numbers, the more traditional ways to cheat the American system, those were complex magics of a kind my ancestors couldn't help me with. Luckily for us, Troy and Del had some insight into how those more mundane back channels worked. They came to check on us a couple of times during those thrilling, bewildering, frustrating early weeks. I showed them how I could lift a Pabst Blue Ribbon out of a case. They made faces at my choice of beer.

I asked whether or not my efforts to "hide my light under a bushel" were doing any good. They assured me my concealment wards were working, that they would never have been able to find me and Kori had they not already been in on the secret.

The next week I took a job busing tables at the same restaurant where Kori worked. My story to explain my strange prosthetics, and my accent, was that I had an accident working in a textile factory back in Tennessee. Folks got used to me and quit asking. Time passed.

Such was the general state of things when the news arrived.

Kori and I had spent a long Saturday night at the restaurant, at the height of summer. An unusually clear evening left the rocky faces of the young, colossal mountains bare, and the setting sun painted them in fiery hues. By the time our shifts finished, night had settled in, and the stars seemed to tremble. Had we taken a walk on the beach only twenty miles distant, their glitter would have shone glorious. Romantic as it would have been, we were both too tired for such a walk.

As we pulled up to our humble mobile home, huge eyes flashed in the headlights of our rust-spotted beater car. The eyes belonged to Del. He paced back and forth in the yard—and continued to pace in human form after we let him inside.

Kori asked before any of us sat down, "Del, what's wrong? What gives?"

He blurted out, "Lilith has a child."

I guess I didn't want to deal with what he was really saying because I laughed. "Doesn't she have a whole lot of children? Like, hundreds? I mean, she's a couple hundred years old. And she's a spider."

Kori didn't laugh. She watched me, her mouth a grim line.

Del didn't know about what happened between me and Lilith, and if he had a trickle of suspicion, he didn't let on. The threat to the balance of power was what had him so upset. "No, no, this isn't one of her dalliances with her spider toys, where she plays with her food. She's claiming this is a human child. A daughter. I mean, sure, they're all as human as me or you if you want to get technical—"

"Del—"

"But this is different. She's claiming her child is rightfully next in line to rule the Day Side of the Silver City. Your grandma, she's—"

My mamaw had told me that Lilith's schemes ran ten steps ahead of what everyone else had on their minds. I still, even then, didn't fully understand why the Silver City mattered so much, but small white spiders crawled at the corners of my mind as I contemplated what Lilith had done to lay claim to it fully for herself.

"She's not disputing it, Nathan. She hasn't said a thing. The only person brash enough to ask her outright hasn't been heard from since."

Oh, yes, *then* I understood what that mesmerizing, terrible night was all about.

But I didn't share that revelation with Del and neither did Kori. We thanked him for warning us and filled the rest of his visit with alcohol and small talk.

Not long after he was gone, we made love, a wordless, jittery, perverse, desperate act, seeking comfort and distraction in sweat and galvanized nerve endings.

Hours later in the dark, both of us still wide awake, Kori asked, "Does your grandmother know what happened?"

I honestly didn't know what my mamaw knew. So I shrugged. I didn't need to speak since Kori could see me fine.

"What are you going to do?"

I surprised myself, how quick I said it. "I don't want Lilith to raise my daughter." A long silence followed.

"Then we'll need to figure out how to get your daughter away from her," Kori said.

No point in saying I didn't see how that was possible. I knew Kori saw the situation the same way I did, but there the idea hovered between us, bearing claws, dripping poison.

Over the weeks that followed, we began to hatch a long-game plan of our own.

"THE CRUELEST TEAM WILL WIN"[1]

A spider with a leg span wider than my outstretched hand squeezed out from the space behind the light switch—and spread its wings.

I froze, finger still on the toggle. Behind me, the dust-draped ceiling fan hummed to life, the lightbulb beneath it flicking on to paint the monster with my shadow. The marks on its body formed a single staring eye above a screaming mouth. Two more false eyes glared red across its dragonfly wings. Another hideous little soul turned demonic, yearning to grow into something far worse.

I showed it my own spirit form.

It made good on its threat and lifted into the air, but its terrifying modification only made my task easier, and my beak closed around it. The poison leaking from its crushed body spread warmth as it slid down my gullet.

The first time I ate one of its kind, that poison made me quite sick. I underestimated how sick I'd get. I told my sweet neighbor across the hall that her three-year-old wouldn't wake up screaming anymore, that her apartment was safe again. Minutes later, I drove to work at the fabric store, nearly crashed my car just trying to park, staggered inside, and barely made it to the bathroom stall, dry heaving over the toilet while my manager clucked behind me. *Leeanne, are you okay? You need the hospital?*

---

1   "The Cruelest Team Will Win" originally appeared in *Corvidae* (ed. Rhonda Parrish, World Weaver Press, 2015) and is set in the same world as *Trail of Shadows*.

But when you eat a ghost, there's nothing to throw up. And the kind of poison a tainted soul puts in you—no doctor can help.

So I told her I'd be fine, that it was just food poisoning, and I'd be over it soon. I couldn't go home. I needed the money too much. So I sucked it up and headed out to the sales floor. And then I found out something else about that poison. When the nausea subsided, a euphoria kicked in, not far removed from the time I mixed my prescription muscle relaxant with peach schnapps, a lava-lamp glow oozing through me. All day, I fought the urge to take my blue jay form right there in the store. My wings, slices of sky, would stretch longer than the fabric tables, and then I'd fly right through the ceiling like a ghost gone giant, melding my blue with the blue above.

I did that once, a couple years ago when I was less weighted with sad knowledge of the world: quit a job at a print shop by going blue jay right in front of my skeevy boss and flapping away through the cinderblock wall into the shimmering heavens of the spirit world. But when I returned to earth, I still needed to pay for my classes, to cover my rent, to eat.

That sad weight kept me grounded that first delirious day of spider poisoning, but the sensation was addictive. The very next time I was asked to "cleanse" a house, I found another spiderling. It was strange that I found another right away and not a perfectly run-of-the-mill, human-looking haint, but it shot out at me from under a closet door, its mutation a second set of legs tipped with pincers, and I didn't hesitate to eat it. And the next one I found and the next one. And the next and many nexts since. And this time too.

The urge hit my brain straight away to keep my form but shift completely into the spirit world and then rise up through the floors and ceilings of this rambling house as if it were mere mirage—soaring at the noonday sky like an ocean dive in defiance of gravity.

But I had already collected my upfront fee from the charming elderly couple that lived there, and now, I needed to collect the rest of it. Classes, rent, normal non-ghosty food. I didn't charge a lot, but it would at least give the debt dog a bone to run off with and chew on.

Emma Manderley was a frequent customer at the fabric store who knew about my specialty in clearing malevolent influences—the word gets around, you know, among those who care about such things—and the Manderleys had just enough sensitivity between them that they would know the thing that had bedeviled their sleep was gone without my even needing to say so.

They were waiting in their station wagon, sitting in the driveway with the radio playing. I had told them I only needed a few minutes. My magic never took more than a few minutes. I looked forward to their relieved smiles.

My brain buzzing pleasantly from the poison, I climbed the spiral stairs out of the musty basement, traipsed through the slightly less-musty ground floor, and glanced out the front window as I crossed the living room.

The station wagon was completely blanketed by a substance like dense strands of shimmering gauze. A slender woman in slate-gray business attire—knee-length skirt and matching jacket—was striding up the front walk.

I didn't slow, didn't want to linger in the window where she could spot me. I leaned to spy through the front door peephole.

I've known since I was a little girl that there are other people like me. My parents weren't spiritfolk but my father's sister was—not a blue jay like me but a raven. She taught me how to be who I am and to be wary of others who do what I do.

See, you might wonder why I don't spend all my time as a bird, and this is why: our world of meat, metal, and bone is a dangerous place, but the spirit world is a hundred times worse. Filled with predators. No laws, no one to force the cruel to rein in their appetites. Ghosts are our natural prey in our animal forms, and they can be dangerous enough—though before I started finding the spiderlings, it used to be that if I rooted out a ghost, I could just order it to leave and it would flee because it knew what I was and what I could do. But there's many out there that don't limit themselves to just ghosts.

I could tell right away this woman had a spirit shadow. It loomed dark around her in my second sight, even though the day was bright. White streaks flared from the temples of her pageboy to frame a narrow face split by sensuous, disproportionately wide lips. She could have been twenty or sixty, her features smooth but not youthful. Behind her, a single strand of blue spiderweb rose straight into the sky, and behind that, I recognized the same webbing, cocooning the station wagon and the poor couple inside. The driver's side door was ajar, bound that way by the webbing.

I wasn't going to get my paycheck.

The woman stepped onto the porch, raising her fist as if she intended to knock. Her dark eyes narrowed, and I had a second to realize she was staring right at me through the door. I leapt back and stretched my wings. She changed too, her fangs missing my head by less than an inch as she phased right through the wood.

A spider large as a minibus, legs longer than my wings, glared at me with eight eyes like black pearls embedded in coal-shiny hide. Her form flowed straight through the walls of the house as if they weren't there—just like mine did as I beat my wings in thunderous panic, shoving as much air between us as I could, my heart shrieking with fear.

I flapped fully into the land of spirits, leaving behind the world of flesh. Surrounded by the sourceless silver light of the spirit realm, I risked a look back and discovered the spider had followed me, clambering after me at terrifying speed on her single strand of blue thread.

I should have easily left her far behind, but the thread moved of its own accord. Its anchor point, somewhere out of sight high in the heavens, kept pace with me as I flew, matching my maneuvers.

I risked a plunge right at it, meaning to snip it in half with my beak. It dodged me and sprang back, and I bet if I hadn't ducked so quickly myself it would have looped around me. And worse, the spider picked up her already impossible pace.

She called after me in a shockingly honey-sweet voice. "Birds eat spiders, but spiders eat birds too."

She didn't have to run anymore. She was level with me, merely had to ride her magic thread until I tired out.

I knew what was hunting me, who she was. My Aunt Audra told me stories about the Night Queen in the Silver City—who savors drawn-out death, who only ever pretends to show mercy because she loves to watch her victims' hopes die before their final agonies begin. "She calls herself Lilith," my auntie said, "but she's not *that* Lilith. They say a couple hundred years ago she was human. But no one calls her one now."

And a few months ago, I met a couple like me, good people like Audra. They were passing through Hagerstown, stopped in the coffee house across the street from my store. An odd pair: Kori's a bird person like me, a killdeer, but Nathan, he's a panther. But missing claws. He had two prosthetic hands. I thought at first he'd fought in Iraq. They were both friendly—super-friendly—but they never told me what did that to him. I mentioned Audra's stories of Lilith though, and they both went pale. "She's not a story," Nathan said, and they warned me to stay away from her. For Nathan, it was like the words got stuck in his throat, but Kori told me what she looked like. And now I remembered her description—narrow face, hair white at the temples. "A black widow as big as a house. I hope you never look on her."

I would not live to tell Kori her hopes had come to naught.

Because I couldn't get away. Not just because I couldn't shake Lilith's magic thread but because out there in the ceaseless silver light, here and there, I started to see shadows suspended in the air. Things with too many legs, emerging from the physics-defying passages that, in the spirit world, are as numerous a mile in the air as they are a mile underground. More creatures like Lilith, at least a dozen—not as big as her but bigger than me. But not close enough to catch me. Not yet. It was just a matter of time before my constant swooping to keep out of reach of the Night Queen put me in range of one of her clan.

I could only think of one thing to do. I didn't have to fake the quaver in my voice. "Your Highness, what have I done to upset you?"

"How droll that you know me," she said. "Someone of your kind should stick to acorns. You keep murdering my pets."

Pets? The spiderlings? Those strange mutant ghosts-things that invade the homes of the mundanes and drive them crazy with nightmares? My stomach lurched at the thought of killing anyone's pet, a terrible guilt twisting through me the instant before my rational side tamped it down. Lilith could not mean that term of endearment the same way as you or I would mean it. The Night Queen grieves for no one.

I continued to avoid her, though as the old joke goes, *Boy, were my arms tired.* "Those weird little ghosts? Why would you care about them?"

"My dear, those weren't ghosts. Surely, you could tell by the taste?"

But I had never eaten a ghost before that spiderling across the hall attacked me. How many ghosts had Lilith devoured over her long lifetime? I couldn't imagine. I gave her a version of the truth. "I thought it was their mutation. I've heard of spirits changing themselves, mutilating themselves, trying to become demons."

Lilith laughed, the sound grotesquely emphasized with a waving of her fangs. "Stupid child. It's our kind who does that. Chooses to modify the forms we're born with. Ghosts have no such power." And surely Lilith knew what she was talking about as the living, breathing, supreme example. "Tasty as ghosts are though, I have found that the little human flies make for finer dining while they're still alive. I've been experimenting, indulging my culinary skills, figuring out the best method to sup from many of them all at once."

I couldn't help myself. "Oh, no."

Her voice brightened with mirth. "You have been eating tiny little pieces . . . of me."

I might then have simply folded my wings together, dropped like Icarus, and hoped quick death on jagged rocks waited below.

I was so, so fucked.

I said, "Your Highness, I didn't know. I am so sorry."

"I am sure you are sorry," she said. "But perhaps you can make it up to me. Let me take you to the Silver City." Her pearl eyes glinted. "You are what you eat, you know. Let me study you and see how your diet has affected you. I bet you've already changed in ways that will surprise you."

"I've never been to the Silver City," I said, vapid as a reality show star. "I'm honored." More of her kind crawled through the air about me, awaiting the right moment to spring. "I'd like to go."

She stretched out her long, sleek forelegs in the most disturbing offer of embrace I have ever seen. "You'll have to let me bind you, I'm afraid. I promise I won't bite."

I flapped away again. I was starting to wheeze, my spirit form unable to stave off the sensation of swimming a marathon. "You don't need to," I gasped. "I'll go willingly."

"My promise only comes with cooperation." She said it so soothingly. I knew I would be better off forcing her to kill me quickly.

"Okay then." I panted the words, flapped my wings in a short, painful burst, and then stilled them, letting that thread drift closer. Easily within her reach.

She continued her ruse, reaching for me gently rather than snatching me from the air. It bought me the time I needed to pull my wings close and dart straight for her face.

Those of us whose spirit forms take an animal's shape can all do the things that that animal does best without need for a second's thought. Lilith proved herself learned when she taunted me with that "acorn" crack. Blue jays like to pin acorns with their feet and break them open with a single peck. We have very strong beaks.

Except my talons closed over her two largest eyes, and my beak struck her hard as a jackhammer in the closest thing a spider has to a brow. Her oversized exoskeleton was thick as a brick wall, and I split it wide open.

I dropped away, but I still wasn't quick enough. No way could I ever have been quick enough. She didn't try to grab me—she was in too much pain, I think—but she struck out of sheer instinct, sheer hate, sheer vengeance. The daggers of her fangs pierced my stomach, and pain exploded through me, like she'd pumped magma into the wounds. I screeched as I fell, flapping my wings to escape the agony, but it was inside me, fire worming through every vein.

Lilith's magic thread came loose from its mooring in the heavens, and she dropped from the sky, vanishing the next second. I didn't notice where her followers went. I was being flayed from the inside out. Those shrill, pathetic shrieks that echoed through all corners of the spirit realm? I was making those noises, so out of my mind with pain I didn't even know the sounds were coming from my own throat.

But the very thing that got me in so much trouble also saved me.

After untold miles, the pain began to fade. Before I had attacked Lilith, I had played at being more worn out than I actually was. Now, I really was that tired, probably a hundred times worse, and I had no idea where I'd flown.

But I didn't care.

All those exorcisms I performed—unknowingly chowing down on extensions of pure, undiluted Night Queen—had built up my tolerance to her venom. Enough that, even though a direct bite felt like flinging myself on hot pokers, it didn't kill me.

And when the agony faded, bliss took its place. A euphoria like no earthly drug could ever induce.

Thoughts of disgust crawled through my mind, that the substance I found so addictive was the venom of the Night Queen herself. But that realization made not a scratch on the joy that buoyed me. Nor did any worries about where I would land or how I would rebuild my life. Nor did the certainty that I would spend the rest of my days a marked woman. I regarded my cares like an airplane passenger watching farmlands scroll by below. I was a piece of the sky, pure sun-painted blue, invincible.

I flew to the east, away from the encroaching dusk, and I didn't look back.

ȣ

Mike Allen wears many creative hats, at least one of them tailor-made
by his wife and partner-in-crime Anita.

An author, editor, and publisher of science fiction, fantasy, and horror,
Mike has written, edited, or co-edited thirty-nine books, among them
his dark fantasy novel *Trail of Shadows*, his sidearms, sorcery, and
zombies sequence *The Black Fire Concerto* and *The Ghoulmaker's
Aria*, and his latest horror collection *Slow Burn*. *Unseaming* and
Aftermath of an Industrial Accident, his first two volumes of horror
tales, were both finalists for the Shirley Jackson Award for Best Story
Collection, and his dark fable "The Button Bin" was a nominee for
the Nebula Award for Best Short Story. Another collection, *The Spider
Tapestries*, contains experiments in weird science fiction and fantasy.
As editor and publisher, Mike has been nominated twice for the
World Fantasy Award: first, for his anthology *Clockwork Phoenix 5*,
the culmination of the Clockwork Phoenix series, showcasing tales
of beauty and strangeness that defy genre classification; second, for
Mythic Delirium, the magazine of poetry and fiction he edited for
twenty years. He's also a three-time winner of the Rhysling Award
for poetry. His six poetry collections include *Strange Wisdoms of the
Dead*, a *Philadelphia Inquirer* Editor's Choice selection, and *Hungry
Constellations*, a Suzette Haden Elgin Award nominee.

With Anita, he runs Mythic Delirium Books, based in Roanoke,
Virginia. Their cat Pandora assists.

BROKEN EYE BOOKS

Sign up for our newsletter at
www.brokeneyebooks.com

Welcome to Broken Eye Books! Our goal is to bring you the weird and funky that you just can't get anywhere else. We want to create books that blend genres and break expectations. We want stories with fascinating characters and forward-thinking ideas. We want to keep exploring and celebrating the joy of storytelling.

If you want to help us and all the authors and artists that are part of our projects, please leave a review for this book! Every single review will help this title get noticed by someone who might not have seen it otherwise.

And stay tuned because we've got more coming . . .

OUR BOOKS

The Hole Behind Midnight, by Clinton J. Boomer
Crooked, by Richard Pett
Scourge of the Realm, by Erik Scott de Bie
Izanami's Choice, by Adam Heine
Pretty Marys All in a Row, by Gwendolyn Kiste
The Great Faerie Strike, by Spencer Ellsworth
Catfish Lullaby, by A.C. Wise
Busted Synapses, by Erica L. Satifka
Boneset & Feathers, by Gwendolyn Kiste
Alphabet of Lightning, by Edward Morris
The Obsecration, by Matthew M. Bartlett
Better Living Through Alchemy, by Evan J. Peterson
The Mosquito Fleet, by Andrew Penn Romine
Trail of Shadows, by Mike Allen

www.ingramcontent.com/pod-product-compliance
Lightning Source LLC
Chambersburg PA
CBHW020819030726
47496CB00009B/2960